Skipping
STONES

Penny Lauer

Copyright © 2012 by Penny Lauer
All rights reserved. No part of this book may be used or reproduced in any manner whatsoever without written permission except in the case of brief quotations embodied in critical articles or reviews. This book is a work of fiction. Names, characters, places, and incidents are either products of the author's imagination or are used fictitiously.

First published in the United States by Createspace, an Amazon company

ISBN: 1477687998
ISBN-13: 9781477687994

Library of Congress Control Number: 2012911231
CreateSpace, North Charleston, SC

To Emily Brasfield and Sandy Streicher, my first readers and two of my dearest friends, there are no words to express my appreciation for the countless ways I depend on you. Thank you, Boake Sells and Ann Johnson for your friendship, trust, and inspiration you provided for memorable characters. This is the second time I turned to Joan and Brian McFarlane for advice and editing and the second time they graciously came to my aid. Judge K.J. Montgomery, Attorney Alexandria Ruden, and my friend Patti Wachowicz provided me with much-needed facts about domestic violence and legal procedures available to victims. I am honored to have been associated with the incredible staff and Guild members of the Naples, Florida, Shelter for Abused Women and Children, whose hard work and dedication is not only providing hope to the victims they serve, but is also bringing about cultural change to our community and future generations. There have been "encouragers" throughout this process whose kind words and gentle nudges have meant so much to me: Cindy Denney, Jane Scholtz, Marti Selhorst, Armand Maran and Pam Bennett. Once again, editor extraordinaire, Mary Linn Roby, brought everything under control and gently disclosed what matters most. Finally, the greatest thanks of all goes to my calm, supportive, and stabilizing husband Bob, my very- loved best friend and my gentle man.

They cranked up the volume on the car radio and sang along, thumping their fingers on the dash and the steering wheel to the beat of the music as they headed north of the city toward Mentor. It took them a good forty minutes to get to the place they'd picked out and another thirteen to unload the bikes and get themselves ready. Fifteen minutes into the ride, Josh was already cursing himself for being so stubborn with her, so determined to prove his strength. He hadn't understood her description of the hill. Or hadn't wanted to. Eight minutes later, his legs were aching. Another five, and they were on fire. His bike felt like an anchor, tethering him to the hot asphalt. He kept his head down and concentrated on the rotation of the tires, visualizing only the distance remaining between him and the top of the monstrous hill. The dark shadows that flickered across the road that sunny day and the distance between him and his mother shut her off from him. She dismounted at the crescent of the long and winding hill and waited for him, shouting muted words of encouragement and making clown-like pantomimed motions for him to push harder when he finally came into view.

Finally, after a very long time for both of them, he made it and weakly returned her gleeful high-five. She praised him for pushing himself and laughed as he gulped down the contents from his water bottle and awkwardly dribbled it over his chin and chest. She grew impatient as he shakily wrestled to get the empty container back into its carrier and took off ahead of him, unfettered and unafraid, leaving him alone to harness the courage he needed to plunge down the narrow road in pursuit of her.

He was slow again. Afraid for both of them, he held onto the brakes and watched for gravel and wished that she would slow down. She was way ahead. She turned to wave. He wouldn't let go of the bar to signal back. She turned again. He saw the car, but his warning was caught up by the wind against them and her interpretation of what she thought she heard. The black sedan completed its turn onto the little-traveled road and increased its speed, just yards away from her. She turned too late and grabbed the brake before she could think of changing direction. He watched as she battered into the hood and, still clutching the bars and still sitting, flew onto the roof and careened back to the road.

He stroked her hand and looked into her vacant eyes. "I'm sorry, Mom," he cried. "Please don't go. Please don't leave me."

They were finally able to pull him away from her. It was his twelfth birthday, and he was forever changed.

PART ONE

Josh

He couldn't do it. He held onto the back of the headrest and gritted his teeth against his guilt and hoped for the zillionth time that he'd die too. Papaw's words were filled with hurt, and when Josh risked looking at him, the gentle man put his big hands around the boy's face and pressed his forehead against his.

"Josh," he whispered, "we need to be strong together and show respect for the memory of her. Let's help each other."

Tears trickled down his creased face, and the sight brought the boy more pain. He leaned into his grandfather and together they shuffled through the new grass to the white tent where the casket lay prominently over the open grave. Josh glanced at the people waiting for them there, searching for the face he hoped to see.

A robin broke through the awful stillness, and the sound of it was like a slap, reminding him how he and his mother had stood smiling at their kitchen window, listening to another robin's song just five days before. "Spring is finally here," she had said.

Spring and the song of a robin could never be the same.

Skipping STONES

They stopped under an old oak tree. The huge limbs were gnarled and brown-green with knobby pale buds jutting out on them. They'll pop open real soon and make it prettier here, the boy reasoned. And they'll spread out over where she is and will keep the ground cool for her when full summer comes. And they'll protect her during long grey winters. He knew there was no logic to his thoughts, but he needed to believe.

He stared up into the tree because he didn't dare look down. Darts of sun poked their way through the branches and stung his eyes. A breeze landed on his face and messed with his hair. It was warm, and the touch of it reminded him of her. He worked hard to blink the tears away and swallowed to get rid of the tightness in his throat. Even now he needed to be her "little man".

Josh caught some of the words that the preacher said about his mother and closed his eyes during the prayer, hoping with all of his heart that the preacher knew what he was talking about, that his mother's spirit was in a better place and was finally at peace. The stories she had told him, but didn't believe, about God and heaven and angels and forgiveness were suddenly important. He needed to trust that they could be true.

The preacher's litany stopped. There was nothing more to add. But Josh couldn't leave her there alone. Couldn't just turn his back and walk away free. She was there because of him. Hands and arms pushed and pulled at him to make him move, but he made his thin, gangly body stiff and heavy and pressed his lips hard together to keep the unmanly sobs that filled his mouth from spewing out. In desperation, his Uncle Bill and Uncle Steve clamped their arms around him and stumbled with the dead weight of him back to the car. Josh knew what an awful sight they made, but he couldn't make himself be better.

He closed his eyes against the pity he saw on the one face and the disgust on the other.

∽

The boy would never remember the ride back to his grandparents' home. He woke up on the guest bed that had been his for the past five nights with a cold drippy cloth on his forehead and his grandmother, Mimi, beside him, whispering his name and rubbing his hands.

He let himself be lead to the bathroom where she embarrassed him by brushing his hair and tucking his shirt in. When she held onto his arm as they walked down to the living room, he stood taller, just in case the tight grip she had on him was to steady her. They stood together while guests hugged them and looked at them with sad faces and whispered comforting words that bounced off him as soon as they were spoken.

"It's a terrible thing to outlive a child," Mimi said to them, "but time is a great healer. We'll heal. All of us. With time."

Josh closed his heart against her words. He would never heal. Someone handed him something cold to drink, and he was grateful for the diversion. Mimi finally released him, and he headed outdoors, as he always did when he needed to ground himself in reality. He was intercepted in the front hall by Aunt Maddie.

"Let's get a plate of food to take with you," she said. "You need to eat something, Josh. You haven't eaten all day."

And even though he promised her he'd eat soon and that he was okay not to talk for a while with anyone else, she hung on and walked with him to the door. They both stepped back, surprised to see someone standing hesitantly on the other side, peering through the screen. They moved closer to get a good

Skipping STONES

look at the man there, and Josh turned to his aunt for confirmation just in time to see the tiny smile leak out onto her mouth. With gradual certainty, he realized that it was, indeed, the same person whose bent and faded pictures he had studied for the past seven years.

Maddie pushed Josh toward him, and he pushed back. Out of character, she stammered hello to the man and said that she was glad that he had decided to come. Her hand was still on the door when she looked to Josh and asked if he remembered the person standing there.

"It's your dad, Josh," she said. "See? It's him. It's Sam."

Josh stared at the floor, embarrassed. How bad is it that a son and his father would need to be introduced? But there it was.

Maddie remembered to ask Sam to come in, but he turned her down and said that he wouldn't be staying long, that he just wanted to see Josh for a minute. And father and son were left alone together.

"Mind if we sit down for a while?" Sam asked, and when the boy hesitated, he led the way to the wide porch steps.

"I know how awkward this is, and how hard," he said as the boy sat down beside him, "but I decided when I saw you earlier at the service that I needed to talk with you. I didn't want to wait. It's as simple as that. God knows I waited long enough."

He cleared his throat to give himself time to gather his thoughts. Again, the words that came out were awkward.

"It's an awful thing that's happened. There's no way to describe it. It's hard to get your mind around it."

He had practiced what he would say to his son, but none of it was right, and he let too much time pass before he tried again.

"I'm so sorry about everything," he said finally, "so sorry for what you're going through."

The boy wanted to study his father's face, the length of his hands and arms, the color and cut of his hair. And he wanted to hear everything about him, every single thing he had done every week and month and year since he had walked out of his and his mother's lives. But Josh looked at nothing and said nothing. He stared straight ahead and made himself as stiff as he had been at the cemetery to protect himself against all of the emotions inside him.

Sam closed his eyes and ran his hands slowly through his hair. "God. This is hard," he said.

Josh was good at reading body gestures. He had learned how from his mother. Ever since he could remember, the two of them had studied people and what their movements and expressions signified. It was a game they had often played, and a serious one. Picking out strangers at shopping malls or McDonald's during nights when they had nothing else to do and nowhere else to go, they watched them closely and decided what kind of people they might be and how they might live their lives. Sometimes if the strangers seemed real interesting, mother and son made up lengthier stories about them and took up their fictional histories and futures for days, maybe even weeks at a time, adding to the tales as fresh insight broke through their imaginations.

Other nights, they read books together and discussed the characters in depth: who were the good ones and who caused pain; who had confidence and who was insecure. They respected the ones who were honest and could be trusted, and they anticipated the fall of the ones who weren't. They praised and rooted for those who were strong and sucked up their disappointments during adversity, and they scorned those who crumbled under pressure. They took their time to form their final opinions about the fictional characters because they realized that people can change. His mother had needed to believe that. The stories they had shared had sometimes helped both of them stand tall in the midst of all their own confusion and sadness.

Sam sat up straighter and put his hands on his knees, a gesture Josh recognized as resolve, and looked at his son with such earnestness that Josh was compelled to look back.

"Look, Josh," he said. "My timing is terrible. Neither one of us can make sense yet out of what's happened. All I meant to do today was to see you, to make sure that you're all right, and I wanted to ask you if you'd consider getting with me soon so that we can get to know each other again and I can tell you everything that's on my mind and you can tell me what's on yours." He blew out air. "This is so screwed up."

Some parts of Josh wanted to help his father, but the parts that wanted to hurt him for the pain he had caused won.

"What could we say to each other now?" He demanded. "Why did you wait 'til she was gone?"

The questions were hurtful but fair.

"I have to begin somewhere," Sam answered. "There's a lot that you deserve to know."

"It's a little late." Josh said it quietly but with as much determination as he could find.

"I hope not," Sam whispered back.

He took another good long look at the young boy he had spoken to only briefly for the past seven years and finally managed to mutter what he felt Josh needed most to hear.

"You were the perfect son to her," he said finally. "You were her rock, the most important person in the world to her. She loved you so much. You know that already, but I just thought it was important to hear it from someone else. You had a relationship with your mother that most other people could only dream of."

"How would you know that?" Josh asked. "You weren't around. Remember?"

Sam hesitated just a moment. "I'll explain that too if you'll give me the chance."

It had been a long time since Josh and his mom had talked about Sam. She hadn't mentioned him except when Josh asked her specific questions, and he had stopped asking several years ago. Her answers never satisfied him. For a long time, the boy had held on to the dream that his father would come back someday and make the three of them into a real family. But holding onto dreams is hard. They get in the way.

Seconds passed, and Josh thought about rushing in to fill the holes in the conversation so his father couldn't leave, but he didn't want to seem too needy or too quick to forgive. And, most of all, he didn't want to sound like a child.

"I'll call you," Sam said, standing up and stuffing his hands in his pockets. "I hope you'll give us a chance."

He realized the irony in what he had just said: they were exactly the same words he had spoken to Becky when he had walked away from her and their young son so many years ago.

It was too much for Josh. All he could acknowledge feeling was an overpowering sense of emptiness as he watched Sam drive away from him. Avoiding the party inside, he walked to the door at the back of the grand house and made his way to the guestroom, where he cocooned himself into the covers and fell into a fretful half-sleep. The house was eerily quiet when he fought his way out of his dreams, and it took him a while to adjust to the pale darkness of the room. Climbing out of bed

Skipping **S T O N E S**

like a much older person, he followed the voices coming from downstairs and stopped outside his grandfather's study.

"Please, let's not get into all of that. Not now," he heard Papaw say. "Who knows what Sam's intentions are? It could be a good thing. I don't know."

"It's okay, Dad," Uncle Bill said. "You're right. Now's not the time."

"I propose a toast," Uncle Steve interjected.

There was shuffling of feet, and Josh visualized his family moving together into a tight circle.

"She's in a good place now," Steve continued. "She's at peace, and we need to move on. She'd want it that way. Here's to the rest of us. Here's to our wonderful family," he offered. "May we continue to support one another and manage to find our own peace and understanding after this terrible tragedy."

Glasses clinked into each other, and Josh strained to hear another toast from Mimi.

"And here's to Steve and Jess for honoring Becky's wishes and taking Josh in as their own son."

The boy found his way back out to the front steps where he had sat earlier with his father and curled himself up against the wrought iron rail. He would never be his aunt and uncle's son. No one, he thought, could ever replace his mom – no one, not even her sister. And Steve? He hardly knew him. Josh turned away from trying to sort through the future and turned his mind again to everything that had happened the day his mother had died and what he could have done to prevent it

୧୨

Just five days before, last Sunday morning, his mother had trounced out of their small house and had been noisy about it.

She wanted him up. Josh knew she'd be on her way down the street to the Jewish bakery where they bought warm bagels on Sunday mornings when they could afford them, and he figured she'd probably pick up some cream cheese and lox too. They had counted the change in their money jar the night before and had a few dollars more than they had thought. She'd be giddy to splurge. He had climbed out of bed to make a pot of strong coffee for the two of them and went outside in his pajamas to watch for her from their driveway.

They had had their breakfast on the steps of the front stoop and celebrated what they thought was finally early summer. Ohio weather was fickle, and they wanted to take advantage of the nice day. Josh wanted to take a bike ride.

Becky was a real biker. Josh wanted to be. Biking was important to her. She said it helped her relax and pull away from her doldrums. She walked, jogged, or biked at least an hour every single day. She was strong physically. The exercise helped her emotionally. She had reminded him often that it gets the endorphins going and produces serotonin. She knew all about all of that. She studied health. She had to.

Her last ride had been toward the end of fall, in mid-October, and she had described it to Josh as "electric." He had understood what she meant. Some experiences jolt you in a way that you'll never forget. Mother and son had shared lots of "electrical experiences" together.

"I pushed myself hard to get up that big hill and then just let go, speeding down like a crazy woman with nothing to lose," she had said. "And I felt such a sense of freedom and well-being."

And she reminded him again that physical exercise is always a much better way to get high than to get all juiced up on drugs. She spoke from experience.

Josh had wanted to feel what she had felt, and he vowed to himself and to her that very day that he would get himself in shape over the winter so that he could take that same ride with her as soon as the weather turned warm. He had done that. He played soccer, basketball, and baseball at school. And in the off-season, he ran on his own. He would have done all of it even without the promises he had made to himself and to her, but the exercise and sports were more fun for him because of his goal.

It had taken his mother a while to make up her mind about the hill that Sunday. Usually she decided things quickly. But not that day. She said that she thought they should start off the season with a shorter and simpler trip.

"I don't want us to be too tired tonight," she told him with a grin, and when he asked what was so special about that evening, she smiled and told him that he'd find out soon enough. "We'll have all summer to bike," she continued. "There's no reason to kill ourselves the first day out."

She didn't kill herself that day, Josh thought. He did it for her.

He had argued with her, saying that he wasn't a kid and that he knew he was strong enough. He reminded her that she had made a promise and she had to keep it, repeated her own words that there's nothing worse than promises broken.

She reminded him how steep the hill was and how even she had to pace herself and gear up and down at exactly the right moment. She told him that she hadn't dared stop because she wouldn't have had the strength to start again and that she had to stay in control on the way down.

"You can't let the bike get away from you. It's important to keep your eye on the road and watch for gravel. Oh, my God. It's a monster."

He had her. He could tell from her voice that she wanted to do the ride as much as he did.

When she poured them another cup of coffee to share, he asked her again why she was smiling so much, and was so fidgety. She reached over to him and messed his hair and looked at him with that too- big smile.

"It's a surprise," she had said. "And, oh how you're going to love it. I'll tell you when we get back. It's going to take a while."

He had never found out what her surprise was. They left for the ride at ten-thirty that morning. She hit the van at twelve twenty-eight. He knew the time because her watch shattered and stopped when she bounced off the hood and hit the ground.

◆

Josh was supposed to move to his Aunt Jess's home the following week, but Mimi and Papaw didn't think he was ready. They asked if he'd stay with them a while longer. He didn't care where he stayed.

Jess and her children, Katie and Ben, visited him frequently at Mimi's throughout the month to give everyone the chance to get to know each other better. He went to their place too, and each time he went, he felt more comfortable. He had been born just thirteen months after Ben, and Becky and Jess had thought back then that the two boys would be great friends, but it hadn't worked out that way. The families' lives had taken different directions, and the sisters realized that they had very little in common to keep them close.

Jess and his cousins treated Josh with kindness and respect and patience that month, and Josh was sure that, beyond the

Skipping STONES

big house, the expensive cars, the designer clothes, and the polite manners and smiles, there was much more to learn about his new family, and he was excited about the discovery of their "real story." He was anxious to please Jess and his cousins and to prove himself worthy to Steve.

Jess's place, which was the antithesis of Josh's old home, gave him a sense of permanency. His mom used to derisively call it a "real show place," but to him it was organized and stable, and he needed that. Jess explained its size by saying that instead of moving over the years, she and Steve had kept adding onto it and that perhaps it felt even bigger than it was because some of the additions hadn't always fit well with the old structure; the end result was lots of hallways and unexpected nooks and crannies. Josh liked it all. The odd spaces made it interesting and unique.

Huge windows and doors let the sun inside, and the crystal lamps and chandeliers and the silver picture frames and trays reflected the light and bounced rainbow colors onto the walls and the floors during the day. Jess had real antiques, and Josh enjoyed the stories she told about their histories and where she found them. The wood floors were covered with rugs that felt good under his bare feet, and she explained that they were Oriental. He asked her specifics about where they came from and how they were made, and she took her time to explain the details of the workers and the looms that had helped create them, leaving fascinating images in his mind. Jess had extensive vegetable gardens, and she let Josh and his cousins pick from them whenever they wanted and eat everything right on the spot. The place felt like it would never change, and he welcomed the feeling of permanency.

A large park and a social club, just down the street from Jess's, took up a big chunk of space in the small community. The village center was comprised of a library, a town hall, a restaurant, a small grocery store with not much in it, and some offices in an historic building. His mother had said that her sister's community was known as the home of the mink and manure clique. The best things about it for Josh were the wide open green spaces, the walking bridge that led to the copse of oaks, the stream where he and Ben caught frogs, and the river that curved in and out the length of the village and was full of fish to catch. He relaxed and began to heal there, certain that nothing but tranquility and graciousness existed behind the black or green doors of its homes' lovely facades.

༄

Sam kept his promise and frequently called Josh, and Josh somehow continued to avoid calling him by any name. "Dad" still seemed too familiar. The word was too much like "Mom." Those were titles that should be earned, Josh reasoned, and should mean something. He hoped that sometime "Dad" would fit. "Sam" was an insult to both of them.

Their conversations were short and mostly one-sided, with Sam explaining his restaurant business and relating highlights of the televised sports he watched in his limited free time. Josh began watching golf tournaments and baseball games with Papaw to have something to add to the conversations.

Mimi didn't approve of the phone calls, and Josh knew it. "Sam is on the phone," she would say indignantly or would simply hold the phone out to him and announce that he had a call. Josh needed to understand her feelings about his father.

"It isn't easy for a mother to forget the hurt someone has caused one of her children," she said when he summoned up the courage to ask her about it.

"Mom said that she didn't hate him," Josh said and wondered why he felt the need to defend Sam. "She said that both of them had decided it was best to leave each other. Actually, she said that, when it came right down to it, she had made the final decision about them because she was tired of trying so hard to keep things going."

"She told you that?"

"She did. She said that sometimes you realize that it's just too damned hard to keep going on with some things, and it's best to get it all behind you and just move on."

"Well," Mimi grumbled, "it was very complicated. I understand how it must feel to hear from him after all this time. I really do. I just don't want you to be hurt, that's all. You've been hurt enough."

She was ready to end the conversation. Josh wasn't.

"Mom told me a long time ago that it was her idea to raise me herself, not his," he said. "She said she thought it was best for all of us."

Josh's apparent knowledge of the circumstances related to the divorce and the custody decisions caught Mimi off-guard. She turned her back to him and busied herself at the counter a few moments to formulate a response to him and a few more to question her head-strong daughter's apparent decision to speak honestly and openly to him about the issues.

"Well. There were a lot of discussions about that," she finally admitted. "We did think, under the circumstances, that it would be best. He agreed to it all, obviously."

"Maybe he didn't give in easily. Maybe she just convinced him. She was good at that."

Mimi stood taller and moved her shoulders back, a gesture that Josh and his mother thought could show either decision or defiance. Sometimes both.

"Well, he is certainly attentive now," she said, trying hard to uncoil. "I think you should enjoy the attention. But we all need to take this new relationship that he's trying to forge with you very slowly."

Josh had been waiting seven years to have a relationship with his father. Forging along slowly was not at all what he had in mind. He continued to challenge his grandmother.

"Because you don't like it that he waited until she was gone?" He asked.

"That's one thing," she admitted. "Yes."

"Do you know why, exactly, they wanted to get divorced?"

He saw her indecision, and he pushed some more. "I'd just like to hear what you think."

"They were ill-suited, Josh," she said reluctantly. "I guess that's the best way to say it. He was very different from the rest of us. They rushed into things. They were young and she was impressionable. And then he didn't give her the time she needed. There were a lot of issues. It's complicated, and I think we need to find the right time to talk about it."

"How was he different from us?"

He read the frustration on her face.

"In lots of ways," she said. "Ways that you can't understand right now. He wasn't brought up the same as your mother or the rest of us. I could see what could happen from the very beginning, and it did."

Skipping STONES

She turned her back to him again and got back to washing the dishes.

"This discussion deserves more time than we have right now, Josh," she said without looking at him. "Let's let it go for now and come back to it at the right time, okay?"

During the six weeks Josh was with his grandparents, there was never the "right time."

Just three days before Josh was to move to Jess's, Sam called to say that he had a scheduled business trip to California to do some research on a new restaurant he was planning.

"I've talked to Jess a couple of times," he told him, "and she said that it would be all right with her if we get together when I get back. Should be about ten days. By then, you'll be all settled into your new home, and you can tell me all about it. Would that be all right with you?"

Josh began counting.

∽

The day before Josh left to move in with Jess, she asked him if he'd like to go back to his old house one last time to make sure there wasn't anything left there that he might want. He weighed his decision seriously, with the same introspection he used in all things, and decided that he owed it to himself and his mother to go back once more to revisit his past and all the things that the two of them had shared together, painful as he knew it would be.

Although their home wasn't more than twenty minutes away from Mimi's, that day it felt much farther. When they finally pulled onto his street, he was surprised at how shabby the old neighborhood looked and how little the house was. Jess unhooked the padlock on the door and let him be the first to go inside.

Someone had cleaned the rooms and had put some things away, but compared to Mimi's and Jess's homes, it was cluttered. And drab.

"We left in a hurry and didn't have a chance to pick up," he explained, and even as he said it, he felt guilty to be apologizing for how he and his mother had lived. He checked the kitchen counter. Someone had cleaned up the cups and saucers and coffee grounds they had left there that morning that felt like so long ago. He hoped it hadn't been Jess.

She brought some cartons from the car to put the rest of his things in, and they packed up the few clothes that were left in his closet, some photos in frames and some in large envelopes, his posters of famous NASCAR racers, the rest of his books, and the jar of coins he and his mother had saved over the winter. He asked what would happen to the furniture and everything else that was left, and Jess told him that it would probably be donated to some charity.

"Why don't you take another look around, Josh?" Jess said, putting her arm around his shoulder. "We're in no hurry. Maybe there's something else you'd like to save for your own home someday. We can keep anything you'd like. Why don't you take some time by yourself? Walk around to make sure you haven't missed something. We'll be outside packing up the car."

He stood in front of the sink and looked across his yard to the garage and could almost see him and his mom pulling out their bikes there that last fateful day. Minutes before, they had read the Funny Papers together, checked out their horoscopes, worked a little on a cross-word puzzle, and talked about his having a job at the deli down the street next summer, as though their life together was going to continue to go on the way it always had.

Skipping S T O N E S

Overcome with memories, he ran his fingers across the two coffee cups he and his mother had made for each other last Christmas and sat down at the chipped kitchen table, thinking about the hundreds of games of Scrabble and Chess and Gin Rummy they had played there. He stood in front of the painting she had made of the two of them many summers ago from a picture she had taken of them at their favorite park, and finally he wandered to the sagging back porch to see if anything important had been left there. A "For Sale" sign leaned against the wall in the corner, and he turned his back to it.

Everything mattered, but having it stored and forgotten or put somewhere to keep him tethered to the memories wouldn't make him happier, he reasoned, and he steeled himself to walk away. But there was his mother's desk.

There was the heart-shaped glass paperweight he had given her one year for Christmas. She had said it was her treasure. And there was her worn chartreuse memo pad with the purple daisies on the front. He opened it and read the list, written in her familiar sloping hand: *coffee, toothpaste, Cascade, silver beads? birthday card*. And there was her old address book. Instinctively, he adjusted the rubber band holding it together and pushed in the loose ends of paper sticking out, flushed with the memory of her teasing him about his tidiness.

He opened her "junk" drawer where she kept paper clips, envelopes, receipts, stamps, and anything else that would fit and moved things around inside it. There, under a pile of papers, was a yellow book he had never seen before with the word *Diary* written across it. Flipping through the pages, careful not to read the words there, he saw that there were at least eight years of her notes there. They stopped the twenty-fifth of April, just over a month before the accident. He decided to keep it – not to read it, but to make sure no one else did.

And although he knew that it might seem like a childish thing to do, he decided to also keep the paper weight, the memo pad and address book, and he secreted them into his duffle bag along with the coin jar. There was nothing left to do. He swallowed hard and made himself not look back.

∽

Jess and his cousins picked him up the next day at Mimi's to take him to his new home, and Mimi and Papaw assured him that they'd visit soon. His grandparents stood at their front door, and the boy waved to them until they were out of sight. It felt like small pieces of his insides were breaking away.

Ben tackled reorganizing his room as seriously as he did everything: slowly, precisely, intent on seeking approval. Katie was breathless with excitement. Jess and the three of them pushed furniture around, pulled a chest in from one of the other rooms so that Ben wouldn't have to give up drawer space, hung Josh's posters on the wall beside his bed, and put his books and car magazines on a new book case that Jess surprised him with. The final items Josh found a place for were his mother's personal things. He put the address book, memo pad, and the coin jar on the top shelf of the book case and hid the diary in a box in the corner of the bottom drawer of his chest, allowing himself to place just the paper weight in clear view on the table beside his bed.

It was all done, and they stepped back to take a good look at the results of their efforts. The room was full and, in Josh's mind, actually looked like someone was finally spending time in there. To celebrate, Katie and Jess brought in a tray of Sprite and chips and Salsa, and, sitting picnic-style on the

Skipping STONES

rug in the middle of the room, they all agreed that they had done a great job getting organized. They were still there when they heard the garage door open, a signal that Steve was home. Jess snapped to attention and glanced quickly at her watch. "He's early!" she said and rushed to the mirror and brushed her hair with Ben's brush, instructing the children to stay where they were. She turned back to them just as she was walking out the door, and said with an eager smile that he must have come home early to celebrate Josh's arrival with them.

"Hi, honey," she called out to her husband. "How was your day?" The scene reminded Josh of the old TV shows, Leave It To Beaver, his mom and he rented once from Netflix. They had laughed, he remembered, all the way through them.

Jess wasn't gone long. "He'll be up in a couple of minutes," she said and took another quick look at the room.

Josh followed Ben and Katie's direction and stood up to wait for Steve's arrival.

"So here you are, all moved in," Steve said to no one in particular. He patted Katie's head when she gave him a hug. "How'd the day go?"

No one seemed to know who should answer him. He leaned against the door frame and crossed his arms and took his time to survey the changes to Ben's room.

"So this is it. You're all moved in," he said again and walked over to the chest Jess had brought in from the guest room. "I figured you'd probably decide to take the other room after all. You'd have everything you need there."

Josh didn't know how to answer, didn't know what the question was. Jess smiled expectantly and answered for him.

"Well, the boys decided it would be more fun to share a room." She told him, locking her arms around her waist. "It's a little crowded, but they don't mind. And this way we can keep the guest room for guests."

Ben shot her a quick, questioning look but said nothing.

"Not what I expected," Steve said. "But I know you'll get it right, Jess."

He rubbed his hands together and smiled at them for the first time. "Okay, everybody, let's go celebrate Josh's arrival. Get yourselves ready, and I'll see you downstairs. It's cocktail time."

He shook Josh's hand on his way out. "Welcome to your new home, buddy," he said.

Disappointment and something else settled like dust around Jess and her children. She checked herself once more in the mirror and wiped the clean counter top even cleaner.

"Don't worry," she whispered as she followed after her husband. "He's just tired. He's had a tough day."

༄

Jess poured a drink for Steve to unwind with while he changed clothes and then headed out to the brick patio to get the table set for the special dinner she had planned for Josh's first night there. Josh offered to help, but Ben said that housework was women's work and stood aside, watching his mother plump up the pillows on the chairs and check for dust on the table. Jess looked up long enough to instruct the boys to get themselves cleaned up and to hurry.

"You should probably change," Ben said as Josh washed his hands. "We don't get dressed up or anything, but we always shower and put on clean clothes. Dad says it's the civilized way to mark the end of the day. You use this bathroom, and I'll use the one down the hall. We need to hurry. We're late, and Dad can't deal with surprises."

Skipping STONES

Josh searched through the closet and hoped that he had enough clothes for his new home.

He was the last one out to the patio, and when he saw the beautiful table Jess had set and all of the snacks she'd put out for them, he was impressed. Everything matched. Even the napkins and tablecloth. They were yellow, the same color as the walls in the kitchen. The blue dishes looked like new and matched the color of the accent pieces that were scattered throughout the house. A white wicker basket was filled with purple, blue, yellow, and white flowers that flowed over each other like they had in the gardens.

"Wow! It looks real great," Josh observed, desperate to please. "Sure isn't like any picnic I've ever been to."

He was sure he heard a snicker behind him and turned to see what might have caused it, but Steve was busy pouring himself another drink. The compliment had the right effect on Jess. She clapped her hands and rushed over to Josh and hugged him.

"Eat 'til you're stuffed. I don't like leftovers," she said in a breathless voice.

When Steve was satisfied that the steak and hamburgers were grilled just right, he motioned to Jess to take them to the table and instructed the rest of the family to sit. Jess served him first, and Josh noticed that Ben and Katie waited for him to take his first bite before they began to eat. They also remained quiet until they were invited to make reports of their day. Josh made a mental note of it all, thinking that this must be the way real rich people behaved.

The reporting began with Katie and was followed by Ben's explanation of his activities, and by the time it was Josh's turn to speak, there was nothing left to say. He had left his grandparents' home and had moved his things to this one, events that had already been reported twice by Katie and Ben. Jess had little to add when her turn came and talked instead about what she was planning for the next day.

When it was Steve's turn, everyone leaned forward to listen intently as he went into detail about the phone calls he had to put up with at his office, the luncheon meeting he'd had to attend, and how, in general, it had been a very trying and very full day. Eventually, he ran out of things to say about himself, and Jess ran out of questions to ask him. Josh rushed in to fill the gap in the conversation and asked his uncle what, exactly, his profession was. The question pleased him, and he took a great deal of time to explain that he was an attorney who specialized in setting up trusts and foundations for wealthy clients. Wealth Management was how he described it. Josh pretended to understand.

"It's a tough profession, Josh," he said, "but you can see that it pays off for someone who does it well. And now you're here to reap the benefits too."

Josh took Steve's boasts as lighthearted teasing and waited for the good-natured laughter he was sure would follow. But there was only silence.

Finally, Steve excused everyone from the table, and Josh jumped up to help carry the dirty dishes to the kitchen counter, just like he had done in his old home.

"What are you doing?" Steve asked, leaning way back in his chair and stretching out his legs. "That's woman's work, Josh." He turned to his daughter. "I'll take some coffee now, Katie. And tell your mother that I need my drink freshened."

Josh followed Ben's lead again and grinned to please Steve, but he understood none of it.

After his third drink and a cup of coffee, Steve suggested that the "men" go out front and throw a baseball around while

Skipping **STONES**

the girls finished cleaning up. Ben's excitement bumped up all over him, and he raced to the garage to find the ball and gloves and brought along a bat for good measure. Steve directed the two boys to positions in the yard and threw to them. The first throws were to Josh, and they were short, but he still caught them easily. Ben waited patiently for his dad to throw to him, and when he finally did, the throws were harder. He missed them, and his father laughed.

"Maybe Josh will give you some lessons," he said.

The hurt expression on Ben's face belied the smile on his father's. Suddenly the game became a competition between the man and the two boys. Unfortunately, youth and sobriety won out. Steve stumbled into a throw from Josh and missed, and Ben made the mistake of showing pleasure in the win and "high-fiving" his cousin. It was a moment that Steve would never forget.

Later, Jess played Scrabble with the children at the kitchen table until the sun was making the final third of its descent into the horizon, its pink rays stretched thinly across the sky. Remembering the sunsets he had watched with his mother, Josh was just about ready to ask Ben and Katie if they'd like to go outside before the dramatic show was over, but Steve interrupted his plan. "It's time to get yourselves to bed, kids," he said. "Time to call it a day."

No one but Josh seemed surprised by such an early consignment to bed, and they trooped past Steve as if on review, with only Katie invited to give him a hug.

Jess visited Katie first, and her soft reading voice floated down the hall to the boys' room. She stopped at their door to wish them a good night, and, almost immediately, Ben was in his bed, turned to the wall with the sheet pulled over his face.

"Are you sleepy?" Josh asked.

Ben's answer was caught in the sheet.

Josh, far too awake to think of sleeping, roamed around the silent room as quietly as possible and moved finally to the window to watch dusk creep its way into the yard outside and fill the room with shadows. Clouds moved lazily across the moon, and somewhere down the street people laughed. Leaning on the sill, he watched as leaves turned black-green and those parts of the lawn not in shadow became silver. Stars revealed themselves and twinkled in the dark blue sky. Mimi and Papaw were probably on their porch now, he thought. And if she were still here, his mother and he might have decided to take a walk on a night like this.

He fought his desire to be outside. He knew how good it would be to walk barefoot out there, the night wetness squishing between his toes. Crickets clicked at each other in the bushes right under the window. A warm breeze came through the screen and circled around his face. A perfect summer night. He took a deep breath and sucked up the earth smells into his nose and throat and held them there as long as he could before he let it go. His spirit hurt.

His decision to leave the room was made with no thought whatsoever. Looking for just a brief moment at his cousin's back, he opened the door and closed it silently behind him, following the direction of the soft light coming from the TV in the den.

Jess looked up the moment he stepped into the wide archway that opened up into the room. Steve lay asleep with his head on her lap. Her efforts to stand roused him.

"What the hell?" He muttered and rearranged himself.

"I can't sleep," Josh whispered to his aunt, "so I thought I'd go outside for just a while and walk around 'til I'm tired."

Skipping STONES

Jess led him to the kitchen, and he accepted the milk and cookie she offered him. They sat in the semi-dark of the room, and he whispered his apologies for waking Steve and interrupting her show.

"This is how our nights are here, Josh," Jess whispered back. "Katie and Ben are used to it, and you'll get used to it too. Steve works very hard, and he needs his quiet time at night. Your internal clock will change. You'll see. Everything will work out just fine. I should have explained the rules to you. Let me walk you back now."

The earth had moved so that the moon was no longer shining through the open window, and Josh lay in darkness, waiting for the night to be over. When the sun finally showed itself, he jumped out of bed, determined to please Jess and not to offend Steve. He was dressed and ready to begin the day when Ben's voice came out from under the covers and stopped him.

"What are you doing?" he whispered.

"I thought I'd get some breakfast and go outside."

"Mom tells us when we can get up. Dad needs to start his days alone with Mom with no hassle from us kids."

Josh's expression upset him, and he asked, defensively, what Josh was thinking and then what he did so early in the mornings.

"We got up whenever we felt like it as long as we didn't have something to get to," Josh explained.

"Well, there were just the two of you. That was different."

Josh had never contemplated the relationship he and his mother had had or the freedom they had enjoyed together. He had always assumed that life with a real family, a mother, a father, and siblings, was the best it could be. Maybe, he thought now, the more people there are to take care of or worry about, the less freedoms families have.

He went back to the open window and put his face flat up to the screen.

"What are you doing now?" Ben demanded.

"I'm sucking up the fresh air."

Josh stayed where he was, and after several minutes of awkward silence, Ben made a brave move and slid quietly out of bed to look outside.

"It's really early," he whispered.

"I'd be up way before now lots of days at home."

"What would you do by yourself?"

The question surprised Josh.

"I don't know. Whatever I wanted to do. I'd go outside and wander around in the yard or watch some TV. I don't know," he shrugged. "Sometimes Mom and I would take an early walk to the donut shop. Or she'd do her thing and I'd do mine. We'd do whatever we wanted to do."

"Like what?" Ben pressed.

"Lots of stuff. Simple stuff. I like to walk barefoot through the grass when it's still wet," Josh went on, and so sometimes I walked around the yard in my bare feet. Sometimes I'd just sit out on the steps and breathe in the fresh air like we're doing now. Sometimes I'd make coffee for Mom and me if she wasn't up yet, but I liked waking up when her coffee was perking. We liked to get on our bikes and ride down the street before the stores were opened and watch traffic go by and people getting ready for the day. Or we'd work on the crossword puzzle in the paper.

He coughed to cover up his ache.

"Want to play some Gin?" he asked, and wasn't all that surprised when Ben confessed that he didn't know how to play cards. "I could teach you, if you want to learn. It's really fun."

Skipping **S T O N E S**

He thought about the yellow legal pad his mother had used to keep track of their scores. On the last day of each month, the loser had to make the beds and fix dinner.

"We'll keep track of our scores," he said, "and at the end of each month, whoever wins gets to choose what he wants to do that day."

The pact was made, and Ben followed his cousin, with some trepidation, to the center of the floor and learned to play Gin Rummy. Early in the morning. Before it was allowed.

༄

Mornings faded into afternoons, afternoons dragged on into evenings, and evenings lasted forever. Everything moved around slowly at Jess's, and she and his cousins reminded Josh of "slow-droning summer bees, drunk on nectar and stupefied by the sun," a word picture he remembered his mom using when she was in one of her poetic moods. The description fit his new family, and it soon fit him too. The lack of spontaneity and creativity, of which his mother would not have approved, was welcomed for a while by Josh. Craving peace and acceptance, he allowed himself to be lulled into inactivity, believing that the sameness - the tedium of each day- was for him, that Jess and his cousins were giving him time to adjust to their home, fancy food, and good manners. But he gradually had to accept that what he was experiencing was the reality of their lives. He tried to adjust, even as he encouraged Ben to break some of the rules with him during those hours before Steve left and after he was finished with his days of personal freedom. The boys artlessly fell into their own routine of card games and quiet talk and learned to trust in each other while they filled the exquisite hours of sunrise and sunset, clueless about the pain their growing friendship could cost them.

On the fifteenth night, Steve, aware that something had changed in his household, positioned himself behind the closed door of the boys' room and listened. He loathed their laughter, their independent conversation, their peace, and his sense of exclusion.

The next morning, Jess had an announcement to make. She rushed through her explanation.

"Your dad and I had a talk last night about the room situation, Ben, and even though you and Josh are excited about sharing the bedroom, we feel that it would be much better – much more comfortable –for both of you if Josh takes the guest room."

"No way, Mom!" Ben snapped.

"Ben, it's crowded, and your father and I feel that you'll soon realize that both of you will need more privacy. It's best to make the move now than wait 'til later. We think we should make the move today sometime. It'll be easy to make the switch. And it will be better. Believe me. You'll see."

"It should be my decision, Mom," Ben insisted, even though he knew that he would never win the debate. "We're not crowded, are we, Josh? We like having someone to talk to. Come on, Mom."

Katie, always the peacemaker, voiced her solution. "We can take turns. Josh can sleep in the guest room for when he needs privacy, and then he can sleep in Ben's room part of the time, and part of the time he can be in my room. I'd like company too."

"Don't be dumb, Katie," Ben argued. "You're a girl. Josh is staying in my room, and that's it. It's stupid to change."

Josh wondered how many arguments Ben had ever won.

Skipping STONES

"It's okay, Ben," he said to stop the arguing. "I don't sleep so good at night. You know that. At home, I usually read or something before I'd fall asleep. I'd get up a lot and just wander around. Actually, I've been thinking about that. If I'm in a room by myself, I could do those things and not bother you." He nodded as though in deep thought and punched Ben's shoulder good-naturedly. "It makes sense to me. Your dad and mom are probably right. It will be better this way. I see that now."

The conversation, such as it was, was over.

Katie got a better grip on the blanket she still carried at times for comfort. "You'll be right next to me, Josh."

They decided to make the change right away, and in less than an hour Josh was moved into a room of his own. He didn't hang his posters, uncomfortably aware that they looked out of place in that house, and he stacked most of his books and personal belongings on shelves in his closet, making his new room as tidy and as impersonal as Ben's. The only treasure he could not set aside and felt was discreet enough to display was his mother's paperweight.

Dinner proceeded just as it had the night before and the night before that, with the children reciting by rote what they had done, followed by a lengthy account of Steve's day. When the sun started its descent and the second-best part of the day began, the children were sent to their rooms. Jess went to Katie's room first and tucked her in, reluctantly closing the door on her daughter's last request of the day, "I wish you could stay longer. One more story? Please?"

Ben was next, and Jess found him at his open window. She paused at his door and asked what he was doing. He simply said that he was sucking up the air.

By the time she tapped on Josh's door, he was determined to turn the mood around and gave her his best smile when she entered.

"I like this room," he said cheerfully and smiled again to prove it. "There's lots of space. And the bed is super-comfortable and big." Remembering something his mom had said once about Jess's house, he added, "Actually, the whole place is like something in a magazine. It could be in one of those house magazines that show people how to decorate."

He spit his words out like rapid gunfire, and Jess understood what he was trying to do.

His need pierced hers. Walking over to one of the windows that overlooked her garden, she straightened the drapes absent-mindedly and surprised herself when she shared part of her story with him.

"I almost became a decorator," she told him. "Right after design school. My roommate and I had it all planned."

He encouraged her. "Design school? No wonder you're so good."

She walked over to the huge armoire and ran her hand lovingly across its doors.

"We found a little place that was coming up for lease in Chagrin," she told him wistfully. "We were going to open a shop and design studio there. We actually talked to the owner and discussed the lease and what changes we could make to the space. We were going to call it Boutique-Deco Des Deux Amies. That means the design studio of the two friends. It's a mouthful isn't it? We were so young and so full of ourselves." She turned back to him and shrugged her shoulders. "We never did it, of course."

Josh was not the kind of child to let questions dangle. He had to ask why.

Skipping STONES

"I married Steve that summer, and we moved to Chicago." She looked back toward the window and let a sigh escape. "Later, he needed my help with his career. He was very busy, you see, and he needed me to be at home. And then Ben came along and then Katie. Oh, well," she added, forcing herself to smile. "Goodnight, Josh. Let me know if you need something."

"Goodnight. Sleep tight," he said and wished she wouldn't go. Jess closed the door behind her, and his mother's familiar response settled on him: "Don't let the bed bugs bite, big guy."

He buried his face into the pillow, heavy with loneliness, desperate to know the story of the family he had become a part of, agitated that he had not heard from his father. As the sleepless night wore on, the big room closed in around him and more slivers of his spirit broke away.

༺

During the weekdays when Steve was at work, the hours passed peacefully enough. Jess cleaned and read, baked, cleaned, and played board games with her children. Some days Ben and Josh fished in the stream or played soft ball in the park with the few kids who gathered there each day. Katie played with her doll Ariel and her Barbies, colored, and walked with her mother. Sometimes the three children had lunch and went swimming across the street at the club. Jess didn't join them, and Ben explained at some point that Steve didn't approve of Jess's flaunting her body in a bathing suit, just as he disapproved of her exchanging gossip with the other women.

And Josh finally began to unravel some of his family's story. There were mornings when Jess hung back and avoided her children's eyes. There were mornings when she refused to sit down because sitting was painful. There were mornings when the makeup didn't cover the black spots at her temples or under an eye. There were afternoons, right before Steve was due to come home, when Josh saw her drink something she kept hidden in a flask at the very back of the cupboard over the microwave or take two yellow pills from a small jar hidden in the same spot. There were evenings when Steve was engaged with his family and made them laugh and feel good about things, but there were too many evenings when he drank one glass of vodka after another and screamed at Jess for things she had done or things she hadn't. And there were nights when the children were awakened by muffled cries and groans seeping through their doors and walls. Those nights, Ben hid in his closet and cursed himself for hiding. Katie crawled under her bed, sucked her thumb, and told her doll to be a good girl. And Josh wrapped himself into his sheets under the open window and cried for the loss of his mother and the realization that he was trapped in a home with its own demons, ones that were much worse than those that had often haunted his mother or made up his nightmares.

No one talked about those nights. No one talked about anything of any significance. Josh had taken his and his mother's zeal for communication and honesty for granted and didn't realize what gifts he had had until those gifts were taken away. He yearned for the conversations he had had with Mimi and Papaw about things important and things inconsequential, and, as the days went by without hearing from Sam, he anguished with the need to talk to him about the loss they shared, even as his gloom and frustration grew over not receiving the call. He began to perceive that his father was, among other things, a promise-breaker.

The one bright light for Josh was Katie, Katie the optimist, the little girl who continued to smile. One evening, long after

Skipping STONES

sunset, Josh was standing at his open window, judging his nerve to climb out onto the roof for a moment of freedom, when he heard a tapping on his wall. He turned to listen and followed its direction as it moved from point to point, changing its rhythm. Realizing that the sound could only be coming from Katie, he tapped back, following her lead and smiling at the game they were playing. He pressed his ear close to the wall that separated them by inches and heard her giggle. Her tapping led to her door, and he held his breath. The house was so still that the muffled creaking of the hinges seemed more like an alarm as it made its way through the divide. He took her dare. She peeked around her door at him, her eyes wide with fear, betraying her smile. Katie had never intentionally broken a rule before. Her lips formed the word "Good-night", but made no sound.

The next afternoon, just before dinner, Josh found a picture from Katie propped against the mirror over his bathroom sink. There were two figures in her drawing, a little girl and a tall thin boy. The girl wore a purple dress and pink high heels. She had brown hair and big blue eyes and a big set of eyelashes. She was smiling with bright red lips. The boy wore chartreuse shorts and a blue plaid shirt and red tennis shoes. His hair was blond, and he had green eyes. The arms of the figures reached out toward each other through a thick black line that went from the top of the page to the bottom and was dotted with small red hearts. "Katie" and "Josh" were written in orange at the top.

༄

Josh and Ben were headed early one morning for the river to fish and catch frogs when they heard Jess call them to come back. She waited for them outside on the steps and handed Josh the phone.

"It's your dad," she whispered through her smile.

Josh had been waiting to hear those simple words for weeks, and he was momentarily paralyzed by them, wanting to relish them and, at the same time, gauging what his reaction to his father should be. Jess understood and gently pushed the phone toward him and signaled with a positive nod that everything would be fine.

"I'm glad I caught you before you got a good start on your day," Sam said. "Going fishing, I hear."

"Yeah. Down along the river."

Josh felt tongue-tied and pushed himself to explain that there were some big bass they might snare there but mainly they caught blue gills. They talked about the size of the fish, what bait he would use, and what kind of rod he had, and Sam asked Josh if he'd take him to see the spot when they got together.

"How would Monday be?" Sam asked.

It was all Josh could do to hold himself back from bouncing around the kitchen floor. His father was going to keep his promise after all.

"I'll have to check with Jess first to see what's planned for us here," he said, trying to keep he voice from cracking and not sounding overly excited.

"Well, I told Jess what I have in mind, and she thinks it'll be Okay," Sam told him. "What do you think about going out on my motorcycle if the weather's nice? I haven't had time to ride it much yet this summer, and I'd like to take you out on it."

"Sure," Josh said, almost choking on the words. "That would be fine. I don't have much planned, actually."

Skipping STONES

As he walked back outside to tell Ben about the plan, he felt a sliver of hope creep inside his mind that maybe things would begin to change for him, that the doors to his freedom had finally been opened. His positive mood was premature.

༄

Josh was sure he remembered Sam when he was still his dad even though his mom had always told him that he couldn't have had many memories of him. He was remembering, she said, what people had told him about his father. But no one had talked about Sam. He remembered the arguments his mom and dad had had just before he left. And he remembered his mother's tears. He had little knowledge about the causes of the harsh words. He understood the tears. But his memories went beyond those times.

No one had ever told him about the walks he remembered taking with his dad to a store to pick up the weekend newspaper and stopping on the way home for a shared root beer. He didn't remember having conversations with anyone about throwing balls with Sam in a small yard with a metal fence around it. No one talked about how, when he was really little, his father tickled him on the living room floor in a house he still remembered and made him say, "Please Daddy, with sugar on top," before he'd stop. And Josh was sure he remembered something about a restaurant with slippery yellow booths and loud music and his dad letting him turn on a milkshake maker after he filled it up with ice cream and milk and chocolate syrup. He absolutely remembered his father pouring the milkshake into one red plastic glass so they could drink it together through green straws. And there was one persistent memory about walking along a big lake close to where they used to live and watching Sam make little flat stones skip three times, sometimes four, along the top of the water before they sank. No one had ever talked to Josh about those things, but they popped up out of nowhere in his head sometimes, and he was sure they had really happened.

He had asked his mother so many times why Sam had left, and each time she'd explained that people grow out of love sometimes; sometimes things just don't work out, she'd say, and it's easier to live without each other than it is to keep trying to make it right, because trying so hard and not having it work hurts too damned much, and it's just too friggin' complicated. She said that he would understand someday.

He tried to understand, but sometimes when they went to the park together for a long walk, or when they'd leave soccer practice, and he'd see dads and their sons play pitch or football together or just walk easily side-by-side, he'd watch them 'til his chest hurt, and he'd tell his mom that he'd like to have a dad like that one sometime. And then mother and son would rush home and get on the computer's match-making sites to look over all the eligible dads out there.

Some of those men looked promising, and she'd fill out the form on the screen and begin a series of "discussions" through email. Sometimes she let him read the responses she received, and together they'd decide if the man seemed okay for her to test out. Josh got to know some of those email men and tried hard to be good around them so they would want to stay with him and his mom so she'd be happy, but she always lost interest or the man did, and it would all end, and a while later, the research would start all over again. As he got older, Josh learned to keep his distance from the dates that looked promising so he wouldn't be disappointed when they didn't work out. After each break-up, his mom would say, "It doesn't

Skipping STONES

matter because I have you, my little man," and he'd hold her tight right back to give her courage and would hope with all of his might that she wouldn't grow out of love for him.

༄

Monday finally came, and Josh climbed out of bed when he expected the sun and waited for it to show itself. He watched as the moon and stars began to disappear onto the other side of the world and the black sky turn grey-yellow. He looked for clouds that could ruin the day.

He rushed to get his clothes on, rinsed the sleepy stuff out of his eyes, brushed his teeth, and checked the clock. Just five-forty-three. He took his tennis shoes back off and tiptoed in his stocking feet back and forth across the floor, wondering what to do with the hours before he'd be allowed out of his room and then the other hours that would have to go by until Sam would be there. Cautiously opening the window, he breathed in the earth smells. Robins and sparrows and finches jabbered and flitted between trees, a black squirrel jumped branch to branch, fresh darts of pale sun flickered on damp blossoms, and breezes wafted around leaves. Life out there made his room feel even more lifeless and dull. He had to escape.

The handle turned easily in his right hand. He shut the door behind him and walked toward the stairs.

"Be still, now. Be a good girl," a small voice said behind Katie's closed door. "Be a good girl and don't cause any trouble."

He opened her door a crack and found her sitting on the floor, holding Ariel on her lap.

"Katie?" He whispered. "Are you all right?"

"What are you doing all dressed?" She whispered back.

Josh would not lie to her.

"I'm going outside to wait for the sun."

"I'll come too!" she said and rushed around her room on her tiptoes, looking for her shoes.

"I can't let you do that. I'm breaking a rule, and if you came along, you'd be breaking a rule too. Be real quiet and pretend you don't know what I'm doing."

She started to argue and he understood, but it was too risky.

"Tell you what. Stand by your window, and when I get outside I'll wave to you," he said. "And I'll bring you a surprise. Be real quiet, Katie. This is our secret, okay?"

She rushed to the window before he reached the door and turned to him with a smile that was almost big enough to wipe his fear and guilt away. The trip down the five stairs to the back hall and the door took no more than fifteen steps, but it felt like one of the most dangerous journeys he had ever taken. The turn he made on the lock clicked so loud in his ears that he was sure it reverberated throughout the house. Holding his breath, he stood frozen for a very long time before he was able, finally, to open the door and step outside.

The freedom he felt out there brought him specks of relief. In his old life, the early-morning songs of the birds, the fragrances carried on the breeze, and the dew under his feet had been gifts served up to him whenever he had wanted them, but today these gifts were tangled up in his guilt from having to sneak and possibly having to lie later and his realization that his freedom was temporary.

He walked slowly through the dawn, squiggling his toes in the fresh dew, and stepped into a small ray of sunlight that fell onto a patch of grass in front of him. His mind was flooded with memories of his mother. She had told him that Native Americans believe that after death a person's soul often passes through to another creature and visits loved ones in order to make sure that they're safe or to make a sign that their spirit is free. He looked around for something that might hold the spirit of her. "I hope you're here, Mom," he whispered. "Are you here?"

Remembering his promise to Katie, he looked up and waved to her, wishing that he could share his freedom. Turning to Jess's carefully tended garden, he twisted off a pink rose, some white daisies, and sprigs of lavender and held them up to her. The bouquet glowed in the brightening light. His time was up. He signaled to Katie that he was going back inside and pointed to the yellow butterfly that came out of nowhere and hovered close to the bouquet in his hand. For just a moment, he thought of capturing it for her, but butterflies are fragile and must be free.

Much later, Josh and Ben were gobbling down their breakfasts, when Katie wandered into the kitchen, sleepy-eyed, carrying the small bouquet to show to her mother.

"What a beautiful bouquet, honey," Jess said. "Where did it come from?"

Katie smiled mysteriously. "Oh, it just appeared in my room real early this morning."

"Really?" Her mother exclaimed. "My, that's very special. Did a fairy bring it in the night?"

Katie giggled and glanced at Josh. "Maybe. Maybe not. There was a butterfly too, but it didn't come in. Butterflies should never be caught. They have to be free because they're so fragile. Well, they're only fragile when they're caught. Some of them can fly for hundreds of miles so in that way they're really strong. Anyway, this butterfly was a sign."

Ben was only mildly interested but voiced his opinion. "That's stupid, Katie," he muttered. He had forgotten how to pretend.

"I used to believe in signs," Jess said. "It's wonderful to believe in a little magic. What do you think it meant, Katie?"

"I don't know exactly. It does mean something though. That's what he…I mean, that's what I thought. Maybe it means that something special is going to happen to us."

"Maybe," Jess said. "We'll all watch for it. We need to be attentive. Sometimes something good can be right here in front of us, and we can miss it if we aren't careful. I hope you get lots more surprises, Katie."

They put the flowers in a small vase, and as the young girl carried it with solemnity and dignity to her room, Jess caught Josh's eye and formed the words, *thank you.*

༄

Ben and Katie had told their friends in the neighborhood about Sam's cycle, and a small crowd was gathered outside when the vroom of the engine came echoing down the street. Katie held her hands to her ears and laughed uncontrollably while Ben worried that the police would be called. It was a sleek machine, a black-on-black Harley Sportster, and Josh had trouble believing he was really going to ride on it. Sam came to a steady stop and lowered his feet to balance the machine, revved up the engine one more time, and shut it down. He took off his black helmet, put it over the handle bars, and slung his leg over the seat.

Josh wasn't sure what to do. His palms were sweaty, and he hoped Sam wouldn't expect a handshake.

"These your friends?" Sam asked easily.

"They want to see your cycle," Josh said, hoping he didn't look as dumb as he felt.

Skipping S T O N E S

Sam greeted Katie and Ben and, after shaking hands with their friends, let them all take turns sitting on it. At some point, Josh remembered to turn off his grin.

After everyone settled down a little, Jess walked across the yard to say hello. Her cheeks were flushed, and she knew it. Her reaction to Sam was still impossible to control. It had been a long time since she'd seen him, but the extra years looked good on him. She touched her hair self-consciously and smiled, feeling younger, absurdly enough, than she had felt for a very long time.

Everyone watched as Sam took out a shiny new black helmet and passed it to Josh, and the boy put it on as casually as he possibly could, hoping it wasn't backwards. Sam got on the bike first and instructed his son to put his left foot on the foot peg and to swing himself up like he was getting on a horse, something else he had never done. "I'll have him back by mid-afternoon," he called out to Jess as they circled around in the road to head back to the center of the village.

Josh told him how to get back to River Road so that he could show him the rest of the village, and they took their time crossing the big green bridge that spanned the river, while he pointed out the waterfall on one side and the foot bridge on the other. Sam parked the cycle in a space in front of the post office, and they walked to the places along the river where Josh and Ben hung out sometimes. He wanted to see the village's arboretum, and they walked through it while Josh explained where the best places to fish were.

"It's a super place," Sam said. "You like it here, don't you?"

Josh thought about his answer. "It's great to be close to the river."

Leaving the village, they followed the narrow, rolling hills through a piece of the neighboring village, and Josh pointed to the river that continued to drift in and out of view. Sam slowed way down so that they could observe horses grazing in the fields, wild flowers growing along the wooden fences that separated private pastures, a red bird flitting across the blue sky, and some of the huge estates peeking out from behind giant trees. They stopped to watch a turkey vulture circle above them and perch on a fence post and marveled at its giant wingspan and ugly small head. Mom would have loved this, Josh thought and realized that he felt more like himself again, the boy that he had been when she was alive.

"Want to stop by the Polo Fields?" Sam shouted over the roar of the engine when they were on their way again.

They found a place to park and joined the joggers, a few teen-age girls soaking up the sun on blankets, and dogs and their owners playing catch- and- return with Frisbees.

"I'd like to have a dog someday," Sam said. "Maybe when I have more time to devote to it."

"Me too," Josh answered. "Mom and I couldn't get one. Our place was too small and, besides, she was allergic to dog hair. What kind would you get?"

"A Newfoundland lab," Sam told him. "Love those dogs."

"I'd like that kind too. At least, I'd like to have a big one – not one of those little yappy things. Labs love the water." Josh felt at ease, and conversation came readily to him. "Want to walk to the river? There's a path to get there right across the road."

Sam had been down that same path many times before, but he let Josh lead the way and said nothing about previous visits. They picked their way carefully over the uneven black dirt and exposed tree roots and eventually cut over to the river where they found a flat boulder they could both sit on. They observed the shallow current make its way over rocks only

Skipping STONES

half-submerged in the sandy river bottom and threw pebbles into the river, watching where they settled.

"Do you know how to make stones jump across the water?" Josh hadn't practiced the question, and it surprised even him.

"I do," Sam answered. "But it's too shallow here. You mean skipping stones, don't you? Whenever I get to a body of water, I think about it. What about you?"

"Not really," Josh said. "I could probably do it now though."

He put together what he wanted to say next and wondered if it would be all right to go on. He needed to know if his memories were real.

"I think you might have tried to teach me," he said in a timid voice. "A long time ago. I think I remember that."

The father took a while to answer.

"I did," he said finally. "You were way too young to learn, but I tried to show you how anyway. Lots of times. I took you out to the lake for walks when you were no more than a toddler." He chuckled. "I figured you were so special you could do anything at any age. You tried so hard, but the stones all just went kerplunk. You didn't get frustrated, though. You were determined."

Determined. The same word Josh and his mother had used so many times to describe each other. Her determination was to rise above her illness and to somehow maintain her independence. For Josh, it had been his promise to himself to protect her and to be the kind of person she had wanted him to be.

"You need to find flat stones that are thin too," Sam continued. "There are tons of them around here, but it's too shallow now. The key's in the wrists. You fling it side-armed and follow through. It takes a little patience, but it isn't that hard once you understand it."

Two of the boy's memories had been confirmed. He got up and walked a little upstream and wondered what else would be okay to ask. There were bigger rocks there, and they stuck up out of the water, making a slippery path across the narrower portion of the river. Josh studied the depth and speed of the water.

"I'll bet someone could cross the river here if he wanted to," Sam said behind him. "Might be kind of fun to try and see how it all looks from the other side. What do you think?"

Josh turned to him in surprise. "I was thinking the same thing."

"Want to give it a try?"

"We'll most likely get our feet soaked."

The current was stronger than either had anticipated, and the rocks were moss-covered and slippery. Mid-way, Josh stood precariously on two of them, wondering where to plant his feet next when he heard Sam cry out, "Oh, damn!" A splash followed, and Josh, turning around too fast, slid off too, and the two of them stood side by side there, ankle-deep in water, bent over with laughter.

"Oh, what the hell," Sam said, catching his breath, and the two sloshed unsteadily across to the other side.

They sat on the bank, took off their shoes and socks, rolled up their wet jeans, and stretched out on the warm bank. Sam didn't apologize for cussing, and Josh was glad. He was being who he was.

"Did you ever come here with your mom?" His father asked.

It was the first time anyone had come right out and asked Josh about Becky since her death, and he realized just how desperate he was to share his memories of her with someone.

"Here and lots of places in the park," he said. "This was one of our favorites."

Skipping STONES

"I'll bet you crossed the river with her too, didn't you? Ever been to Squaw Rock, on the other side?"

"Oh, yea. We went there a lot of times."

"That was one of our spots too," Sam said, pitching pebbles again. "In fact, I think one of the big reasons I want a Lab so bad is because of one of my memories of her." He settled himself, taking a few moments to adjust to his thoughts. "Right after we were married, we took a picnic down there at Squaw Rock. We were living in Brecksville then, but whenever we wanted to get away, take a ride somewhere, she usually wanted to come back to the east side of town where her family lived. We'd usually drive out here for a walk or something."

Josh held on to every word. It felt strange, he realized, to hear stories about his mother that he had not been a part of. He had naively thought that all of their memories belonged to just the two of them.

"So, anyway," Sam continued, "one day I'll never forget, we were eating our sandwiches on the rock. Nobody was around, and we were just sitting like this, talking about this and that, when all of a sudden a Lab puppy bolted past us, barking its head off, as puppies do. Its owner, an older woman, finally made her way down the steps. Remember those steep rock steps down to the river? Anyway, she apologized for her dog and called for him to come, but the little thing was too excited and too interested in the river to obey. Remember the rapid waterfall just beyond the rock, just downstream? The water's deep there, and the current's strong. Well, that darned dog saw a big tree limb floating in the river toward the falls and decided he was going to fetch it."

Josh watched his father's intent face and held onto every word he said. The memory, he knew, was strong and important to him, and Josh was grateful for the telling of it.

"Well," Sam continued, "the pup realized too late that the limb was too big for him and he had made a mistake, but by then he was caught in the current. He paddled like crazy to get to shore, but he was stuck, and we were sure he would drown. And suddenly, out of nowhere, was your mom. She rushed into the river, up to her waist in that cold water, balanced herself against the force of it and the slippery river bed until she reached that puppy. She grabbed him and held him in her arms, for God's sake, and got him back to the bank, never once giving one single thought to the danger. She just did what her instincts told her to do, and when it was over, she acted like it was something anyone would have done."

Sam was quiet for a while then. They both were. And then, as if it was the most natural thing in the world to do, Sam put his hand on his son's shoulder.

"She was quite a gal, your mom," he said in a low voice.

The significance of that gesture and those words went deep into Josh, and even after his father took his hand away and his words faded into the air, Josh could still feel his touch of intimacy and the strength of his respect for his mother. Happiness in a person's life is often measured by single moments of warmth.

They walked through the water again to the other side, dried their feet on a small towel Sam had in the saddle bag, and decided to ride into the neighboring community of Chagrin Falls to see what was going on there. The ride was uneventful until they reached the stop sign at the top of the steep hill that goes down to the village. Josh had been down that hill many times, but he couldn't go down it that day. He became light-headed and disoriented. He panicked and fell awkwardly as he leaped off the bike.

Skipping STONES

"Hey, buddy, hey," Sam cried, cussing himself for his lack of judgment. "It's okay. We're fine. We're not going down. Hop back on here. There's a better way to go."

Sam gave Josh time to recover from his panic and traveled slowly through the longer, flat way into town so that he could settle down even more. Finally, they pulled up in front of Starbucks and waited for an elderly couple to maneuver their bike out of a parking space. A line of bikers of all ages stood leaning against the railing overlooking the waterfalls below and greeted them as comrades. Josh hoped he wasn't swaggering as he walked towards the cafe.

They drank their iced mochas while they walked up to the Popcorn Shop to get a couple of bags of Kettle Corn, and Josh assured his father that he was fine with their plan to head out for Burton, the small town noted primarily for its maple festival . Following the back roads that wound through Amish country, they eventually found their way to the center of town, where they bought maple candy for Katie and Ben and Jess and a maple-scented candle for the grandmother Josh didn't know. They walked around the square and were drawn into a place called Cogan's Diner by the sign outside that claimed "Bad Food and Lousy Service" and ordered up cheeseburgers and fries. Josh gladly accepted his father's request for a future taste test between his restaurant's food in Westlake and Cogan's. The challenge meant that the day had been successful and they would see each other again.

And suddenly it was time to head back. Jess would be expecting them soon, and Sam had to drive clear across town to get to his restaurant in time for the evening rush. On the ride to his new home, Josh thought mostly about the choices his mother and father had made that caused him and his father to go in different directions and call different places "home."

Katie and Ben ran out to meet them when they got back and begged Sam to come inside. To Josh's delight, he accepted and acted as though he had all the time in the world to spend with them. For Katie, the highlight of the visit was when he magically pulled a coin from her ear.

"Maybe we could all get together again soon," Sam suggested to Josh before he left. "I'll call you, and we'll set a date for everyone to have lunch at my place and do that taste test."

Josh's new small world seemed even smaller as he and his aunt and cousins went back inside. It was late, and Jess rushed to begin her ritual of making everything perfect. The pillows were plumped, Steve's glass of Vodka was set out on the silver tray, and dinner was shoved into the oven. Katie had a conversation with Ariel, and Ben shut himself up in his room with his Game Boy. Josh went out on the front steps and thought about his day with his father, and Jess had a quick drink from her flask.

Steve arrived punctually at six o'clock. Had his Vodka. Had another. Changed clothes. Told the family when to sit. Described his day. Invited them to speak.

"I didn't do much after Josh left," Ben said and instantly regretted what he had started.

"And where did Josh go?" Steve demanded.

Ben turned to his mother, and Jess hesitantly explained that Josh had a meeting with his father. It took seconds for Steve to absorb the news and several seconds more to calm himself for his response. The family watched the process and waited anxiously for the outcome.

"So you met your long-lost dad again," he said, clearly making an effort to appear relaxed. "Well, good for you two. So tell me about it. Where did you go and what did you do?"

Skipping STONES

In the short time Josh had lived there, he had learned that no question from Steve should be taken lightly, and he read the tenseness in everyone around the table. He would need to be very careful with his answer, even though he didn't understand why.

"Well, first we just rode around here for a while and then we went to the park and on into Chagrin," he said, trying to show no enthusiasm. "Then we checked out Burton. We just rode around, and he dropped me off back here so he could get to work on time."

Steve studied Josh, and the intensity of his look made the boy avert his eyes. Then he turned on Jess.

"Why didn't I know about the visit? Was there a reason you didn't tell me?"

Clearly flustered, Jess said that she had forgotten about it until after he had left.

"Josh reminded me no more than a half hour or so before he was supposed to arrive," she lied.

He turned to Katie. "What about you, Katie? What can you tell me about today?"

Katie rushed to fill in the blanks. "His motorcycle made a bunch of racket, and it was funny. We all got to sit on it. He's real nice. Ben wanted to take a ride on it, but Mom wouldn't let him. Today was Josh's day. We're going to try to meet him again. They brought us back some surprises."

His look made her flinch, and she realized too late that she had said too much.

Steve studied his wine glass, and the four watched as he swirled the deep red liquid around in it. He spoke to the glass.

"I'd forgotten about Sam's interest in motorcycles. It's been a long time since I've thought about him at all. Of course, you kids never really knew the man. He left the family a long time ago. Becky never talked about him either after he took off. No reason to." He looked piercingly at Jess. "And here he is again."

He looked back at his wine. "I've always wondered what the fascination is with motorcycles and the people who own them. They always seemed to me...let's see. How should I say it? Common, maybe? Yes. 'Red-necks' comes to mind too. 'Macho'. Yes. That's it. That's the word. They like being 'macho'." Wouldn't you say so, Jess? Isn't that your feeling about bikers?"

He kept his eyes on the glass and waited for her answer.

"I've never thought about it," she said. "I'm sure Sam's intention was to let Josh have a different kind of experience."

It was coming. She ticked off the progression: the calm, the reasoning, the innuendoes, and then the sudden outbursts. She braced herself. *Let it be over quickly.*

"But wouldn't you say they are a little different from the rest of us?" He persisted. "Wouldn't you say they're kind of out there on the fringe?"

"I don't know. I suppose some of them are."

"You have very few opinions about anything, do you, Jess?"

Let it be quick.

"And what do you think, Ben? Do you think men who ride motorcycles are grown boys trying to be macho? Or red-necks? Or are you like your mother and have no opinion?"

Ben squirmed. He was caught. No one would be satisfied with his answer. *He's after us. He's coming after us.*

"I don't know," he said. "Maybe. I don't know anyone else who owns one."

Steve took his eyes off his glass and turned to Ben. "You don't know? Maybe? You have so much trouble thinking. And you, Josh. What do you think?"

Josh had also learned in a short time that even partial honesty was unacceptable there, and yet he felt the need to justify his father's hobby.

"He likes the feeling of freedom it gives him," he explained. "He likes the feel of the open road and the wind in his face. He's not trying to be macho or anything." He ploughed on, desperate to prove Sam's kindness and value.

"You get to see things close up, things you could miss in a car. You're right there, close to the road. It's like when Mom and I rode our bikes. It just feels good."

"It feels good," Steve repeated. "I see. He likes the wind in his face. Uh huh. Tell me more."

"We went down to the river and walked through the water," Josh went on, surprised and relieved to find this unpredictable man so interested in his father. "He told me a story about how my mom saved a puppy at Squaw Rock."

Steve interrupted him. "How sweet. She saved a puppy."

He motioned to Jess to get more wine.

Katie took a risk and spoke without being asked to. "Tell him about it, Josh," she suggested.

"You just interrupted, Katie. You know better than that," her father insisted.

Katie held her hands clasped in her lap and, unable to help herself, she whispered to Josh, "I really like your dad."

"What was that?" Steve demanded. "How would you know enough about that man to form an opinion that quickly?"

She looked to Jess for support. "He's really nice, isn't he, Mama?" She said.

Steve's face turned deep red. "And just how would you know that he's really nice when you were with him for such a short time?" He sputtered. "How can you make such quick decisions about someone you've never known?"

Katie was trapped again, but she had no choice but to answer her father's question.

"Well, he told us funny stories and showed us a magic trick with a penny. He pulled one out of his ear, and…"

"He was in this house?" Steve exclaimed. "That man was in here talking to you? You entertained him in my home?"

Katie's little arms swept out to everyone at the table. "Mommy's nice and you're nice and Josh is nice and Ben's nice. Everybody's nice."

Nothing she might have said would have curtailed her father's feeling of betrayal. Steve stood up so abruptly that his chair crashed backwards to the floor. He kicked it for falling. The children cowered.

"Get out! Everybody get out! You," he said, pointing his finger at Jess, "you stay here."

Katie and Ben ran to hide in their rooms, and Josh walked with as much dignity as possible to his. He stood rooted just inside the door, wondering what had just happened. What rule had been broken? What had he done wrong? It didn't matter. It was about Sam, and so it was about him. He would apologize and set things right.

He practically ran back through the hall to get it done before he lost his nerve and followed voices to his aunt and uncle's bedroom. Ugliness stopped him at the door.

Bitch. Whore. Tramp. Something heavy crashed to the floor and something lighter fell against the wall. *Pathetic.* Someone moaned. *Your dead sister's husband. In my own goddam home.* A slapping sound. And more. And more. Jess's muffled voice. *Please. Sorry.* Another moan. Whispers too hard to make out. *Prove it*, he said. *Prove it, bitch. Prove it.*

Josh didn't know how, but he understood exactly what was happening behind that wall and was embarrassed by it. And ashamed. Forcing his body to move, he backed away, holding his hands over his ears, trying to expunge the real groans coming from the room and the pathetic scene in his mind. Back in his room, he opened his window and took big gulps of fresh air. He had barely begun trying to put the pieces of the story together when he heard Steve battering down the hall.

Finished with his wife, the man was ready to diminish the children.

"Everyone up. Get up. Get the hell out here," he shouted, pounding on Josh's door. "Get out here, you little son of a bitch, you needy little bastard." He banged on Katie's door. "You too, little girlie. All of you, everyone out."

He lined the children up against the wall and instructed them to "Take the position." Ben and Katie bent their knees into a sitting position and slid their backs half-way down the side of the wall. Josh did the same.

"See what you've caused?" Steve said, standing over him. "See? You break rules, you insult me in my home, you pay. Understand?" He stood in front of Katie. "Take your thumb out of your mouth, and get rid of that damned doll," he said and threw Ariel down the hall.

Sweat poured down his face and onto his open shirt. He breathed heavily. "We're going to get some things straight around here," he slurred, slamming his fist on the wall again and stumbling from the force of the blow.

"I'm sick and tired of what's going on in this house. No discipline. No respect. You break rules. You defy me. Damned mother treats you like babies. Turned this place into a goddammed zoo. That's what she's done. A zoo. Do you hear me?"

He turned to Josh. "You go ape-shit over that man, and he's nothing. Nothing. A damned lady's man. Macho man, that's what he is, a damned macho man. Your own mother didn't want him anymore. He's nothing. Never was. Never will be."

He bent down and put his face close to Ben's, and Ben turned away from his breath.

"And you," he said. "Playing gaga over his little toy. You're a disgrace."

One perceived insult after another took shape in the man's mind, and his own insecurities leaked out.

"And another thing," he said. "Look at me. Tell me what was so damned funny the other day when we played ball. Was that funny, to see your father stumble because your cousin there is showing off? Look at me and stop shaking. Weakness makes me sick. Answer me. I want to know why you thought it was funny."

The boy had no answer, and Steve didn't expect one.

"And that business about sharing a room with your cousin over there," he continued. "I will not have you turn into a damned faggot. You hear me?"

The man never forgot, and he never forgave.

He checked his watch and smiled as he watched the children's legs quiver and their backs arch involuntarily to find relief from the ache there. He knew they had reached their limit when they pressed their lips against the all-over pain in their young muscles and joints and breathed shallowly.

Katie was the first to yield. Her legs quivered and she fell to her knees. Josh couldn't watch.

"Do you have anything to say, girlie?" Her father asked.

She shook her head and wiped her tears on her shoulder. He let her go after she repeated after him that she would be a good girl.

Worn out but not yet finished with his punishment, Steve turned back to Josh. His sudden calm was terrifying. Josh tried to concentrate.

Skipping STONES

"You know, Josh," he said, "that I'm the one responsible for you now. You're in my care, and I take that very seriously. It's what your mother wanted. She chose me over him. Without me, you have nothing and no one. He's a loser. Everyone knows that. And, just for the record, so was your mother."

He bent down to Josh, his voice a whisper. "You are not to see that man again, do you hear me? Not tomorrow, not next week or next month or next year. I'm in charge of you. That man is out of the picture. Understand?"

He was finished and was thrilled with his win. Stumbling past Ben, he instructed, "Get your sorry ass to bed."

Josh let his body sink to the floor and watched Ben crawl into his room. Ariel lay twisted down the hall. He struggled to his feet and picked up the doll and set it gently against Katie's door.

Once back in his room, he gathered up his mother's belongings and held them on his lap in the same way he had done every night since he had been delivered to that house. He didn't belong. He was an interloper, an additional sore in the core of everyone's lives. What was it? What was the story? Nothing in Josh's past had prepared him for what he was experiencing there, and he struggled to define it. But his efforts were overshadowed by the one declaration that his young mind understood absolutely and didn't want to accept: he would never see Sam again.

The edict was too crippling to even think about. And so were the things Steve had said about his father. They not only collided with Josh's own recent perceptions of him, but they also interfered with all of the hopes and dreams he had had about Sam for as long as he could remember. Sorting through what he had been told about his father and what he had actually experienced, and what he needed to believe were tantamount to the violence he had experienced.

The diary seemed to pulse under his palms. Opening it, he riffled through the pages to his mother's final entry and the blank pages that followed. He found a pencil in the chest beside his bed and wrote "My Memories" on the first blank page. And below the title, he wrote down everything he remembered about the day he re-met his father and the hours he had spent with him. And he wrote about the goodness of his mother.

Jess

It was late the next morning when Jess was able to call the children out of their rooms, and she turned her back to them to give herself a few more seconds to compose herself as they walked to her in the kitchen.

Katie went to her first and touched her hand. "Mama?" She whispered around the thumb in her mouth, knowing that Jess would need comforting. "I'll help you, Mama. I'll help," she said. But Jess's pain was much deeper than even Katie's loving touch could reach.

Jess turned around and said that she was all right. But she wasn't. She was dressed well as always. Her hair was brushed back, and she had a pretty band around it. But she knew her makeup didn't hide the blotches of red on her face and the dark black mass above her eye. She had trouble moving, and Ben and Josh turned their eyes away from her, the way you do when you really don't want to see. Or when you're embarrassed by what's there.

All day long Jess and the children pretended that nothing had happened. No one asked questions. No one offered answers. Instead, they feigned busyness. Three of them had mastered denial over the years. Josh had come into it late, but he was a good student.

At four o'clock sharp, just like every other afternoon, Jess went into action again. She searched for dust, brought in fresh flowers, turned on the warming drawer, and checked to make sure the silverware was perfectly perpendicular to the table's edge. Then she took a pill from the cache she had hidden in the cupboard.

When Steve came home, he was carrying two big grocery bags and was smiling.

"We're going to celebrate us," he told Jess. "Put away whatever you fixed for dinner, and see what I brought home from our favorite restaurant. It's a veritable feast."

She went to him and thanked him for what he had brought. He lifted her face to his and kissed her gently and whispered that he loved her so much.

He had had a good day, he told his family as they settled around the table. It was clear that he expected them to forget the events of the previous evening because he had. Dinner went well enough, and he even played a game of Scrabble with the boys while Jess and Katie cleaned up.

And then, just before the children were sent to their rooms for the night, he turned to Jess, as if suddenly remembering something fairly inconsequential, and said to her, "Don't you have something important you want to say, honey?"

He smiled at her and waited while she stumbled over her words.

"We've decided that you're too big to be talked to in your rooms at night," she said, dreading her children's reactions. "We'll all say our good-nights together before you go upstairs from now on."

"Even me?" Katie wanted to know. "Aren't we still going to read to each other before I go to bed?"

"It's time you all grow up," her father interjected. "You're a big girl, Katie. You need to learn to do things on your own. Being tucked in at night is for babies. Starting tonight, no more baby stuff around here." He said a simple goodnight, turned his back, and walked away. "Come on, Jess, it's adult time."

The children stood uncertainly in front of her.

"Can I kiss you goodnight, Mama?" Katie asked.

Jess watched them walk up the stairs away from her and returned the kiss Katie blew in her direction.

Steve rubbed his wife's back and massaged her feet and told her again how much he loved her. He put his head in her lap and wrapped his hand around hers.

"Tell me you love me like I love you, baby," he said.

She stroked his cheeks until he fell asleep and cautiously reached for the TV remote to turn the mindless program off.

There was no peace for her. She wondered if Katie had cried herself to sleep and was reminded of the night almost thirteen years ago when she had closed the door to Ben's room and had left him crying in his crib for the first time. The rule had been set by Steve: as long as everything was in perfect order and dinner and drinks were ready when he got home, he hadn't cared how much she catered to her son, but the nights had always belonged to the man of the house, and they began whenever he returned to his home. The rules about bedtime had been adjusted over the years and had nothing to do with the children's ages or the hour of the evening. Instead, they depended entirely on Steve's sense of power and the size of his ego. Now both had just been threatened again, and this time the threat had come from his nephew and ex-brother-in-law.

She had known from the beginning that she had made a huge mistake bringing Josh into her home, but she reasoned that she had had no recourse. She and Steve had agreed, with very little thought, to Becky's request that they become Josh's guardians if she died young. No one imagined that she would. But just two months ago, that agreement they made had the full authority of law, and Josh had become a part of Jess's tragic life.

If only she had told her sister the truth all those years ago when she had had the chance. But she had been too proud and too frightened. If she had told Becky the story of her married life, her entire family would have found out that she was living a lie. They would have judged her, and she couldn't face either their pity or disgust.

And now there was terrible guilt to work through. She had failed her sister and the boy. She understood that Josh would continue to be dragged down with her and Ben and Katie, but she couldn't think through what could be done about it. After all of those years of groveling to please her husband, she no longer had any faith in her own convictions. And so she made the same vow that she had made every night since Ben was born: *I'll try harder to please my husband. I'll change him. I'll protect the children. I'll endure it. Someday the violence will end.* She clung to the dream, just as desperately as a drowning person would hold on to flotsam.

༄

Steve announced that they would all be going to the family cookout at the club that weekend, and Jess and the children looked forward to it. If nothing else, it would be a diversion. He came home from work early on the afternoon of the party to make sure his family was scrubbed and properly dressed, actually lining them up for inspection. Ben and Katie passed but Josh's clothes didn't suit him, and he considered the pros and cons of leaving him behind. Josh was once again the source of consternation for the family. Steve finally decided that not having the grieving boy at the party would look worse than taking him wearing the wrong style of clothing. The family had listened attentively throughout the harangue and had sympathized with the man's indecision.

Once at the party, Steve became the devoted husband and loving father, smiling at Jess and engaging his children in conversation. He introduced Josh to everyone and told them how proud he was of "the boy" and how he was handling the "situation." Ben and Katie basked in their father's praise and graciousness, holding on, as they always did, for any sign of affection from him. Josh felt like he was an actor in a play.

Flushed with success among his friends at the club, Steve continued the ruse throughout the following day and called his in-laws to invite them over for dinner.

"Things are finally settling down since we saw you last time," he told them. "Josh is doing great. It's good to have him here, especially for the kids; the three of them have become very close. There've been some detours along the way, but we've worked it all out. It's been harder on Jess. She's taken a lot on, and I'm proud of her ability to cope."

Cocktails and wine and conversation flowed. Jess kept up. After dinner, Steve and Papaw went outside to the patio to have cigars, the children grabbed the opportunity to escape to the park, and Jess tried unsuccessfully to remain steady enough to refill glasses of wine for her and Mimi.

"Here, honey. Let me do that," Mimi said to her. "Are you sure you want more?"

The question embarrassed Jess, and she poured the wine down the sink. Now, both of them were upset.

"I thought it would be fun for the two of us to relax together," Jess snapped, "but if you're thinking I've had too much, then we won't." She instantly regretted her sharp words.

Mimi apologized and, filling both of their glasses, suggested that they sit alone in the front yard for some girl talk.

"I didn't mean to upset you," she said as they walked toward the door. "It's just that you look so tired, honey."

She put her hand on Jess's cheek and turned her face a little toward the light of the chandelier. Some of the blotches from the beating Jess had taken several nights before and the dark spot over her right eyebrow had broken through the makeup; the ones on her arms were covered by her blouse.

"What's this?" Mimi asked. "Did you fall?"

Jess turned her head away and fell back on an answer she had used before with someone else.

"Oh, I bent down to pick up a lid I dropped in the kitchen and forgot the counter ledge was there," she said. "It's nothing."

Even as she spoke those words out loud, she thought to herself, *I could do it. I could tell the truth now and set us free, if only she'd really look at me and see.*

"I'd like to get together with you soon," she said, the words slipping out unprotected. "I'd like us to have a good talk alone."

"So there is something wrong," Mimi said. "I thought so. You've been quiet all afternoon. It's about Josh, isn't it?"

"It's not just about Josh. There are other things," Jess admitted.

"I can imagine, honey. Of course," her mother said. "One thing always leads to another and before you know it, everything feels out of control. I understand how tired you must be. And how stressed you are."

Mimi rubbed her forehead and sighed, and Jess saw the fatigue around her eyes. She has just lost a daughter, Jess reminded herself and regretted adding to her strain.

"Now probably isn't a good time to talk about things, Mom," she said. "Maybe we should talk another time when it isn't so late and we aren't so tired."

"Let's do that, honey, and real soon," Mimi said. "If it's any help, I'm having trouble too," she continued. "I'm having trouble sleeping. I have a real good sleeping aid. I don't like to take it, but I can't function well without sleep. My head feels muddy when I'm so tired. I make mistakes. I'd be happy to let you try one to see if it helps."

They settled into the wicker chairs on the front lawn, and Mimi prattled on.

"Ahhh. This is better," she said. "The kids seem so happy together, Jess. That should give you comfort. Josh is a little quiet, I think, but I'm sure he'll be more like his old self with time. He's a strong, self-assured little guy. I have to admit that I miss him being around. He got your dad and me going when he was with us, that's for sure."

She stretched and yawned. "Are you sure you don't want to tell me what's on your mind now, honey?"

The right question finally came, but at the wrong time and in the wrong way.

Josh

Even though Josh had been told in absolute terms that his father was no good and that he was off-limits, he kept waiting for Sam to call. The memories of the day they had spent together had meshed perfectly with the ones he had of his mother and brought him happiness. But always behind the happiness were the pictures that Steve had drawn of the two of them. Those images gnawed at him and made him doubt. The goodness and quality of his parents were the first things the boy thought about when he got up each morning and the last things he thought about when he went back to his analyses at night. He needed confirmation. Contact with his father became all important.

Before, in his previous life, when he had trouble sorting things out, his mother had told him to write down what was on his mind because affirming his thoughts in writing and in some order would help make sense of things. She had always done it. So many nights he had been awakened by the light in their old kitchen, and he'd get up quietly and find her making her lists. Sometimes she'd invite him to sit with her and give her his input; most often she asked him to go back to his room and leave her alone with her concerns, saying simply that often holing yourself away alone is the only way to find answers to your dilemma. What he didn't know was how often she tore her lists apart and flung them into the waste basket, frustrated by the scope of her fears and her realization that she was incapable of surmounting them on her own.

Josh decided that he'd try to work things out the way she had and walked down to the river where it would be easier, he thought, to think clearly. He sat under a huge pine tree and wrote whatever popped into his head, just the way his mother had told him to.

1. *I miss my mom*
2. *I miss my old life, my friends*
3. *I want to laugh and be loud*
4. *I wish I could be honest about how I feel*
5. *I miss my freedom*
6. *I don't want to be afraid*
7. *I don't know what to do. I don't know what I'm not supposed to do*
8. *I'm afraid it will never get better*
9. *I want Sam to be my dad*
10. *I don't know what's real about my mom and dad and what isn't*

Listing his thoughts made them more real, and his concerns enormous. As he re-read them, he could no longer control his emotions. He let go. He cried. And then he ran. He ran faster and faster until his body hurt. He ran until he couldn't run anymore and there were no new tears to shed. Finally, with dread, he turned back to the house.

"Where have you been?" Ben wanted to know.

"I was getting worried," Jess said.

"You're all sweaty." Katie looked at him, and her look went deep.

That night he threw away his fear and gave into his need to be outside of the house. He gathered his diary and his blankets and climbed through the window to the roof and simply sat for a very long time. Finally, weariness took control, and he climbed back inside, where sleep finally took him over.

Katie

She sat in the darkening room and wondered what to do with herself until she got sleepy. She sang a song her mother had taught her a long time ago and rocked Ariel to the rhythm of the simple tune: *You are my sunshine, my only sunshine, you make me happy when skies are grey, when I'm alone dear, I am forsaken, please don't take my sunshine away.*

The flowers Josh had given her weeks ago were hidden behind her Oz books, and she pulled them out again. She hadn't wanted to throw them away because they reminded her how brave he had been to break the rules. She wanted to be brave too.

Carrying the vase to the window, she stood looking out onto the massive garden outside and made a frightening decision. Waiting until the house was absolutely quiet and clothed in darkness inside and out, she took a deep breath and tip-toed to Josh's door.

She held out the vase to him. The flowers inside were brown and brittle.

"I want to pick a bouquet like you did out there, and I want to catch a lightning bug, just like you used to do. We can put the new flowers in here and the lightning bug too," she whispered. Her eyes were wet, and the wetness was ready to overflow.

He shook his head and closed the door behind her.

"We can't do that, Katie. We can't break the rules. If we get caught...I can't even think about it. I won't get us in trouble again."

"You didn't get us in trouble. He gets mad at us a lot. It happens a lot. It happened before you came."

She looked down at the flowers and broke off their dead blossoms. They crumbled in her fingers, and pieces of them fell to the floor.

"Usually, we don't know why he's mad," she whispered. "Even when he tells us why. He tries to teach us to be good, but his lessons hurt. We have lots of stuff. Sometimes he throws our clothes and games out the window and makes us go out and see what a big pile they make so that we know how lucky we are to have so much. Once he gave away my doll. But then he got me Ariel. He says he'll take Ariel too if I don't follow the rules. He said he might even give us away. Or Mom. Or all of us. He said he could do that. But he says nobody would want us because we're so bad. He could make us homeless people."

Josh had no words for her.

"I want to catch lightning bugs like you used to do. So does Ben, but I don't think he will. Will you take me outside? Please? Ben told me about how you used to go outside at night whenever you wanted to and felt the wetness between your toes and sucked up the air. I want the wetness in my toes too. I want to really suck up the air at night like you do."

It was impossible for him to turn her down.

She smiled her big smile even as the tears rolled down her cheeks and bounced on her toes in what Josh forever would call "Katie's happy ballerina dance."

They walked like thieves down to Ben's room and let themselves in. He was curled up, buried under the covers.

"You can't do that," he whispered. "You know you can't do that, Katie. If you get caught…Don't be stupid."

"We'll bring you back something, Ben," Katie whispered. "Let's go, Josh."

The lawn glowed from the rays of the moon and the beeping lights of the fireflies, and the two children walked through the light as if they were walking through magic. He tapped her on the shoulder and pointed for her to look back to see their footprints in the dewy grass, and she squiggled her toes deeper, her smile more than making up for his fear.

They lay down side-by-side on their backs and searched the sky, and he pointed out the constellations he knew and whispered their names to her. She giggled at her wet backside and shook herself like a wet dog to make him laugh too. They had a silent race from one side of the yard to the other, and he let her win. Finally he led her to the pulsing bushes and caught one of the magic-makers and put it in the palm of her hand. It tickled her, and she let it go. He caught another one and gently formed her fingers into a cup and placed his hand over hers, and together they watched the glow there.

She picked out the flowers she wanted, and he helped put them into the vase. He caught three more sparklers to put inside and added a few blades of moist grass. Then he showed her how to put her hand on top so the occupants couldn't escape but could breathe, and again they stared at the bright world they had created inside.

Taking one sorrowful last look at the beauty behind them, they crept back upstairs and stopped at Ben's door. Katie wanted to share her discovery with her brother. And for the first time in a long time, Ben was coaxed out of the protective cocoon he made for himself each night. All three added a few more drops of tap water to the vase and secured a piece of paper over it with a rubber band. Katie held it tightly as Josh punched three tiny holes in the paper so that the captives could breathe and explained that they would have to be released first thing in the morning.

"It's wrong to keep any living things – no matter how small they are – penned up," Josh explained. "Every creature deserves to be free."

Katie solemnly carried the vase to the twin bed, and the three children sat together and watched the wonder they had created. It was a victory, a fresh beginning. Together they had found a spark of magic, a splice of freedom, a small escape from their insular world.

And from that night forward, whenever the three children were confident that Steve was pleased, whenever he wasn't mad at Jess, whenever he had drunk enough vodka to put him to sleep, whenever they felt safe, Katie or Josh tapped on the wall that separated them and signaled that it was time to sneak into Ben's room where they whispered their deepest thoughts to each other, listened to stories Josh related from his "other life," enjoyed simple games, and stood at the window sucking up the air.

Through those secret talks and secret games, Katie and Ben realized how different their lives were from Josh's old one. They were fascinated by his experiences with his mother, the spontaneity they had enjoyed together, and the freedom Josh had been allowed for discovery; and they realized that the way they lived was not the only way. They began to understand the monotony of their days, the lack of empathy and stimulation they had experienced. And little by little, step by step, Ben and Katie learned to look outside the walls that imprisoned them and dared to dream about participating in that other world Josh had once known.

~

Katie and Ben asked Josh questions about his mother's nature, her quirkiness, her apparent disregard of her extended family, and they asked what it had been like to live without a father. He answered as honestly as he could, but often his search for answers to their questions hurt. And sometimes he didn't have answers.

He had never known, really, why his mother and her family didn't see eye to eye on things. He didn't know what had caused her bad days and why or how they suddenly changed into better than good ones. He'd never understood why she couldn't keep her jobs. And he had never understood why his father and mother had fallen out of love with each other and why she had asked him to leave. Katie and Ben's questions made him need to know the truth of things.

Sam became a source of fascination to all three of them, the unknown factor, the mystery. Two weeks had passed since Josh had talked with him – at least a week beyond when he thought he would hear from him again – and it became impossible for Josh to hide his disappointment and creeping sense of loss. He had been told that he wouldn't be able to see Sam again, and yet he continued to hope that if his father really cared at all for him, he would call, they would talk, and someday, just maybe someday soon, Steve would change his mind about Sam and no longer enforce his edict.

Initially, Katie and Ben tried hard to assure him that the call would come and helped him make up all kinds of excuses for the ex-father. At the end of the second week, however, when there was still no word from Sam, their assurances turned to sympathy and then shared anger until, for self protection, Josh retreated back inside himself and turned down his cousins' invitations for more deep discussions and Josh's memories. He began to ignore Katie's anxious taps on the wall and, alone in his room, sorted through his old pictures, counted the coins in his jar, and recorded memories of his old life in his mother's diary.

Late on the first night of the third week since he had heard from Sam, he made another list:

1. *It doesn't matter that he hasn't called. I can't see him anyhow*
2. *He promised to call. It's a bad thing to break a promise*
3. *He never meant to call. He was messing with me*
4. *Mimi was right. He isn't like the rest of us*
5. *Maybe what Steve said was true about him. He's nothing*
6. *He's a liar. He probably lied to Mom and that's why she threw him out*
7. *He could have fought to see me when Mom kicked him out. He was glad to get rid of us*

And still he held on. Every day for a chunk of the day, Josh waited on the front steps for Jess to call out to him that his father was on the phone. Finally, he pulled out the diary from its hiding place again and wrote,

8. *I don't want to see him*
9. *I hate him*

And then he tore out every single page he'd written there about Sam and the time they'd spent together. He ripped away at the stories his father had told him, the descriptions of the way he had looked that day, the tricks he played on him and Katie and Ben out on the patio, and everything Sam had said that caused him to believe that he had loved his mother and him. He tore them to shreds and tore them more and let them drop to the floor. He ground his feet into the pieces – one last humiliation for the man who might have been called father.

And he told Katie and Ben never to mention Sam's name in front of him again. He carried his grief disguised as armor, but Katie saw what lay beneath and confronted him.

"Don't be sad,'" she said. "I know you're sad. I know you want Sam to call. And he will. I just know it."

Ignored, she decided to take matters into her own hands.

"Josh acts like he's mad at us," she told her mother. "But he isn't mad. He's sad. He's sad because Sam hasn't called him. He's been sad for a long time. We're not supposed to talk about Sam again because he's a bad person. Josh thought maybe he'd be his real dad someday, but now he knows that won't happen. Sam lied to him."

Jess

When Josh ignored the knock on his door, Jess knocked again and said, "It's me, Jess, and I need to talk to you."

She walked to the window and looked out for several minutes, and the way she turned back to him told him that she had made a decision. It frightened him. She sat next to him on the bed, and her hand on his shoulder felt like a wisp of air.

"Josh," she said, "please listen to me."

His immediate fear was that Steve had told her to send him away. It was even more complicated than that.

"I'm sorry for how you're feeling," she said. "But your dad will call. I promise he will. Please don't think bad thoughts about him. He's a good man. He didn't lie to you."

The boy's emotions fell all over each other.

"Yes he did," he said. "He said he'd call, and he didn't. He was bad to my mom, and he was bad to me. I don't want him to call, and I don't want you to talk about him either. He'll never be my dad."

She seemed to shrivel in front of him.

"He's not a bad man," she insisted. I know that."

Skipping STONES

The fight downstairs began early that night. To cut off the sound of the barrage, Josh sang in silence, "A hundred bottles of beer on the wall, a hundred bottles of beer..." But it was no good. The ugliness penetrated everything, and he knew it would always be with him in the same way it was always with Katie and Ben.

༄

Jess tried everything she could think of to change Steve's mind that night, even though she knew that when it came to Sam and Josh, it was impossible for him to be objective. She appealed to his ego with compliments, praised him for taking Josh in, and even attempted seduction. She pleaded with him to allow Josh to see his father again, but he was as adamant as he had always been about allowing Sam into any crevice of his life. Finally, she pushed too hard, and his jealousy pummeled out through his fists and his feet. Hurting her, she knew, made him feel stronger.

The ice cold shower she had learned to take when he was finished with her washed away some of the pain and cut back on the bruising and swelling to her legs and back. She spent the night in bed beside Steve, wondering if she had the courage to defy him and contemplating her added punishment if he were to find out. It was morning before she finally found resolve.

She put on a cloak of cheerfulness while she fixed Steve's breakfast, and he watched her first with amusement and then with suspicion. He got up from the table and pinned her into the corner of the kitchen counter.

"What's up with all these smiles and this happy drivel?" he asked her. "And don't bother to lie to me," he hissed. "I can read you like a book. Still thinking about how to get him over here for a little fun? Huh? Is that what you're planning?"

He shoved himself against her and ran his hands over her body before claiming her roughly on the kitchen floor.

"You are mine, Jess," he whispered when he entered her. "All mine." And when he was finished, he reminded her again, "You belong to me. I'd destroy you before I'd let you have that man back in our lives."

When it was over, and he was finally gone, she cleansed herself again and nervously carried out her plan. Her sister Maddie answered her call immediately and agreed to make a call of her own.

"It's done," Jess thought to herself. "God help me, it's done."

She called the children to come downstairs and was pouring out their cereal when the phone rang. It was Sam.

Josh

Josh's happiness was immediately overtaken by suspicion, and he wasn't sure how to respond to the sudden call. He backed away from the phone.

Jess understood. "There's been a huge problem," she said. "I've talked with your Aunt Maddie. Sam's been trying to call for over a week but couldn't get through. No one can figure it all out, but he's on the phone now. That's the important thing. Trust me, Josh. It's all right. You'll see."

She and the children left the room, giving Josh the privacy he needed.

"This is Josh," he said, determined not to sound excited.

"Josh, I'm so glad that I finally got through to you," Sam said. "I've been trying to reach you for almost two weeks. I don't know what happened. I was sure I was calling the right number. I left messages, but I guess you didn't get them. I even called Maddie a couple of times to make sure everything was all right."

He waited for some kind of reply, but Josh had no idea how to respond.

Skipping STONES

"Hey. I'm just glad you're okay," Sam went on. "I was real worried, that's all. I want to get with you again, like we said. I've been looking forward to catching up and seeing what you've been up to. So let's make a plan, okay?"

Josh would have none of it. Things had happened too fast, and he couldn't catch up. He refused to react to anything his father said.

"Josh? Are you there?" Sam continued. "Look, I swear to you. I've lost track of the times I've tried to get in touch with you. I can understand how you feel, what you must have been thinking when you didn't hear from me, but I swear it's the truth. First I thought maybe you'd all gone somewhere on a trip. I've left some pretty detailed messages on someone's answering machine this past week. But, hey, let's forget all this. I want to take you to Edgewater Park and do some fishing. I know a guy who owns a boat and takes people out. I don't think you've been there before. It's a huge marina and beach area. He'll take us to the best spots. Then I thought we could go to my restaurant afterwards for lunch. We can take Ben and Katie if you'd like to have them. Jess too. I've had it all planned ever since our last trip together. Josh?"

"I don't know," Josh said. "I'll think about it." And he hung up without saying good-bye.

He needed proof. What was the rest of the story?

If what Sam had said was true, how was it possible that he'd dialed the wrong number over and over again? But if his father was telling the truth, if he had called and left messages, maybe some of them might still be on the answering machine. He walked back to the counter, found the "Play" button, and turned the volume down.

There were several old messages from Mimi and Papaw, one from Jess's dentist to remind her about a missed appointment, one from an insurance person, and then…there they were: a string of calls from Sam asking Jess or Josh to please call him back, a call from Maddie saying that someone needed to call Sam, more messages from Sam asking if everything was all right and that he was worried, and another concerned and angry call from Maddie just four days ago.

Josh felt Jess behind him before he saw her. He looked up as the last message from his aunt was being played. She stood with her arms crossed tightly across her chest. She had been found out.

"I can't give you any excuses that would make any sense to you, Josh," she finally said. "I'm not going to lie to you. I heard those messages, but there was nothing I could do about them. I couldn't get myself to erase them. I don't know why. I'm glad I didn't. I can't give you answers that I know you need now. Not now. I will. I promise you I will. I'm working on things. I'm going to try to make things better for all of us. I'm so sorry."

Josh had always been quick to forgive, and he would find reasons to forgive Jess.

"If you had just told me," he said. "If I could have just called him back… I know Steve doesn't want him here. I know he doesn't like him. But he doesn't have to come here. I just wanted to talk to him."

He looked at Jess again, and the sight of her shut him off. She's hurting because of me, he thought. It's all because of me.

"I need to leave." He blurted out the words. "I need to get out of here and leave you alone. I'm making everything worse. It'd be hard for anybody to take on another kid like you've had to do. I'll go to Mimi's or maybe Aunt Maddie's. They don't have anyone to take care of like you do. I'll call Mimi and Papaw and see what they say. I won't tell them anything. I'll just tell them that I miss them or something. I'll tell them something."

He meant to help, but he could tell that his grief and confusion hurt her even more.

"I don't want you to leave," she said. "I couldn't stand that. Katie and Ben love you like a brother. You're like a son to me. We want you here, Josh. I'm going to try to make it better."

He searched for a way to help her.

"Mom did stuff sometimes too that didn't make a lot of sense," he confessed. "She said that sometimes it feels like life is just too damned hard, but sometimes we need to pitch around in the dark before we can see the sun."

He looked into her with his wide eyes and waited patiently for her to catch up to him. His patience drew her out.

"She was so right," she told him. "Sometimes things are just too damned hard, and I need to help us see the sun. I'm starting by telling you not to listen to your uncle about Sam," she continued. "He's a good man. I've known him for a very long time, and I respect him and trust him. He was one of my best friends. Your uncle Steve knows, deep down, that he's a good man too."

She took a deep breath and went on.

"Steve was jealous of our friendship," she said. "I'm simplifying things. There were a lot of issues, but it really gets down to that. And, Josh, please don't listen to what he says about your mother. I know how it hurts you, and I'm sorry that he does that to you. Please try hard not to listen to him. She was a wonderful woman. An incredible woman. She was a fighter. You know that. And you need to know that you're a wonderful combination of both of them. Your mother and father loved each other, Josh, and they both loved you. More than you could possibly know."

She squared her shoulders, and Josh saw her resolve. "I'm going to take you to see your father," she said. "Call him back and tell him you'll meet him tomorrow."

Jess

The children were dressed and ready to go the next morning when they went downstairs to have their breakfasts. They were meeting Sam at nine-thirty.

"Don't forget that we need to keep this trip a secret," she warned them again. "If we can do that, maybe we'll be able to have other fun trips. Are you sure you can do that? Katie, do you understand? Can you keep the secret?"

"Sure! Let's go!" She was dancing her ballerina dance.

Ben rolled his eyes at his sister. "Katie. Think," he said. "Are you thinking? You screw this up and we are in big trouble."

Jess asked the same thing of Maddie when she called, and, reluctantly, Maddie agreed not to tell anyone in the family about the call or the outing. She would wait to have her questions answered.

Sam's friend, Captain Zeke, had a lot of rules about his boat and safety, and he went over them all and made sure everyone understood them before they were allowed to board. The two boys attempted nonchalance, but Katie did nothing to hide her excitement. The lake was calm, and Zeke was finally able to relax and entertain his crew with stories of famous people he had led on expeditions over the years, the history of the Islands they were passing, and the record fish he had caught.

He threw the anchor just off of Middle Bass Island where, he assured them, the fish would be swarming for their bait. He was right about the fishing spot, and soon all of them, even Katie, caught several Walleye and Perch. She squealed as the small things wriggled at the end of her hook, and Ben accused her of being delirious. Nothing they caught was big enough to keep, but that was all right. They were there for fun, not for dinner.

Just after noon they said good-bye to Zeke, and Sam promised to bring the children back for another trip before the end of summer. They wanted to share their day with Jess, and Sam called her on his cell phone and asked her to join them for lunch. It took some doing, but he turned to the children with a thumbs-up sign, indicating he had won the debate, and they took off to his place in West Lake to meet her.

Sam's Place was the first restaurant Sam had owned, and when Josh walked through the front door, he stepped into his memories.

"I remember this," he blurted out. "I remember the booths and the juke box over there, and the bar over there and the milkshakes you made there."

Sam took the kids behind the counter and showed them how to run the milk-shake machine and let each one of them whip up their own concoctions. Ben's was a traditional blend of chocolate syrup and chocolate ice cream, to which, at the last minute, he daringly added a big spoonful of caramel sauce. Josh combined a banana with chocolate and strawberry ice cream. Katie's was the most creative, a mix of pineapple and raspberry syrup, coffee and cookie dough ice cream, chocolate sprinkles, and a dollop of whipped cream. It came out looking purple but tasted good. Even Jess took part, putting together her version of a turtle sundae, heavy on the caramel sauce.

Everything felt familiar to Josh - even the glasses they poured their shakes into. The only thing that was different from his memory was the straws they used.

"How do you remember that?" Sam asked. "My supplier stopped carrying the green ones years ago."

They finished off the shakes and sundae while Sam gave them a tour of the place and introduced them to the cooks and waitresses, and when he called Josh his son, it made Josh feel at least eight feet tall. Finally, they gorged themselves on hamburgers, fries, and applesauce, and everyone declared that the burgers and fries were the best they had tasted. Nothing was said about the phone calls, not one bad or sad issue came up at all. Josh was proud of his father. Jess searched in her mind for the words to describe him.

Sam stood with his arm across his son's shoulders as he said good-bye to everyone, and Josh was careful not to move away until he had to.

"I'll get in touch with you," he said as he slipped a small folded envelope into his son's hand. "Keep this in case you don't hear from me by the end of the week."

Jess and the three children talked non-stop about the exciting day they'd had, the fish they caught, their funny guide, and the milkshake machine. Katie asked to see what Jess had in the fancy bag on the floor of the front seat, and Jess handed it back to her. Inside was a blue cardigan sweater. It felt silky in Katie's hand, and she said that it would look beautiful on her mother.

"This is so much fun, everybody," she squealed as she jammed the sweater back into the bag. "I really like Sam. I think he should be your dad again, Josh. But if he was your dad, you'd have to leave us, and I don't want you to leave us."

Skipping STONES

She tapped her lips with the fingers of her right hand, like a grown-up who's seriously thinking about something.

"This is a real problem," she said.

Ben suggested that she should think before she opened her mouth again. He didn't do well with issues of love and relationships. He asked, simply, if they could all get together with Sam again.

"We'll see," Jess said, knowing that the answer depended on her courage. And her willingness to lie.

༄

Jess and the children had little time to get ready for Steve's return, and as she hurriedly prepared for dinner, she warned Katie again to stick to the story they had invented about their day and to be brief with any questions her father might ask.

Ben was the first one Steve asked to give an update on his day, and Ben studied his plate as he repeated the story that had been decided on.

"We went for a ride to the park just for something different to do," he said, "and afterwards we had lunch at a hamburger place close by."

Steve asked which park they had gone to, and Ben looked to Jess for help.

"A part of the Metro parks up north," she explained. "I can't remember what they call it, but it's one we haven't been to before."

Katie was next. She shrugged her shoulders and said simply that she had just gone to the park too. Steve asked her what everyone had done at the park. "Oh, we just walked around a little bit," she answered.

"Where did you have lunch again?"

"Oh, some place that had good hamburgers and fries and shakes." She too looked to Jess for help. "Right, Mama?"

Steve put his elbows on the table and studied them as though they were specimens under glass.

Jess asked how his work day had gone, and when he moved on to describe the important events that had filled his time, the others breathed again.

The children were sent off to bed the same as always, but for the first time since he made the rule that Jess couldn't go up with them to say goodnight, Steve went to each of them, Ben first and then Katie, saving Josh for last.

He walked through the room, touching the few things Josh had there. Finding the paperweight, he picked it up, examined it, and let it fall carelessly on the bed. Finally, backing Josh into a corner of the room, he whispered, "Do you have anything to tell me?"

And when Josh shook his head, Steve looked at him with such intensity, cold shivers shot down the boy's back.

"Watch yourself, nephew. Watch yourself."

Jess

Maddie called the next morning and asked if she could have lunch with Jess that afternoon, and when she arrived, she was all business as usual, needing to *dash off* soon to an important meeting. She asked the children about the afternoon with Sam and gave up on them when their guarded answers didn't satisfy her. She visited with them as long as she thought it was necessary and dismissed them.

She was rushed and got right to the point. "So tell me what's going on with Sam and Josh. What about the phone calls? Did you figure out what happened?"

"Have you and Mom talked about it?" Jess asked.

"I wouldn't do that," she answered, "and you know it. So why are you and the kids so evasive?"

"We're not. Like I said, the kids had a good time. He took them out fishing. Hired a guide. Everybody caught some fish but had to throw them back in because they were so small. We all had lunch together..."

"That's great, but it's not what I'm asking. When are Josh and Sam going to see each other again? Is there some sort of plan? Is it all finally going to happen?"

"There is no plan, Maddie. I don't know what's going to happen."

"No plan? No plan to finally get a father and son together? There has to be a plan, Jess. What's happened? It's what I was afraid of. You've changed your mind, haven't you?"

Jess was so weary. *I could tell, I could tell and end it all right now,* she thought, but all she said was that she didn't know how to answer all of her sister's questions.

"Well, it seems pretty simple," Maddie hammered on. "Did you get those calls from Sam or not? It's as simple as that. And if you got them, why didn't you talk to him?"

"I got them," Jess admitted. "But I couldn't talk to him. Josh knows that now. We've moved on. We're making it right."

"Why? Were you afraid of Mom's reaction? We're big girls, Jess. She'll get over it. She has to." Maddie threw her hands up in desperation. "Why are we going over all this crap about the past?"

"It isn't that, Maddie. Mom has nothing to do with this. I don't care about all of that."

"So you ignored the calls. Why? Christ, Jess, I feel like a defense lawyer badgering away at a witness. Talk to me. Is there something going on in your head about Sam? Is it you? Maybe you're not sure about what you're feeling? Is that it?"

"Oh, Maddie, don't even go there."

"So? What? What?"

Jess hesitated just a moment before she began her testimonial.

"It's Steve. He doesn't like Sam. You know that. He doesn't want me to talk to him. Doesn't want the kids to get involved in any way with him. He told me that Josh is not to see Sam again."

"Okay," Maddie sighed. "Finally we're getting someplace. Why would Steve care if Josh sees his father?"

"It's just the way it is, Maddie"

"And?"

It was just like it had always been between Jess and her big sister, and Jess felt the old angst creep in again.

"That's it. I broke my word to Steve. I don't know if I can do it again or not. You have no idea what you're asking me to do."

"I can't believe this," Maddie shot back. "You knew that Sam was calling, and you ignored the calls because Steve told you to because of some stupid misunderstanding on his part over eighteen years ago. Is that what you're telling me?"

"I don't know. I guess so. It's more than that. He said that it wouldn't look good for him and me to move forward like you and I talked about. It's too fast, he said. It's all just happened too fast. He'd agreed to take Josh on, and he's uncomfortable about anyone interfering right now. It's too soon, Maddie, to talk about custody. It's too soon for everyone, especially Steve."

Even as she said the words, she knew that it sounded like she was defending Steve, and that wasn't what she had intended. Tell her, she thought, just tell Maddie the truth and get it over with.

"Interfering? That's ridiculous," her sister scoffed. "Didn't you tell him how ridiculous that is? He shouldn't be thinking about himself on this issue. I'll talk to him. I don't mind telling him he's wrong. My God, Jess, you have to stand up for yourself. Stand up for Josh."

"No. Don't do that, Maddie. Please don't say anything to Steve," Jess implored her. "Please. You don't understand. I can't argue with Steve. I can't. Just give me time to make things right."

Maddie lost control. "And so that's it?" she demanded. "Steve decided not to let Sam and Josh see each other, end of story. It's all about him. This is so wrong. You're wrong. You're not making any sense, and I'm out of here."

"You just don't understand, Maddie," Jess implored, following her to the door. "Listen, please. Steve can never find out about any of this. Don't tell Mom or Dad. I can't afford to have any of it to get back to Steve."

Maddie stopped and turned back to her. "So what will he do if he does find out?" She demanded. "Yell? Have a temper tantrum? Take away your privileges? So what if he gets mad. He isn't the only one around who has feelings. It's not about him."

Jess was totally deflated. And so tired. Another opportunity for truth had just come and gone.

Dinner with Steve went well. The children had no new lies to tell.

Josh

Josh was supposed to meet Katie in Ben's room, but the sound of thunder somewhere close kept him at the window. A storm was coming, and he watched for lightning.

In his before-life, he and his mother had watched summer rainstorms together. In fact, just a couple of weeks before she died, the two of them had sat out on the steps of their stoop, watching thunder clouds roll in. They reminded each other how dangerous lightning is, but ignored their own advice, unable to pull themselves away from the beauty of it. They watched the entire storm right there and got wet from the pieces of rain coming in with the wind, and when the downpour settled and the lightning stopped, they stood under the warm left-over drizzle, soaking up the therapy of it.

Becky had loved everything about nature and had imparted to Josh the same respect and awe for it that she had. She had told him that the bond people have with it matters and makes a difference in their lives. She talked about the beauty of living space, the perfect natural order of things. He remembered her words: "If we stay in touch with our Source, with Nature, we'll be taught the rhythm of life itself, where we belong in the order of things, and the pettiness of our daily problems." She believed that nature gives us beauty, strength, and wisdom if we get ourselves outside in it. Everything, she said, is tied together. Whenever she had needed quiet and peace and comfort, she had turned to the great outdoors. "It gives my soul sustenance and strength," she had told him.

He needed to get outside. The screen came off easily again, and he climbed through the opening to the roof and was waiting for the rain when he heard Ben's voice.

"What the heck are you doing?" Ben whispered to him.

"I'm waiting for the storm."

"Me too, me too! I want to watch it with you," Katie chimed in.

She was waist-deep outside by the time Josh was able to get himself turned around to help her. Ben followed her, talking to himself as he climbed outside about how crazy the three of them were.

The boys put Katie between them, and the three lay down together and let the rain cover them. The earth was cleansed and so, for a while, were they. The sun was low when the deluge stopped but still had time to dry them off. They remained close together and watched in awestruck silence as the sky turned red-pink and lavender.

At last, Josh told himself, they're beginning to understand.

༄

Filled with peace, before he climbed into bed, Josh took the note Sam had given him out of its hiding place in the closet and slowly read it again.

Penny Lauer

Hi, Josh.

I'm so glad that you were able to get away and come for a visit today. I had a terrific time, and I hope that you and Katie and Ben and Jess had a good time too. Actually, it was better than terrific. Tell Jess thanks for making it possible. I'll look forward to getting together again. Be thinking about where you'd like to go. Here's my phone number – (330)225-5253. Call me soon if you don't hear from me for any reason. Promise. And call if you need anything, anything at all. Say hi to everyone and take good care of each other. Sam

Josh had no reason to believe that he would see his father again, but the note filled his mind with a wealth of possibilities. Pulling out his Mother's diary from the box in the closet, he flipped through the pages to where her words ended and his began and put Sam's note there. The book now belonged, in a sense, to all three of them.

He couldn't put it away. He had been so careful to honor his mother's privacy, but because Steve had upset his faith in everything he believed and needed to believe, he looked at it in a different way. There could be words, sentences, pages from her that might help him understand things. His mother's thoughts and stories, written in her own words, might contain truths which, since she was no longer here to explain to him, she might want him to read. Maybe, he thought, that had been her purpose for writing in the first place: to leave something of hers that would tell the whole story.

With a great amount of unease and the same amount of anticipation, he turned to the first page and read.

Fri. – The counselor says that I should write my thoughts down as they come. It's some kind of a new therapy shtick. And I thought

Skipping STONES

I knew them all. Anyway, so here goes. I feel lousy. I feel worse than lousy. I don't have any idea what I should do. I loved my husband. Maybe I still do. He says he loves me. We fight. I need more of him. He says that he doesn't know how he can give more. We've screwed up. It's just too damned hard! I need more, but I don't want to lose him. I'm afraid. I'll have Josh, and he'll be enough. I've always been screwed up. I know that.

Tues. – The arguing hurts too much. I don't think I can take it anymore. Mom's right. There are too many bad memories, too many ugly words, too many accusations dangling in front of all of us. I'm sick of counselors. I'm sick of everything. But how will it affect Josh if Sam and I split? He's the one to think about. I've always thought it was bullshit for people to stick together because they think it's best for the kids. What about the tension the arguing creates? I can't think anymore. I wish we could just run away somewhere peaceful, where we could just be alone. I wish. I don't know what I wish.

Mon – Been lost. So much going on. Dr. put me on meds again. Hate it. Second-guessing everything. Almost everything of his is gone. He's fighting me about Josh, but I'm sticking to it. Mom and Dad are right. Can't stand the thought of tearing him apart between the two of us. What if Sam refuses? What can I do? I'm trying to hold it together. But I'm so afraid.

Fri. – Okay. So I'm trying to think rationally. He's still my best friend but he has no time for us. He's busier than ever now and I need more. But do I really want it to end? Or did I just get caught up with all the talk? When did I begin to feel small next to him? Why do I feel like he's condescending? It was wrong for him to talk to Mom and Dad so openly about my health and the issues between us. Or was it? There are so many words that can't be taken back. The decision's mine to make and I can't make it. Would the old proverbial grass be greener if I left? Screw it. I'm going for a ride.

Josh put the diary down. He had been so young back then, he could barely remember now what all had happened. He thought he remembered his mother's sadness, but it was hard to separate that period from all of the others that had made up her sad days. He remembered less about Sam. Reading her words was hard to do, but he needed to know the entire story behind his parents. And so he read on.

Sat. – Jess and Maddie called to make sure I'm okay for Monday. No. I'm not okay, but I couldn't tell them that. I'm so scared. Holding tight to Josh. Can I do it alone? Will I be enough for him? I'm going to be better for him. I must be better than better for my son. I'll be his only parent. Oh my God.

Sun. – Wandered around in a daze the whole day. Josh is sleeping on the couch beside me. I can't let go of him. Sam called. I'm falling apart. He said again that we don't have to do this, that it isn't too late to pull away from the proceedings. I almost said that we might wait, but then I'm thinking about the past year and all the hurt – arguments, spiteful things. Family. It's too late. I'll never get through tomorrow. Do I still love him? Oh, God. What am I doing?

Sunday – Been at Mom and Dad's all week. They didn't think I should be alone. Josh with Jess today. Cleaning up the place for my new life without Sam. It's done, and I will never forget Monday. Sam agreed to everything immediately except my having sole custody, with visiting rights for him only when I allow it. His attorney asked mine one more time if I still thought it was best. I almost changed my mind, but Mom and Dad reminded me about all of the pros and cons we had gone over thousands of times before. Finally I told my lawyer to tell his that we would go to trial. Hours went by – message after message. We wore him down. We won. What did I win? What price will I pay? Taking a pill and going to bed.

Tues. – I'm going to get it together. Went out riding, and it cleared my head a little. I will survive. I'm not the only gal in the world who has gone through this. I'll do it. I will do it. I'll be better for Josh. I'll make a good life for us. I'll show them all. I can't look back. The only thing I can control is today. And, by damned, today was a good one. I'm going to take charge. Meds are helping. I hate taking them.

Fri. – Okay. Getting back to writing because the doc reminded me that it can help. I'm ready to go out for interviews. Dad's helping with plans for Josh. I'm scared. How many times will I be turned down? Living day to day, but I can do it. I can do it!!!! Cannot crash. I will not allow it! Wish I knew how to pray...

Wed. – This place is a wreck, but I'll get to it. Josh is doing great at his school. I hate taking Dad's money. I'll pay it all back someday. Time out. Going for a run. Back from the run and feel better. The sun is shining so bright. Life is good. I'll make it all work. The doctor said that it's time to get some order into our lives. I will. Josh deserves it. I can do anything for him.

Tues.- Shrink says I'm better. Took a long walk. Trees are beautiful. Josh and I will play in the leaves.

Josh couldn't read any more-couldn't see through the tears. His mother's diary entries had brought back vivid memories of her struggles and the constant attempts by the two of them to push away her darkness. He had been a part of it all. But there had been more good times than bad, better-than-good -times, and they had laughed and walked in sunshine until the happiness crumbled around them again.

He climbed back out to the roof to see the beauty of the remnants of the day and felt as though he were a part of the universal mix, including his mother's spirit. And he wrote, "She didn't give up, ever, and neither will I."

༄

Josh rose early the next morning to cooler temperatures and lower humidity, filled with energy and no way to work it out. In his old life, on a morning like this one, he would have been preparing for a bike ride already, and he longed to ride again. But would he be able to stare down his fears?

Grab the tail of the wind and enjoy the ride, his mother had told him so many times, explaining that it meant that we each have to grab hold of what life has to offer and ride it through, enjoying every minute of. *Get right back on and ride, kiddo,* she'd also say to him when he lacked courage. She called those and a number of other expressions "truisms." He called them "momisms" to make her laugh.

An idea began to grow inside him, and by early afternoon it had shape and depth and demanded attention.

"Have you guys ever been to Peninsula?" He asked Ben, and when he said no, they headed for the computer and Googled facts about the village and the old canals and bike paths that ran out from it. They called Jess and Katie in and explored more websites, and after little debate, they decided that Josh's idea was a terrific one and that they would go biking there the following morning, their second adventure in four days.

They headed to the grocery to get supplies they thought they would need, and on the way Josh told them about Fisher's Pub where he and his mother had always gone for breakfast when they visited the village. They always got the biker's special, he told them – pancakes, ham, and eggs however you want them – and everyone decided that they would go there too and have the same thing. Back home, they set out the camera, sunscreen, hand sanitizer, and sheets of information they'd printed from the computer, and stuffed everything into their bike bags. And they waited anxiously for morning.

As soon as Steve's car disappeared down the street, the family loaded up theirs and took off for Peninsula. Josh taught Katie and Ben the license plate game and the song about

Skipping **S T O N E S**

working on a railroad to help the time pass faster on the highway, and they soon found themselves turning off Rt. 271 and onto Rt.303 that leads to the town. The countryside was exactly the way Josh remembered it: twisting hills wrapped around low valleys, woods on both sides of the narrow and winding road, huge homes behind iron gates, and little farm houses set beside streams.

After breakfast at the pub, they unloaded their bikes and walked them along the main road, dissected by the Ohio and Erie train tracks, toward the paths along the old Canal.

Josh thought that everything was fine until he actually mounted the bike and began pedaling. Jess and Katie took the lead, and Josh struggled to follow. He was off balance. His hands were sweaty, and his heart beat fast in his chest. He put his right foot on the pedal but couldn't push off.

Ben waited and watched. "It's okay. Take your time," he said. "I'll wait for you."

Josh remembered his mother's words: *Get back on and ride, kiddo,* and he reached down deep for courage. He kept his eyes on the path in front of him and fought to keep his mind blank, pushing away memories of the last time he had ridden.

The two boys slowly got into the rhythm of biking again, and Josh began to feel a little more comfortable. They took their time and stayed out of the way of the fast bikers and were careful as they passed joggers and families with strollers. Eventually, Josh took the chance to look around a little, and he and Ben stopped several times to check out concrete ruins of the canal. They rode at a leisurely pace side by side until they came upon a long curve in the path and realized that they were way behind Jess and Katie. They agreed to pick up their pace to catch them. Josh geared up, sat low, and concentrated on his speed and the path in front of him. Everything went well until they finally came within shouting range of Jess and Katie, and Ben decided to offer Josh more encouragement.

"Mom, hey Mom, look," Ben yelled. "Look at Josh."

Josh looked up in the direction of Jess at the same moment she turned toward him. She smiled and waved and gave him the thumbs-up signal to show that she was proud of him, just as his mother had done right before she ran into the dark SUV on the shadowy road on the awful day.

The boy slowly gained consciousness on the path, and it took him a while to realize that it was Jess, not his mother, rubbing his hand and saying his name. It took longer for the voices of his cousins to reach him. And it took him longer still to process his thoughts and to claw his way through the mire of his emotions.

There were many times that day when Josh could have told Jess the truth about how his mom had died the day of their last ride together. It might have been easy to go from explaining his fall that morning to explaining that other morning with his mother. He could have admitted to Jess that the accident had been his fault.

He could have told her that he had been too slow to get his water bottle back into its holder at the top of the hill, that his mother was way ahead of him before he began his way down and that when he finally got started he braked too much because he was afraid. He had been afraid. He could have told Jess that his mother was going very fast and was laughing out loud and had wanted to see where he was, and that she took her eyes off the road and turned around to find him and smiled a huge smile and waved to him. He could have told her that his mother couldn't have seen the big van come out of the dark driveway and pull out onto the road in front of her because she was watching him. He could have tried to explain that when she hit the van she flew, still on her bike, over the hood and slammed into the pavement on the other side. He could have told her that his mother's eyes stared up at the canopy of trees overhead and didn't see any of it, and that he sat beside her body and rubbed her fingers and screamed at her not to leave him and he was sorry that he hurt her. And he could have told her straight out that they pulled him away from her when they announced her dead at the scene and put him into the police car to wait for the men to contact another member of his family to get him away from that place. He could have explained all of that, but he was afraid of the truth and what it could mean to everyone. He was afraid that his entire family would turn away from him because he had taken so much away from them and had been such a coward.

Because he was ashamed and filled with guilt and fearful of what would happen if anyone knew the truth, he kept it all hidden inside. He, like Jess, kept the silence.

Ben and Katie and Jess stayed close to him all day long, and he felt their love. And then it was time for Steve.

༄

The children showered and put away everything that might show what they had done all day. Jess checked dinner, scrubbed the counter top again, looked for dust on tables, plumped pillows, lined up the silverware, checked the vodka, showered, took a white pill from under the sink and drank it down with the liquid in her flask. She and Katie picked a fresh mass of flowers from the garden, and Jess took a lot of time to arrange them in the elaborate silver cache pot.

The home was the perfect picture of Perfection except for the gloom that entered the house like fog at precisely five-thirty, the hour Steve was due. Katie held onto Ariel and Jess's skirt; Ben retreated to his room where he paced and worried what the night would bring; Jess set out Steve's favorite glass and opened the red wine bottle so that it could "breathe" and be ready for her man; Josh showered again to wash away his shame.

Steve entered the house ready to party. He had, he explained, been given another huge account, one of the potentially biggest that his firm had ever received, something to do with managing a multi-million dollar family foundation headed by a billionaire in Maine.

"I knew how to talk to him about incidental things," he explained proudly, pouring his first drink, "thanks to the fact that I knew something about the area he's from. At least something came out of that God-forsaken camp my parents made me go to every year as a kid," he said.

"It's huge, Jess," he continued. "A huge break. This is the one I've been waiting for. This guy rubs elbows with the best of them. Jeff and I and Tom have been working for months to close the deal. Baker himself has been involved. I'm going to take it over, leave the others in the dust, and then I'll be in line for that place at the top. I know it."

The children smiled appropriately and acted like they understood it all. Jess asked the right questions at the right time and encouraged her husband to continue talking. Toasts were made. "Here's to my beautiful wife, my partner," he said. "Here's to our family." He winked at them. "Christmas has come early."

When it was finally time for Jess and the children to be questioned about their day, Steve was already on his third glass of wine and clearly prepared to be bored. Ben was the first to be called on, and he was careful to down-play their day. Katie was next.

"Well, we had fun," she said, "for a while." She looked over to Josh and put on a sad expression. "But then Josh fell off his bike and hurt himself and so we had to stop. But it was okay. He wasn't hurt bad. We didn't want to do too much because Mommy wanted to make sure Josh's head wasn't hurt. It's fine. Right, Josh? And...let's see. Then Mommy and I picked some flowers and made this pretty arrangement for us, and...."

Steve interrupted her and turned to Josh, instantly interested. "So you fell off your bike? How did that happen?"

Josh was uncomfortable with the sudden attention and was on guard. He explained that he looked up too fast, probably hit some gravel, and lost his balance.

Steve took a sip of his wine and leaned back regally in his chair.

"Lost your balance on the path?" He leaned forward again and rubbed his chin like he was deep in thought. "Well, that's too bad. I assume you got up and tried to ride again."

"I was a little dazed from the fall, I guess," Josh responded, "and Jess thought I should keep quiet for a while."

Steve's voice was calm and reminded Josh of the southern drawls he'd heard on TV shows.

"You know what they say, Josh. When you fall, you have to get right back on and ride or you'll always be afraid. Only sissies would be afraid to get back on. Now. Let's look at this objectively. You're not a sissy, right?"

He watched Josh for a second and waited for an answer. Then he turned around to the others at the table and smiled as if he had made a good joke.

Josh felt his face turn red. "I'm not a sissy."

"Well, I think there's a good lesson to be learned here," Steve slurred. "Josh has had some problems with biking since his mother's accident. We all know that. But he needs to know that he has to hang tough, try not to be afraid. Has to move on. Get over his fear of things. I wouldn't want him to turn into a scared little prissy, that's all."

He raised his glass. "Ben and Katie and you, Josh, here's to being strong. Damn the sissies!"

Because they always did what Steve told them to do, the children raised their water glasses.

"You too, Jess. Raise your glass. That's it. Once more, let's all say, 'Damn the sissies'."

They clinked their glasses and damned the sissies.

Steve struggled to get out of his seat and lurched his way to the den, waving his hand at the children.

"Get to bed, kids," he said. "Jess, hurry up and get in here. I'm on a hell of a roll and need some attention. We're going to celebrate, baby."

Katie and Ben argued as they followed Josh up the stairs.

"See what you've done? Why do you have to tell everything?" Ben asked Katie as they left the room.

Josh thought about defending Katie, but he couldn't get it together. He was sick to his stomach and madder and as embarrassed as he'd ever been. He kicked his door behind him. He wanted to throw things, to bang the walls, to yell out loud, but he was afraid. He was afraid, and he hated it. *I'm no sissy. I'm no sissy.* But doubt crept in. Maybe he was.

He opened his window and gulped the air. A mourning dove cooed from somewhere above him; robins sang from the trees above the gardens; sunshine flickered and created shadows that changed size and shape and made abstract patterns on the green lawn. *I'm no sissy.* A brown squirrel chattered and hung upside-down on the bird feeder, stealing the seed; yellow and orange butterflies and groggy bees zigged and zagged together in and out around the rainbow of flowers. Life and freedom and normalcy were out there. *I'm no sissy.* He felt as though he were suffocating. He knew what he had to do.

He went to Katie's room and told her his plan so that she wouldn't worry if she tried to find him later.

"I'm going outside and ride. Don't worry. I have to do it. Your dad's right. I have to get back on. Mom would have made me do it. If your dad comes and asks where I am, you tell him you don't know. That's important. You have to pretend that we didn't talk. Promise. I'll let you know when I'm back."

"I'm sorry," she said. "I'm so sorry I told him."

One more apology in the house of deceit and sadness.

༄

Josh felt removed from himself as he sneaked out the back door and stealthily wound his way through the bushes to the garage. He found his bike and ran with it to the end of the street, wondering what would happen to him and the others if Steve found out what he was doing.

I'm going to do it, he said to himself as he got on. I have to do it now, or maybe I never will.

And he did. Alone on the road with nothing else to consider, he eventually found his balance and, easing his grip on the handlebars, shifted into a higher gear to gain speed. The air felt delicious to him, and he found himself smiling. Eventually, he relaxed even more and took the chance to look around him.

He'd been in those same spaces many times before – most recently with his father -but that evening they looked and felt different to him. There was nothing enclosing him to cut off any part of it, and he was in charge of his body. As he pushed himself through space, he sensed his growing strength and internal drive.

The sun was low, and its thick, long rays filled the pastures and lawns in deep magenta. White fence rails popped out against the green grass at the sides of the road. Stands of tall corn weaved in the breeze, and horses bowed and shook their heads and nudged each other in the open fields. Crickets and grasshoppers jumped in the grass beside him, and a frog hopped unafraid across the road in front of him. Josh's senses were acute. He felt all of it.

The road began to climb. Its incline wasn't steep, but it was long. Very long. Just in time, he remembered to shift down, knowing that the ride was going to be harder than he had anticipated. He hadn't used his leg and back muscles since the day of the awful accident, and he hurt. But the ache was good. He was conscious of his body again. *It's like a machine,* his mother had told him, *and we have to keep it well-tuned.* He shifted down again as the incline increased and concentrated on the road and the spin of the front tire.

Sweat ran down his forehead and into his eyes. His legs burned, and it was hard to breath. His heart pounded in his head, and he thought of quitting many times, but every time he did, he heard Steve say, "I wouldn't want to think you're a sissy." He risked looking up again and saw that there were maybe no more than forty yards to go and, bending over his bike and gripping the bars, he willed his legs to move.

And finally he was there. Finally he was at the top.

Skipping STONES

His legs were like putty, and his shoulders burned from the strain of leaning forward and supporting the rest of his upper body. It took him a while to get off the bike and longer still to walk to the other side of the road. He could see for miles. I did it, Mom, he whispered. I did it.

He raised his face up to the darkening sky, watching the clouds slowly change form and wondering again how birds let each other know their flight patterns, and he made a vow that no matter what happened in that house from then on he would not give up. He would remember this moment and find ways to be strong. He would find the same strength he had read about in his mother's diary. Leaning against the white rail-fence that enclosed the verdant pastures, he tried to look at his new family the way he and his mother had looked at strangers, to see them as they really were. He was not a sissy, and Katie was no girlie girl. Ben was stronger and brighter than his father thought he was. Jess shouldn't have to be afraid, and Sam was good.

Most importantly of all, he understood that he and his mother had had everything that mattered all along – important things that Steve and Jess would never have. And he wished that she had had the time to realize that.

He turned his bike around and realized that he had to go down the same hill he had just come up. It looked longer and steeper from there, and its curves looked deeper. He tested the brakes and searched the road for danger and forced himself to shove off.

"Keep your eye on the road ahead and don't let the bike get away from you," his mother had always told him.

The rest of her words came to him so clearly, it felt as though she were there.

"Enjoy the ride, kiddo, and feel the thrill!"

He eased his grip on the brakes, breathed deeply, and pushed back his fear. He rode down that hill like a banshee, and it felt better than good.

Whoohoo! He heard someone yell and realized it was him. This is what it's all about!

The speed, the wind, the danger, the freedom he felt was what his mother had tried to describe to him so many times.

"To be strong and to test your strength, to challenge yourself and face up to the hard stuff is what life is all about," she had said. "Being simply safe is not enough."

That evening Josh finally and absolutely understood.

He stopped by Katie's room like he had promised and tried to explain to her how he had felt out there.

"We have to catch the wind, Katie." He told her. "We have to 'go for the gusto'."

She listened, leaning toward him, but her eyes had a faraway look. There was something there inside her, and Josh saw it and stopped. He looked around the small room where Katie had sat shut up and alone early evenings and dark nights and sunny early-mornings most of her life, kept away from the beauty and freedom that he'd just ridden through.

"Will you take me outside to the garden again?" She asked.

They sneaked out like before and sat at the edge of the garden to try to repeat the happiness of their first trip out there together, but the newness of it, the mystery and magic weren't there for her. Something else had taken Katie over.

They lay down in the grass and watched the clouds make faces on the moon.

She started to speak but gave up as though there was simply too much to say. Instead, she reached for his hand and held on.

Skipping STONES

⁓

Josh wanted to show Jess and his cousins how to defend themselves against Steve and to prove that truth was not dangerous and that misunderstandings can be avoided if people communicate openly to each other. He would be brave and show Jess and Katie and Ben how to win a battle, and he would do it at the table during dinner.

The following evening, he half-listened to his cousins' tepid reports, silently practicing instead how he would begin his, and when it was his turn to describe his day, he took a deep breath and explained that he had taken a bike ride the night before, just like Steve thought he should.

"You told me to get back on and ride, and so I did," he said. "I listened to you, Uncle Steve; I decided I didn't want anyone to think I was a sissy."

He told them about the big hill about a mile or so out of town, how steep it was, and how hard it was to get up to the top. He tried to find the words to describe the coast down, how it felt to just let loose and let the speed take him and not be afraid.

"My mom loved to bike," he reminded them. "She was never afraid. I'm not going to be afraid again either. I'm not a sissy," he repeated.

No one spoke, and taking their silence as affirmation, Josh suggested that on Saturday, Steve and Ben and he should go for a ride together through the village, down through River Road and on to the Polo Fields.

"It's a long way," he said, saving his best salvo for the last. "I've never done it, but I'll bet we could. Mom used to do it all the time."

Josh turned to Steve and asked him directly if he thought he could do it.

Steve grinned at him and took his time to respond.

"I have nothing to prove, Josh," he said.

Josh's come-back was weak.

"Well, I just thought you'd like to go out with Ben and me. Do a man thing together," he added, risking a hint of sarcasm, but not quite able to pull it off. Even he heard the doubt in his voice.

Steve leaned back in his chair and again took his time, swirling the red wine around his glass, checking its "legs."

"You know, Josh," he said in a low voice, "I see more and more of your mother in you every day. I wonder how I can explain." He rubbed his chin as in deep thought and went on. "Well, she certainly had a wild streak in her, that's well known. Arrogant. Yes, that too although I can't imagine why. Let's see. How about irresponsible? Yes, those words all describe her, and I'm beginning to see that they describe you too."

The change was way too fast for the boy.

Jess knew where the conversation was going and decided to deflect it even though she had no doubts about the consequences of her actions. Bracing herself, she hoped that her punishment would be swift.

"Steve, please don't," she intervened. "There's no reason to talk like that about Becky. Josh only did what you suggested."

He looked questioningly at her, as surprised as the children were to hear her protest.

"Did you just interrupt me?" He demanded.

"I'm sorry, but I just don't think that we should talk about Josh's mother – my sister - like that," she told him as firmly as she could. "I'm sure that you don't mean those things."

"Oh, so now you know what I mean and don't mean."

"My mother wasn't wild," Josh interjected, bolstered by the unexpected support. "She got excited about things. She was fun. She was always doing something – painting, making jewelry, hiking and biking and…"

When Steve held his hand up for silence, everyone obeyed.

"That was part of it." He looked thoughtfully at his wine again, working on his swirling technique. "We remember what we want to about people. You must know, though, that your mother had some tough times."

"I think we should move on to a different subject, Steve," Jess said, and Josh detected a note of desperation in her voice.

Steve leaned toward her and jabbed his finger at her, still under control of himself.

"That's the second time you've interrupted me, the second time. Don't challenge me," he said.

Josh remembered his vow and interrupted, attempting to come to Jess's aid.

"She was a good person," he said. "We didn't have a lot of money like you, but we were happy. You don't need a ton of money to be happy. There are other things that are more important. You're wrong about her. She was not wild. She was a super mom. She took good care of me. She couldn't help her moods. But she always made her way through them. She'd go to bed and rest and…"

Steve leaned slightly forward, still in control, intent on diminishing. "You're right about the money. You didn't have any. You led an entirely different life style. That's why I've been lenient with you. And, oh, yes, she'd go to bed. For lots of reasons."

No one could miss the sneer on Steve's face, and the humiliation was just too great for Josh. He knew his plan had failed and the battle was all but lost, but he couldn't stop defending his mother and the way they had lived. He insisted on having the final word.

"You are so wrong about her. You didn't know her."

The man was absolutely shocked that the boy had the audacity to continue to disagree.

"Are you kidding me?" He shouted. "You've lived in a dream world, kid. There's something wrong with you. You apparently had no clue what was going on in your own home with your mother. You're the one, boy, who doesn't know what he's talking about. You romanticize her rebelliousness, her disrespect for authority, her irresponsibility."

Jess did what she knew she had to do. She stood before she was told to and brought the attention to her.

"Steve. This has to stop," she said. "That's enough."

Her plan worked. His reaction to her was instantaneous. He shoved his plate away, and it clanged against his wine glass and knocked it over. He banged his fists in front of him again, and everything on the beautiful table jumped from the blow. He looked at the mess he had made as if the plate and glass were co-conspirators against him.

"What did you say, woman?" Steve demanded and rose so abruptly, Josh was shocked to see him standing over him.

"Look what you've done," Steve bellowed. "Do you really think you're going to get away with mocking me?"

Josh braced himself for the attack, but Jess grabbed Steve's arm, and all of the man's attention finally turned to her.

"You!" he shouted and struck her face so hard she sprawled to the ground.

"Mama, Mama," Katie cried out as she rushed to Jess.

But Steve's arm reached out and stopped her. She pulled to break away and her father let go, knowing what would happen. She fell hard onto the floor. Ben moved toward his sister, but stopped and put his hands to his ears against the crying and the yelling and turned away.

"Wimp!" Steve shouted to his back.

He focused back to Josh. "Now you, you arrogant son-of-a-bitch."

Josh was ready for the blow. He wanted it. But Jess was somehow there again and stepped between them. Her voice was amazingly quiet.

"He doesn't understand, Steve. You're right. His life has been different. But punishing him won't help. I'll make him understand the rules. I'll work harder to make things right. Let him go. I'm the one. I haven't taught him well. I'll do better. I promise."

"You are fucking worthless!" The man screamed at her.

"I know. I'll make it better," she said. "I promise I'll try harder."

"This place is a fucking mess. He shoved her around to face Josh. "You brought this arrogant kid into our home. Thought only about yourself and your dead sister and that stupid promise you made to her. Didn't give any thought at all to me and how he would impact all of us."

He turned her to face Ben. "You've turned your son into a pussy. Look at him sitting there whimpering like a damned fagot." He turned to Katie. "And you, you stupid little girlie-girl. Jesus. Stop crying. You're just like your mother."

"Don't blame them," Jess insisted, locked in his grasp.

"It's my fault. I'll do better." She looked at the children. "Go to your rooms," she said.

"I'll tell them when to go and when to stay," he seethed.

"Go to your rooms!" she repeated.

The children ran to their rooms and covered their ears to the sounds of the man releasing his fury onto their mother.

Penny Lauer

∽

Josh stood at attention behind the door in the twilight of his room, transfixed. He would leave, he decided. He would leave and his leaving would make things better. His mother had told him that overconfidence brought nothing but defeat, that as soon as you thought you had something figured out and allowed yourself to think you were in control, just like that you could be struck down to size and be reminded that you are never really in control at all. That afternoon, he had proved that she had been right. Some day he would come back and make it all up to Jess.

And then there was no sound. The sudden silence was deafening. Still the boy could not move, grounded by fear and shame and guilt. Minutes went by, and he stood paralyzed until a tiny rap on the wall from Katie's room broke through his concentration.

He crept to her door and stepped over into the dusky room.

She was wrapped in her piece of old blanket, lying on the floor facing the wall that separated her from him, tapping, tapping. She wouldn't unwind herself. He bent down to her and half-carried her to Ben's room.

Ben's bed was empty. They found him hidden in his closet, stabbing the wall with a pencil.

The three children lay that night in a pile there, hidden from the enemy.

∽

Jess and the children stayed inside the next day and the next and the next to hide the truth about themselves. Ben and Josh and Katie pretended that they were unscathed, and they pretended not to see the effects of Jess's punishment. To acknowledge any of the violence or to question why it was allowed would have been a betrayal to her and the image she worked so hard to keep.

Sam called every day, and Jess let him and Josh talk. The boy hung on to the conversations as he would a lifeline, soaking up the communication and the expansiveness of his father's world like a sponge. And with each call, he invented new excuses to put off his invitations for visits.

He thought every single day about leaving. But he knew that if he did, his aunt and cousins would pay dearly. Truths would be made known, and Steve would lose face and would punish. Turning inward, he became consumed with his mother's diary and the truths and insight he hoped it would hold.

Tues. Hot Damn! Woke up this morning to a beautiful day and a good, happy feeling. Can't remember when I felt this good. Took Josh out early for a bike ride. Got ourselves gooey cream-filled donuts and sat outside and ate them. Delicious! Needed to take Josh back inside to clean up. Chocolate and whipping cream all over him. Got stuff cleaned up around the house too. Josh ran the sweeper for me. Worked a little on my painting. Looks good. Josh and I sat outside for a long time after the sun went down and made up stories. What an imagination he has. Maybe he'll be a writer when he grows up, but I'll never tell him what he should be. Low on $$$ but getting by.

Fri. Mom invited us over for dinner. Everyone was there, and things went as well as can be expected. Bill's a love. Steve's an ass. Wish Mom could relax a little. She fusses, and it makes me crazy. I know I'm too hard on her. Working on a necklace for Maddie's birthday. Took some beads to Mom's for her to pick out. Some day I swear I'll be able to go to a store and buy whatever I want. Nope, probably not. Who am I kidding? The art show's just two weeks away. Hope it all sells. If it does, things will be much better. I didn't think of Sam once today – except just now.

Fri. Another weekend and nothing to do. Need some adult time. I'm seeing Jess and kids with Josh tomorrow. Going to the zoo. I'm thinking about signing up for an art class to meet some people with a little of the money I've set aside. Should spend it on clothes for Josh. Maybe I can do both. We'll see. I'll clean this place up this weekend. Then what? Should have asked all those counselors what to do about loneliness. I have to get myself to move on. Need to work on my appearance. I can just hear Maddie and Mom saying, "She looks like hell."

Tues. Surprisingly, the visit to zoo over the weekend was nice – even though Jess checked her watch constantly. I came right out and asked her if she was bored. All she said was that she had to be home before Steve got back from whatever he was doing. How does she live like that? Then again, she has a husband and I don't! Drove in today to Maddie's with her necklace, and she actually seemed to like it. I'm trying hard to have more family time because it's good for Josh. Decided to sign up for class with the $$$ Dad gave me. Baked some sugar cookies with Josh. Mom wouldn't approve because she doesn't think a young boy should be in the kitchen. What the hell? It worked for Sam. But I'm not going to think about Sam. But I do.

Sat. I went out with Cindy tonight. Sat at the bar before dinner and got into some conversations with a few people. One guy hit on me. Remembered when I first met Sam. God, was I blown over! What good times all of us had – crazy, fun times. Anyway, I felt alive again tonight. Hell of a thing to come home alone again though. Think I'll go watch Josh sleep. Maybe he'll wake up and we can take a walk. Am I nuts?! Everyone knows I am.

Fri. God! Mom and Dad stopped by unannounced. I hate that! The place was a wreck. I shouldn't care. But I do. Got me and Josh cleaned up so that we could all go out to dinner. She's so hard to talk *with. Dad's such a jewel. We talked about Josh's going into third grade. Where has the time gone? Dad wants to take him shopping for clothes. I'll be able to find a steadier job once he's back in school, and I'll be able to buy him some things. I'm going to miss him. I feel like things are closing in on me. Mom still thinks I'm on the meds. Does she really think I could pay for them? A beer would help right now.*

Tues. Sam called! Said he wanted to make sure Josh has everything he needs for school. I can't write about it or think about it.

Mon. It's beautiful outside - the Indian summer we've been waiting for. Can't stay inside. I've cut back the garden. Finished a painting for the art show. Hope something sells. Being poor is so hard. Achy. Feel the panic coming on. No meds. Need to do this on my own. Taking a long jog to work it off.

Another call from Sam interrupted Josh's reading, and Josh hung on to the conversation as long as he could, but it was hard to keep it on a positive course. As always, he had little to say, and Sam pressed hard to see how he was living his life and why he was being so evasive. Josh couldn't come up with answers that made any sense even to him. And still he took care to disguise his unhappiness.

Finally, Sam came right out and asked if everything was all right. Josh's skin was prickly. He was so close. So close to telling the truth, but he was too caught up with all of the reasoning he had done over the past several weeks. What good would the truth bring, he had thought. He belonged to Steve and Jess. There was no reason to share his unhappiness with his father. There was no point in sharing anything with him. And then there was Jess. If he were to tell Sam the truth and Sam were to believe him, he would confront Steve. There was no question about that. And he didn't even want to think what might happen to Jess if that happened. And so they said goodbye, each wanting more, and Josh went back to his room and immersed himself again in his mother's story.

Mon. My first day of work at the Senior Citizen Center. Four little old ladies and one not so old showed up for class. Half-way through, a bent- up old man with a great sense of humor came in and entertained the ladies. He's a doll. I think two of the ladies are hot to trot for him. Hope he comes again. We're working together on a Paper Mache bowl to decorate the front hall. They call me "honey" and "dear." Josh loves school. I worry if he's safe and treated well. He must be or he wouldn't be happy! A little jealous of his teacher. Too damned confident and sweet. Josh loves her. She sent me a note telling me what a good reader he is. Now she's sending home special books for him to read. Says he's advanced for his age. I could have told her that! Going out for girl's night out Fri. to a bar Cindy and Donna know about on the West Side. Beginning to enjoy girlfriends. Shouldn't spend the money, but what the hell. Will limit myself to two beers. Maybe I'll run into Sam! Now, wouldn't that be the berries?!! Must be careful what I wish for...

Sat. The bar was filled with tweny-somethings last night and was a real bore. Felt like my students at the senior center. Gotta be honest. I need a man in my life. Where will he come from? No single friends. Bars bad choice. The internet? Time out...Sam sent a Hot Wheels car to Josh – a red '65 Ford Mustang. He took it to bed with him. Should I call and thank him? Probably not a good idea. We'll write a note. I can't write what I'm thinking.

Tues. Something's wrong with Jess. Not herself, according to Mom. I wouldn't know. I should call her and get the kids together. Wondering if I made the right decision for Josh. Not sure she's the right one to take care of him, but who else is there?

Skipping STONES

Fri. So damned lonely. I'd kill for a cigarette. Time out. Just went out and bought a pack. Why kill myself? Who the hell cares if I smoke? Will only do it outside so Josh isn't hurt by it. Time out. Called the doc. He'll work with me. He's a good guy. Got some meds. Beer tastes delish. Can't sleep. Took half a pill. I'm so friggin' weak.

Wed. Called Jess for tomorrow. She seemed glad to talk to me. Said she had something important to tell me and that it would take some time. Asked her if it was about Josh. She said no, not really. What does that mean? Sometimes she talks in circles. Class at the old people's home is growing. A couple more ladies signed up. Toby's mad because another guy came, and now he's going to have to share the ladies. What a hoot. I guess these old guys still get it on somehow. Had some $$$ left over from my pay check. Put some change in Josh's jar, and we counted it. Whoopee! We're stinkin' rich! $101. Saving to take him on a road trip next summer. He's all excited. Signed up to be a room mother at his school. Might take a little cash out of the jar to get him some new clothes. Saw Jess. She didn't have anything special to tell me after all. What a good life she has. Beautiful clothes, gorgeous home, shiny new car, no worries. God. Just for one day in her shoes. Wrong. I'd go freakin' crazy with all that stuff. What does she do all day?

Sat. Splurged and went to the Science Museum with Josh. Walked the mall and looked at all the stuff we can't have. Kept him up as long as I could. I think I'm falling. I want Sam back. I want to be a better mother. I want a life. I'm fucked up.

Tuesday. Back home from Mom's. Josh and I there two weeks. Fell deep. What's my excuse this time? No one to blame it on. Work was going well. Josh is great. Exercising to get back in shape. Good-bye lecture from Mom and Dad. They make it sound so easy. It's always the same with Mom - thinks it's simply a matter of wanting to be strong. Working my way up. Heard from the state. Can start with counseling again. On meds. I'm a lousy mother. I'll get better. This time I'll really get over it. I'll do it for Josh. I swear.

Mon. The two things that make me happy are Josh and nature. Everything and everybody else make me sad.

Sunday I gave up the one person – besides Josh – who could have made me complete because I didn't want to hear what he told me – didn't want to accept the facts. I screwed up. Look at him. Look at me. What am I?

Josh wrote his words in his own part of the book, behind hers.

Mom still wanted my dad to be with us. He didn't want to give me up. He helped us with presents and money. Mom thought maybe something was wrong with Jess. If only she had found out about it. Mom tried hard not to be sick. I wish she had been happier. She always made me happy. But she didn't know.

༺

Things were going very well for Steve. He had become the crown-prince at his law office and the absolute monarch at his home. He conferred daily with his managing partner and reminded Jess and the children on a regular basis what was necessary to keep him comfortable and content. The children were respectful and quiet, and Jess was as compliant and as lovely as she had ever been. He was living the dream and felt magnanimous. He noticed that the physical bruises he had been caused to inflict on Jess had healed. He was unaware of emotional ones. He took his family out to dinners, treated them to movies, arranged visits with Mimi and Papaw, escorted them on shopping sprees, patted the children on their heads and reminded them and Jess that many more good times would be had so long as they understood their responsibilities. They followed him like good pets, anxious to please and wanting to trust his kindness, thinking that they had finally mastered the proper behavior to warrant his love.

Skipping STONES

He was called into the managing partner's office on Wednesday, three weeks after the last attack on his family and was told that he would be going to Boston Monday morning to meet with his big client and his managers. Monday morning finally came, and Jess and the children stood by the door to say good-bye to him. He kissed his wife and patted her on her behind, reminding her that they'd celebrate when he got back.

The weeks of non-thinking had made his family dull. They had at least three days of freedom ahead of them and didn't know what to do with them. Josh had an idea. He would begin to pay Jess back for the kind things she had done for him. He had nothing to offer her and his cousins except the contents of his and his mother's coin jar, but it was a start. He rushed to his room and counted out the quarters and dimes and nickels and hoped it would be enough. He would take them to the DQ for lunch.

"My treat," he said. "And then let's go to the park and hike around. I'll show you some really cool places."

They scrambled ant-like in their excitement and packed up fishing poles, towels, Handi-Wipes, and snacks for the park in case they got hungry or thirsty after lunch, and climbed into the car for their big day out together. Josh directed Jess to his old neighborhood, and they parked at the local strip mall not far from his old home and enjoyed going in and out of the quirky shops before they could justify eating again. Finally, Josh led them to the place he and his friends from his previous life went to for special treats when they were out riding their bikes. The pretty girl behind the counter, whose name was Allis, recognized him immediately and happily served them Chili Cheese Dogs, fries, and colas. There was still enough from Josh's cache to cover Billy Bars and Peanut Buster Parfaits for dessert.

Josh had been to the South Chagrin Metro Park the previous fall, but it felt like it had been years ago. He and his cousins sat forward, pushing against their seat belts, anticipating getting outside and being children again.

"Wait! Stop here, Stop here," Josh called out as they slid past Sulphur Springs Picnic Area. "Pull in here, Jess. I want to show you something."

They pulled into the parking lot and followed Josh through the picnic and play area, along the stream that broke off from the river. He found the worn path that led them down the steep drop to the shallow riverbed, and as they sloshed their way across the layers of slippery stone, their excited reaction was exactly what he had hoped for. Eventually, he came upon the exact spot he was looking for and invited them to raise their eyes and to turn around real slowly. They looked into a wall of slate on the right and, on the left, into a horizontal wall of trees. Small pools of water remained trapped in rounded hollows of rock at their feet, a waterfall gurgled somewhere beyond them, pines grew out of bare rock beside them, and streaks of sunlight poked through leaves above and made the crowns of Maples, Elm, Oak, Spruce, and Dogwood glow.

"Man this is awesome," Ben whispered, awestruck. It's like those pictures of canyons out west. I can't believe that we didn't know this was here."

Jess tried to remember how long it had been since her son had been so excited about something and watched with delight as Katie whirled in a circle of speckled sunlight, full of joy.

"Kind'a makes you feel filled up, doesn't it?" Josh said to her.

Skipping **S T O N E S**

"Yes," she answered. "Filled with wonder. And with peace."

They might have stayed longer, but Josh was eager to show them more. Following the signs to Squaw Rock, they passed bikers, joggers, dog walkers, and people of all ages giving it their all at the exercise stations along the path by the road. When they reached their destination, Katie jumped out of the car and ran ahead to the walking path where she barely missed stepping on a baby black squirrel which had obviously fallen from its nest. It was agitated and walked erratically toward the grass.

"What's wrong with it?" She asked when the others caught up.

"Stay away from it," Ben warned. "It looks weird. Maybe it has rabies."

Suddenly there was a noisy chattering in the tree behind them, warning the intruders to stay away.

"It's the mother," Jess explained to Katie. "She's afraid for the baby, but she's afraid of us too. She's not sure what to do."

"She'll come get it when she knows it's safe," Josh suggested.

Katie was distressed and grabbed her mother's hand. "Are you sure the mother will save her baby?"

"I'm sure she will. She needs to figure out the safest way to do it. Moms never give up their babies. Even squirrel moms figure out how to protect them." Jess gave Katie a kiss on her forehead. "Just like I would never give you up," she said. She looked back up into the tree. "Josh is right. The baby must have fallen. There's nothing we can do."

Ben broke the mood by challenging them to a race to the bottom, and they all took off down the steep dirt path to the other branch of the Chagrin River and the rock where Josh and his mother, and his mother and father, had gone so many times before.

While Jess took pictures, the children splashed their feet in the water, and Josh explained again how Sam and he had trekked across to the other side of the river that first day they were together. Ben and Katie wanted to do the same thing, and Jess quickly gave her permission. As they made their short journey, she found a flat boulder to sit on and dangled her bare feet in the cool stream. Turning her face to the sun, she thought of the joy that simple pleasures bring and wished for simple things in more abundance. On the other side of the bank, her children wished for the same thing in their own ways. The three of them took their freedom and play seriously and not with total abandon, understanding that the time they had to exercise their bodies and spirits was limited.

Still their leader, Josh directed them toward the falls where the rescue of the puppy had taken place, and he pointed out the flow of the current and how much deeper and swifter the river was there. He told the story again, and to make his point, threw a heavy limb into the water close to the falls. It spun and dove and resurfaced and spun again before being carried over the cascade.

"Sam told me the water was above Mom's waist," Josh told them.

"Wow," Ben said. "Your mom had to have been really strong."

"She didn't think about herself at all," Josh said, fighting back his emotions. "She just wanted to save that puppy."

They pulled themselves away from the park late in the afternoon and stopped by the local grocery store to pick up cheese and crackers, chips, trail bologna, and popcorn, all of which, Josh told them, had been staples in his and his mother's diets. It was growing dark when the movie they had rented was over, and there they were, still up and needing more. Josh asked if they could go outside and stand under the moon and stars for just a while, and their slow and deliberate pace made him feel as though he was walking into a church where something profound was about to take place.

Ben separated himself from the others and stared into the night as in prayer. Jess walked to him and put her arm around him, and Katie and Josh shyly followed and watched her wipe something off her son's cheeks. The four of them stood together, their arms around one another, soaking up the beauty and the vastness of the glittering sky.

Josh and Katie made beds for themselves in Ben's room, and Jess joined them there, staying with them until they fell into deep and peaceful sleep.

PART TWO

Jess

Jess followed the moonlight and wandered around her beautiful home. She touched photos and paintings and curled her toes into the rugs and carpets. And she wondered how much she would miss those things if she were ever to lose them. She took a long, hot, leisurely shower and wrapped herself into her silk robe and wandered again back to Ben's room to watch the sleeping children. They were exactly the way she had left them, breathing softly in luxurious rest, the boys sprawled without dream-tethers across the two beds with Katie between them on the floor, her arms above her head and Ariel on her tummy.

Jess was at peace, but was still unable to direct her thoughts away from Steve, trying, as always, to sort her way through how her life with him had progressed. She went outside again and lost herself in thoughts about the boy-man with whom she had immediately fallen in love.

He had stared at her that first night and had said her name slowly as if tasting each part of it on his tongue.

"Jessica", he had repeated. "I've never known a Jessica. I like your name. It fits you."

And he looked her up and down just as slowly as he had said her name.

He was the first and last boyfriend she had ever had. She was seventeen.

She had thought about turning down the invitation to the party that night they met because everyone would be on the prowl to find dates for their last high school Homecoming, and she had already decided that she wasn't going to go to one more event with a boy who had no other date choice and who would treat her like a sister.

Her major contribution to her small group of friends had always been listening to their ideas and problems and worries, sympathizing and encouraging. She was the one they went to, to unload their problems or to seek advice. "Shrink" had appeared under her picture in her high school yearbooks, and she had been named "the most helpful" in her class. She had strived to be a pleaser to make up for her shyness. Back then she had no idea how beautiful she could be outside her five foot, ten inch frame, nor what talents she possessed.

Her future was determined that night twenty years ago when a girl whom she had met sometime before but didn't remember well at all, came up to her and told her that there was a boy who wanted to meet her, and although she had trouble believing that, she let herself be led to a group of young men who grinned a lot. Eventually, all but one of them wandered off. The one who stayed was Steve Selby, and Jess thought he was gorgeous. Standing next to him, she felt much smaller within her tall, athletic frame, and almost fragile. He had an easy, amused smile that she didn't quite understand and the confidence she had always wished she had. And there was the way he had said her name.

Steve focused all of his attention on Jess that momentous evening. He asked her questions about herself and gave her the time to answer them. His conversation had purpose. When he had asked her if she'd like something to drink and put his hand on her back to help guide her through the crowd, his touch took her breath away. She forgot everyone else there and was surprised and disappointed when her girlfriends found her and told her that it was time to leave.

"I could drive you home," he said in a low voice. "We could drive around a little and get to know each other better."

She had wanted, more than anything, to go with him, but was afraid that, somehow, the spell would be broken. He asked for her phone number and promised that he would call her the next day. His call came just as she was getting ready for bed, and at the end of their long conversation, she had her date for Homecoming.

Jess's mother was so happy for her daughter that she had insisted that they go shopping the very next morning for clothes for the big game and dance. Her father had winked and reminded her that her best color was blue. Becky followed her everywhere, wanting more details about Steve and the party. Jess called Maddie at her college in New York and told her the good news. She was Cinderella.

Steve showed up for the Friday night football game and looked even more handsome than she had remembered him. He shook hands with her parents and was so at ease, it felt as though they had all known each other for years. When she opened the door to greet him the following night when he picked her up for the dance, he whistled and told her how incredibly beautiful she looked, in a way that made her believe it. She felt beautiful.

Skipping STONES

She never dated another man after that. Steve called every night, came to her home to study at least once a week, and took her out every Friday and Saturday. Often, she went to his home on Sundays to have lunch or dinner with his family. His mother was a small southern lady whose lovely voice was so soft you had to listen closely to hear her speak, a gentle and elegant woman whom Jess never tired of watching. His father was tall like Steve. He had a big voice. He had presence.

Steve helped her with math projects; she helped him with his English papers. He took her mother flowers. His mother bought her *Veranda, Southern Living,* and *Décor* magazines because she knew that Jess was interested in interior design. The couple attended all the high school sports games together, rode home from school together, went to the library together. They did it all together. Mostly alone. Just the two of them. And in the process, she discovered passion she hadn't imagined she had, and he was free to use her naiveté and inexperience to mold her like a piece of supple clay to meet his needs.

They took long walks in the parks and talked about their dreams. Steve wanted to be an attorney, rich and respected, a man of power and influence. She wanted to be an interior designer to help set design trends. He assured her that she would succeed.

Jess remembered the night her future was determined as if it were yesterday. They were at Steve's house after school on a warm May day, lying together on the sofa and watching an old movie on TV when suddenly he turned to kiss her with new urgency. When he pulled away, he looked at her more seriously than he ever had.

"I've been thinking about what we want for ourselves," he had said. "And, basically, we want the same things. We could do it together. If we had each other, we could make it all happen. We could be an awesome team. With the two of us working together, babe, there isn't anything we can't accomplish. What do you say?"

"I don't know what you mean," she'd said, but she knew exactly what he meant.

"I need you, Jessica," he'd told her. "I need you to be beside me all the way. I love you. And after we graduate from college, I want to marry you."

They kept their plans secret for that entire summer, and their secrecy brought them even closer together. The intrigue was exciting to Jess for a while, but as the end of the season approached, the novelty of the affair wore off somewhat, and she was able to step outside of herself and him and analyze her other relationships.

Jess had been a trusted friend to many people, a devoted daughter to her parents, and a caring sister to Becky and Maddie, but she had cut all of them off for months during her whirlwind romance with Steve, and she found herself missing everyone else who had been important to her. For years she and her friends had talked about having summer jobs together at camps out of state after they graduated, taking trips over college spring breaks, and meeting up in their family homes for holiday reunions. But now Jess was on the outside looking in.

She decided to make an effort to see them more, and she was grateful when they welcomed her back into their group. She helped plan nights out to see movies or to have dinners with them, but when the movies or dinners were over, there was Steve, ready to drive her home. She asked him if he ever wanted to be with his old group of friends, but he assured her that she was enough for him. He was content. She loved him for loving her so much.

Skipping S T O N E S

It was the same with her family. She made an effort to spend more time with them, but each time she planned to stay at home, Steve showed up to surprise her, appearing on the scene as if he were expected. Clearly, in his eyes, they were extensions of each other. When Steve's parents invited her to spend the last two weeks of summer with them and their family at their vacation home just outside of Bar Harbor, it seemed the most natural thing in the world for her to go.

Steve had applied to all of the schools that she did and accepted her choice of Miami of Ohio. She became a Delta Gamma, the tradition of the women in his family, and Steve joined the Phi Delts and pinned her immediately. In their junior year, he gave her an engagement ring. She was his girl. Her future was fixed.

༄

Emily Bennington and Jess were roommates their first year at college, and they became best friends. They joined the same sorority and eventually shared the same dream of having a design studio together after graduation. Emily was from Connecticut, but she was willing to move to Shaker Heights, Ohio, to set up their business. The two friends were young and confident. Their plans were huge. They would travel the world to collect antiques and beautiful accessories and meet exciting people who shared their love of design. They would work hard to make a name for themselves. Jess shared their plans with Steve, and, at the time, he said that he supported them. With her own business, Jess would have had a sense of identity. She might have been someone whose talents made a difference.

Steve applied and was accepted to Northwestern University Law School in Chicago, and, unwilling to be separated from

Jess, he insisted that they be married in early July, after they graduated and before he started law classes. They would set up their apartment as soon as possible, get married, and settle in together. Jess preferred an early fall wedding so that she would have more time to plan, but he convinced her that fall would be too challenging for him, and both families began immediately to make arrangements for the wedding. Plans with Emily for the design studio took a back seat, and the two friends reasoned that a couple of years' experience working for someone else would help both of them understand the business aspects of owning a studio. It was understood that Jess would definitely move back to the Cleveland area after Steve graduated, and the girls would look for space for their place then.

Jess had been excited to move to Chicago, heady with the possibilities and the novelty the big Windy City would provide her. She and Steve would entertain, make contacts for their future, and she would attend advanced design classes and find part-time work.

As for Emily, she interviewed for a good job in Boston as an assistant to a prestigious designer there and got it. Jess researched design firms in Chicago but didn't follow up, primarily because of Steve's advice that she get settled in first and then interview for jobs. They could manage financially on what he had saved, he said, and what his parents were willing to provide for them. Jess's mother and father praised him for his consideration of Jess and her time.

That spring before they graduated, Steve went to Chicago for more interviews and arranged his schedule at Northwestern. He also found a place for him and Jess to live and quickly furnished their new home. For the first time, Jess was not a part of decisions that impacted their future together.

Skipping STONES

Jess's parents put aside any concern about expense for the wedding and reception, and her wedding day was incredibly beautiful. The church was packed with family members and dear friends, and the couple's parents were overwhelmed by the generosity of their gifts and the distances people were willing to travel to be with them for their children's "big day." Jess had been so caught up with all of the showers and shopping and florists and photographers that she didn't stop to think that the minute she walked down the aisle, her life would be changed forever.

The fact that, from then on, Steve would be the person who would bear the ultimate responsibility for her happiness and well being hit her at the church when she stood beside her father behind her bridesmaids and saw him waiting for her at the altar. When she linked her arm with her father's to begin the wedding procession, he gripped her hand and held her there and told her that if she had any doubts at all about the marriage, it still wasn't too late to back out. She told him that she was incredibly happy. He kissed her forehead and said, okay, my precious one, let's go. And he added, in a whisper, *I will always be here for you.* She would never forget his promise even though she had no idea at the time how much she would need to count on his love and support years later.

Steve had planned a trip to Paris for their honeymoon, and it was wonderful. He had made all of the arrangements and was her guide, directing her through the city, surprising her with reservations to the finest restaurants, picking out souvenirs to take home. He held her hand and kissed her at intersections and listened attentively to her explanations about what they saw in the museums and galleries. Their last night there would be the best, he said, and he bought her an expensive dress to wear to "show her off."

That final evening at the restaurant he had selected for their farewell to Paris, Steve ordered after-dinner drinks and made her stand beside him as he made two elaborate toasts to her for all to hear. The first was to praise her - his beautiful, classy, and loving wife. The second toast was to them, a respected team, the envy of all their friends, partners forever. They drank, and he kissed her. The other diners applauded. He was her prince, her knight in shining armor.

They were both excited about Chicago and everything that it would have to offer them. Steve immersed himself in his studies. She searched the want-ads for jobs with decorating studios and galleries but settled with a job at a temp agency, initially working in their office as a secretary. The managers quickly recognized her potential for them and began sending her out to the most influential businesses in the best parts of town. Her take-home salary increased dramatically, and she was happy to be able to contribute more to their budget. She was equally excited that the jobs were interesting and required her to work directly with top management. When she was offered a permanent, full-time position with a public relations firm, she was ecstatic. Steve balked but eventually gave in, but questioned her every move. He was angry when she had to go to meetings that required her to leave their apartment early or return late, and she tried to make up for his anger by pleasing him in other ways. The job lasted three months. When he attended an office party with her and realized how taken certain managers were with her, he demanded that she quit. They had argued, but he insisted that the men weren't trust-worthy, that they were using her and didn't have her best interests in mind. He accused her of being naïve and putting herself and her job before him.

Skipping STONES

She fought his edict for a while, but his displeasure with their situation confused her and made her sad. She was conciliatory. She eventually gave in and turned in her resignation.

Bored, she began to study cooking and designed pillows and tablecloths and napkins for their apartment. She joined a women's book club in their building and made friends easily. And she entertained on weekends when Steve wasn't too tired. He found fault with everyone she met and derided the book club and the guests she invited to their home. Finally, she confronted him.

"This isn't exactly what we had planned, honey," she said over dinner one evening. "We were going to work together. But it isn't happening that way. I don't understand why you don't want me to work and why you don't want me to learn more. And I don't know what you expect from people. We need to be involved to keep our friends."

"This is law school, Jess," he had protested impatiently. "I'll be the main bread winner when it's over. We said we'd work together, and we are. You're helping me complete my education. We're beginning our dream right here, and we'll continue it back in Cleveland."

He'd leaned across the table and given her a kiss on the cheek. "You're my little woman, honey," he'd said. "My wife. You're helping me. You'll have your chance."

Part of what he said made sense to her. Law school was, of course, the most important thing to accomplish. But she needed a challenge too.

"I can still take care of our little place and support you in what you have to do if I have a job," she'd told him. "I'm sorry that I let some things slide before, but it wasn't all that bad, was it? I just don't feel that I have enough to do here. I don't feel like I'm contributing at all. I'm not used to having so much time with nothing to fill it.

He was defensive. "So now you don't like our home. It's too small for you. And you're bored already. Six months of being married, and you're bored."

"No, honey. That's not what I mean at all," she'd said. "I just want to do more. And I want to keep learning too."

He pushed back his chair and shoved his plate away. "I can't believe this. We're barely settled in, and you're complaining already."

She'd tried again to explain how she was feeling, but he shut her off. He leaned in close to her, and the intensity in his eyes was frightening.

"You wouldn't make enough money to pay for your transportation. You'd be a gopher again. You let people take advantage of you. They laughed behind your back. I saw it at the party that night. They ridiculed you, and you smiled along with them."

His words stung her, and she considered the truth in them. Had she been a fool?

"I would never have thought you could be so selfish," he continued. "You've been spoiled all your life, Jess. I saw it, but I thought I could change it. Apparently, I was wrong. I'm giving everything I can. I'm working my butt off for you. For our future. And you're complaining and thinking only about yourself. Get this through your head. You're a wife now. You have a job. Right here. It isn't all about you anymore."

"I'm not complaining," she said. "It's just that you said…"

"I said that we would help each other," he interrupted. "I'm helping you. I'm supporting you. Even though I'm going to school, I'm supporting you. You're acting like some prima donna. You're a small fish in a big pond here, Jess. You need to grow up."

She was devastated. "I'm sorry," she said. "I want to be a part of the team. That's all."

"You want. You want," he shot back at her. "Listen to me. I know you're in love with the idea of being a big designer, running around for wealthy clients, playing the artistic role. Listen to me, and listen good. Designers are a dime a dozen in this city. So are pretty women to run around for wealthy, sleazy men. Looking for a job and flitting your ass around all over town isn't worth the time and effort it would take you, and it isn't worth the frustration it would cause me. I need you here. Period. I can't be worrying about where you are, whether this place is cleaned up or not, whether dinner will be made. I have to concentrate, and you're making it a nightmare."

For a moment, she had been speechless. He had started in the middle of a story, and she had no idea what the beginning was. She made one last attempt to be understood.

"I just don't feel very worthwhile."

He walked away from her. "So I don't make you feel worthwhile now, is that it?" He grabbed his coat and walked to the door. "I'm going to the library for some peace and quiet. Maybe someone there will make me feel 'worthwhile' for a change. Don't wait up."

By the time he returned, she had convinced herself that he was right, that the most important thing for her to do at that point in their lives was to see to it that he graduated from law school high in his class. Her role was to make that possible. Her time would come later.

But everything had suddenly changed. They attended parties the school hosted for Steve's class, and he commanded the same respect he had in high school and undergraduate school, but once he and Jess got back to their apartment, he derided everyone he had befriended. Jess continued to arrange casual dinner parties for a few people she met in the building, and Steve was the perfect host, but when they were alone again, he complained about how boring or aloof or argumentative or assertive they were. The more Jess tried to meet people and make friends on her own, the more Steve accused her of being flighty and self-absorbed.

She involved herself in projects at the apartment building. Chicago was a treasure-trove, and she continued her education by taking advantage of free classes at the Museum of Art and special exhibits at local galleries and antique shops close by as well as the many inexpensive architectural tours offered from the heart of the city. She taught herself to prepare gourmet meals to help her get ready for when she'd be able to entertain on a grand scale when Steve was an important lawyer.

He praised her. As long as she was home when he was there and made their place comfortable and clean and organized and had his clothes pressed and placed in the closet the way he wanted them, he was the old Steve. She learned how to please him and put out his temper. His praise made up for the times when he made her feel stupid and worthless.

At night he held her in his arms and thanked her for molding her life around him. He told her how hard he was working and that he would make a wonderful life for them if she would continue to help him. One day, he said, we'll relax and realize our dream of being that model couple we had decided to be. He guaranteed it. Behind every great man is a great woman, he'd said, and you're my woman. She flinched at the cliché.

Skipping **S T O N E S**

Jess stayed in touch with Emily. In her letters, Emily described her job and everything she was learning from her employer. She was growing, she said, and was understanding basic business practices that would be helpful to both of them when they opened their own place.

Jess had never felt jealousy before. It was ugly and it hurt.

Jess counted the years and finally the months that were between her and all of the things that she missed back home. Finally, the day came to go back, and she immersed herself into decorating their new place and getting back in touch with her old friends and family.

Steve went to work at a large and respected law firm. The first months were as hard for him as it always was for all new lawyers, and he had to work late in the evenings and most Saturdays. He was driven. His goal was to set a record for being the youngest man in the firm to make full partner. Jess was proud of him and supported him. She worked hard on their home and joined organizations in order to meet women whose husbands Steve thought could help him in his career. She waited for her turn. One month turned into another and another and finally Jess asked him again if she could go to work. He told her again that a woman's work is in her home.

Appearance was important to him. His favorite motto was that you have to look the part to play the part. He dressed impeccably, and he made certain that Jess did, picking out her clothes and buying her expensive pieces of jewelry. Jess went along with it all, playing the perfect hostess, the beautiful wife, the impeccable home keeper, calming him when he was furious over some perceived slight and suggesting ways to hide his contempt of people. She became a part of his game.

She gave up her dream. Her focus was their home and socially supporting Steve. Even then, she refused to let go of the fairy tale. She could still be a princess. His princess.

∽

They had been back home in Cleveland two years when Steve made a sudden announcement.

"It's time to have a baby," he said. "Get off the pill."

The downward slide of her life suddenly grew steeper. She had been ecstatic about having a baby, but she had totally misunderstood Steve's motivation. His reaction to the pregnancy crushed her. The larger her belly grew, the more unattractive he found her. Her swollen body repulsed him. On one of her really bad days, she asked him why he had wanted her to get pregnant in the first place and why he was so unhappy.

"If we didn't have a child, people would think there's something wrong with us," he had told her. "The timing is perfect, but you look disgusting."

Eventually, his embarrassment over her appearance became unbearable, and they stopped going outside of the house together. She tried to hide her morning sickness, vomiting in the bathroom with the doors closed and a pillow over her head to hide the sound of it because it was so abhorrent to him. He eventually relegated her to the guest room to sleep. She watched every calorie she took in and walked to keep her body as tight as possible. What she had entered into with joy, she endured with disgrace.

Once Ben was born, Steve's demands for orderliness in his home and silence from his son became intense. Too many times, he demanded that Jess choose between caring for him and caring for their child, and Jess felt that she was constantly disappointing someone. She read articles that led her to believe that what she was going through was nothing unusual, that new mothers often experienced what she was feeling, that some amount of stress and anxiety were normal after childbirth. She didn't understand what constituted normal anxiety.

At times, Jess hinted to her mother about Steve's demands over her son's and how she felt about having to choose between them. Her mother supported the articles.

"It's all normal, honey," she would say, patting her daughter's hand, "all normal, and you have so much to be thankful for. Every woman has to adjust after the birth of her first child and work through a little depression."

And she added that Jess should keep in mind the fact that Steve was a man with a lot of responsibilities and pressures of his own outside the home, and that he was going through a huge adjustment too. Jess was fortunate, she said, to have such a strong, virile, and respected man who had a wonderful career ahead of him. Jess accepted the words of the authorities on the subject and agreed that she simply had postpartum depression and that things would change. But they didn't.

Ben's late-night cries or temper tantrums, his messiness at the table, his toys, occasional colds or tummy aches infuriated Steve. Jess learned to adjust her son's eating and sleeping schedules so that she could accommodate Steve's personal needs, but the effort did little to satisfy him. Too many nights, she lay in bed, filled with regret that she had not been able to finish the story or song she had started with Ben, but had rushed out the door, ahead of his cries, to satisfy his father.

As Ben's needs grew, Steve's appetite for sex increased. He was rough and had specific acts he demanded her to perform. Much of what he asked from her was distasteful to her, but she wasn't sure what her role should be since he had been her first and only partner. And she never found the courage to refuse him.

⁓

Within the next several years, Steve was well on his way to becoming a junior partner, sure that he would reach his goals. They were doing exceedingly well financially. He purchased several rental properties with some of his trust money and made substantial monthly earnings from them. He had also been directed by one of his clients to a financial advisor, and his significant stock investments grew and became increasingly profitable. Jess knew nothing about their net worth. Steve handled all of their finances and laughed when she asked if he would explain his investments to her so that she could learn and understand. He refused. According to him, women weren't supposed to be involved in those kinds of things.

"Just enjoy it, baby," he often said. "You don't need to be bothered with the details."

Jess was amazed when, after four years, Steve said that they needed to have another child. She reminded him how terrible her pregnancy with Ben had been for him and how much time another child would require. His response was chilling.

"People are always suspect of one-child families," he'd said. "I don't want anyone to think that either one of us is sterile. You'll arrange it. We'll get through the pregnancy the way we did before."

She had always wanted a boy and a girl, and so, against all reasoning, she prayed for a little girl who she would name Katie. Her son would have a sibling. Maybe Steve would learn to love him more.

Skipping STONES

The physical attacks began her fourth month of pregnancy. What started as slurs and derogatory remarks when she couldn't respond quickly enough to Steve turned into shoves and small smacks to her arms. It went downhill from there.

She was seven months pregnant the first time he hit her hard. Ben had been home from kindergarten with a bad cough and fever, and Jess had spent the entire day taking care of him, reading, playing quiet games, and making him take cool baths to bring the fever down. She lost track of time. When Steve walked into the house, she was still in the clothes she had thrown on when he had left that morning. The sink was full of dirty dishes, books and games were scattered all over the coffee table, and dinner wasn't even a thought yet. Worse still, she wasn't at the door waiting for him with smiles and kisses and cocktails.

She had put on extra weight with Katie, and getting up and down wasn't easy. When she struggled up from the sofa, Steve looked at her like she was some deformed creature, and the disgust on his face was undeniable. He surveyed the clutter, and something terrifying broke inside him.

Screaming at Jess, accusing her of being lazy and unappreciative, he threw the books and games off the table, and when Ben cried, he yanked the little boy off the sofa and shoved him through the room. Jess raced after them as fast as she could, and when she grabbed her husband's arm to stop him, he turned on her and pushed her away. She landed against a side table and lost her balance and fell. He looked at her as if she were foul.

"My God, look at you," he had said. "Look what you've turned into."

He prodded her legs with his foot, and the prods became kicks. Again. And again. And then he stood her up, looked at her coldly, and hit her across her cheek. It was a calculated and deliberate act, and one that clearly gave him pleasure.

"Get this place cleaned up and then get yourself cleaned up and don't you ever let this happen again," he said through clinched teeth.

He stormed out, telling her that she had thirty minutes to get the house in order. Jess was afraid to move, terrified for her unborn child. Ben sobbed and stared at her with absolute terror, and she struggled to find comforting words to offer him.

What should she have done, she asked herself now, eight years later. It's easy to say that she should have left with her son that very minute, gone to her parents and asked for their help. She should have admitted that her marriage was a failure and she was afraid for her and her children's safety. If only she had.

She had packed and unpacked suitcases day in and day out, determined to leave one moment and convinced that it would be a mistake the next. It was the most important decision she would ever make, and in the end, she chose not to put herself first. Instead, she based everything on changing Steve. She wouldn't tell. She would suffer silently.

༶

Shortly after Katie's birth, Steve began to come home late every Thursday night. At first, he offered Jess excuses: he had to work on a special project or meet with a client for dinner or show up at a meeting someone had called at the last minute. But over time, the excuses stopped, and when Jess asked if she should expect him home late every Thursday, he refused to give her an answer, saying only that she'd know when he knew.

Not wanting to believe the story her imagination created, she used the time he was away to visit her parents or to take

Skipping **S T O N E S**

the kids on special late-afternoon outings. The phone calls started two months after the Thursday night sessions began. An unfamiliar woman's voice asked her if she was Steve's wife. Off-guard, Jess answered that she was, and the caller laughed and hung up.

The second call came the following week.

"Do you know where your husband is every Thursday?" the same voice asked. "Do you know who he's with? Do you know what he does?"

Jess hung up.

The third call came the following Thursday evening just before Steve came home.

"He just left me," the woman said. "He'll be back to you soon. Just thought you'd like to know."

Jess sat for a long time, listening to the dial tone. Someone out there knew about her. Probably knew about her children. Might know where and how they lived. To Jess, the invasion of her and her children's privacy was as bad as the fact that Steve was cheating on her.

She practiced what she would say to him, envisioning denials or pleas for forgiveness. Whatever his response, she would forgive. Her husband would realize how he had hurt the two of them and how valuable she was and how loyal. He would leave the other woman, everything would be out in the open, and life would be better. The victory would finally be hers.

She waited until the following morning to tell him about the calls, but instead of the remorse and shame she had expected, he turned on her, blaming her for his having to go to someone else for sexual relief. She was frigid, he said, and had no idea how to please him.

"Fucking you is like banging a brick," he had told her. "You learn how to please me, and I won't have to go out for it. And don't you ever question me again. You should feel damned lucky I'll still have you."

He came home the following day with a beautifully wrapped box that contained a diamond tennis bracelet. It was his way of saying he was sorry.

The calls stopped, but the voice continued to haunt her.

Now, seven years later, after two days of unexpected and joyous freedom, her children were finally sleeping peacefully together in her son's room, and she, standing in the middle of her perfectly manicured garden, could finally see everything for what it was: a barren foundation built on lies.

She was nothing more than an object to her husband, something to be used only for his pleasure. As long as she performed effectively, she was safe. When he no longer found her desirable and serviceable, he could, whenever it pleased him, punish her. Or throw her away. The cold reality of what she had become brought her shame. She was chattel.

The only things that mattered now were the children: her son and daughter who were sleeping their best sleep in years because their father was not at home, and the child who had lost everything that had been real in his previous life and had showed her and her children in just a few months what they had been missing in theirs. She would, she vowed, make everything right for them somehow. But how would she do it? Steve had threatened to take them away from her, and she had learned to believe in his ability to carry out his threats.

PART THREE

Josh

    Mimi and Papaw called the next morning and invited Jess and the children to their home for a visit. Maddie and Bill would be there too. Papaw grilled barbeque chicken and shrimp and corn on the cob with the husks still on, and everyone, laughing and chattering, overate. After dinner, the conversation became even more animated as the adults reminisced. Time, as Mimi had said so many months ago, is a great healer, and enough time had passed since Becky's death to ease the family's pain and allow reflection. The children curled themselves up on the massive sofas and listened with attention.

    Light conversation bounced around in all directions for a while until Maddie brought up the sisters' summer camps. All three of them had gone to a place in Michigan, just outside of Petoskey, throughout junior high and the first year of high school. The three were carefully placed in separate cabins, even though they were close in age, and there had been friendly, but intense, competition among them.

    "Your mother was the most athletic girl at camp," Maddie told Josh, "and the most imaginative. Her reputation preceded her each year."

Skipping STONES

Maddie and Jess explained that Becky had won awards for archery, rappelling, climbing, and canoeing, and that she had always been in constant motion.

"She was always the first one out in the mornings and the last one to leave the campfire at night, and she drove the camp counselors crazy," Jess said.

"She was everywhere," Maddie continued. "She might just decide during chores to run to the lake and take a swim with her clothes on." She laughed and added, "Then, of course, everyone would want to do it, and there we'd be, the entire camp totally wacked out because of Becky. Or she'd talk some people into hanging back from campfire songs before bed and scare the pants off us on the way back to our cabins."

"So she had a lot of friends back then?" Josh asked.

It didn't escape his notice that the sisters had trouble answering that question. They said that people had trouble keeping up with her. They said that she was friendly but was real independent.

"She had her off-the-wall hilarious moments, and that's where her zany reputation sprang from," Maddie explained. "You see, your mom was respected for her talents. She was very bright. I think people wanted to be her friends, but often-times she gave them the impression that she didn't need them. She'd pull them up close and then back away," she added, and Jess agreed.

Papaw had a memory to share.

"There was one Christmas Eve, Josh, when your mom was around fourteen, that none of us will ever forget," he said. "The whole family and some very good friends were together here at our house for our annual holiday party. We were all seated where we are now, in this very room, all of us around the big tree we always have, ready to sing some Christmas songs, when we realized that your mom was missing.

He paused, and the smile on his face fought with the pain in his heart from the memory.

"Mimi and I went through the house, calling for her," he went on, "and eventually we became alarmed. We came back here and tried to decide what to do next, when we heard something like footsteps outside on the roof. *Clomp, clomp,* they went over to this chimney right here. We all ran outside and were greeted by a *"Ho, Ho, Ho,"* someplace above us. We looked up to find where the greeting had come from, and there was your mom, rappelling down the chimney in the snow and freezing cold. Rappelling down the chimney!"

Josh swelled up with pride. "I can just see her doing that," he said. "She'd do something like that. She sure would."

"It didn't really surprise us either," Uncle Bill chimed in. "She was always doing something crazy. How would you describe her? I'll tell you what, when she was on her game, she was unbelievable. I think 'exuberant' is a good word for her. She was full of energy. You just never knew what she was going to do. And she was so witty. She was so much fun."

The words were like manna to the boy.

Maddie and Bill talked about the high school parties the sisters had at home when their parents were gone, and the children had trouble believing the stories until Papaw confirmed them.

When Bill and Steve's names came up, Josh relied on the good mood of the adults and took the risk to ask where and when Sam entered their lives. The silence that followed was uncomfortable, and he was afraid that he had ruined the rest of the evening. Finally, Maddie spoke up and said that he had been brought by one of her friends to a party she'd had at her family's house the summer of her sophomore year in college.

"We liked him right away, and he became an instant friend to everyone. From then on he was invited to every party we had."

Josh asked if his mother and Sam had liked each other right away.

"Oh, yes," Maddie assured him. "There was something cooking between them in no time. In fact, your aunt Jess and I had crushes on him for a while too, but we were already spoken for."

She winked at Bill, and he grinned back at her.

"So they knew right away that they loved each other and wanted to get married." Josh wanted it all, the entire story.

"Absolutely. They got married right away, before Becky graduated."

Becky had told Josh about the family's reaction to her wanting to get married, and he knew that Mimi and Papaw were not happy. She had explained to him that she had threatened to elope and that the family had finally given in and gave her a small but respectable wedding. They had allowed her to finish school at a small community college in West Virginia when Sam got an attractive opportunity as a sous-chef at a renowned resort. Josh had always thought of his mother and father's defiance as romantic.

There was another awkward pause in the conversation, and Jess broke through it. It was late, she said, and they had a long drive back to their home. They said their good-byes and promised to get together again soon. It had been, everyone agreed, a wonderful evening together.

The children were tired, but they wanted to hold onto the evening. Katie made a small request.

"Would it be okay for us to have a hot chocolate and a cookie before we go to bed?" She asked. "Like Josh and Aunt Becky used to do?"

They changed into their pajamas and entered into the simple act of having a late bedtime snack together with deep seriousness. And when they were ready for bed, their sleep was filled, once again, with peace.

Josh was the first one to awaken, and he walked immediately to his closet and took the diary from its hiding place. And then he brought out the box of pictures he had saved of his mother and him and finally allowed himself to look through them. He found the one he was looking for – the one he had taken of her on their front steps, the day of the big rain. She was soaking wet and radiant, wearing a big grin, her hair plastered to her head. He was able to look at the picture and not cry. Finally, he tucked the picture inside the diary, over the note from his father.

And then he wrote.

Uncle Bill said my mom was exuberant. I looked it up and it means lively, high-spirited, effusive, cheerful, excited, irrepressible. And she was witty, he said. They thought she was great. They loved my mom. I wish she had known how much. My mom was everything I thought she was and maybe even more.

I wish every day could be like yesterday and the day before. I wish I could see my dad.

Later that morning, after breakfast, Sam called again. He wanted to see Josh, and he wanted him to meet his other grandma. Jess said yes. There would be time before Steve got home.

Skipping STONES

It was Jess who decided that their outing would begin at the Natural History Museum. Sam would meet them at ten and bring Josh back after a late lunch.

"Are you sure you can keep it a secret?" She asked the children once more before they loaded themselves into the car, and they assured her that they could. No further questions or explanations were necessary.

Josh's other grandmother's name was Annie. That he knew, but not much else. Sam told Josh that the two of them and his grandfather had spent a lot of time together when Josh was little. When he told him that his grandfather had died just seven months ago, Josh felt cheated again.

Turning off Highway 90, they drove through narrow streets lined with old oak trees and winding sidewalks, and finally they turned onto Lake Road where they stopped in front of a square white stone home with black shutters. A wrought iron fence covered with miniature pink roses spanned the yard, and a stone walkway curved its way from the sidewalk up to the front door.

When Josh hung back a little, Sam seemed to understand.

"You're going to get along great," he assured him. "She's a super lady."

She was outside within seconds, waving to them and smiling in a way that made Josh want to smile right back. She was a tall, thin, straight woman with brown wavy hair. She had a flowered apron on over a simple beige dress, and she wore green no-nonsense Crocks. Josh sensed that he was going to like her.

"Let me take a good look at you," she said in a voice that was deeper than he thought it would be, and he grinned under her good-natured scrutiny.

"You've got your father's tall, thin body and his smile," she told him, "but your eyes are your mother's. What a fine looking guy you are. And so grown up. My gosh. Where have all the years gone? Oh, if only your grandpa could see you now."

She looked up into the sky with that same big smile. "Maybe he does," she said. "Do you see this handsome young grandson of yours, Paul?"

Father and son laughed and shrugged their shoulders at each other.

"Come on, come on," she said as she shooed them into the house. "We've given the neighbors enough to talk about for the rest of the week. Come on in, and let's get re-acquainted, Josh."

She had a pot of coffee ready on her kitchen counter and poured a cup for Sam and herself. And when Josh said he'd like some too, she was pleased.

"Good for you," she said. "Good for you. My dad gave me coffee as soon as I learned to walk. Paul always said that's the reason I'm so high-strung. All that caffeine. He always said that he'd give his first dollar to know what I'd be like without it, and I assured him that he'd never know and just as well."

The talk never stopped. She asked direct questions, and Josh answered them easily.

She listened. And she heard.

She told Josh what she knew about how Becky had died in that same voice she used to talk about everything, as if accidents and dying were things that were matters of fact and should be dealt with in that way. She said that she understood how hard it was on him to lose his mother because she'd lost people she loved too and would miss her husband forever.

"But I'm going to continue to push on, to live my life just the way he'd expect me to and just the way he'd do if the tables were turned," she told Josh.

And she told him that she was sorry she had lost touch with his mother, because she was a "terrific gal," whose spunk and honesty she had always enjoyed. She knew where he had been living and came right out and asked how that was working out. The question threw him off-guard.

"It...it's real different," he offered, "but it's okay. It's good to get to know my cousins better. And Aunt Jess is real nice."

"It's tough to be moved around," she offered, "especially after what you've gone through. It takes time to adjust to new rules, different ways of doing things. Works both ways. Your Aunt Jess is a good lady. Always liked her. She'll never replace your mother, but she's a good one to stand in for her for a while."

Josh saw the quick glance she and Sam shared and wondered what was behind it, but then she was off again, asking him what kinds of things he liked to do, and when he mentioned cooking as one of them, she wanted to know more.

"Mom and I used to work together in the kitchen a lot," he told her. "I make pancakes and real oatmeal. My best is French toast – it's better than Mom's. I made it a lot for us on Sunday mornings when I had plenty of time. Hers was good, but I put secret stuff in mine to make it different. She liked it."

"Well, I'd like some of that sometime," his grandmother told him. "Come over for breakfast next time and you help cook. Maybe you can teach your dad how to make it so he can offer it as a special at one of his restaurants on Sundays."

When it was time for lunch, she put a big pot of Sloppy Joes on the stove and pulled a peach pie out of the oven, saying that it was his dad's favorite. And while the one got hot and the other cooled down, she brought out some deviled eggs and celery sticks stuffed with peanut butter for them to munch on. That was food Josh could relate to.

After he and Sam helped her clear the dishes away, she showed Josh around the house and the yard out back. There wasn't much left to pick in her garden, but she said that the pumpkins would start growing soon and that she'd give him and Katie and Ben some for Halloween. They sat in the small screened porch, and Josh told her about his mom's and Jess's gardens, and all three of them agreed that there's just nothing better than digging in the dirt and watching things grow.

Time flew by so fast that when Sam checked his watch, he discovered they had just a little over an hour before he needed to get Josh back to the museum, and he still wanted to take him to his favorite spot on the lake. She shooed them out as fast as she had shooed them in and asked if it would be okay for her to give Josh a big hug, and he answered by giving her one.

"Take good care of yourself and give it time," she whispered to him.

Josh and his father pulled off a quiet street onto a narrow lane marked as the entrance to a beach and walked down stone steps and through a friendly park with grassy knolls, picnic tables, and a new playground. The beach area was small and was partially protected by a broken break-wall. The two stood side-by-side for a while and watched sail boats languidly skim across the sparkling water. And then Sam turned around and pointed to a bench on top of one of the knolls and said that he and Becky had liked to sit up there and look out on the water and dream about owning a home on the lake one day and a boat to travel over it.

"I didn't know Mom liked to sail," Josh said. "We never went out on a boat together."

"The boat was my idea," Sam told him. "I kinda' grew up boating. Your mom was willing to go along with it. We both dreamed about the house. She said the lake made her peaceful when it was calm and got her creative energies going when it was churned up."

"Do you still want to do that? Have a house on the water and a boat?"

"Well, actually I have both. Not the same kind of house that she and I had planned for, but it suits me fine. I'd like to take you there the next time we get together. We'll hang out, and if the weather's good, maybe we could go sailing together. What do you think?"

Josh wanted to do it right there and then, but of course he couldn't say that. "Sure," he said. "That would be okay. I think that would work."

Josh watched a while as Sam searched the beach for small flat stones.

"The lake isn't always calm like this," Sam explained. "You can't trust it from one minute to the next. It can stir up and play havoc in no time at all, and so sailing can be a real challenge. You have to know how to read the weather and be prepared for anything and everything. So you've never been sailing?"

"No. Never been," Josh answered. "We biked a lot. And hiked. Fished some. That's about it, I guess. I think I'd like it though, probably." He looked out across the horizon. "It's huge," he continued. "This must be how the oceans feel."

"It is huge, but nothing like the ocean."

Sam began throwing the stones side-armed onto the water and watched as they skipped across the smooth surface.

"From east to west it extends over two hundred miles," he continued, "and I think it's close to sixty miles across at its widest point north to south."

Josh studied his father's technique and gathered some of his own flat stones and threw them into the water. They fell heavily.

"Lake Erie has the best Walleye in the world," Sam continued. "Too bad we couldn't have taken some home when we went out with Zeke."

He skimmed four more stones across the small waves, and Josh tried it again. The second attempt was no good, but the third stone skipped itself three times before it sunk into the water. He tried another and another and another and all but one glided across the surface, and then he gathered more and skipped them too, one after another, until he was satisfied that he wouldn't forget how. His concentration was so deep that he didn't see his father watching him.

Sam walked over to him and ruffled his hair like fathers do when they are proud of their sons. "Good job, Josh," he said. "Good job."

They grinned at each other and sat down on a slab of concrete, and Sam moved to the next step that he hoped would help deepen their relationship.

"You know, don't you," he said, "that if you go straight across from here north and then east, the lake dumps into Niagara Falls."

Josh's chest grew tight, and it was a moment before he could speak.

"Mom and I were going to go to Niagara Falls this summer," he said. "Just for a weekend. We were going to go on that boat ride that goes under the falls. We had a trip jar we put our change in, and she opened a special account at the bank to keep the money when the jar filled up. We probably wouldn't have gone, but maybe we would've. I used most of the money from the jar the day before yesterday. Took Jess and Katie and Ben out for lunch. I hope it was the right thing to do."

Sam bent down and grabbed a couple of sticks from the sand.

"Sure it was. Absolutely," he said. "You made a memory for them."

He took his time and traced designs through the sand.

"I knew about that trip to the falls. She was real excited about it."

"How did you know about it?"

"We talked, Josh. We had talked a lot, starting around Christmas time last year."

He took a deep breath and went on.

"She and I went to Niagara Falls together once, a long time ago right after we were married. It was kind of a late honeymoon. She said she wanted to share our memories with you. Your mother had so many ideas for you and her and..." He dug deeper into the sand, holding on to something in his mind or struggling to push it out.

"What?" Josh asked. "And what?"

"You'll get to Niagara Falls, Josh," Sam finally said. "And you'll get to all of the other places she wanted you to go."

He stood up suddenly and dropped the stick. "Come on, buddy," he said, putting his hand on his son's shoulder. "I have more to show you right here."

He asked Josh if he would like to see the first house they had lived in, and they left Rocky River and headed east to Lakewood, toward Cleveland and Jess. He explained how the area was being redone and pointed out the new restaurants and shops that had recently moved in. He slowed down as they passed by one that looked better than the others.

"There's the second restaurant I put up. Just re-did it."

"Looks good," Josh said. He took a good look and added, "It's a lot different from the other one we went to. Fancier, but I like it."

Josh was struck by how little he knew about the man who had helped create him.

"So how many restaurants do you have?" He asked. "I don't think I asked you before. I should have."

"Three now," Sam told him. "I'm re-inventing the last one. That's the one I went to California to do some research for. It'll be a little different from the others. We're going to run a little catering business from it. I'm hoping I'll get to do one more."

Sam circled back and weaved in and out around the streets off the commercial area and slowed down in front of a duplex on Edanola.

"There it is. That's your first home," he said. "It looks small, but it was plenty big for the three of us. It was a great place to start out."

It looked good to Josh, as good, if not better, than the one he and his mom had lived in, and he asked why they moved out of it.

"Well, as you got older and started needing bigger toys, we were pretty cramped. And we wanted a nice yard for you to play in."

"There was one here, wasn't there? A yard with a metal fence around it?"

"There sure was. I can't believe you'd remember that. You were so little at the time. How can you remember that and the straws and the booths at the restaurant?"

"I don't know," Josh said. "I just do. I don't ever forget too many things. So you moved to get a bigger place? A bigger yard?"

Sam pulled away from the curb and headed back to Jess and the kids. "We did. To do that and to get your mom back to her side of town. She missed the east side where she had grown up, and so we figured out how to make it all happen."

"Did you miss your side of town after we moved?"

"A little. I think everyone misses their roots when they relocate."

"I liked our house in Lyndhurst," Josh said and braced himself to ask a question that he knew would be difficult for Sam to answer. "Did you miss it when you left?"

"I missed it a lot," his father said in a low voice. "I missed you a lot. And your mom."

"I miss it too," Josh told him.

"But you have a beautiful home to live in now."

"But it isn't the same," Josh said and wondered how much more he could say.

"I remember the home I grew up in," Sam told him. "Every single room of it. It wasn't so great, but the memories I have of it are. I don't think anyone ever forgets where they grew up. Sometimes you remember it being better than it was."

Josh wanted to tell his father about all of his memories. And he wanted to tell him about his mother's.

"Do you have any of your old stuff from back then? Did you save anything when you left your home where you grew up?"

"Your Grandma Annie saved everything. It's still all packed away in boxes in her attic. Someday I'll go through it all, probably. I should do that."

Josh decided to take the risk.

"Mom and I didn't have a lot of stuff. We didn't save much." He paused briefly and decided to say what was on his mind. "She had a diary. I found it the day I went to our old house to get the rest of my stuff."

"I didn't know about that," his father said in his easy, non-judgmental voice. "What'd you do with it?"

"I kept it. I thought I should."

"That's good. I hope you have other things of hers too."

"I do. I have a paper weight and an old address book and a few pictures. Don't know why I kept the address book, actually. And I have the coin jar."

Josh was tired of cautious statements and innuendos and half-truths. He wanted to be the way he had been before when he had nothing to fear. He wanted to tell Sam about everything he had read about him and his mother in the diary, but he was afraid Sam would tell him that he had been wrong to look into her private thoughts. Instead, he admitted to keeping his own notes about what he was feeling and what he remembered inside her book.

There was one more, and by far the most important, truth he felt he needed to disclose.

"I think you should know that she didn't hate you or anything when you left. She always thought you were great. I just thought you should know that. I think it's good for people to know how other people think about them when it's good. That's all."

He rushed on before he could lose his nerve.

"Actually," he blurted out, "she really missed you. There were times when…when she was confused about things."

Sam pulled over to the curb and turned to speak directly to his son. The words came out like they'd been hurt in his throat.

"I know how difficult all of this is for you," he said. "I'm glad you told me these things. There's a lot more for me to tell you too, and it's going to take some time. I've put off the things I've wanted to tell you because they're too important to rush through. Phone calls won't work. I want us to have a face-to-face conversation about a lot of things. I think we're ready. But I want to tell you right now that your mother and I never stopped loving one another."

Josh held his breath and willed his father to begin the path to understanding right then and there. He had no idea when Steve would leave again and Sam and he would be able to meet.

"I'll talk to Jess and ask for more time with you," his father was saying, as much to himself as to Josh. "She'll understand. We'll work it out." He turned back to Josh and said, "I'll never lie to you. Lying only brings more pain. And I will never give you half-truths. I want us to trust each other."

They already did.

༄

It was Labor Day weekend, and everyone in the village was celebrating. Soon, outdoor parties would be set aside until the following spring, warm weather clothes would be packed away, trees would soon turn bright colors, birds would migrate south, gardens would be cut back, and pumpkins would be put out on porch steps. School would start Wednesday, and Jess would be alone in a house with nothing to do and nowhere to go. The thought of her children being away from her saddened her.

Things were going fine on Saturday. Steve took his family to Jess's favorite annual antique show and treated them to lunch afterward. They invited Mimi and Papaw for dinner. Sunday, the family went to early church, and Steve took the children to the mall to pick up some new back-packs to start school with. They planned to attend the annual Labor Day parade the next afternoon, and Jess rushed to the grocery to get things for the village picnic on The Green.

Everything was still good after a late lunch. Steve went outside to clean the cars while the others relaxed in the kitchen, Jess fixing a complicated dish for dinner from an old Julia

Child's cookbook, Josh and Ben mastering a new computer game, and Katie coloring in her new Disney Princess book.

And then, suddenly, the peace was shattered by a small pink piece of paper.

Steve had been outside for over an hour when suddenly he barreled through the door and slammed it shut so hard behind him that the chandelier in the hall clattered into itself. The children sat paralyzed, recognizing pending danger, and Jess's mind clicked through all of the possible reasons why Steve might be angry. And there he was, waving a sales receipt in her face.

"What is this?" he shrieked. "What is this?"

She stepped back, but he grabbed her wrist and yanked her to him.

"It's a sales receipt," she whispered.

"And where did you get it?"

He grabbed her chin with his other hand. "Where is the goddamned dress shop?" He shouted. "Where is the dress shop? It's in Rocky River, isn't it? And that's where Sam lives, isn't it? Damn you! You went to see him, didn't you?"

He pulled Jess to where Katie sat.

"That's right, isn't it Katie?" He asked her. "You'll tell me the truth. Did you kids and your mother go to Rocky River to see Sam?"

"We went fishing," she whispered.

"Was your mother with you?"

"No. Just me and Ben and Josh."

"And your mother?" He pressed.

"She came when we had lunch."

"Steve," Jess said, "it was just fishing and a lunch. It was simply an outing for the children. Nothing more. Let's stop this."

Skipping STONES

He turned and narrowed his eyes at her. "Get the sweater," he demanded, shoving her to their bedroom door. "Go get that damned sweater!"

The children sat rooted to their chairs, afraid to move and afraid to stay, listening to their father assault their mother. In a few minutes, he was back to them, holding scraps of the blue sweater he had shredded, panting and sweating from the effort of Jess's punishment.

"You disobey. You pay," he said. "I warned her, and I warned you. That man is history. Consider him dead."

He turned directly to Josh. "You will never see that man again. Never. Whatever you were thinking about for a future with him will never, ever happen. Do you understand?"

He ordered the children to get out of his sight and to stay away until he decided what their punishment would be. Josh was ashamed at how fast he ran for safety.

They hid in their rooms and wrapped themselves inside blankets and draperies, forcing their minds to go empty, unwilling to think of Jess's pain. *Ninety bottles of beer on the wall, ninety bottles of beer. If one of those bottles...You are my sunshine, my only sunshine, you make me happy...I'll show him what he is, someday I'll show him.* At some point, very late, each of them fell into fitful sleep.

Josh awoke gasping from another nightmare and struggled to push its image aside. The moon's rays shined through the window, blanketing the room in white light, and he stood in the middle of the glow and watched the shadows wash over his arms and hands. Without thinking, he sought the outdoors and climbed to the roof where he slept until the sun began to show itself. Marveling at the glorious colors of pink, lilac, and finally the pure blue that filled the sky, he questioned how everything out there could be the way it should have been.

Penny Lauer

∽

The children were in their rooms the rest of the holiday, their detention interrupted only by a very late breakfast and then a late lunch. Everything was in its place downstairs except for Jess and her blue sweater.

During the two meals, Steve lectured the three of them on the importance of family members supporting one another, the necessity of rules, and his hopes that they would develop into mature and productive adults, something that could only be done if they were imbued with strong values and self-discipline. He told them that he was giving them time to think about their lies and insubordination and that they would all join together again as a family that evening for dinner. In the meantime, they should think about how to be better people and begin preparing themselves for school.

"We're making some positive changes here," he finally concluded. "I'm taking over. From now on, you report only to me. There will be no more lies, no more sneaking around. This home needs discipline and order, and since your mother is incapable of enforcing them, I'll have to take care of it. She's developed some unusual traits," he continued and turned to Josh. "You probably recognize them, Josh; she's becoming more and more like your mother."

Josh played solitaire in his room and leafed through the books Jess had bought him for school. And he slept. Never in his life had he slept so much.

Late in the afternoon, Steve called up to the children and told them to get themselves washed up and dressed and to come down soon for a celebration.

Katie finally appeared, all dressed up in a party dress and a bow in her hair.

Skipping STONES

"Come here, little princess," Steve said, holding his arms to her. She walked into them, and he gave her a hug that hid her and a deep kiss on the cheek. "There's my little girlie-girl. There she is."

He pointed to the food spread out on the coffee table. "We're going to have a little snack before dinner to celebrate your going back to school," he told them. "What an exciting time in your lives. I remember those days well when I was a boy, anxious to learn, to impress my teachers, to make friends. These are the best of times."

His efforts to revive them continued throughout dinner - a sergeant rallying his troops. His empty words slid off them.

He was there the next morning, knocking at each of their doors, telling them it was time to get dressed. At breakfast, he showed concern that they eat everything Jess had prepared for them and that they had all of their supplies in their back-packs. Jess came from behind the counter finally and followed them to the door. There were no good-bye hugs, no wishes for a good day from her. When the children turned from the end of the drive to wave, she had already gone inside. It was Steve who took them to the corner to wait for their busses.

༄

Every year before, Josh had looked forward to school. Making friends, participating in sports, working hard for good grades were things he had always enjoyed, but this day he was disoriented, unengaged, and unprepared. The noise in the halls, the confusion finding his classrooms, the laughter and joking among the other kids at their lockers, the anxious attention of the teachers, the free-for-all in the cafeteria, and the abandon of free period felt like absolute chaos. His mind would not accept the freedom there, and he blandly walked through it. His spirit was shriveled.

Jess was waiting for her children on the front steps when they came home and tried to engage them in conversation. But no one even pretended to be interested in answering her questions. Mid-sentence in mid-thought, Jess pulled herself up and slowly walked away.

Back in his room, Josh brought the diary down from its hiding place. His entry was short: *I'm messed up.*

Then he read more of his mother's words.

Thursday

God, how I love the home! Took Josh in yesterday on my day off because they all wanted to meet him. Some of them never see their own families and feel abandoned. He wowed them, and I promised to take him in again soon. So glad I have the additional morning there. Still need another job so I can make our lives better.

Sam's place is doing well, I've heard. Would love to see it but can't very well just walk in and order up and ask to see the owner, can I? Made a point to tell Mom about it. No reaction.

Feel like I'm sliding again. Putting on weight. Too much beer. Need to exercise more and get some damned money! I don't know where to go for conversation.

Sun.

Picnicked with Josh and took a bike ride in the park. Walked through the mall. Stopped by Mom and Dad's – anything to kill time. I wanted to talk seriously, but we always seem to skim around real issues, avoiding what's hurtful. Thinking about seeing a doctor to help me. Mom said that what I need is a change in scenery and offered to send me to a spa. A spa? My God, now there's an idea, isn't it? How does she come up with this crap?

Skipping STONES

Mon.
Called the doctor. Don't know how I'll pay for it. Not enough time to apply for more assistance. Not telling anyone. Praying he'll work with me again. I can't do it alone.

Fri.
Hallelujah! Got the job at the community center! Working total of 4 mornings/week. That will really help. Have a date tomorrow night with a guy I met at Sandy's party. Mom's watching Josh. Cleaned out the garage and pulled weeds in the garden. I'll clean the rest tomorrow with Josh. I think things are going to really pick up now.

Sun.
Last night was a disaster. Guy was about as interesting as a tuna casserole and still thought I should jump in bed with him. Aren't there any good men out there?!!! Dinner at Mom's. Jess looks like hell – way too thin. Maddie is way too direct. She came right out and asked Jess what her problem is, and the party broke up pretty quickly. Thought about dinners there with Sam. And dinners he couldn't make it to. And how I ridiculed him.

Tues. Took a huge ride after work. I'm falling.

Mon. Got into the doc. He recommends a psychologist and wanted to order up a battery of blood tests to get started until I told him about my money situation. He's a good man and will work with me just the same. Talked about chronic depression. An old guy at the home told me a while ago I just needed a good sex life and volunteered to assist – with a wink. He could be right! Love that guy. Talked to Jess and Maddie. They want the three of us to have a girl's weekend out. Can't afford it and will not take their charity. What a stupid idea...

Page after page showed his mom's struggle to get control over how she felt. They showed her happiness and pain and her battle with her moods – her depression. Going to his computer, Josh Googled the word and saw that its source could be genetic, biochemical, or environmental, and that it had to do with chemicals in the brain being out of balance. Doctors on all of the web pages he clicked to said that victims of depression have trouble sleeping or sleep too much, lose interest in things, feel empty, and need to turn to others for help. They could be restless, irritable, angry, violent, and have difficulty concentrating. Exercise was recommended, as well as meditation and journaling. His mother had been unwavering in doing all three, and he finally understood why.

He went back and forth between websites and went on to read about a condition called bi-polar or manic depression, and there they were, a summary of her ups and downs: sleeplessness, sadness, chronic pain, and then there was her extreme optimism, hard physical activity, substance abuse, hopelessness. He had experienced it all right along with her and had watched her try everything she could think of to help herself. There had been countless victories, followed by countless heartache.

His thoughts went between his mother and Jess. He had stood beside his mother and had tried to do whatever was necessary to help her. She had done the same for him. He belonged to Jess now, and his arrival had increased her problems and had caused her greater pain. He had to help stop the pain. He had known what he should do for a long time, and he would finally do what was necessary to help Jess and his cousins. He turned to a fresh page on his side of the diary, and he wrote.

Skipping STONES

1. *I belong to Jess. Mom made that decision*
2. *Jess is being punished because of me and Sam*
3. *Katie and Ben are too*
4. *I can stop the punishment that I'm causing*
5. *I have to give up trying to see Sam. I've been selfish*
6. *I got along without him for a long time - I can do it again.*

Because calling Sam and telling him about his decision would be too hard, he once again turned to writing. Finally, after many bad attempts, he settled on being direct and to the point.

Dear Sam,
We talked about getting together again soon, but I'm writing to tell you that we can't.
It isn't because of anything that you did or didn't do. I'm not mad at you. It's just not a good idea to talk right now. Please don't call me again and don't call Jess. This is between you and me. I hope you will do what I say. I'm glad I got to see you, and I'm really glad that I got to meet Grandma Annie too. You can tell her that if you want to.

He read and re-read. It was too final. Because he needed to leave room for some future contact – when he was grown up or when Jess had changed Steve - he added:

If you ever need to get in touch with me for any reason, you could write me a letter. But make sure that you don't send it when it would get here on Saturday. If you write, I might write back, but I don't promise for sure. Well, that's all.
Josh

Jess

Jess had learned how to survive her husband's physical attacks by compartmentalizing them in her mind and, she thought, by keeping her children removed from them, but she doubted her ability to endure the emotional punishment he put in motion after Labor Day. The new rules were intended to cut her off from her children. Not only was she not permitted to talk to them at bedtime, she was also forbidden to be alone with them in the mornings. He adjusted his schedule and theirs so that he could have breakfast with them and could walk them to the corner to catch their school busses. She would be alone with them from four o'clock to six o'clock five days a week.

Katie clung to her in the mornings at the door and at the stairs at night and shadowed her in the hours they had together before Steve came home. Ben, filled with anger and frustration because she had allowed his father to make these changes, turned further and further away from her. The excuses she continued to make for the way they were living sounded hollow even to her. Yet she continued to offer them.

Meanwhile, she filled her hours with cooking, cleaning, shopping, and an occasional visit with her mother. During solitary walks, she considered her options to make change and returned to her home thinking that she didn't have any. Throughout each day, she constantly picked up and put down the phone, thinking that she would finally explain to her parents or sister what had happened to her life and ask for help, but she was always deterred in the end by her fear that Steve might carry out his threat to take her children away from her. She was incapable of developing a plan.

Then, in the midst of everything else, she received a desperate call from Sam about a letter he had just received from Josh.

"I thought everything was fine when I dropped him off at the museum that day," he said. "We had agreed to get together soon to do some real in-depth talking about the past and our futures. He had a lot of questions to ask about Becky and me. I told him we'd go to my place and hang out and really have a conversation. Then out of the blue I get this letter telling me he can't see me again. We can write, but he even set specific times when he could receive my letters. He asked me not to say anything, but frankly, Jess, I'm worried. Do you have any idea what's going on?"

She was caught. Should she tell him that Steve had set the rule that Josh couldn't see him again? If she did, where would that conversation lead? And she couldn't pretend not to understand anything about the letter. That would get them nowhere. Finally, she decided to tell a half-truth.

"Josh is mixed up," she said. "There's no doubt that he's confused about you and Becky. He's still grieving her death, of course. He's trying hard to adjust to his new life here, and it hasn't been easy for him. If you think about it, he's done very, very well, all things considered. Probably seeing you again has opened up a lot of old issues. I think maybe he's just saying that he needs some time to sort through things. Maybe he's decided he's not ready for that conversation yet. Don't worry. He'll be fine. It's just been a little over four months. He's still grieving. He's still confused. I know you are too, but we need to give it time. It's going to be okay. It's going to be okay."

She knew that she was weaving another blanket of lies, just like the ones she had grown accustomed to covering her children with to protect them from the reality of Steve, but she couldn't get herself beyond her method of protection.

"I can understand that, but why the restriction on the time when he can get the letters from me?" Sam was saying. "Why can't we at least continue to talk on the phone? I don't feel that I've ever pushed him. When we talked after visiting Mom's, he seemed as anxious as I was to get together again. I can't understand the sudden change."

"Maybe he doesn't want anyone to know that the two of you are communicating until he sorts everything through on his own," she responded. "Maybe he simply needs privacy. Weekends are busy here. Before, it was mainly just Becky and him. It's a huge adjustment."

She'd had a lot of practice in half-truths. She hated lying, especially to Sam. She hated lying about Josh. But she didn't know what else to do.

"Maybe," she continued, "talking on the phone is as hard on him as talking face to face. I don't know. But it's going to be okay. Just give it time."

There was a long pause before Sam asked, "Jess, you'd tell me if something was wrong, wouldn't you? If he's suffering more than is normal with all of this, you'd suggest counseling, wouldn't you? Maybe that's what he needs. I could find a good counselor if you think that would help."

She began to panic. If Josh went to a counselor, it could open up everything. And where would it lead them? What options would she have? What options would any of them have? Arguments and cross-arguments went rapidly through her mind. Maybe, she thought, that's exactly what should happen. Everything would be brought out in the open, and the counselor could advise her too. But there was absolutely no way that she could set it up without Steve's finding out, and she dreaded to think what would happen if he did.

"No," she said. "He doesn't need counseling. He just needs time. Let's talk again in a while and see how it goes."

She hadn't satisfied him. She could hear it in his voice. He was worried, and he had every right to be. But she couldn't help him. Not yet.

༄

The children put their time in at school and studied at night in their rooms, intent on meeting their father's expectations for high grades – not out of self-motivation, but mostly out of fear. And so the family settled into a routine and felt blessed when Steve seemed pleased with their performance. Life was stabilized for almost an entire month before his ego was challenged again.

It happened when his major client from the East Coast, his wife, and his financial advisor planned a meeting at the law office the first week of October. A big dinner following the day-long meeting was scheduled with Steve and everyone else involved with the account, including their wives.

From the beginning, Steve wanted the big dinner to be held at his club. He had insisted that the client and his entourage would be impressed by the place and that it would provide an intimate, quiet setting for whatever additional discussion might need to take place that evening. After much debate, his suggestion was accepted.

Steve took full responsibility for all of the arrangements, consumed with planning the event, and tended to the minutest details.

There were some logistical problems because of the distance from the office to his community, but he solved the problem by hiring two limousines to get everyone there. The senior partner was concerned, but Steve assured him that the camaraderie that would result from the setting would more than compensate for the small inconveniences the location presented. He was in control and enjoyed the power. But, at the last minute, the client balked and insisted that the dinner be held at the Four Seasons Hotel downtown where the client was staying, within blocks of the law firm and minutes to the airport. When Steve was told that going at least forty-five minutes outside of the city during rush hour made no sense to the guests, he was furious and took the change as a personal affront, but he had no choice but to acquiesce. As always, he turned his frustration on Jess.

It was important to Steve that the decision to change locations would not in any way reflect negatively on him. He and Jess, he said, would have to show even more power and class than before. He selected what she would wear to the dinner: a black, slim dress, a single strand of pearls, and her diamond studs. She felt that what he had chosen was way too dressy for the evening, but he insisted that it would impress everyone. The evening before, he had her "model" the outfit and watched as she pulled her hair up into a twist, before finally deciding that she would be presentable.

Around four o'clock the day of the dinner, Steve called Jess to tell her that he couldn't get out to their home to pick her up and get back in time because of some last-minute work he had to do for the client. She would have to take a taxi into town. Traffic was terrible that evening, and she was thirty minutes late. Everyone was there when she arrived, enjoying their cocktails and waiting for her in the library, the special room that the firm was able to reserve. Seeing the other wives dressed simply - some even in pants suits - did little to put her at ease, and she was further embarrassed when Steve apologized to everyone for her tardiness, saying that she always tended to take too much time "dolling herself up," as he put it, a joke that fell flat.

Eventually they were escorted into the small private dining room the managing partner had reserved for them, and Steve found himself seated at the center of the table, between two of his colleague's wives and across from a mid-level protégé. He was not happy, and Jess knew it. She prayed that he would remember the discussions they had had in the past about setting his frustrations aside at social gatherings and being subtle. He was beyond that. Feeling snubbed, he chugged his vodka and snapped his fingers at the waiter to take additional drink orders from everyone before they had made their choices for dinner. And when the guests declined the offer, Steve asked his managing partner if he could take a look at the wine menu, only to find that the selection of two very fine wines had already been made in advance.

Talk around the table initially was broken up into small groups, but once orders had been taken by the wait-staff and the wine had been poured, conversation turned to the economy and politics. Jess had always been a good listener and waited before she formed questions or comments. She spoke quietly and deliberately, and when she said something, people listened. She had been seated across from the client's wife, and the two of them, discovering a meeting of the minds, eventually found themselves at the center of the conversation at the table.

Looking back, Jess knew that the biggest mistake Steve made that night and, without a doubt, the one that had the biggest influence on his client was when he suggested that she was monopolizing the conversation. From then on, the tension in the air hung like a net around the table. The more Steve drank, the more the others shut him out. As he and Jess waited for their car, the client suggested that perhaps Jess might drive Steve home.

The evening was a fiasco for Steve, and because he had to have someone to blame, he turned on her. The disastrous evening was her fault. He accused her of trying to outshine him by talking so much, of belittling him in front of everyone by asking questions to everyone but him, and flirting with the men in front of their wives. He even blamed her for the dress she had agreed to wear.

The road out from the highway to their home was winding and hilly, and by the time Steve pulled onto it, he was driving so recklessly that, at times, Jess felt that they were airborne. And all the while he berated her, saying that she was responsible for the way things had gone, that she had shamed and embarrassed him. She braced herself against the dash and pleaded with him to slow down.

He slammed on the brakes suddenly and turned onto a narrow dirt road that led to an old cemetery, a road that she had passed thousands of times before and had paid little attention to. When they reached the top of a hill, he stopped the car and pulled her to him, his breath hot on her face and smelling like tin. The blow to her head was sudden and so strong that she hit the window behind her. He pulled her back to him

Skipping **S T O N E S**

and hit her again and watched for the strike's impact on her. She held onto consciousness and begged for his forgiveness, complimented him on his ambition, his ability to care for his family, his intellect, anything and everything she could think of to counter his rage. Finally, drugged by the alcohol and tired from the stress of the last several days, he lost his will to punish. With one last push to show his strength, he told her that if her behavior had affected his career in any way, he would destroy her.

For a week, there was another stretch of calm in the home. Steve was attentive and engaged. There were no threats. And when he was called again to Boston to meet with more of the client's legion of advisors, he was ecstatic.

"I guess that night wasn't as bad as we thought, babe," he said.

The one thing that worried him was that another partner was asked to go too. There were now three men working directly on the project.

Josh

Josh checked the mail every single day for a response from Sam to the letter he had written him. It arrived on Monday, just four days later.

Dear Josh,

I got your letter today, and I'm trying to figure it out. I can't help but think that maybe something is wrong, but, for now, I'll do what you asked me to. If there's a problem at home, at school, if there's something that I said or did that made you feel uncomfortable, I hope that you'll let me know and will be honest with me. Sometimes we can get ourselves in deep water if we aren't open and frank with people.

We'll do this until you feel comfortable telling me what it is that's bothering you. I have so many things that I want to do with you, and I hope we'll be able to begin doing them soon.

Is school all right? I know you've always liked school and have done really well in the past. It must be hard to start out in a new place and make new friends, but I know that you can do it. You've always been good at friendships. Did you sign up for any sports or other activities?

I'm doing well. Business is good. The renovation of the restaurant will be complete in time for the holidays. It might have been easier, looking back, to tear the place down and start over. Nothing like hindsight, is there?

By the way, I told your Grandma that you said hi. She was as concerned as I am when she found out that we won't be seeing one another for a while. She said that I should just march right over there and find out what "the story" is. Sounds like her, doesn't it? She's a no-nonsense gal and always deals with issues head-on. She and your mom were alike in that way. Your mom wouldn't tolerate secrets and half-truths; but you know that better than anyone.

Well, I'll look for your next letter. Take good care of yourself and tell Jess and Ben and Katie that I said hi. Steve too.

One more thing: I hope you're still writing in your journal. I think it's a good idea to write things down. It helps us sort through things. I keep one too, and every now and then I go back and read what I wrote. It helps me see things more clearly and lets me see how far I've come. Let me know how you're doing on that.

Sam

And there it was. His father wasn't going to give up on him. They would still be a part of each others' lives through writing.

Josh liked the word "journal." And he went back to the first entry he had made in the diary and put the word JOURNAL at the top. Then he wrote.

Monday

Sam said that he isn't going to give up on me even though I wrote the letter to him. My grandma Annie is worried about me. I didn't mean for them to worry. But in a way I like it that they are. He's just like my mom. It's not good to keep your problems and questions and real feelings inside. You just get filled up with worry and have more questions when you do that. And if someone asks you something, why not be honest? They may not like what you say, but at least they know what you think. Why is it so complicated? Sam understands and so does my grandma. I'm tired of fishing and thinking so hard about everything. I'm tired of being afraid that I'll make someone mad or hurt their feelings. I'm going to try to be more like Sam. I'm going to talk to Jess as soon as I figure out how.

◈

School was too hard. The lessons were easy, and ordinarily Josh would have made good grades, but he couldn't get his mind around everything. He felt tired. He didn't make friends because he had no desire to get involved in any activities. He couldn't laugh.

He was becoming an outsider just like Ben.

After school, he took long walks, continued his research about depression, and wrote in his journal. He craved activity and change and tried to implement both into his life with small steps. One morning, he sneaked out the back door and cut off a blossom from one of Jess's mums and had Katie and Ben sign a note to her that read, *Have a great day*. Ben thought the note was pretty stupid, but he signed it anyway. Katie drew a heart at the bottom and put the gifts on her bed where she knew Jess would find them later.

Josh felt better when he got on the bus that day, and the feel-good feeling lasted all day long. He looked for Ben after lunch, and the two of them hung out together during their free time with several kids they knew from their PE classes. Josh asked if anyone was interested in playing basketball sometimes on their lunch breaks. Everyone but Ben thought it was a good idea; he said he'd think about it. The others designated Josh to be the one to talk with the coach to see if they could play in the gym, and the following day, Josh and his new friends got a game together; Ben watched from his seat on the floor.

Late that night, Katie tapped the signal on the wall between their two rooms that told him she wanted to talk, and she tiptoed to his door to show him a picture she had drawn of four stick figures holding hands – another surprise for Jess.

"This one is you," she told him, "And these are Ben and me and Mom. I didn't put Daddy in. Do you think that's okay?"

On each of the figures' chests was a big heart. A butterfly sat on Jess's head, and Katie was holding flowers.

Josh thought for a few seconds before he added his own note under Katie's: Just for fun, take a walk down to the river for some exercise and fresh air. And find a flat stone to skip across the water and think about good things.

༄

Being sent to their rooms was more bearable for the children as the days grew shorter. They didn't have so many daylight hours to look outside the window and wish they were somewhere else. Josh spent more time on his homework, thanks to the interest his core teacher had taken in him. She had clearly checked his school records and knew about his mother and his moving to Jess's, and she told him that he could count on her to help him adjust at school. She also encouraged Josh to join in after-school sports and even had the coach meet with him about it. As the days and weeks went on, some of his self-confidence returned. But Ben and Katie showed no signs of improvement.

Ben remained moody and as reclusive as ever and was ignored by almost everyone at school. Katie clung to her mother whenever Steve was not at home, and often cried as Steve escorted her to the bus in the mornings. Steve's behavior became more bizarre, checking on the children in their rooms at different times throughout the evenings. Eventually, out of fear of being found out, the children no longer tried to visit each other, and Josh learned to lock himself in the bathroom and turn the shower on when he had the diary out.

Every single morning when he got up and every night before he fell asleep, Josh told himself that if he tried harder to stop the hurt there, it would happen. At school, he found it easier to pretend that he was like the other kids. When the dismissal bell rang, he steeled himself for the life he'd return to at Jess's. Football practice started, and Josh participated the first two weeks and then dropped out. He was adding to Jess's burden, he reasoned, by having her pick him up after practices, and, besides, he felt like he was participating in a vacuum. He had no one to talk to about what he was doing, and somehow he felt like a traitor to Katie and Ben for enjoying an activity outside of his home. At the end of the second week, he informed his coach that he was dropping off the team.

He lay awake at night, nagged by what more he could and should do to try to change things. The pictures and notes to Jess and his instructions about how she could spend her time alone had had little effect on her. So, after several days, he decided that there was no other option: he would break the unspoken rule of silence about their sadness and talk openly with her.

Skipping STONES

"It's nothing big, don't worry," Josh assured her the next afternoon. "It's just that I've been thinking a lot about the way things are here, and I'm wondering if we couldn't talk about them and see if we could change some things. I mean, I know you're sad. Katie is too. And so is Ben. But we never talk about it. If we'd just get everything out in the open and explain how we all feel to each other, maybe everything would get better. I think it would. It's a start anyway. Maybe we could sit down and really try talk to Steve about everything. Get it all out in the open. Maybe that would help."

Jess was very quiet. Finally, she whispered, "I can't, Josh. I just can't."

He whispered back. "You can trust me."

She wrapped her arms around her stomach, and he understood her kind of pain.

"My mom had depression," he told her. "I know because – well, because I'm reading her diary. I want to know those parts about her that I didn't get to know or didn't understand."

He hadn't meant to tell her about the diary, but he understood somehow that he should risk telling the truth if it would help her.

"Anyway. She had chronic depression," he went on. "That's what her doctor told her. Maybe something called bi-polar, where you're way beyond happy for a while and then you come crashing down. I don't know it all yet. I'm checking it out on the internet. But she got herself some help. That's the important thing. She went to a therapist and a psychologist. She worked on her denial. That's when you don't admit that you're having trouble and need help. I'm not saying you have all of that. But maybe we could all help each other if we'd just talk about it. Or maybe you could go to a counselor or something like Mom did. The most important thing is for all of us to talk so everyone knows what's going on and we can work together sort of like a team."

He pulled out the notes he had printed off from the computer and put them in front of her, pointing to each fact he had found about depression and adding his own insight.

"See here," he said, "it says that depressed people need to have someone to talk to, even if it's just a doctor, but friends would be better. Everyone needs friends. And look here where it says that laughing, exercise, meditation, getting outside, and being religious are important to help people feel good about themselves. And writing your thoughts down helps a lot too. I'm doing it. Sam does it too. Maybe it would help you."

He watched the water from her eyes make spots on the table cloth and was sure that he had made things much worse for her.

"I'm sorry that I made you sadder," he said.

She looked at him with such sorrow that his stomach hurt too.

"Sometimes," she said in a voice so low that he had to lean closer to hear, "sometimes it's best not to know everything, Josh. Sometimes talking can make things much worse."

༄

Sam and he continued to write to each other. Jess knew about the letters, but not once did she ask Josh about them. It was just one more thing that was kept hidden inside those walls, one more thing that was impossible to discuss openly because of their fear about where the discussion might lead. Most of the letters from Sam were full of encouragement, reasons why Josh should do well at school and take advantage of opportunities offered there. And he asked when the two of them could meet again.

His letters were full of news from the outside, and they made it even clearer to Josh how small the space was that Jess and Katie and Ben and he inhabited, how little their world was. Sam talked about boating and fishing on Lake Erie and a trip he was planning to Cincinnati. He asked if Josh watched certain shows on TV, what football team he was rooting for, what movies he had seen recently. Josh couldn't communicate about specific things because time and issues and specifics slipped by him daily. His letters to his father were general in nature and flat.

Josh struggled to hold on to the bigger thoughts he had carried around before the awful day when his mother had died. At school he chose desks closest to windows so that he could watch the wind in the trees and birds flying and could feel the sun hitting his skin. After lunches he quickly made his way outside and played hard at whatever game the other guys put together and sucked up as much of the free air he could. He listened silently to their news and banter, but no matter how hard he tried, he was, still, an outsider.

Alone in his room at night, he opened the window and stared out at the sky and often climbed out onto the roof to feel a part of something larger than the miniscule space he inhabited. One evening in late October, the sky was so clear and so filled with stars that the realization of the immensity of the universe and the minuteness of that place where he was fell on him hard. The night left him both diminished and hopeful.

He reached deep inside for insight. Ben and Katie and Jess and he couldn't be the only ones feeling the way they were, he thought. Whatever pain and unhappiness they were experiencing, others had to be too. At any given moment, millions of people must be trying, just as he was, to figure things out. And to help him remember what he was thinking, he wrote his thoughts down in his journal:

We aren't the only ones like us. We can't be. There have to be other kids out there like us. And there were other kids just like us before who lived like we live. Other people had to have figured out how to make themselves happy. We can too.

And even though it was late at night, he tapped the wall for Katie. Soon her little hand made the four-knock signal back, and they found their way to their doors. He wrapped her up in his blanket and helped her out onto the roof so that she could see the immense sky unimpeded.

"Look, Katie," he said. Just look at how big it is. We aren't alone, and we'll get better. We'll make things get better."

Jess

Josh had no way of knowing it, but following his brief conversation with her, Jess set up a strict weekly schedule that would force her out of the house and make her a more active member in the world at large. Eventually, she signed up for yoga classes and bought herself a mat and suitable pants to wear; she baked elaborate cupcakes for Katie's classmates and took her mother out for a special lunch. And since the children had outgrown their heavier jackets, she took advantage of the pre-season sales. She began to have her nails done once a week instead of twice a month, and she signed up for a lecture series at the Museum of Art. Having been cut off, long ago, from her friends by Steve, she had no one to call for games of tennis or bridge. But that was all right; it was easier and safer to be alone, away from probing eyes and questions.

She particularly began to look forward to Mondays, her day she set aside to go to Barnes and Noble for a cappuccino and book searches. On one of her visits, she bought a lovely notebook with a simple grass-cloth cover. The unlined pages were like crisp linen, and at the bottom of each was a proverb that she read daily to help her reach some clarity about what she could do to make her life, and the lives of the children she was responsible for, more meaningful and prosperous. She made notes to herself and carried the small journal with her everywhere.

Her relaxed and intentional Mondays were short-lived.

On her fourth trip to B & N, she bought her cappuccino with cash, entered her to-do list in her journal, and carried her choice of magazines to the checkout counter and waited patiently in line. She and the cashier recognized each other and engaged in small talk while he rang up her purchases. His embarrassment for her was obvious when he discreetly told her that her credit card was twice declined. She searched her purse for her checkbook. It was gone. Leaving everything at the counter, she rushed home and called the bank to report the declined card and the missing checkbook. The kind representative hesitantly announced that both had been cancelled the previous Friday by Mr. Selby.

When Steve got home that evening, he told her, in response to her questions, that he had decided to give her a weekly cash allowance, and when she asked why, his answer had the effect of acid. He had been following all of her activities by way of her checking and credit card accounts.

"You're irresponsible," he told her. "You've used poor judgment. You've squandered away too much time and too much money on those classes you've been taking. And all that time at the book store. What's that all about? Your place is here. I'm protecting you from yourself."

There wasn't enough cash for her yoga or her days at the bookstore. She couldn't sign up for additional lectures. She rationed her gas money. The sneaky shots of wine she took from the flask she kept hidden under the oven increased. Her self-recriminations kept her awake at night, and she practiced the story that she would give her family doctor for wanting sleeping aids and anti- anxiety pills in case he needed an explanation.

☙

The office was full when Jess arrived, and the wait to see Dr. Joseph was so excruciatingly long that she got up to leave several times but changed her mind because her need for medication was so great.

The nurse, whom Jess had known for years, greeted her in the examining room and, after a brief conversation, checked her history to make certain that the office records were correct. Then she asked, quickly and matter-of-factly, if she felt safe in her home. She didn't bother to look up at Jess when she asked the question; it was a required inquiry and had become a permanent part of every patient's annual update. A check-mark had to be recorded in the box provided, and she anticipated a positive response. But the abrupt, unexpected question threw Jess off.

"What do you mean? I don't understand."

"Oh, it's just a question we have to ask everyone now," the nurse muttered, busy with the office computer. "It's a policy our health group adapted."

She looked up to check Jess's reaction and made a note in Jess's file that confirmed the question had been asked. "You'd be amazed," she added. "Violence in the home is a huge problem, much bigger than what you'd think."

When the doctor came in, he examined her in his usual perfunctory way and, accepting the explanation that she had not been sleeping well lately and felt anxious because of her added responsibilities with her nephew, wrote out the prescription.

And then there was another shock. Stopping by the desk and waiting for her bill, Jess saw on the counter in front of her a sign that read, "Do You Feel Safe in Your Home?" Beneath it was a pile of cards with the hotline number for the local shelter for abused women and children. As casually as possible, she picked up one of the cards and turned it over. Listed there, on the back, were eight circumstances that indicated abuse. She read the list, and every one of them characterized her relationship with Steve.

She walked as straight as she could, as normal as possible, out of the office and somehow got to the car. It took her a long time to pull away. She finally acknowledged the name for her: I am an abused woman. I am one of them.

How was it possible, she asked herself, that she had never, all of those long years, put herself in the category of an abused woman? Was it because the abuse had been so subtle when it started and had grown so slowly over the years that it had become something she accepted as normal? She had wanted the hurt to stop, but never had she realized that she had a right to make it stop, that there were laws to protect her. Was it denial, as Josh had suggested when he had made an attempt to talk honestly with her?

The subject of domestic violence had been totally outside her family's circle of reality when she was growing up. They had never been touched by it, and certainly didn't expect that anyone else they knew had either. It didn't happen to people like them, they thought: abused women were women of poverty, women from "bad" families who had grown up with violence and couldn't get themselves out of their situations. It was sordid and yucky.

She parked the car on the side of the road and sat for a long time reading over and over again the information on the back of the card and analyzing her life through each point made there. Finally, she forced herself to move again and was almost home when she realized that she had totally forgotten her reason for going to the doctor's office in the first place and had left without the prescription. It would have to wait.

The children were waiting for her on the front steps. She was late, and they were frightened. She forced herself out of her self-analysis to go through the routine they always went through after school, even though it led to nowhere, and after the children talked briefly about their day away from her, she retreated to the kitchen, her place of escape, and managed to prepare dinner as she sorted through the mire of her new insight. Steve, as usual, was right on time.

Along with checking the children's activities, their nighttime habits, their appearances, their rooms' tidiness, Jess's spending habits and cash on hand, Steve had also been checking phone messages and scrolling through the phone numbers of incoming and outgoing calls on both their land line and Jess's cell. That evening, after all of his other inspections, he clicked on the play button of the answering machine and found the message from the doctor's office. He listened as the receptionist said that Jess had forgotten her prescription and asked if she wanted her to phone it in to the pharmacy.

When he demanded to know what the prescription was for, Jess explained that she had seen the doctor because she was having headaches that were keeping her awake at night and that he had prescribed something for the pain that was also a kind of sedative. Steve stared at his wife intently but said nothing. She had seen that look many times before: he was filing information away that could be used against her later.

The next morning after everyone was gone, she sat down with her notebook, and, ignoring the proverb for the day, she copied the list from the card she had taken from the doctor's office and wrote beside each statement how it applied to her and her children. There was no way to deny the truth.

She needed to get out. Needed new air. Needed to get anywhere as long as it was away from her home and community. She would drive somewhere and try to decide what to do. Checking her purse to make sure she had sufficient cash, she inserted her notebook and a pen in case she had additional moments of clarity. Satisfied, she went to the key rack. The car keys weren't there. After too many minutes of frantically searching for them, she called Steve. His response to her question took her breath away.

"I have them," he said. "Your days of self-indulgence and roaming all over town are over. I've checked the mileage. We'll do what you need to do together over the weekends. I'll repeat what I've told you before: you have a job, the same as I do, and your workplace is your home. I'm busy, and you should be too."

The time alone, her loss of what little control she had felt she had regained, diminished her further. She realized that she was involved in a game of power, and she was a bad player.

Josh

Hi, Josh. Thanks for your letter. I'm sitting out on my deck one last time before I put the furniture away for the winter. It's so much cooler now, and the evenings are downright cold. I'm holding out as long as I can to come out here and enjoy the view with a hot cup of coffee before I go to bed. By the way, are you still drinking coffee? Wish you were here to share mine.

There are still some boaters who refuse to admit how cool it's getting and how riled up the lake has become. I've put my boat in storage until next spring, and I'll take one more ride on my cycle before cleaning it up and putting it away too. This is definitely the season of transition. There are lots of good things to do in the winter, though, like reading some good books I've put off and revving up some community committees I serve on. I'm trying to be positive! The challenge in the winter for me is forcing myself to get out and move.

I'm glad you like your teachers, especially your core reading teacher. What was her name? Mrs. Jamison? It seems as though she's definitely in your corner. I'll never forget my fifth and sixth grade teachers. I'll tell you all about them sometime. By the way, how's your geography report going?

Skipping STONES

I'm wondering if you would mind writing to Grandma Annie. She asks about you a lot and hopes that she'll be able to see you again soon. If you want to, you can just send your notes to her with mine, and I'll make sure she gets them. No point wasting envelopes and stamps. I see her often.

We've set the grand opening of our new place for December 1. I'm inviting our best customers and some close friends and, of course, Grandma Annie in for a wine tasting and canapes. I'd like you and Jess's family to come too. Let's try to make it happen, okay? Mention it to Jess, if you'd like to, and I can follow up with an invitation.

Not much else going on. You take good care of yourself. Say hi to everyone and write again soon. I'll be waiting.

-Sam

Josh slugged through one day at a time through late fall and the beginning of winter, bolstered by Sam's letters which had become his most important tie with the outside world. Fall apple-picking, pumpkin carving, and Halloween's beggar nights and parties slipped by the family and were non-events. The Thanksgiving dinner Steve had Jess organize at their home for their extended family provided a small respite, and finally the Christmas holiday season arrived, unwelcomed, serving as a somber reminder of a happier past.

Ironically, it was Josh's art class that provided him with some of his old enthusiasm for the season. His art teacher instructed her students to make small ceramic pieces to give as gifts to members of their families, and since he and his mom had make ceramics together for years, it was easy for him. The first gift he made was a small container for Jess to keep her everyday jewelry in, choosing a yellow and blue glaze, her favorite colors, and decorating the lid with a small yellow rose. It was so well done that the teacher used it as an example of what the others might do and made Josh, in effect, her assistant.

He felt that he should make something for Steve, but he just couldn't do it. Instead, he made a small white ceramic rectangle and painted "Sam's Place" on it. On the back he made two hoops and threaded a small piece of wire through them. He hoped that maybe someday Sam could put the sign on his front door or in his kitchen or maybe somewhere in his new restaurant. Getting it boxed and mailed would, he reasoned, be too much of an imposition on Jess, and besides, if she couldn't get it mailed, he didn't want to make her feel bad. So he hid it away in his closet and hoped that someday he'd be able to present the gift to his father himself.

Katie had worked hard at school decorating and applying pictures of the family to the cut-out wreath that would be her Christmas gift to them, and she decided to give it early so that it could be added to the decorations as soon as they were put up. She chose to present it at the dinner table and hid it under her chair, anticipating everyone's surprise and delight. When it was her time to speak, she pulled it up with a flourish and a wide smile, but the response was not what she had hoped for. Steve barely acknowledged it, saying that it was cute and passing it back quickly to her. Jess whispered a thank you in her direction because it wasn't her turn to speak, and Katie quietly folded it and let it drop back to the floor. Watching it all with sadness and anger, Josh decided that the box he had made for Jess should be hidden away with Sam's gift until he could finally make things right.

Skipping STONES

The next day he received another letter from Sam.

Hi again, Josh. I put my tree up last night – always do it on the 17th. Your mom and I started that when we first got married because her family had always done it that way. That was her birthday and so it was a double celebration. Did she tell you about the time we bought the huge tree that took up most of our house? It didn't seem all that big out there in the field, but by the time we got it on the roof of the car, we were sure we'd never get out of the parking lot. I drove practically all the way home with my head outside the driver's window so I could see where I was going!

Long story short, we had to take out most of the furniture in our small living room to fit it in, and because our tree holder was way too small, we had to attach the tree with a rope tied to the overhead light fixture to keep it upright – not the smartest idea, but we were young and stupid back then. Anyway, you were absolutely mesmerized by that tree and insisted that you go to bed under it every night. Your mom and I spent a good two weeks that year lying with you there until you finally fell asleep and then carrying you to your little bed. Those were good times, and they just prove the point that there are all kinds of good ways to create super memories and find happiness.

I think I'll fix myself some coffee and sit out on the porch a while. It's cold as anything, but the Christmas lights from the houses on my street are pretty. They light up the lake with their colors. Maybe you'll help me decorate my tree next year.

Tell everyone hi.

Sam

That night, Josh got his mother's diary out, locked himself in the bathroom, turned the shower on, and read what she had written about their last Christmas together.

Sat.

Christmas is right around the corner. Love this time of year. And hate it. Wish that just for once I could buy whatever I want for everyone. Josh and I decided to make ornaments for everybody's trees this year for gifts from him and necklaces and picture frames from the two of us. Such fun when we work together. Making cookies today for everybody at the home and the art class at school. Josh is going with me for the sing-along at the home.

Sun.

The 17th. Going to the farm to cut the tree. Thank God I have enough money saved. Sam called again to see how we're doing. Calls every Dec. 17. Decided next time he calls to come right out and tell him how I feel. Had a blast at the farm! Cold as hell, but such a good time. It snowed, and it was beautiful walking through it, surrounded by those majestic trees. Such memories, but not going there. Tree was damned expensive, but worth every cent. The house smells delicious, and the lights add so much warmth to our little place. Josh and I had our usual hot chocolates and cookies on the floor with just the tree lights on before bedtime. He is my life.

Thurs.

Finished shopping for Josh. Think I have almost everything he asked for, including bike stuff to go with the new bike Mom and Dad are giving him. Had great fun at the home. Lots of visitors there this time of year. I feel a part of the clients' families too. Making pins for the ladies in my section and book marks for the men.

Fri.

What a terrific day! Received a carton from Sam filled with gifts for Josh and one with my name on it. Going to keep it for a surprise for

Josh Xmas Eve. I called. Yes! I called him to thank him. Oh, my God, talking to him was wonderful. He said he'd call me back. I'm so giddy. Dumb! Feel like a young girl. Told Betty, my client, how I feel. She thinks I'm on to something and that I'm right to call. She's my buddy.

Xmas. Eve. Went to Mom and Dad's to have dinner with the family. Our tradition. Had a wonderful time. Came home and Josh and I sat under our tree and had some more cookies, and each of us opened one gift. Then I gave him the gifts from Sam. He was so incredibly happy with the gifts, but his happiness really came from knowing that Sam had still remembered him. Hung our stockings and brought out the rest of our presents for each other for tomorrow morning. Josh is in bed, sound asleep. Enjoying a glass of wine by myself. Life really is beautiful, I must admit. But I need someone else to share it with. Next year will be better.

I'm back! He called! He called! Late at night when his company left. Annie was there and had just gone to bed. She told him to tell me hi. He wanted to wish me Merry Christmas. Wanted to just talk. We talked for almost an hour! Touched on so many things but kept it light. I can barely write! Can hardly breathe! It was wonderful!

Wed.

Lonely. Allowed a guy I met on the internet a couple of weeks ago to stay over. Pretended he was Sam. God. I'm weak. And needy. I hate this. Last time. Going to get my shit together.

Mon.

Went to the doc for stronger meds and a good talk. He told me that I have nothing to lose by talking honestly with Sam. I'm going to do it.

Josh held his breath and scanned the final pages to find the answer about his parents' love for each other.

Fri.

Talked to Sam again. The walls are going down. We're talking honestly and openly to each other. Have to run. Going to Mom's. Wondering what to tell her. I'm not telling her anything. Way too soon. We're moving very, very slowly. Josh asked me if something's wrong 'cause I'm "acting weird". I'm truly happy!

There were very few entries until late January. *Let it be here,* Josh thought. *Let the truth be here.*

Tues.

Sam and I met for coffee. I drove over to his side of town because we thought it would be safer – no chance of being seen by anyone we knew or family. What can I say? He hasn't changed. Looks the same – beautiful. He's so easy to talk with. He gave me a hug, and I thought I would cry right there, right on the spot, but I kept myself in balance. We touched on light things and filled each other in on our lives. He's doing so well. He praised me for my work and for how I've parented Josh. I'm calm. Calmer than I've been in such a long time. Trying to be sane, adult-like. Moving slowly. Oh, how I wish I could tell Josh. I want him to know his father. Now. But we don't want to make any more mistakes.

Mon.

We talked about our split-up and were very honest. We were so immature. And we listened too much to everyone else. We talked about my health. The way he explained it made me feel well. I'm all right so long as I take the meds. It's nothing to be ashamed of. I'm continuing with therapy and know I have a long way to go, but I can do it. He supports me and is so interested. Oh, if only we could have talked this way all of those long years ago. If only we had been more mature. So much time lost.

Skipping STONES

Fri.

Met with Annie. Such a loving and wise woman. She supports us.

Nothing else seems to matter to me, yet everything else is going so very well. Because I'm happy. I'm getting answers. I'm moving forward. What will my family say? What impact will this have on Josh? I know that Josh will be better for it. I want my family to be happy. But if they aren't, well, so be it. I pray they will be happy for me. Finally, after all of these years, all that I've hoped for is beginning to happen.

The pages were filled with hope and happiness. His mother and father saw each other once every two weeks. They took walks at the park where Sam and Josh had gone. They went out for dinners, met for coffee after she got off work. They talked on the phone.

Josh was happy, but he also felt cheated that he hadn't known about it. And he wondered why she hadn't told him. He remembered asking her why she was so happy. He had even asked the day of the accident. She'd just smile - that beautiful, secretive smile.

He read on. The last entry in the diary had been written three weeks before her accident.

We're sure of each other. We don't know where all of this is going to lead, but we're happy and are ready to move onto the next steps. We've waited long enough to know that all of the hurts and doubts are erased. It's time to get Sam and Josh together. We're just thinking of the best way to do it. It has to be slow. Mustn't force it. Let it develop. And then we'll tell the family if all goes well. A picnic? We'll see.

There is a God. I feel free and pretty and good and hopeful. And so alive!

Josh's fingers ached from grasping the diary so tightly. He searched through the left-over blank pages. Where was it! Where was the ending? He choked on the sob that became a groan. The ending was at the bottom of the hill on the fourth of June.

He finally knew most of the truth, and the truth hurt. What if the three of them had met before that day? Maybe that ride wouldn't have happened. Maybe Sam would have gone with them, and he and his mom would have waited for him to get things ready at the top of the hill. Maybe she'd still be here. How different everything might have been if he had only known.

There were still unanswered questions. Why was he here and not with Sam? Had Sam had doubts about him? Were he and his mother just going to date and not pull him in to make a family together? But that made no sense. If that were the case, Sam wouldn't be so interested in him now.

And so with a new resolve, he wrote to his father and asked him. The reply came immediately.

Dear Josh,

You asked me an important question in your letter. You asked why you went to Jess's after your mother died in the accident. The truth is hard to tell, and it will be hard to read, but I promise never to lie to you. The truth is that, when she and I divorced, I gave up custody, as you know, and she wanted to make sure that you would be taken care of by someone she could trust if anything ever happened to her. She chose Jess for all of the right reasons. When your mom and I made our new vows to each other last spring, she was going to have her will changed. It never got done. That is the awful truth. Maddie and I tried to contest it, but the law is very clear. Steve and Jess held firm to your mother's decision.

Skipping STONES

Josh, this is too involved and too complicated to explain in a letter. We have to talk. I have a feeling that your question is the reason for not seeing me. I understand. But please trust me that we have a plan. I want to be your father more than anything else in the world. And I want you to live here with me. We have to talk. I'm breaking my promise to you: I'm going to call Jess.

Sam

Jess was the answer to everything. Josh had to talk with her again. And soon.

༄

Christmas was nothing at all like those Josh had with his mom in the past, when they had made their own wreaths, strung lights inside and out, and lovingly hung the familiar ornaments, most of them home-made, on the tree. Instead Steve assembled a white, artificial tree with lights and ornaments already on it.

Josh waited for someone to be asked to place the angel on top, what he had always thought was the "finishing touch" on any tree, but when he asked about it, Steve laughed and said that no one with any taste used an angel anymore. It was no longer "de rigueur", he added. Angels, he laughed, had gone the way of tinsel.

He told Josh that he had explained to Ben and Katie from the get-go that there was no Santa. He didn't want them to believe in the foolish tales about him. Without Santa, there was no point in hanging stockings.

And the Baby Jesus? "Jesus had been a wise man," Steve said. "There's proof of that, but the virgin birth and all of that about being the son of god? Sheer fabrication."

Steve had, Josh realized, single-handedly stripped the most wonderful holiday of the year of all its magic.

The next week was the school Christmas performance, an evening that would bring change to all of their lives.

꩜

Everyone was expected to participate in the boys' school's holiday concert, but Ben and a few others, whether because of stage fright, lack of confidence, or honest boredom, put up a fight about it, and finally the music teacher and the others in charge decided it was easiest to just let the half-dozen or so sullen students sit alone and watch others practice. No amount of Josh's pleading with Ben could make him change his mind about sitting out. Josh had never seen his cousin so defiant, and he worried about the consequences.

The big night finally came. All participants had to wear black pants or skirts and white shirts or sweaters - not exactly Christmas colors, but their school's population included students from multiple ethnic and cultural backgrounds, and the faculty was determined not to offend anyone. Ben and Josh scrubbed themselves, put on the required outfits, succumbed to Steve's inspection, and the five of them packed themselves into the big Lexus and headed for the school. The ride was what Josh had anticipated. There was no feeling of excited anticipation, but simply endurance. And then Ben made the announcement.

"I want to tell you right now that I am not going up on that stage. The teachers know it. I'm sitting it out. You can watch Josh, but I'm not doing it."

Steve turned around in his seat, his face incredulous. "What? What did you say?"

"I'm not singing. Josh is, but I'm not. I'm sitting with some other kids and watching it. The teachers know it. I didn't practice."

"And just why is that?" Steve's voice was controlled.

"Because it's dumb." Ben blurted out. "We don't believe in any of the stuff about Christmas. Why should we go and pretend we do? I don't want to sing those stupid songs and pretend I'm happy and that I believe in Jesus and God and all that stuff. I'm not going to sing about Santa coming down the chimney. And I don't care about what other cultures believe in. I'm not going to fake it."

Steve was astounded by Ben's sudden audacity. Slamming the brakes, he pulled over to the side of the road and turned to face his son.

"You listen to me, boy," he said, jabbing his finger at him, "and listen good." His voice was confident and heavy. "You are going up on that damned stage and you are going to sing. You will smile just like all of the others. Whether you want to or not, you will look like you are enjoying yourself. You will not embarrass me and your family, and I will not listen to one more word from you about it."

And then, turning to Jess, he said, "How in the hell did you let this happen?"

The school parking lot was packed, and Steve had trouble finding a place to put the car. And since there was little time to spare, he pulled up to the school building and told everyone to get out and find their places and that he'd join them as soon as he could.

Ben refused to get out. Steve went berserk. Backing the car up against a snow bank, he leaped out, slammed his door, walked around to Ben's side, and told everyone to get themselves into the school.

Jess tried to calm him, but there were a few people still arriving, and she quickly realized that she was making matters worse.

"You take care of things inside. I'll take care of Ben," Steve snarled.

"I can't do it," Josh told Jess in the hallway. "I can't go up on that stage and sing. Not now. Let's forget about the performance. It doesn't matter to anybody if we're there or not."

Jess whispered her pleas, telling him what he already knew: if he didn't go up, there would be hell to pay later for all of them. They calmed Katie down, put on the correct faces, and walked toward the auditorium.

The three of them waited for Steve and Ben, and finally they saw them coming. Steve's hand was on the back of Ben's neck, and he was pushing him forward. What had to be a bruise was beginning to appear on the right side of his face, and his damp hair was sticking to his forehead. Josh heard Jess gasp and took her hand.

Ben stood on the stage that night and mouthed the words of the holiday songs. Josh thought his punishment was over. He was wrong.

After the last song was sung and the applause died down, the music director thanked the children and their parents for being there and announced that coffee and punch and cookies were set up for everyone to enjoy in the school cafeteria. Happy Holidays, she trilled. As the performers cleared the stage to meet their families, Josh looked for Ben and found him alone in a dim corner of the stage. His bruise was darker. Welts had formed at his neck. They agreed to meet at the car.

Josh found the rest of the family in the cafeteria, where Steve was involved in an animated conversation. Josh had no intention of interrupting him. He whispered to Jess about Ben's appearance and rushed alone outside to meet up with him. The two boys stood silently in the cold and waited.

Skipping STONES

Once home, Steve ordered Josh and Katie to their rooms, and Josh stood behind his door, braced for the possibility of Steve's coming after him. But Ben was the only one the man wanted that night.

It was just minutes until the eerie silence in the home was broken by curses and shouting at the bottom of the stairs. Then suddenly the stillness returned, interrupted only slightly by the bang of the back door slamming shut, and all was still again. Josh stood rooted to his spot for several minutes more until he finally harnessed the will to move. Slowly, he crept to the window. And there was Ben.

He stood in the snow alone, his arms straight by his side, with nothing on but his undershorts. The snow was deep. The frigid iced air swarmed around him and covered his body with slick wetness. His toes were numb. His fingers burned. The pain in his ears was so sharp that he wondered if he would lose his hearing.

With no thought at all, Josh ran outside, and Steve, incredulous, watched from the warmth of his vantage point inside as Josh stood ramrod-straight next to his cousin.

"How dare you," Steve sputtered at Josh. "Get your sorry ass out of here. This is between me and my son."

"He's my cousin," Josh managed to say through his chattering teeth. "Whatever happens to him happens to me."

And suddenly, Jess was there. Outraged and defiant, showing more courage than she felt, she hobbled unsteadily past her husband and gathered her boys into her arms and, without saying a word, directed them past him into the warmth of their rooms. For the second time in less than two hours, three members of his family had stood up to Steve, and their defiance and solidarity impacted him in ways they would not have imagined. He let them go.

PART FOUR

Ben

Josh could scarcely believe the contrast to the darkness of the night before and the beauty of the morning. Snow fell in big puffs that hit the ground and stayed there. Bare tree branches bent under heavy ice and sparkled in the white light, turning the familiar space around the home into a sculptured crystal palace. The sun shone for the first time in weeks and sent its rays through the windows to dance on the walls and crystal and silver.

"It's all sparkly," Katie said as she made her way to the bright kitchen to join her mother for breakfast.

Jess forced a smile and made a valiant attempt to be cheerful for her daughter, but she couldn't work through her reverie. Besides comforting her children, she had spent most of the night considering her options for getting them and herself away from Steve and his nonsensical violence. But every path her mind took her had led nowhere. There seemed to be no good options. It was Christmas time; she would wait until after the holidays to do anything.

Jess wasn't the only person there considering alternatives and trying to come up with a plan. Upstairs in his room, Ben took another good, long look at his face in the mirror and ran his hands over the bumps and bruises on his forehead and neck. And then he put a sweater on over his flannel shirt and wondered if he would ever feel warm again. He wasn't ready yet to show himself to his mother or Katie or Josh. He didn't want their pity and didn't want to hear more of his mother's excuses for his father. And so he lay back down on his bed, wrapped himself again in the cocoon of his blankets, and thought again about how his life and theirs had come down to this terrible, incomprehensible debacle.

Ben had always wanted his father's love, but he knew it had never been there for him and never would be. He hated his father in so many ways even as he continued to love him. And he wondered why he still wanted his respect. He knew what the man did to his mother at night. For a long time, he pretended not to know, but he knew, and it sickened him. He loved his mother, but for a long time he couldn't forgive her for not making the hurt stop, even though he understood that she couldn't stop it. He berated himself for not being able to do it for her and lived with guilt. If only he had been stronger, more athletic, smarter, or better looking, perhaps his father might have been different. If he were stronger and less afraid, he might have been able to help his mother.

His memories of his father were a mixture of good times and bad ones, and he was often confused about how he should feel on any given day. Whatever pleasure his father gave was always followed by pain and defeat for his family. A long time ago, Ben cried from disappointment and ridicule, until he was told that only sissies make a display of their emotions and weaknesses. He didn't want to be a sissy. He learned not to cry.

It took him a long time to recognize the fact that all play with his father was meant to hurt, that all acts of kindness had malicious motives, and yet he was never able to say "no" to him or defend himself or his mother. He knew that he was a coward.

He had tried to make his father proud of him. He had been good at sports, had done well at practices, but he froze under his father's judgmental eyes and looked foolish and performed badly at the games. And so he had stopped playing. He was a quitter.

His father was usually bored with whatever he had to say, and so Ben lost confidence in his ability to communicate and had trouble getting words out in good sentences. He feared he'd say everything wrong, and the fear made it happen. He felt stupid.

He was most afraid at night. He had always been afraid of visits from his father, and when he was little, he thought he could hide under his blankets and be invisible. But that changed. He didn't feel safe anywhere. Not even in his closet. He remembered how, when they were real little, he and Katie were afraid to be alone in their rooms and so Katie often sneaked into his room to sleep. Their father found them one night and spanked them and said that they were not going to turn into perverts. They didn't know what that was back then. He learned later and was ashamed.

Why can't I be better, why can't I be good, Ben asked himself that morning. He tried to be good and follow the rules, but he was never good enough. Why did he pull that stunt yesterday and ruin everything? The answer was that he had determined to stand up to his father and to show some gumption in front of the rest of the family, the way Josh had done. And he had messed up.

His father had threatened to send him away before. He just might do it this time, Ben thought. He had packed to leave by himself so many times, but as bad as it was at home, he couldn't leave his mother and sister. He had never been able to protect them. But he thought that someday he would. Sons don't leave their mothers. He was sure of that. There was always the chance, though, that his father would send all of them away. He said that he might, and Ben believed he could do it. After all, his father was very smart and strong and could do anything. Ben wished that he were smart and strong too.

His mind went back to when he was eight or nine and actually thought about telling someone – his teacher maybe or his school principal or maybe even the police - what was happening to him and his mother and sister in their home, what their father did to hurt them, but he didn't. He was too embarrassed to admit it to anyone and was too afraid that his father would find out if he did, and things would get worse.

Ben was afraid for Katie. Often when she hid under her bed at night, he heard her talking to her doll, telling her to be quiet and to be a good little girl. Their father called her his "girlie-girl." Ben knew that his name for her wasn't meant to be nice. Ben loved Katie, but he couldn't let her know that. He couldn't let anyone know how he felt about anything. He tried not to feel.

The boy burrowed further into his bed, hiding, as he always did, against his thoughts, when he was brought back to the present from a knock on the door. Josh came in to rouse him.

"I know you're not asleep," Josh said to his back. "Let's go out for a while. I need to walk."

The two cousins made their way over the crunchy snow down to the footbridge and their favorite side of the river. They walked aimlessly and silently, neither one knowing how to breach the unspoken agreement not to talk about how they lived. They stood mute for some time, simply watching the water gurgle under the thin ice, when Ben broke the silence.

"We have to make it stop," he said.

"I know."

"But how can we do it?"

"I don't know. We have to talk about it. And then we have to talk to your mom."

It was small, but it was a beginning of a plan.

Josh

The UPS truck was sitting in the drive when they got home. The driver was at the door, presenting a package to Jess with Josh's name on it.

There were gifts inside, wrapped in bright red paper with white snow men all over it and big red sparkly bows. One had a gift tag that read, "Merry Christmas, Josh. Miss you, Grandma Annie." Two more gifts were also tagged for Josh and were from his father. And finally there was a box for Jess, Steve, Katie, and Ben. At the bottom of the carton was a large card with "To My Grandson, Josh," written in big letters on the front.

Josh encouraged the others to open the package with their names on it first. Inside were two dozen cookies cut out in Christmas symbols and decorated with green and red and white icing and silver sprinkles. They decided that they should sample them right then while Josh opened his presents. He went for the larger one from Sam first and found Angry Birds, a game he had been hoping for but didn't think he'd ever receive. He decided to wait until Christmas Eve to open the other boxes from his father, because that was the way he and

Skipping STONES

his mother had always done. He hid them in the bottom of his laundry basket in his closet.

But his curiosity proved too great by evening. When he was sure that everyone was sleeping, he pulled them out from their hiding place, locked himself in the bathroom again just in case Steve wanted to make another inspection, and, for several seconds, simply held them in his hands, savoring each moment of good expectations. Which to open first? Which to save for last? He opened the surprise from Sam first.

Inside the small box was something wrapped in a packet of white instructions. Josh pulled off the rubber band that held a brochure in place and found a camouflaged deep green leather case. Could it really be, he wondered, what he thought it was? Flipping open the Velcro piece on top, he pulled out the steel gray cell phone. A short note was taped over the buttons:

Your number: 440 269-5674

My number: 330 225-5253 (quick dial on #1)

Grandma Annie's number: 330 928-2425 (quick dial on #2)

911 (quick dial #3)

Call whenever you want to. I miss you.

His own cell phone! Josh imagined Sam searching for the perfect gift for him, picking out the colors and designs of the phone and case, working with the sales clerk to program the numbers, wrapping it, and taking it to the post office. All that time spent. On him. Just him. Did he know why Josh couldn't talk on the house phone? Did he understand that Steve would trace the calls? Had he figured out, or at least suspected, what was happening in this house?

Josh ran his hand over the smooth metal of the phone and the velvety leather of the case and felt strength in knowing that his father and grandmother were just a button away from him. He could press either #1 or #2 and talk to them right then and there if he wanted to. And if he ever needed help in any kind of emergency, someone would be there for him in minutes. There couldn't have been a more perfect gift, and he loved his father even more for it.

Grandma Annie's package was next. He knew from the weight and shape of it that it was a book, and so it was, a book with a brown leather cover with its title written in gold. The first and last pages were gold too, and on the first page she had written, Merry Christmas to Josh with love from Grandma Annie. It was called *Jonathon Livingston Seagull,* a curious name for a book. He would, he decided, start it that night.

And finally there lay the cheery card with the letter from her inside. He made his bed under the window and sat down on the covers, put the phone and the book and the game carefully on his lap, and opened it.

My Dear Josh,

I've wanted to write a real letter to you ever since you came to my house that day in August, but Sam thought I should wait to tell you what's been on my mind and not upset you. Well, I've waited long enough, by golly, and here I am. It's Christmas-time, after all – the most beautiful time of the year – and families are meant to draw close together and share things. I've enjoyed your notes to me and the ones you sent your dad, and I've enjoyed answering mine, but it isn't enough for me. Plain and simple, I miss you.

I keep reminding myself that you are twelve years old. Hard to believe that all of those years have gone by and so much has happened. You had always remained, in my mind, a little blond toddler filled with curiosity and determination. I can still see you coming to me when you visited with your lovely mother and grabbing my hand to pull me up. "Walk, Gummy," you'd say. And out we'd go, you leading the way. We discovered all kinds of wondrous things on our walks together: smooth

Skipping **STONES**

stones of all different shapes, bird feathers, dandelions, caterpillars, and perfect twigs – terrific treasures. And then there you were that day I finally saw you again - a strapping young man. I'm wondering if you still collect special things and still enjoy walking and searching for them. I suspect you do. Your mother always had that sense of adventure. And so does your father.

I've been baking up a storm here, and I'm almost ready to take big paper plates full of cookies and fudge to my neighbors. I hope that you and Katie and Ben enjoy the goodies I sent. You probably have lots of Christmas treats, but a few more won't hurt, right? I'll bet Jess is a great cook. She always did everything so well. Tell her that I said hi, will you?

Sam told me that I should just be quiet about what I'm going to say here, but I've always been one to speak my mind, and I don't see any point in changing at this point in my life. So here it is. You asked him to send letters that would arrive during the week and told him that you can't talk to him on the phone. Now, if you don't mind my saying so, that sounds a little unusual to me. And it's troubled your dad ever since – even though Jess said that everything was all right. I just hope that you aren't angry with him for some reason.

These past six months have been awfully hard on you with all of the changes that you've gone through, and no one can blame you for being confused about all of them. You should know that your dad loves you and always has, and that he wants only the best for you. You should know that. Sometimes things just don't make any sense in the way they happen. But sometimes the good Lord gives us a chance to finally make things right. Your dad wants to do that as soon as possible.

Now, I'm going to get to my point. Here's what I've been worrying about: is it possible that you won't talk to Sam because you can't? Is someone setting rules about that? It might sound crazy and a little presumptuous of me to suggest to you, after all of these years of being away from you, that you can call on me or Sam any time you want to if you need someone to talk to. But that's what I'm saying, just the same. Sam wants you to have the phone so that if you ever feel you need to talk, you can call and no one else needs to know about it. For reasons that you may or may not understand, your father can't just go charging over there and demand to know what's going on. But he's working on all of that. There. That's it. Your dad is a little hesitant to speak his mind. He doesn't want to undermine Jess or the rest of the family, and neither do I, but...well, so much water has flowed over the dam, as they say, that I just don't want to leave anything left unsaid.

I hope that you have a wonderful Christmas just filled to the brim with beauty and joy. And I'm sending all kinds of wishes your way for a new year of all kinds of possibilities. You just keep thinking good thoughts and stay as precious as you have always been, and good things will come your way. I love you.

Grandma Annie

PS: I hope you like the book. It's always been one of my favorites.

Josh checked the clock. Nine-thirty. Still early enough that he could call Sam or his grandma. Should he? What would he say? He would just thank them for the presents, maybe. Would he have to tell them why he hadn't been able to call before? How would he say that? He pushed the button to turn the phone on and listened to the music play as the screen turned red. Verizon. And then the screen turned blue and showed the time. Nine thirty-two. Maybe Sam would call him to make sure he'd received the phone.

Nine thirty-four, and he was still undecided. For the moment, he would simply keep the phone next to him while he started *Jonathon Livingston Seagull*.

The small section he read gave him a lot to think about. He understood Jonathon Livingston, the gull, and his determination to push himself to be the best he could. His mom had always told him to be his own man and never settle for mediocrity. "Dare to soar," she had always said. And there was Jonathon, proving her point and making it real. Josh read until he couldn't keep his eyes focused. And then he sank into a deep, dreamless sleep, one cheek pressed against the lighted screen of the most precious present he had ever received, a link to his father.

෴

This is good," Josh said absent-mindedly. He and Katie were in Ben's room, killing time until Jess and Steve were ready to leave for Steve's big annual Christmas party.

Katie scooted closer, glad to have something to focus on. "Tell me what it's about," she said.

Josh explained that the book Grandma Annie had sent was about a young seagull who isn't like any of his family or friends, that he isn't content to simply look for food all day. What he really wants, more than anything, is to become really good at flying.

"Most gulls just fly low, close to the ground," he said, "looking for food. But he wants to learn how to go higher, see different things, do tricks in the air like other birds. He has an imagination. So every day he goes away from the flock and practices flying. He doesn't have any friends, and his mom and dad are worried about him because he's so different from the rest of the seagulls. They think he should give up flying and be like everybody else."

Katie looked up from her dolls and asked if Jonathon was happy, and Josh told her that he was happy to be doing what he was doing, that he was excited about using his imagination and improving himself, but, at the same time, he was sad because no one understood what he was trying to do and because everyone seemed stuck in their old lives, not able to move beyond what every gull before them had done.

"What happens to him?" Katie wanted to know. "Do they punish him and make him do what they want him to do?"

Ben finally looked up. "So he's not worried about not having any friends? It doesn't bother him that he's different?"

And Josh answered that he hadn't gotten far enough into the book to know for sure, but he had the feeling that Jonathon would do whatever he felt was right. Katie wanted to know more about the book, and so Josh read a few pages to her. They were into the section in which Jonathon was on his way back to his old flock when Josh decided that maybe he should ask Grandma Annie about the book's deeper meanings. Josh didn't know how much he should discuss with Katie.

Ben was somber. "I could be like Jonathon," he said, "and just do my own thing. I could do that. I could learn how to sail and go on a trip around the world all by myself or just start walking somewhere and never stop." He stood in front of the closet. "I could decide not to grow up at all."

Katie put her hands out to make her strong point. "We have to grow up, Ben," she said. "We all grow up sometime."

"No we don't," he said. "We don't have to. I could decide that I don't want to. I could do that." He was at the window. "There are a lot of ways."

"You just want to stay a kid," Katie offered.

"I hate being a kid," he answered.

Katie looked at Josh and shrugged. She whispered, "What does he mean?"

"It means life sucks," Ben said.

"Hello, Sam here."

When Josh heard his father's voice, it was all he could do to keep his voice steady.

"Hey! Josh! I'll be darned," Sam said, clearly delighted. "Wait a second while I turn the music down. It's so loud that I almost didn't hear the phone ringing. Hold on."

Christmas music was playing in the background and there was laughter. Thinking about how the holiday had been in this house so far, Josh felt even more miserable.

"Sorry about that," Sam said, returning to the line. "I always have people over for brunch on Christmas Eve day. Grandma Annie's here with a few of my friends to get some of the food prepared ahead of time. They're a rowdy bunch. It's like we have a party to have a party. Anyway, I'm so glad you called. Are you calling on your new phone? Do you like it?"

"I like it a lot," Josh answered him. "I didn't have time to call you before, so I thought I'd just call now. We aren't doing much yet. Thanks. I like the color and everything."

Sam led his son in the conversation, and Josh was grateful for that. Sam told him what he had made for the brunch and described the new chair he'd bought for Grandma Annie's living room. He asked about Jess and Steve and Katie and Ben, and how they were celebrating Christmas. And then he put Grandma Annie on the line.

"I got that book, or a copy of it, over thirty years ago," she said when Josh thanked her for the gift. "Still have mine. It's one of my all-time favorites. Let's get together again real soon so that we can discuss Jonathon.

"Does he die?" Josh asked. "Did he die from trying so hard? Or was he so good at flying that he just changed because he was so happy?" He had to have answers for Ben.

"Well, there are a lot of different thoughts on that. The way I see it," she said, "is that our job is to strive to be the best we can be, to seek perfection right here and now, just like Jesus did or the Great Gull. 'Course, most of us don't get as far as Jonathon did, but God rewards us for trying. All of the really great people in the world have followed their passion. They worked hard to be the best they could be, and that brought them incredible happiness. I think the author was saying that if you have a gift, you should use it and be the best you can be at it and face up to doubts others might have. Finish the book, and you and I and your dad will sit around my table with some good strong coffee and talk about it. We'll do our own book review. Let's make arrangements soon, okay?"

Sam came back on. "When is the best time to call you?"

Josh told him that night time during vacation would be best and that after school on weekdays would be great once school started again.

There was an uncomfortable pause, and Sam finally asked Josh point-blank if he was all right.

"I'm okay," he lied.

Jess

The next several days were dedicated to wrapping gifts, baking for the family's Christmas dinner, and Steve's taking Jess to find a new dress and shoes for the firm's annual Christmas Ball. Because of some recent problems he had had with his two biggest accounts, the fete would be especially important to him this year. He and Jess would have to out-dress, out-talk and out-perform everyone else there. He galvanized himself to prove his superiority. Jess hoped that she could make it through the onerous evening.

The night of the elaborate party, Jess got herself dressed and presented herself to Steve. Even she could see that she was too thin, her skin and hair lacked luster, and the smile she forced onto her mouth was not convincing. She didn't want to go.

"You look like shit," he told her, and she went back to her dressing table and applied more makeup.

She turned down the offer of wine when they walked into the beautiful ballroom the firm had secured for the evening, but Steve whispered that she should carry a glass around so that she wouldn't appear to be a "damned pris." As she sipped it, the warmth of it, and the tranquilizer she had taken earlier, relaxed her somewhat.

She made it through the cocktail hour by staying close to him and allowing him to carry the conversation. She smiled and nodded appropriately through the first three courses at the dinner table. And she made it through the toasts that were made to the partners and their staff. She made it through the close dances with Steve and his intimate whispers in her ear. She made it through all of the talk at their table about the opportunities that would be available to all of them in the New Year.

And then, with the help of the expensive wine, the conversation had turned nostalgic and introspective. Holidays and families and how people there spent their Christmases became the end-of-the-evening topic, and Jess allowed herself to relax more; it was almost over and she didn't try to follow the flow of conversation. And then one of the senior partners from across the table looked directly at her and asked her a question: "Tell us, Jess," he said, "what are the holiday traditions that you and your family value most?" And all eyes turned in her direction.

It was a frightening moment for her, and she asked him to repeat the question and turned toward Steve for help, but he sat there, a smile pasted on his face, and waited like everyone else around the table for her reply to the simple question. But it wasn't simple for her. They had no traditions. Christmas and all other holidays were lies like everything else in her home. They were endured.

She managed a smile, and, to give herself more time to clear her mind and form her answer, she reached across her dinner plate to pick up the glass of wine in front of her. The table was crowded. Stemmed water glasses and wine glasses, bread plates, candles, flowers, and small favors for the women were everywhere. Her hand shook. She put her damp fingers around the tall glass and slowly attempted to remove it from the clutter and bring it to her lips. But the direction her arm took wasn't accurate, and the etched crystal banged into the water glass next to it and shattered against the china. Its contents flew over the linens and the shirt of the man beside her.

Nothing she had been through compared to the hostile and dead silence in the car after the party. Her punishment would be severe.

River Road was perilously black. The sky was empty. The raw wind whipped at the snow and sent it scattering in every direction, as if even it was filled with fear and fighting for escape. Steve drove slowly and deliberately. The park sign flashed in front of the headlights, and he turned deftly into the entrance to the parking lot, searching for the narrow service road that would drop them into the dense woods that edged the river.

"Get out," he demanded.

He stood her in front of him and held her there with one hand and hit her head and her shoulders with the fist of the other. The fourth blow to her stomach knocked her down. He watched her try to stand. In full control, he kicked her side and legs. The trees and river and blasts of snow absorbed his threats. The freezing damp air cloaked her body, and his slurs slid off her. He turned and walked away through the darkness.

She lay curled in a heap over a drift of ice and snow and wondered if she would die there. And then wondered if she really cared.

It took a long time to make her legs move. She had lost a shoe somewhere, and for some reason that became very important to her. Struggling to feel her toes, she forced herself to her knees and ran her hands through the snow to look for it. Katie, Ben, Josh. The images of her children gave her strength as she crawled to a tree. Circling her arms around it, she pulled herself up and searched through the trees and black sky for direction. She walked aimlessly, one numb step at a time through the woods in the direction she thought she had come from, towards her children, stopping only when Steve's car finally pulled up in front of her and hurled her towards them.

He carried her inside and wrapped her cold, dirty body inside a blanket and put her on the chair beside the bed. The last words she heard were, "Have you finally learned?"

Josh

    Something was wrong. The children had heard Steve leave a while ago, and still Jess hadn't called them to come to breakfast. They gathered in the hallway and made their way to the kitchen where they expected to find her and then to the bedroom and its closed door. Katie knocked softly.

    "Mommy. Mommy? Are you in there?" she asked.

    They stood in a close huddle, listening for her footsteps.

    "I don't like this," Ben muttered. "I don't like this at all."

    Finally Jess spoke, and they tentatively stepped inside. The heavy drapes were pulled, and the only light in the room came from the small brass floor-lamp beside her. Covered by a blanket from her shoulders down, she sat in the big blue and white plaid chair, her legs stretched out on the ottoman. The children could just see her face and the top of her turtleneck sweater. Katie and Josh inched forward as she explained that she was just not feeling up to par today, was just a little tired. Ben stood like a piece of cement, grounded just inside the door.

    There was no preamble.

Skipping STONES

"He hurt you, didn't he? You're in here because he hurt you again," he said. It was a statement, not a question. "You haven't come out because you can't. For once, just tell the truth, Mom. He hurt your really bad."

Jess continued with the story she had thought up, but this time it didn't work.

"Stand up then," Ben insisted. "Get up, Mom, and let's all do something together. Come on. Show us how good you are."

Katie reached out and gently touched her mother's cheek. "I'll help you," she said.

But Katie was too helpful, and, even as her mother was protesting, she pulled the blanket off of her lap. "There," she said encouragingly.

And then they saw the huge splotches of black bruises and broken skin on Jess's legs.

"Mommy," Katie whimpered.

Ben could no longer pretend not to see. All of his old anger and hurt and frustration finally let loose, and he ran around the room, kicking at the furniture, the walls, the door, anything that came in his way, like a child possessed.

Do something, Josh thought. But the crying, the kicking, the yelling, and Jess's pitiful attempt to stand made him incapable of action. Finally, he forced himself to act responsibly: who's hurting the most, he asked himself, and went to Katie just as Ben ran out of the room.

He got her to lie down on the sofa and put Ariel beside her before he ran to follow Ben.

He found him throwing clothes into his back pack.

"What are you doing?" Josh asked.

"I'm leaving. I can't stand it here anymore," Ben answered.

"But that won't do anything. It'll make things worse," Josh pleaded. "You can't just leave. We'll change things. We said we would."

"Nothing will ever change," Ben yelled back. "You don't know. You haven't been here long enough to know. It'll never change. Never. She should leave," he continued. "She should leave and take us with her."

"Maybe she will now. Please don't leave. She needs us to help. Leaving will make it all worse," Josh said. We have to take care of Katie too. Come with me. Please. They need both of us."

He ran back to Katie and coaxed her to her brother's room. Ben didn't help comfort his sister, but neither did he leave.

Josh made a decision. He walked deliberately back to Jess.

"You have to make it stop," he said. "You have to do something. Ben wants to leave. Katie is hurting so bad. We need to leave before Steve gets back."

"I don't know where to go," she whispered.

"It doesn't matter where we go," he said. "Mimi's. A hotel. Let's just get in the car and go. We'll figure it out. Sam's. We could go there. Sam will help. Let's just get out of here! He'll be back soon. Come on, Jess, let's leave now!" He realized he was yelling.

But still she pushed back. "I can't get family involved. Not yet. I need to talk with someone who knows what to do. He'll take you kids away from me. He'll make a case against me. He's told me he knows people all over town who will side with him."

"He can't do that," Josh protested. "He's the bad one. I'll tell everyone what he's done. So will Ben."

He ran to his room and got the cell phone.

"Here," he said. "Call someone. Anyone. It doesn't matter who. Steve won't know."

"Do it, Mom," Ben echoed from his place at the door. "Do it before he comes back."

"Go into my closet," she told her son. "There's a pair of navy shoes. Reach into the toe of one of the shoes. There's a card there. Bring it to me."

Jess dialed the number on the card.

The woman who answered had a pleasant voice. "This is the shelter. How may I help you today?"

Jess answered that she might need help and asked how the shelter worked. The woman asked if Jess was calling for herself or someone else and, when Jess told her that she was calling for herself and her children, she asked if they were in immediate danger and then if they were in a safe place. The questions were put kindly, but firmly. She asked how many children were involved and if they could get themselves to the shelter if they needed to. Jess admitted that she didn't have a way to get there. And then she changed the course of the conversation.

"Will you tell me more about the shelter? Where is it? What is it like?"

The woman explained the living conditions there and said that families were welcome. She would not say where it was.

"Pets are welcome too," she added in her kind, calm voice. "We offer temporary shelter unless more is required. We help you set up a safety plan and provide counseling for you and your children and legal assistance if you need it. We want to help you, but we'll need a little more information first."

Jess shut the lady off. "Can you give me the name of the attorney who can help? Could I come in and talk to him?"

She was told that there would be an assessment and counseling. An attorney would be called if it was appropriate and if they were ready to pursue legal aid. Jess thanked the woman and hung up.

"I can't take you children there," she said. "I'll come up with something. I'll figure it out." She looked nervously at the clock by her bed. "He'll be home soon."

She reached her hand out to Ben to help her up. He held back for a moment and then put his arm around her waist and helped balance her while she walked unsteadily across the room.

"Don't worry," she said. "He was in a good mood when he left."

And then she turned directly to Ben and promised him that this would absolutely never happen again.

Steve came back into the house as if he were Santa, with a big smile and a Ho, Ho, Ho.

He called her and the children to the living room and presented her with a beautifully wrapped box from Tiffany. Inside was a diamond heart necklace that glimmered by the light of the fire and tree. She put it on, at his insistence, over the turtleneck sweater that covered her bruised neck and shoulders. He kissed her and told her how much he loved her.

Josh

Josh lay in the dark for some time before he picked his phone up from its hiding place. Careful to make certain the bathroom door was locked, he turned the shower on and pushed the button numbered one. Sam answered immediately.

The boy's throat tightened, and he swallowed quickly to try to push back the sobs swelling up inside there. It was an old trick that didn't work for him that time.

"Are you all right?" Sam asked. "What's wrong?"

And when Josh still didn't respond, he became more alarmed. "Josh?" he said. "What's happening? Talk to me."

"I can't. I don't know what to say."

"I'll wait. I'll wait right here until you can talk. Take your time."

"Things aren't very good here," the boy began. "In fact, things are, well, they're really bad."

He paused and heard the intake of his father's breath.

"What kind of bad things?" Sam urged. "It's okay. Take your time."

"It's Steve," Josh finally answered. "It's everything. Steve does bad things. We hear him at night when he's drunk and sometimes in the mornings. He hurts Jess. We see the black and blue marks. He hurt Ben before the concert and then made him stand outside in the snow with almost nothing on. Ben hides in the closet and digs at the wall with his fingers. Katie sleeps under her bed most nights. I'm so scared. And I don't know what to do."

Sam quickly put it all together. His reaction was swift.

"Josh," he said firmly. "Listen to me. I understand. We need to call the police. Uncle Bill or your papaw and I will come right over. You and Katie and Ben stay in your rooms and lock the doors."

"No. Please don't do that!" Josh cried. "Steve told Jess that he can get the judge to take us away from her. She's done some things. Not bad things, but they make her look bad to people who don't know. He told her that. It's all messed up."

Once the wall of resistance came down, the words fell onto each other.

"She has to find someone to tell her what to do, but you can't come here," he blurted out. "If you showed up it would be awful. Steve hates you. He hated Mom too. I'm not supposed to see you or talk to you. Jess got in awful trouble when he found out that you had been here. He found out that we went to see you. He called her terrible names and said that if she tried to leave he'd tell everyone she's the bad one. Then they'd give us kids to him. He knows a lot of important people."

"Josh. Take a deep breath. Listen, okay? No one will do anything to Jess if we get help. No one will take the kids away from her. Steve's just saying that to keep all of you under control. Will you believe that?"

"I don't know." Josh was sobbing now. "I don't understand all that stuff."

"I'm going to hang up and get the police," Sam told him. "You stay in your room."

"No!" the boy pleaded. "You can't do that. I promised Jess. She's working on a plan. Just talk to her tomorrow, please. Everyone's in bed now. We're all right. For now, we're okay."

Sam fought against his impulses to rescue his son immediately, but even he wasn't sure what the ramifications might be if the police arrived with him and Bill trailing in later. He didn't know how it would all work. If Jess was afraid or unsure about leaving her husband, he and Bill could make everything worse. What would he say once he got to the house? What if Jess wouldn't press charges? He had no legal right to Josh. He had already begun the process to change all of that, but the legal system moved slowly. Breaking in to the house could slow it down even more.

"If Jess tells the police the truth," he reasoned, "we could get all of you out of there, Josh, or Steve would have to leave. Would Jess do that?"

"I don't know. She's afraid to leave. She needs a lawyer or something. Would you get someone to help her? If she knew someone would help her, she'd leave, I think. Would you please get someone?"

"I can do that. I'll tell her that right now."

"No. Steve might wake up. He can't know what we're doing."

There was a long pause and Josh knew that his father was working out a plan.

"Josh, I'm going to get help. I have a friend who will know what to do. And I'm not making that up. He's a lawyer, and a good one. Steve won't find out about it until we're ready for him to."

For the first time, Josh felt a ray of hope.

Skipping STONES

"Are you sure you're safe right now?" Sam asked, and Josh assured him that they were all safely in their rooms.

"I have to talk to Jess," Sam went on. "Listen. Keep your cell phone on at all times and keep it with you. There's a way you can turn the ring off and put it on vibrate. There's a button to push. Go to "Tools" and you'll see how to do it. If anything happens, you call me immediately or dial 911. You have the button for that. Call me early tomorrow morning to let me know you're all right and when I can talk to Jess. Or call me tonight – anytime you want to. I'll get to work on this first thing in the morning. The man who will help us is a good friend of mine. He'll talk to me tomorrow. I know he will. Will you be all right 'til tomorrow?"

Neither one of them wanted to hang up.

"Josh, I will not let you down," Sam pressed. "I'm here for you. I will not let you and Jess and the kids down. I swear. Do you believe me?"

Josh believed in him absolutely.

෴

The following morning was Christmas, and after all of the gifts were opened, the children were told to shower and to change into one of the outfits Steve had given each of them to wear to Mimi and Papaw's for the family celebration there. Josh cringed while he put on the navy slacks, white button-down shirt, and green sweater Steve had selected for him. He didn't bother to take his other gifts out of the boxes they had come in. He simply stacked them in his closet.

Jess had her coat on and was sitting hunched over in the foyer when the children came out of their rooms, ready to go. The diamond necklace Steve had given her earlier sparkled at the neck of her clean turtleneck, looking garish and out of place there.

"We're going to make a stop at the Emergency Room before we go to Mimi's," Steve told them. "Your mom might need some medication. Nothing to worry about. She'll be fine. Let's go. We're going to be late as it is."

Josh thought the emergency room would be empty on Christmas day, but there were about eight people signed up ahead of Jess to get help. Steve went to the registration desk to get her signed in, but immediately came back for her. The lady at the desk needed to ask her some questions. Steve stood anxiously behind his wife.

The family waited at least thirty minutes before Jess's name was finally called to see a doctor. She and Steve followed the nurse into the examining rooms behind the big metal door, but Steve came out minutes later, clearly upset.

They waited another hour or more before the door opened and the nurse brought Jess out into the waiting room in a wheelchair. They rushed to her. The nurse looked directly at Steve and was abrupt.

"Your wife had quite a fall, Mr. Selby. She has three cracked ribs and multiple lacerations. We've given her some strong pain medication. The ribs will heal on their own, but it will take a while. You understand, of course, that she should be quiet and not do anything strenuous." She paused, and her look was intense. "We've made a detailed report about all of your wife's injuries. We're going to call her to check on her progress to see if additional care is required."

Once in the car, Steve let loose.

"Arrogant sons-of-bitches. Talked to me like I was some kind of flunky, ordering me out that way. I'll write a letter.

That's what I'll do. Maybe press charges. I'll show those sons-of-bitches."

He handed Jess his cell. "Get your mom on the phone," he instructed, "but let me talk to her."

They were travelling west on Mayfield Road, going way too fast and barely stopping at signals, but somehow Steve was able to control himself during the call. He told Mimi that they were on their way from the ER and that Jess had three cracked ribs from a fall and would have to take it easy.

"She has some pain medication and should rest as much as possible. Please don't fill her with a lot of questions. And no drinks for her. We'll be there in about fifteen minutes. We're looking forward to a nice family visit. It's just what we all need. Tell Dad I'm ready for one of his Manhattans. It's been a hell of a Christmas season, I'll tell you."

He clicked off and turned back to Jess. "No dramatics, you hear?" And to the children, "Don't make a big deal out of this. I'm warning you."

When they arrived, pillows and blankets were piled on the sofa for Jess, soft Christmas music was playing in the background, the fresh tree was sparkling under the green, yellow, red, and blue lights, the bright fire was roaring in the massive fireplace, and the air carried the fragrance of an evergreen forest. It was Christmas the way Josh remembered it, but of course much grander; and the cold and sadness and fear he felt dissipated slightly from the warmth and affection he felt there.

"So how in the world did you fall?" Maddie asked while Mimi served the hors d'oeuvres.

Josh lowered his head and held his breath, waiting to hear what story Ben and Katie and he needed to remember.

Jess told her family that she and Steve had gone to an office party at the Laurel Hills Country Club, and when they were leaving to go home, she slid on some ice on the porch steps and tried to catch herself on the banister. She lost her footing and slipped, mostly on her side, down five steps. She said that her side hadn't really started to hurt until last night. She was going to be fine, she said. The ribs would heal themselves.

Okay, Josh thought, that makes sense and it was simple enough that Katie and Ben and he could repeat it.

"I've been to that club. I don't remember steps or a porch," Maddie persisted.

There was an awkward silence. Jess turned to Steve.

"We won't file charges against the club," he said, ignoring Maddie. "We were careless. Jess was in heels. We weren't prepared for the weather."

Josh saw the piercing look Maddie gave Jess.

The rest of the afternoon and evening was festive. Katie and Ben relaxed and laughed and seemed restored under the affection and attention the rest of the family showered on them. Jess smiled through the pain from her ribs and the bruises on her back and legs.

Josh continued to touch the phone hidden in his pocket.

The family exchanged gifts and moved to the dinner table and their Christmas feast. Papaw said a heart-felt prayer of love and gratitude, and at the end of it he asked if anyone had anything to add and paused to give each of them a chance to think about what they might say. Josh waited for the others to respond -waited for someone to recall the memory of his mother. It had been only six months since she had died, and this was his first Christmas without her. He had thought about her often throughout the day, and when the entire family sat at the table together, memories of her welled up into his heart and made it heavy. He had to honor her.

Skipping **S T O N E S**

"I would just like to say hi to my mom and tell her that I love her and that I'm sure she's in heaven, and I hope she's happy there. 'Merry Christmas, Mom.'"

༄

Josh called Sam again that night from his bathroom. He wanted to talk about normal things and asked his father how he had spent his day. Sam had wakened early that morning and had made a thermos of coffee to take with him on a long walk by himself to the park where he had taken Josh. Later, he had gone to Grandma Annie's for their traditional Christmas breakfast and to give her a few more gifts. Late morning, they had gone together to deliver huge containers of sliced turkey, potatoes, and green beans from his restaurant to the local men's shelter and helped serve the homeless people there. Finally, they had wrapped up the evening driving to Vermillion to have dinner with his father's side of the family.

"Next Christmas you and I will be together," Sam said. "We'll have a feast and invite all of our relatives and celebrate big time."

"Can Jess and Ben and Katie come too?"

"Of course. And your Mimi and Papaw and Maddie and Bill. We'll work on that. We'll really work on it."

Josh let himself picture all of them together. "Where do you think we'll have our celebration?"

"Well, let's see. We'd want to include your grandpa's family too. Grandma Annie wouldn't consider not having them. That's four more people. I guess that would be eleven of us. My place holds that many people. We'll see. There are all kinds of possibilities."

"I've never seen your house," Josh said, and the statement reminded both of them of the senseless chaos and the precious time wasted in the past six months of both of their lives.

Josh asked him what he got for Christmas. Grandma Annie had given him a big apron with his name on it and a gift certificate from Barnes and Noble. He gave her the living room chair she had picked out to replace her old one, a new robe, and a book she had asked for. The trouble was, he joked, that the new chair made everything else in the room look old and faded, and they'd probably end up having to redo the entire room around it.

"I made you something," Josh blurted out. "It's dumb, but you might be able to use it sometime. I was going to mail it, but I thought I'd rather give it to you when I see you."

Finally, the question they both had been anticipating needed to be asked.

"Did you talk to your friend? The one who will help?" Josh ventured.

"Yes. This afternoon. He'll help. I knew he would. We're going to talk more tomorrow. But I'm going to have to talk to Jess, and she's going to have to talk with him."

Josh wondered if he should tell Sam about the emergency room and Jess's broken ribs, but he decided that it was up to Jess to finally tell him. So all he said was how difficult it would be to get Jess to talk, that she had never really wanted to talk about it.

Not even he knew how very hard it would be.

Steve stayed home the rest of the week, and there wasn't a good time for Sam to make the call. Josh walked to the river every morning after breakfast to talk with Sam on the phone, and he closed himself in the shower each night when he was alone in his room so that they could talk more. He assured his father that he was safe, and Sam shared with him what life was like outside of the walls he was living in and how it would be for him and Ben and Katie when Jess left Steve.

Sam reinforced Josh's sense of who he was and what he was capable of, and he assured him that freedom is the norm for most people and is absolutely necessary for everyone: Jess and Katie and Ben and Josh had the right to be free, to love and to be loved unconditionally, he said. It was a basic premise that Josh needed to remember, and one that Jess needed to finally understand.

Son and father girded themselves with details about abuse and how to approach Jess when Steve finally left the house, and they gave themselves permission to discuss their future together. Their conversations filled them with hope and purpose.

Sam made it clear over and over again that no man has the right to hurt anyone. He shared with his son a slogan that he had recently read during his research to help Jess: "Hands are for helping, not for hurting." When the time was right, Josh would repeat those same words to Jess and Ben and Katie. Talks with Sam filled Josh up with courage and compassion and empathy. When the talks came to an end each evening, he was left with compounded loneliness.

Josh had finished the short book about Jonathon the seagull, and it had raised a lot of questions. It was complicated, and yet he had the feeling that it was important for him to understand or Grandma Annie wouldn't have given it to him. He had asked Jess to read it so that they could discuss it. She did, and whenever Steve left unexpectedly to run an errand, Jess and the children talked about Jonathon's pursuit of perfection and his love of his flock and how, because of that love, he sacrificed everything to convince them to set themselves free.

It took some doing, but Jess was able to satisfactorily explain her version of the story to the children that Jonathon and Fletcher hadn't died and gone to heaven, but because of their strong wills and quest for knowledge, they had entered into a different stage in their lives and had become wiser and stronger. And they never gave up trying to help others. She didn't go into the deeper, esoteric, messages of the book because none of them had enough background in spirituality to understand it, but the message she took from her reading, and helped them to understand, was powerful enough. It gave Josh and, perhaps, her and Ben and Katie something profound to contemplate in their hours of isolation. The messages of strength and sacrifice and absolute love were not lost on any of them, and neither was Jonathon's will to convince his flock to seek a better life for themselves. Josh's esteem for his grandmother reached new heights.

On the fifth morning, Sam reported that he had an appointment with his friend later that afternoon. He would have some answers for his son that evening and would be ready to talk directly with Jess.

"Can I tell Ben?" Josh asked.

Sam thought that it might be best to wait until they had some real answers before he told his cousin.

"And maybe it would be better for Jess to tell him in her own way," he said. "We're on the road to helping them change their lives, Josh. I'd think Jess would want to tell her children herself."

༄

The first thing Sam disclosed when he called the next day was that the attorney said that the chance of Steve's changing and things getting better in that home were slim. He also explained that one out of every five women in America experience violence from their husbands or boyfriends at some point in their lives. But, he said, they didn't have to accept it. There were laws to protect them from their abusers, and there were people and organizations to help them work to make change within those laws. He wanted Josh to understand that none of the abuse was Jess's fault. It was no one's fault. Katie and Ben had done nothing to cause Steve's violence, and neither had Josh. There are men out there, he said, who can only feel powerful if they hurt or diminish other people. Josh asked him what causes men to be that way, and Sam acknowledged that he didn't have an answer.

"All I know, he continued, "is that Jess needs to admit to being abused and to ask for help. But my lawyer friend said that we need to understand that it's very hard for a woman who's lived as long as Jess has with an abuser, to have the courage to start all over. She's really afraid, and she needs our help and everyone else's who loves her. We can change things, Josh."

Josh felt empowered. If Sam and his friend thought that they could help Jess, then he was sure that they could.

"He gave me a lot of information, and one thing that really caught my attention was about your role in all of this," Sam continued. "You probably don't realize it, Josh, but you're stronger than Katie and Ben because you had a loving mother who provided you with years of happiness. You had unconditional love and laughter and freedom. You have her strength. From what you've told me, Katie and Ben have never had those things on a regular basis. Love has been given and taken away all of their lives. They've had Jess's love, but Steve's put limits on how much she can show. And the consequence could be, if they don't get out of that situation soon, that they could be damaged emotionally the rest of their lives. Without you, change might never have taken place. I hate it that you're there, but Grandma Annie sees it all differently. She told me to tell you that God works in mysterious ways and according to His plan and that we have to trust in Him. And she said he's working through you."

The boy felt the weight of responsibility push down upon him.

"Nothing's happened for a while. Maybe she talked to him and is making it right."

"Think of the times, Josh, when things felt better. But have they ever stayed that way? Our lawyer told me that abusers confuse their victims. They can be real actors. They'll make you believe that they're filled with love for you, if it suits their needs, and then they'll turn on you if they feel threatened by you. It's intentional. It's all about them.

"Josh," he continued, "I want you out of that house. I'd get you out right this minute if I could. I would have gone to you the night you called when all of this got started, but I have no legal right to do that. Jess and Steve have custody of you because of a very bad decision I agreed to almost eight years ago. I screwed up royally, and I've paid for that ever since. Once we get Jess going and she gets away from Steve, I can start custody hearings again. I have to talk to her tomorrow. Mr. Karnanski will meet with her immediately. Call me as soon as Steve's gone so I can call her.

He had an additional fact that he hadn't shared: the danger from an abuser is magnified if there is evidence that the spouse is thinking of leaving. They were going to have to be very, very careful.

Skipping STONES

Steve didn't leave them that day. Instead, he took the family out for lunch and to the mall to hunt for some deals on some things he thought they all needed. That night he took Jess out for dinner and a movie. Josh was frantic and so was Sam.

As soon as Steve finally left the next morning, the phone call was arranged and would take place within minutes. Josh was too nervous to stay and witness Jess's reaction, and so went again to the river, praying that Sam would be able to convince her to make the break. Without thinking, he knocked off shards of icicles and threw them into the water, watching as they floated downstream and mixed with the thick water. He formed perfect balls of snow in his gloved hands and dazedly threw them at the barren trees and watched them splatter against the grey trunks. And for a while he simply stood looking across to the other bank, thinking about spring and the birth that would surely come with the new season. And he hoped with all of his heart that the budding beauty that he always anticipated at that wonderful time of the year would also include a miraculous transition for him and his father and Katie, Ben, and Jess. Finally, deciding that his father and aunt should have had plenty of time to talk through things, he headed back to the house, anxious about what he would find there, gripped by a ghostly sense of doom.

"She's afraid, and she's shocked and embarrassed." Sam said when Josh called him. "She needs a little time to get over the humiliation of someone knowing her secret.

"She'll get back to me," he added. "I'm sure she will. We go back a long time, and we've always trusted each other."

If Sam believed it, Josh told himself he would too. He wandered aimlessly through the house, waiting to see Jess. When she finally came out of her room, her appearance cut him short. She had been crying, and she looked so tired.

༄

Jess's self-incriminations and indecision were so great that she could think of nothing else but her perceived failure as a mother, her shame for having held onto a marriage that had been a sham from the beginning, her humiliation from her secret having been discovered, and her fear for her future and her children's.

It was December 31, a day often filled with nostalgia, happy and sad memories of the old year and hope for what the New Year might bring. Josh experienced every emotion. In his old life, it had always been just him and his mother to celebrate their past and future, and the celebration had been one of his fondest memories.

"It's an excuse for people to get drunk and act crazy," she had told him, "and then they can't do anything the next day because they feel so shitty. And, besides, it's dangerous out on the roads."

And so, each year, they were alone to bring in the new one. They'd put on the silly hats that she had bought years before at the party store down the street, turned up the volume of the TV, and carried lids from their pots and pans out to the porch where they'd count down with the Times Square partiers to twelve o'clock. And then they'd shout "Happy New Year!" to each other and anyone else within hearing distance and bang the lids. Once back inside, they'd make a toast and drink their champagne, a tumbler-full for Jess and a shot-glass full for Josh. How simple it had been. And how special.

Josh needed something to do. He found Katie and Ben and suggested that they make hats to celebrate and write resolutions for themselves. Ben refused to be a part of it, but Katie eagerly set to work. Jess shook off some of her gloom and encouraged them and even sat down with them to participate in their project. When they finished, Katie insisted that they put their hats on and work on their resolutions, the way Josh and his mother had always done. But one by one they gave up. Each intention Josh wrote down would require some amount of mastery over himself. He didn't have that yet, and neither did Jess and Katie.

Steve was in a celebratory mood and permitted the family extended time together that evening. Music played during the time set aside for cocktails, and dinner began late. The feast was served at a table set with Jess's finest china, crystal and silver. Seven candles in tall crystal holders twinkled under the chandelier overhead, and soft music played in the background. It was the fanciest sight Josh had ever seen and he told Jess so, but although she smiled, he could see that her mind was elsewhere. He could only hope that she was seriously considering the possibility that this was the last New Year's Eve that she would spend in this house.

Steve slowly and deliberately filled his wine glass with more of his new French wine and turned to Jess and raised the glass to her. "You do have a knack, wife, I'll give you that. Here's to your talent and your beauty."

The children raised their water glasses and acknowledged his toast, careful not to appear too filled with praise for their mother, lest they insult their father, and, after a couple of sips of the deep burgundy Steve called the elixir of the gods, he walked over to where Jess was sitting and refilled her glass. He kissed her on the cheek and ran his hand across her breasts and whispered something in her ear. Her embarrassment and discomfort were apparent.

Later, Katie suggested, with more enthusiasm than was called for, "We should put on the hats we made, Mom!"

And then she turned to Steve to explain how Josh and his mom had spent their New Year's Eves.

"They both had champagne too," Ben interjected, "and made toasts to each other."

"My, my," Steve said. "Josh and his mom did it all, didn't they?"

It was an uncomfortable moment, and he thought for several seconds before telling Jess to get the Dom Perignon he had brought home that day.

"Let's pop that sucker and really start to celebrate," he said. "Oh, and bring out those pretty little snifter glasses for the kids. You're going to get your wish, Ben, and you're going to start with the finest. That stuff is damned expensive and shouldn't be wasted on kids, but what the hell."

Steve popped the cork with bravado, and when the bubbles and fizz came to the top and trickled over the bottle, Katie was mesmerized. "Oooo," she said, "it's so pretty."

Her enthusiasm pleased him, and he poured a little of the golden drink into the glasses and stood to make a toast.

"Here's to a great new year for us," he said. "May it be filled with success."

Finally, Jess and Katie cleared the dishes, and Steve retired alone to the sofa. By nine-thirty, he had fallen into a sotted sleep, and Jess and the children stood by and wondered what to do next. Remembering Josh's experiences, Katie pantomimed putting their coats on and pointed to the door. She wanted them to go outside.

They made a bold step into the night. The black sky twinkled with tiny silver sparkles, and the crunchy fallen snow glittered at their feet. They inhaled deeply and twitched their noses as the frosted air froze the hair there, and they lifted their faces and stuck out their tongues to catch fresh snowflakes, even as they blinked to remove their light heaviness from their eyelashes. The delicious music of quiet was interrupted only by Katie's occasional delighted giggles. They huddled together on the cold brick steps with their arms around each other to stay warm, and Josh had an epiphany.

"I know what I'm going to try to do," he announced. "I'm going to try to study how to make people strong and happy and learn how to write about it. I'm going to be like Jonathon, the Gull, but I'll do it by writing like that writer did. My resolution is to say and write what I think is right, no matter what - as long as it doesn't hurt other people. I'm going to help people by writing books that will get them to do what's good for them. And I'm going to start practicing now so that when I get older I'll be really good at it."

"Me too!" Katie said. "I'm going to help too. I'm going to be nice to everyone and make people happy too." She thought for a split second. "But I won't write to make people happy. Maybe I'll help people dance to be happy. Or maybe I'll draw. I could make pictures to make people happy. Maybe that's what I'll do." She looked at her family for approval. "I'll practice now too. I'm going to be an artist and dancer."

Jess drew her children closer, amazed by their depth and resiliency. Finally, she asked Ben if he had decided on a resolution. It took him a while, but finally he responded.

"I'm going to be stronger."

"In what way, honey?" Jess asked.

"In every way. No matter how hard, I'm going to be strong. I'm never going to let anyone hurt me, and I'm going to try to keep other people safe. Especially you, Mom. I'm going to find a way to keep you and other people from being hurt. That's my resolution."

There was a moment of silence among the four of them as the impact of his words settled on them. Katie was the first to respond.

"That's good, Ben. That's really good." Then she turned to Jess. "What about you, Mommy?" She whispered. "What's your resolution going to be?"

Jess couldn't get started. The children's resolutions were profound to her, and, in a sense, she had been diminished by them. It was Ben who came up with an idea for his mother.

"When things change, you could be a decorator for other people like you've always wanted to be. That would make you happy and other people happy too. You could do it. You could do so much, Mom. You deserve to do something good for yourself. You should start thinking about ways to do it."

Jess couldn't speak.

"Jonathon the gull would do it," Josh offered. "That's one of the things we're supposed to remember from the story: never let go of your dreams. No matter what."

He arranged them in a kind of huddle and asked everyone to hold hands.

"Remember Jonathon," he said. "Be the gull!"

The simple words became the children's mantra.

~

The following day went well enough. Mimi and Papaw and Maddie and Bill came to the house for the family's annual gathering to bring in the new year, and everyone was in a festive mood. The following day, Steve returned to work, and Josh was certain that Jess would immediately call Sam back and continue the discussion about leaving Steve. But the hours clicked away, and still the conversation hadn't taken place.

A neighbor invited the children over for lunch and to sled on their hill, and Katie and Ben gladly accepted, but Josh was too tense to do anything other than wait. He made several calls to Sam to confirm that the call had not taken place, and by midafternoon he was so frustrated that he decided to take matters into his own hands. Perhaps, he thought, she just needed a nudge, someone to encourage her to see how important it was to act. And he needed to make sure that she wasn't mad at him.

He knocked on her open door. She was sitting at her dressing table, examining her face in the mirror as if she were looking at a stranger.

Josh attempted some pleasantries that didn't work, and finally he took a deep breath and went directly to the point.

"I know you talked to Sam. And I know that you might be mad at him and me."

He waited for a response, some encouragement, but Jess remained very quiet.

"I couldn't help it," he continued. "I kept everything a secret until the night when you were so hurt. Things were so bad. I couldn't help it. I just needed to talk to somebody, and I called Sam to just talk. But he came right out and asked what was wrong, and things just kept coming out of my mouth about how you were hurt and how Ben had been hurt and how he was thinking of leaving. I didn't mean to tell everything. I just couldn't help it."

Again he waited for a response, but it seemed as though Jess had no words left in her.

"Please don't be mad at us," Josh said. "We only want to help. That's all. Sam has someone to help. I think we should trust him."

Jess waited so long to respond that he was ready to leave, but finally she found her voice.

"I'm not mad," Jess said. "I know you meant well. I know Sam is trying to help."

Indecision stuck out all over her.

"But you don't understand," she began again. "You think you do, but you don't. Neither does Sam. There are so many things to consider. He makes it sound so simple. It isn't simple."

Josh could feel the heat rise in his face.

"But I do understand," Josh went on. "So does Sam. We've looked it up on the computer. He's talked to his friend. Other families leave. Moms and kids go to Shelters or they live with someone else. Everything we've read on the computer says you need help. Sam and his friend are ready to help."

When she said nothing, he decided to take another approach.

"It isn't right for you to keep letting Steve hurt you and Ben and Katie. No one has the right to hurt members of their family. Ben needs help. And Katie does too. Sam's trying to help us. He's trying to protect us."

Jess buried her face in her hands, and Josh saw again how incredibly tired and disconsolate she was. She seemed totally hopeless.

"I was going to work it out, Josh. I didn't want to get everyone else involved. It's my problem. I don't want their pity or their disgust. I was going to sort it all out myself."

And just like that, all of the boy's confidence and good intentions imploded, and he couldn't make the thoughts that he had had get back into focus. He couldn't get past his disappointment in her inability to act even as he experienced guilt for talking about her behind her back. And quick, electric thoughts went through his mind about what his life would be like if she didn't accept his father's help. He could be like Ben.

He got up and walked to the door. He had done a bad job and had ruined everything. He put his hand on the door knob and looked back at Jess. There was no victory for her either. She sat like a lost child. When she looked up at him, her eyes were filled with hopelessness. But it wasn't over. Something inside him – a very fine thread of consciousness - wove itself slowly around through all of his other thoughts and finally shoved through them.

All of the promises they had made to each other just two days ago to be strong and to follow their dreams, all of the plans for his own future, and all of the memories of the struggles and the strength of his mother cried out to him.

Never give up and never give in, she had told him over and over again. *One more time*, a voice inside him said; *trust what you know to be right.*

He turned back to Jess.

"I know you want to change things, but you're afraid," he told her. "If it's any help, my mom was afraid too. No one knew how afraid she was about her depression. And there were times when she was so lonely. But she stayed strong. She got help. Sam and I just want you to know that you don't have to figure it all out alone. Doctors and lawyers can help you. And we can too. Families help each other."

His father's words came back to him crystal-clear.

"There are thousands of people out there, millions even when you think about the whole world, who have had the same problems we have, and they get help. There are laws and people who will help us. We shouldn't hide anymore. We don't have to. We have the right to be happy and free. Remember our New Year's resolutions? Katie and Ben and I made a pact. We're going to be The Gull."

He went to his room and sat on the floor, feeling hollow. He had nothing else to give. He was done. All of the planning with Sam, all of his own research, his practicing to get ready to talk with Jess, his worry and frustration and his hope, his desperate hope – it all clamored around him and left him exhausted. He curled up on the bed, wanting to shut down, to feel nothing.

And suddenly Jess was standing in front of him.

"You and Sam are right. I know that. I'm not mad. It's just that once I start the process, that's it. There's no going back. As horrible as it's been, there have been some good times. It's hard to let go of the good times. I know that's hard for people to understand."

"No, it isn't," Josh told her. "Not for me. I understand how mixed up you can get when people are sick. Mom and I had some pretty bad times, and it was hard sometimes to get over them. But the good ones made up for the bad. She tried so hard. She never gave up. She was a fighter. When it was good – when she was good – it was the best. And when it was bad, it was really horrible. And she hated that. But she never tried to hurt anyone. She couldn't help how she was. She hurt herself mostly. She wanted to be better. She loved so deep. You don't know how deep she loved. She never, ever hurt anybody on purpose."

Jess sat down beside him, and to give herself just a little more time to get the courage to make the call, she asked him to tell her more about the relationship he had had with his mother. He told her everything from start to finish - everything about his mother's diary and his journal, about what a good person his mother was and how wrong Steve was about her. He showed her the diary and let her hold it. He told her how happy his mom had been most times even though she had serious problems and depression and that she was happy because she was free and saw the beauty in everything, every little creature, every little rain drop, every leaf, and every good person. He explained that they had been poor, but they were happy most of the time, even during her bad times, because she was a fighter and went out every day she could to suck up life around her and be a part of it all. And she had taken him along with her. He had never doubted her love.

"Mom believed you have to grab the wind by the tail and enjoy the ride, and when things don't always go right and you fall off, you just have to get right back on and keep trying. And especially, she told me that we have to be honest with ourselves and with others or we get confused and mess up. Sometimes I swear she comes to me to remind me about that. I feel her here."

And then he told her about how his relationship had grown with Katie and Ben and what that meant to him.

"I had always wanted a real family with brothers and sisters," he told her, "and now I have it. I want to live with my dad when all of this is over. But Katie and Jamie will always be like a brother and sister. It's going to be hard to leave you and them."

He smiled at the good memories of them together and told Jess about how he had taken Katie outside to the garden at night and how they ran races together in their pajamas and how such a simple thing had meant so much to her. "We caught lightning bugs," he told her.

"And we signaled each other on the wall and met in Ben's room a lot just to talk and play games. I taught Ben Poker and Gin Rummy. Katie and I colored together sometimes and played Boggle. One evening we all sat out on the roof during a storm and got ourselves soaked. We read books together and made up stories. We really like going to the river and fishing and catching frogs. We've had a lot of good times."

Jess began to cry, harder than Josh had ever heard anyone cry before - even more than his mom who had cried often for her inability to control her moods and to bring stability out of the chaos of their lives. Jess cried because of the decisions she had made and not made, and the years of unhappiness and loss she and her children had endured because of her fear and indecision. And there was the guilt.

"What should we do now?" Josh prodded.

Jess gripped her sister's diary and, not yet filled with the confidence it takes to be decisive, looked to him for the answer.

He handed her his phone. "We can talk to Sam right now. All you have to do is press #1."

PART FIVE

Jess

Josh's honesty, his fear, his love for his cousins, his defense of his mother and father, and his unbelievable wisdom broke Jess's heart so that it could finally be put back together again.

When he handed her the cell phone Sam had given him for Christmas and told her to push #1, she began the process that would lead to freedom. She took it to her bedroom, the place of so much unhappiness.

Sam's compassion and gentle strength opened other wounds, and she cried again. He waited for her, and when he spoke again, his words fell like drops of soothing oil.

"Starting today, right this minute, you are changing your life and the lives of your children," he told her. "It's all good from here on, Jess. There have been hundreds, tens of thousands of women all over the world just like you who have discovered that the people they chose to love weren't the men they thought they were. They believed in the image that was presented to them. They wanted to believe in the dream. You aren't alone, Jess. You and Katie and Ben and my son have the right to be safe and happy. Starting today, you are going to

Skipping STONES

make it happen, and you will have all of the love and support and direction you need."

She turned back the covers of her bed and slipped under them, too exhausted to think of anything else, and she cried again until she was, blessedly, empty.

∽

She was awakened by pounding on the locked door, and for the first time in years, she took her time getting up to answer her husband's summons.

"I'm coming," she said in a voice she didn't recognize. "I'll be out in a minute."

Jess walked out the door. The dim light coming through the windows cast dreary shadows. The house was quiet. It had, she realized, been hours since she had talked to Sam. Steve stepped through the gloom.

"What in the hell is going on here?" He hissed, suddenly beside her.

She simply looked at him.

"I asked you a question. What's going on?" He was demanding but surprisingly quiet. "Why are all the doors locked? Why are the kids locked in their rooms?"

"We were resting," Jess told him calmly. "We're tired."

"Resting? You were resting? From what? What the hell is that?

"I don't know how else to answer you."

He looked at her in disbelief.

"What's going on, Jess? What are you hiding?"

"I'm not hiding anything," she continued. "It's been a very hard week. You know that. The kids and I have been together for over two weeks in this house. Sometimes when you go out, we go away to our own rooms for a little privacy. There isn't anything more to tell."

She had no idea where her answers were coming from.

He grabbed her by the arm when she stepped away from him.

"Let go of me," she said, and, miraculously, he did.

༺༻

School started the next day. Sam had instructed Josh to give his cell phone to Jess so that she could make calls and not be worried about Steve's knowing about them. Josh pressed the phone into her hand and gave her a quick "thumbs-up sign" just before he walked out the door.

She waited until after lunch. The mood between her and Sam was less urgent, but the conviction on his part was the same as the afternoon before. It was clear that he expected that the two of them would move forward, and his decisiveness and optimism encouraged her.

"I'm so sorry that you and Josh became involved in all of this," she said again.

"No apologies," he told her. "Let's not do those. I can't begin to tell you how often I've beat myself up for some of the decisions I've made throughout my life. I can't undo them, but I can learn from them and try to make things right." He chuckled. "God, life is just one big screw up after another if we really think about it. I try like hell not to worry about things I can't change. The past is gone, and because I can't get it back, I try to let it be a lesson and concentrate on each new day at a time."

Skipping STONES

And then he asked her, as if it were the most logical question in the world, "So what will your first step be?"

The question was meant to empower her, and it did. There were decisions to be made, and she would make them.

"I need to let my family know the truth," she told him. "I need to assure the kids that they're going to be all right. I should see a counselor who knows how to help with these kinds of things. Probably in that order."

She felt the strength that comes from decisiveness. Sam encouraged her to make the call to her parents as soon as the two of them hung up and suggested that she set up a time for them to come over. He reminded her that she was on her way to living without fear.

She wrote down on the pad in front of her, in big letters, *Call Mom and Dad! Live without fear!*

Before they said good-bye, Sam had a favor to ask.

"I would like to begin seeing Josh on a regular basis, if it's all right with you," he said.

It would, he explained, be very simple. All Jess would have to do was to write a note to Josh's principal, giving him permission for Josh to leave school and have lunch with him every Wednesday, beginning that week. She agreed. Decision-making is easier when it's done in a climate of trust.

"You're going to want custody right away, aren't you?" Jess asked.

"As soon as possible. Once you get the divorce, things should move faster. But let's take first things first."

"I know that he should be with you," she told him, "but I'll miss him so much."

Jess sat with the phone in her hand for a very long time. Finally, she reached for the note she had written to herself: *live without fear.* And slowly, very slowly, she dialed her parents' number. There were no preliminaries. When Mimi answered, she simply arranged for them to come to see her at ten the next morning.

"It's very important," she said, adding, "if you call between now and then and Steve answers, please don't tell him that we're meeting. And please don't tell Maddie. We'll talk with her later."

"What's wrong, Jess?" her mother asked. "Something's terribly wrong, isn't it? I can tell from your voice."

"It's a long story, Mom, and it's complicated," Jess told her. "Please, just come and give me time with you."

After the conversation, Jess spent a long time thinking about how she could possibly explain the past fourteen years of her life to her parents. Out of habit, she went back into the kitchen and climbed onto the counter to find one of her "sanity" aids that she kept hidden on the ledge above the sink. Automatically, she poured one of the sedatives into her hand, ready to tranquilize herself for the day. But something stopped her.

You don't need this, a voice inside her said. *You can manage this day on your own.* She studied the pill she was holding. The drugs had become her antidote against feeling and had dulled her resolve. She gripped the bottle firmly and climbed down from the counter and stood in front of the sink. Her hands and face were clammy, and she breathed hard. *Do you have the nerve? Do you have what it takes?*

She threw the entire supply down the disposal, one at a time, and felt a thrill run through her with each quick grind. Emboldened, she got down on her knees in front of the huge Viking stove and opened the drawer beneath the oven. Behind the grills and trays was the metal flask Josh told her he had seen her use. The contents of the flask followed the same path as the pills. It was liberating. She couldn't remember another time throughout her entire years of marriage when she had been so pro-active as that morning and the afternoon before.

She took an unhurried walk throughout the house. The children had made their beds and had rinsed out their sinks and put away all vestiges of their being children. Pillows on the sofas were still fluffed, tables were dust-free, closets were organized. The rugs didn't need to be vacuumed, she decided, and the few clothes in the clothes bags could wait to be washed. All was perfection, like a model home waiting to be bought and finally lived in.

Bundling up, she went outside for a long walk in the sunshine and made her way to the river where she sat on a log, absent-mindedly throwing small broken slivers of ice into the slow-moving current. There was so much to think about, including the fact that Josh and Sam would soon be together to work out their future. She was happy for them both, but she also envied their freedom to have that opportunity together. She thought about Katie and prayed that she would laugh and run and sing and dance that day with her teacher and friends and be truly happy. And she prayed that Ben would be able to push away bad thoughts and would also experience some kind of happiness that afternoon. *Our time is coming,* she repeated to herself. *Our time is coming.*

Later, after a very hot and deliciously slow bubble bath, she loaded the stereo with jazz and sat in her robe, letting her mind wander to wherever it wanted to go, suddenly aware that, for the first time in a very long time, she was at peace.

And there, prominent in her reverie, was Sam, the last person she had ever thought would come back into her life and help change it.

She had met him during Christmas vacation her first year at college when Maddie had a party to get all of her old friends from home together. One of those friends had brought Sam along. Jess was helping in the kitchen, putting snacks on trays and pulling things in and out of the oven, and in walked the tall, lanky, blond, and very handsome stranger who introduced himself and asked if she needed help. She had trouble looking into his vibrant green eyes without blushing.

She and Maddie were taken, their future lives planned with Steve and Bill. But Becky was still available, and immediately after they introduced her to Sam, their passionate romance began. Sam brought solidarity and purpose and balance to Becky's life, and she brought to him spontaneity and unrelenting support. They were opposites, ying and yang, but it worked. For a while.

Sam had been a part of all of their lives, and Jess and he were especially close. They had been drawn together from the beginning, and their fondness for each other was apparent. Sam was guileless, incapable of deceit of any kind. He said what he meant, and he meant what he said. And he was creative and saw beauty in the simplest things, and that creativity ensured the bond between them.

Jess was in love with Steve, but she let Sam into her heart. Steve was never able to accept the friendship. His jealousy was always seething just beneath the surface, no matter what kind of assurances Jess gave him that the relationship she had with Sam was purely platonic.

Sam dropped out of Ohio State at the end of his third year and enrolled in a renowned cooking school in West Virginia.

Skipping STONES

Mimi was disappointed in Sam and had no desire to have a daughter of hers married to a chef. She refused to believe in his plan to someday own a string of restaurants. The fighting began, and Becky's solution was to drop out of school too and marry the love of her life and finish her education at a small community college close to Sam.

Their marriage was a tempestuous one, not because of lack of love, but because of Becky's health issues and Sam's dedication to fulfilling his dream. They struggled financially, and Becky needed much more time from him than he could give at that time. Mimi and Papaw wanted more for their daughter and placed blame for her unhappiness onto Sam, refusing his explanations of what he had learned about Becky's condition. In the end, Sam had lost the battle.

And here he was again, back in the lives of the family whose love and acceptance he had sought and had never grasped, giving his old and dear friend the chance to turn her life around and to fulfill her own dreams.

꿍

Jess almost lost the courage to talk with her parents, knowing that once she told her story, she would never be able to take it back. All of the ugliness and deceit and failure would be exposed. And the sadness. She and Steve had loved each other once. At least she had loved him. Once, he had been all that she had ever wanted in a man, and the memory of her love for him still hurt. Exposing the truth would be closing the door to everything good that they had once had together. Ironically, what she was about to confess felt almost like betrayal.

Mimi and Papaw arrived a few minutes before ten, and at first Mimi made an attempt at light chit-chat, but it was awkward and fell flat. It was her father who asked Jess to sit down at the table with them and tell them what was on her mind. And so her cleansing began.

"Things aren't what they appear to be here," she told them. "This isn't the happy home we've pretended it is. It's all a lie, all made up. I've pretended most of our married life, and the children have endured it since they were born. The truth is that we have no life outside these walls and we live in fear inside them. Up until the past month or so, I didn't know the name for the way we live, but now I do. I've kept it all a secret. But I can't keep the secret anymore."

Jess took a deep breath and forced herself to go on.

"Steve isn't Mr. Perfect, like you think he is," she said. "He's successful, obviously, but beyond that he isn't anything like what you think. He's cruel. He hurts us."

Her parents stared at her, unsure of what they had heard. Papaw was the first to begin to understand.

"Are you saying that Steve is deliberately hurting you and the kids in some way? That he's violent? Is that what you're saying?"

"He punishes the children, but not in the ordinary way," Jess explained. "If he gets mad at one of us, he punishes us all. Things have gotten worse this past year. He didn't hurt them physically before, but that's changing. And the emotional abuse…it's been going on for a long time. They believe they're bad children. He tells them they are and threatens to send them or me away. He hurt Ben before and after his Christmas school performance this year. It's just a matter of time, maybe, before he hurts him and Katie like he hurts me.

Her parents felt the cold of hurtful discovery seep through them.

"And this has been going on for a long time?" her father asked.

"For years, Dad. Ever since Ben was born. I've tried hard to change it, to make things right, but nothing I do helps. It's getting worse. All three of the children know what he's doing to me. Their lives aren't normal. I know that now. They are not normal. Josh has made me see the truth. I denied it all until Josh and Sam confronted me about it."

It took a while for her father and mother to register the enormity of what she was telling them.

"Start at the beginning, Jess," her father finally said, taking her hand and holding it tightly. "Take your time and tell us the whole story. We're with you, Jess. Tell it. Tell us everything."

And so she did. She told them everything, from the very beginning when she had met Steve to their lives in Chicago, the birth of their children, the progression of his sickness. And as she talked, she became aware of the enormity of her denial. Originally, she had made excuses for Steve because of her continued belief in him and their dream; later she had rejected the truth because of her pride; finally she had hidden behind fear.

"I've made such a mess of things," she confessed. "I've failed everyone."

"Oh, Jess," her mother said. "You've never been a failure. Please don't say that. Why, look at what you've created. Look at your beautiful children. You're a wonderful daughter."

"But my beautiful children are suffering, Mom. They always have. And I've let them. This home I've created is filled with sadness. I let it happen. And I've lied to you."

"So Katie and Ben and Josh know what Steve has done to you?" Papaw confirmed.

"Yes. Up until recently, they never saw what was happening, but they knew. They heard the arguments. Now he doesn't try to hide anything. He lashes out at me and them whenever and however he feels like it. And it's more deliberate. It's almost as if he plans when to hurt us sometimes. We all prepare ourselves for it in our own ways. And his punishment is much worse than ever before."

"Oh, my God," her mother said. "How's it possible that we didn't know any of this?"

"The story about your ribs was a lie, right?" her father said. "Steve did it to you."

He cried then, and his tears completed the break in Jess's heart.

"Oh, Jess, honey, why didn't you tell all of this when it started?" he said. "All of these years…you've been suffering all of this time, living in hell, and we didn't know. Why didn't you come to us at the beginning?"

That was the one question that Jess knew she could never answer satisfactorily. Even as she tried to explain, she knew that none of it would make sense to them. They could somehow understand the abuse, but they would not be able to understand why she stayed. The telling of her story was turning out the way she had feared it would.

She did her best to explain.

"I kept thinking that it would get better," she said. "I didn't want to disappoint anyone. I didn't want to be a failure. For a long time, he would hurt me but then tell me how sorry he was. He told me what I had to do to make things better, and I tried. I really thought that I could change everything. He had meant everything to me. We had had so many dreams. It wasn't all bad all of the time. But over the years, it kept getting worse and I didn't know how to get out of it. He told me that I would lose everything if I left him. I didn't know how I could support myself. I thought I could protect the kids, but I can't.

"I've been so scared. Scared to leave and scared to stay. He said he'd get custody of the kids. I can't imagine that. I can't lose them. I just can't. I'm so sorry, Mom and Dad. So sorry. I don't want to hurt you. I don't want to be a burden to you, but I can't do this without you. I see that now."

She told them how Josh initiated the talks between her and Sam and how he showed her the packet of information about domestic violence he had put together. And she showed them the cell phone Sam had given Josh so that they could talk together without any danger of Steve's finding out about it.

"Sam and Annie gave Josh courage, and Josh helped me find mine."

"He's broken you off from everything and everybody," Papaw said. "He has total control over all of you. That was his plan from the beginning."

Papaw walked around the table and sat down beside Jess and hugged her like he used to when she was a little girl.

"Oh, my dear Jessica," he said. "We've been so blind. But it's going to be okay. We're going to make everything all right again. We've let you down. We should have seen it. But we didn't. I'm so ashamed that I never looked closer."

He wiped his eyes and looked directly at her.

"I'm going to get you and the kids out of here. Today. You'll live with us for as long as you want to or need to. We'll do whatever we have to do because we love you and those children. We will never let you down again. I give you my word. We're getting you out of here right now, and then we're going to call the police and press charges. He's done."

"It isn't that simple, Dad," Jess said, panicking. "Steve's told me that he'll fight to get sole custody of the kids if I ever think about leaving him. He knows half the judges in town. I have to have a plan, Dad. I can't just walk out. There's no proof that he's hurt me. I've never reported it. I can't ask the kids to back up my story. I would never put them through that. Oh God, Dad. I can't even pay for a lawyer to represent me."

"Money is the least of your concerns," he assured her. "Your mother and I'll take care of all that. We're going to get all of you to our home. Your old home. That's all we're going to think about right now."

It made all the sense in the world to leave right then and there except for what she had read about the danger of leaving.

"He could come after us," she insisted. "Or he could say that I abandoned him, and it would end up being my fault," she said. "Sam has a lawyer friend who knows all about this. He said that there are procedures to follow. It's taken me a long time to get to this point, Dad. I have to do it right, or I could lose the kids or worse. And he can't find out. The lawyer said that if the husband suspects that the wife is leaving, the violence gets worse."

"He can't get to you and the kids if you're at our house, Jess. If he tries, we'll call the police and lock him up."

And still she was undecided.

"I need to prepare the kids. They need some time."

"For what, honey? Time for what? What if he comes in tonight furious about something? What will happen then? No. We'll get you out of here and figure out later what we're going to do."

But still she hesitated, imprisoned by old habits, able to only think in small pieces of time.

"Let's talk again tomorrow with Maddie and Bill if they're available. And I'd like to have Sam here too."

Mimi bristled when Jess mentioned Sam's name.

"He's been wonderful, Mom," Jess told her. "I know you don't think much of him, but there's a story there too. There's so much to tell. I wouldn't be here having this conversation if it weren't for him. And he's Josh's father. Josh confided in him first. Sam's been right there for him in so many ways since Becky's death. He's a good man, Mom."

"I don't have a problem with Sam's meeting with us," Papaw intervened. "If he's helped Jess and the kids and is willing to help more, then he should be a part of it. As Jess says, he is Josh's father."

And he encouraged Jess again to begin packing to leave. It was too fast for her.

"I haven't talked to the kids about any of this," she protested. "I can't just pack them up in a matter of minutes and make them leave the only home they've ever known. We need to have a plan of some kind. I need some professional advice. I need to talk with Sam's friend."

"Let's at least start to get some suitcases packed," Mimi suggested. "Just enough things to get you and the kids through a few days while we figure things out. The courts will see to it that you can move back here once it's known what he's put you through. We'll take some essentials and make more trips as we need to."

Finally, Jess was convinced.

They were heading for the attic room to get the suitcases when the doorbell rang. They had lost track of time. Katie was home, and her arrival put them in a tailspin. And since the boys would be home soon too, Jess whispered to her mother that their leaving would have to wait until the next day.

෴

All of the family, including Sam, gathered at Mimi and Papaw's house the next day and discussed the situation in detail.

As Jess suspected, Maddie was quick to react.

"That bastard," she said. "I knew it. I thought about it right after I left your house the day we met the last time when I was so mad at you. I almost turned around. But I told myself that it couldn't be true. And then when you had your "accident," it seemed even more possible that I was right. I almost came right out and asked you, but I figured if it was anything like that, you'd step forward. My God, Jess. Why didn't you leave him at the beginning? Why in God's name did you stay?"

Just as the day before with her parents, Jess couldn't offer reasons to her sister. She would no longer offer excuses. There was an uncomfortable silence around the table until Sam broke through it.

"I'm amazed at how much information there is on the internet about all of this," he began. "I started looking it up when I realized how guarded and uncommunicative Josh was. Something just wasn't right, and my gut instinct was that he was somehow being mistreated. He broke down during Christmas vacation, and that's when I called my lawyer friend, Boake Karnanski. He confirmed what I had read."

He glanced at Jess to try to determine if he should go on, and her expression was one of relief.

"But getting to your question, Maddie," he continued, "Boake told me that women like you and Jess would be called 'women of means' in the world of domestic violence. They often stick it out their entire lives because talk about abuse among affluent men and women is almost taboo or it's simply something that no one would imagine was going on with people they know. Just like you, most of us just simply can't understand it. But, thankfully, there are attorneys and judges and police forces and people high up in state and federal governments now who are beginning to see the enormity of the problem and are trying to do something about it. My friend is one of those people."

He had turned the conversation around, and Papaw kept it moving forward.

"Tell us more about this attorney," he said.

"Well, as I said, he's a friend of mine," Sam continued. "I've known Boake for years and have a lot of respect for him. He has quite a background. He's actually a trial lawyer who got interested in domestic violence issues years ago. I've never asked him why. For whatever reason, he's been pro-active here in Ohio to get laws passed to protect victims and is very involved in initiatives to provide state funding for shelters and educational programs in schools and various agencies and has represented a lot of women in court on a pro bono basis. He's now on the board of the local shelter here in town."

"He sounds like our man," Papaw said.

"I've had several conversations with him, and he said that we need to move quickly, but cautiously. Divorces are never simple, but separating from someone who's an abuser is something entirely different. There are procedures to follow, things to do to guarantee the safety of everyone involved and to get it over with as quickly as possible. As we discussed yesterday, if you'd like to meet with him, he's available."

General conversation broke out at that point, and the consensus was that Jess would meet with Mr. Karnanski immediately and get out of her home as soon as he told her to. Jess listened to it all as if she were an impartial observer until, finally, all faces turned back to her.

"I'll try to explain everything to Katie and Ben," she said slowly but with an edge of determination in her voice. "I have no idea how they'll react – especially Katie. I'll pack. I'll move in with you, Mom and Dad, and I promise we won't be a burden.

We'll stay just as long as we have to. I'll call Mr. Karnanski. And I'll try to keep it all hidden from Steve."

She was close to panic. The list of things that she needed to do immediately seemed impossible to her. It had been a very long time since she had made any decisions, and she had never been required to do anything as dangerous as leaving her husband. She needed every single person around that table to help her.

"I'd feel better if all of you, if you can, would go with me to talk with Mr. Karnanski. I can't begin to tell you what it means to…" She couldn't finish.

Josh

Everything moved fast. Jess told Josh about the meeting with Sam and her family, and she confided that they would all meet soon with Mr. Karnanski. She also told him that he couldn't share any of the information with Katie and Ben because she was afraid that Steve would be able to trick them - especially Katie - into telling him everything. It was a tall order for Josh, especially after his and Ben's brief conversation at the river, but he quickly agreed to it. There was only one thing that worried him. Jess was different. Josh could see it, and he was afraid that Steve could too.

Josh filled the pages of his journal with his dreams about how things would soon change for all of them and tried to sort through what would happen if things turned out wrong. At the top of his list of bad things that could happen, he wrote that he could be given to Steve and would never have Sam as his dad. At the top of his list of good things was that he would live with Sam and have a real father. The hours and days crept along, and he went through them wrapped up in himself, unable to think of anything except his "what if's."

Skipping STONES

Josh walked to the school office the following Wednesday at eleven-forty-five sharp and found Sam already there, talking comfortably with the principal and his secretary. Walking out of the school with his father felt better than good.

They had lunch at a busy and very noisy restaurant not more than twelve minutes away. To begin, they ordered up a huge platter of the specialty, Heart-Stoppin' Potato Skillet, a layered combination of fried potatoes, cheddar cheese, sour cream, and chives, followed by grilled cheese and ham sandwiches. Josh convinced his father to try a chocolate and cherry coke, his mother's favorite.

"By the way," Sam said with a big grin, "when am I going to get that Christmas gift you made me?"

Josh had forgotten to bring it and promised he'd bring it along next week.

They talked then about Jess and the big change that would soon take place in all of their lives, and Sam encouraged Josh to "hang tough."

"It's going to be tough on everyone for a while," he said, "and Jess will need all the help she can get."

When it was time to leave, Sam reached across the booth and put his hand on his son's arm.

"You're a very brave and very caring young man," he said. "I'm proud of you. You've been through so much, much more than anyone should have to go through at your age – or at any age– and yet I know that you'll be all right. I want you to know that I..."

He paused, clearly struggling with his emotions. And Josh knew exactly how he felt.

"I just want you to know," Sam continued, "that I'm glad I'm back in your life. I'll never let you down again. I promise."

There wasn't enough time to get through all of the news, plans, and emotions they had to share, and they were late getting back to school. Sam walked Josh back inside and remembered an envelope in his coat pocket. "Please give this to Jess when you can."

Jess

When the children came home on Wednesday, Jess searched Josh's face for some sign of how the lunch went with Sam and was relieved to see his broad smile. Later, when Katie and Ben were engrossed in their games, Josh ran back to her with an envelope in his hand. "It's from Sam," he whispered to her. She went to her room and opened it.

Dear Jess,
Thank you so much for making this special day possible for me. I hope your day has gone well. Call me so that we can talk about it.
I have a habit of picking up posters or pictures that have meaningful pithy sayings on them – just a silly way to help me remember how to live my life and to remind me to "stay connected and be real." Here's one that I especially like. Maybe you will too. "I stand, I reach, I yearn, I bellow, and finally I live. What do you do?"
I love that! In the end, it's all up to each of us, isn't it? Finally you're going to really live too.
Take care of yourself. Call me!
Sam

Skipping STONES

Jess read the note several times and memorized the saying. It summarized the stages in her life. She had reached. Oh, how she had yearned. She had bellowed silently. Finally she was going to live and recapture joy. Tearing the note into tiny bits, she stuffed them into the bottom of the trash compactor, reminding herself to be careful: Steve continued his mindless search everywhere for everything.

The meeting with Mr. Karnanski couldn't be arranged until the following Thursday, and Jess decided to stay where she was until she could get his advice. That week was one of the longest in her entire life. She and Josh carefully maneuvered their way around the incredible situation they were in, and Ben and Katie continued to walk through their lives, oblivious to the undercurrents that could splinter the base of their lives and alter them forever.

With Sam's encouragement during their long phone calls, she began to involve herself in new activities such as surfing the web to acquaint herself with the latest trend in the design industry, watching news programs that would make her feel more a part of the bigger world, and journaling for self-discovery. She was aware that Steve knew that something was different. He called frequently to make sure that she was where he wanted her to be and probed her and the children with frightening calm to find evidence of betrayal. When he came home from work angry, he didn't strike out. He was almost solicitous of her. His control over himself increased Jess's fear and imbalance.

On Wednesday, Sam and Josh had their second lunch together.

Josh

    Josh and his dad went to a popular pizza shop Sam had heard about but never tried. They settled into the booth together and ordered their lunches and initially made a point of talking only about positive things. Josh asked about his Grandma Annie, and Sam told him that she was buying decorating magazines by the armful to help give her ideas on how to bring her home up-to-date.

    "It's a good diversion for her," Sam explained, "but it's also frustrating to her."

    "That reminds me. I brought your Christmas present," Josh told his father, taking a package out of his backpack. "I hope you don't think it's anything big. It's just something I made. You don't even need to use it if you don't want to."

    "Should I close my eyes?" Sam teased.

    Josh laughed. "Mom used to make me do that. She'd say, 'open your hands and close your eyes, and I'll give you a big surprise.' She made me do it even when I got older. It was pretty babyish, but I went along with it."

    Sam was clearly impressed by the workmanship Josh had put into the "Sam's Place" sign.

"It'll be perfect in my new restaurant," he said, "but something could happen to it there. Might even get carried away. You know what? It would look great in my kitchen at home. That's where it's going. I have the perfect place for it there in a prime spot in the kitchen. That's where my friends and I spend our time. They'll get a big kick out of it, and I'll see it every day and will think of you."

Josh was beyond happy, but behind the happiness loomed all of the ambiguities of his life. There were so many questions to be answered and so many issues to be resolved in the next several weeks, but there was a question – one of the biggest questions of all for him – that could be answered right then and there. His mother had always told him that, if something was bothering him, it was always best to put it out there and deal with the answers he got. He decided to follow her advice while he still had the chance.

"I need to tell you something," he said, blurting out the words. "I told you before that I have Mom's diary, but what I didn't tell you is that I've read it."

He waited for Sam to react, but his face was inscrutable.

"I...I know that you and she were thinking of getting back together, that you talked a lot on the phone and you saw each other. She always told me everything, but she never told me about any of that. She wrote that you and she were going to really get back together when the time was right. Is it true? Were you going to come back for Mom and me? Were you going to be her husband and my dad again?"

Sam had thought for months about how he would explain to his son the new relationship between him and Becky- contemplated when the time would be right, waited for the perfect moment. And here was Josh, asking the all-important question. The directness of it caught Sam off-guard, and he took some time to respond.

"We had started seeing each other again several months before…before the accident," he began. "It was right around that Christmas, as I told you."

Josh sat very still and tried to control his breathing while his father searched for the right words.

"We thought we should take it slow," Sam finally said. "We didn't want to ever hurt you again, and we didn't want to face your mother's family until we were sure it would work out. We were sure. It didn't take us long to get there. Yes. We were going to be married again, and I was finally going to be a real dad to you."

The affirmation made Josh unbelievably happy.

"That must be why she changed last spring," Josh said. "She even looked different. I asked her what was going on because there was such a huge difference. I knew she was back on her pills to make her feel better, and they had always helped, but this was different. She told me that I'd find out soon. She was more than happy that day we went on the bike ride. I think that was her happiest day maybe."

Sam leaned back and covered his eyes with his hand, and something frightening embedded itself into Josh. It took a huge effort for him to ask the next question.

"When were you going to tell me?" he whispered, and he realized he was trembling inside. "When were you going to start being my dad again?"

"Oh, Josh."

The boy knew. Deep down, he had known for a very long time but couldn't accept it. He asked the question again even though he dreaded the answer.

"It was that Sunday, wasn't it? It was going to happen that day we took our bike ride."

Josh heard Sam release his breath as he reached out for him.

"I decided the day of her death that I would never lie to you about anything," he said. "Lies get in the way."

Josh couldn't control the moan coming out of his throat.

"Let's get out. Let's get out of here, Josh. We can't talk here. Hold on," Sam said.

Josh let his father guide him to the car and, once inside, out of the way of questioning eyes, he released everything inside, every bit of sadness, every piece of guilt he had borne for the past eight months.

"Why didn't you come with us that morning?" He yelled. "Why did the two of you shut me out? It didn't have to be that way. She turned around to look at me. She didn't see that van because she was looking at me. She looked to see where I was. The van came right out of the driveway, and she never saw it. We didn't have to be there! We could have been with you. I begged her to go. She said no, but I begged her. And I killed her! You could have stopped it! Why didn't you tell us not to go?"

Sam had asked himself the same questions and had fought with his own guilt and remorse for the outcome of that ride day after day and night after night ever since the accident. The questions and accusations hurt even more when spoken aloud by his son.

"I can't tell you how many times I've asked myself those same things," he said through his own tears. "Why did we wait so long? There was nothing I wanted more than to be a part of your lives again. We thought we were doing the right thing. That's all that I can tell you, Josh. We made plans, planned it all, including how we were going to tell you and the rest of the family. We wanted to make sure that we had all of the answers ready for all of the questions we knew we'd get from everyone. You have no idea how many times I've thought about how I could have called that morning. I ask myself every single day why I didn't. And every single day I think about how different everything might have been if I had. It isn't anyone's fault. I've spent every day since her death thinking about all of the "what if's," analyzing every single decision your mother and I made together and the ones I made without her. She was going to tell you that afternoon. And if you were happy about it, I was going to meet you that night or the next one. The last time I spoke with her was that morning when she was on her way to pick up breakfast."

Josh had wanted the truth, but the truth was too hard to accept. All of that time lost. All of those days and weeks and years that went by, and he without a father. And the one day when all three of their lives could have come together, he had insisted on going for a bike ride.

"My God," Sam went on, "for months, I blamed the driver of the van. I hated her for not seeing Becky. I called her and went to see her. I needed to know how it happened. She was in pain too. She'll never get over the accident either, and she's angry at the hurt it's caused her and her family. She didn't see Becky, and Becky didn't see her. There were long shadows. She eased her way onto the road and suddenly Becky was there."

Josh closed his eyes against his pain. His mother didn't see the van because she was watching him. If only he had been closer to her. If only he hadn't been so afraid. If only.

"It's a horrible combination of things, Josh. But you know what? We never know from day to day what's going to happen to any of us. Most things are out of our control. It's easy to say, once we know the sequence of how things happened, that we might have done this or changed that and things would have been different. But life isn't like that. We have no way of knowing what the future holds for us. We do our best to protect ourselves, but in the end, we're just like leaves in the wind. We try to hold on, but we're carried along by chance, by the direction the wind blows. Why did that woman choose that minute to pull out in front of Becky? All of our lives were changed by just a few seconds."

To Josh, it felt as though his entire life had absolutely been carried on by chance, that all the pain and unhappiness and joy and love he and his mother had experienced had been beyond their control. Just like his father was saying, they had been like leaves in the wind, even that awful day when she died.

"And you know what else?" Sam continued. "There's no way we can change what has already happened. All we can do is be the best we can be today and hope that we're prepared for whatever comes at us tomorrow. And we can make up our minds to be happy. I've wallowed in my guilt, but I can't continue to do that because if I do, my life will become meaningless. I choose happiness over sadness. It's a choice we all have."

Josh weighed his father's words. Life had been terrible since that awful day, made even worse by having been sent to Jess's home. But if he hadn't been sent there, he would never have known her and his cousins the way he knew them now. He loved them. They were family. He would never have lived with his grandparents and learned about their deep love for him. Things were changing. Jess and Katie and Ben were, in a way, starting all over again. Their lives were going to be so much better. Would they have gotten to this point if Sam and he hadn't become such an important part of their lives? With the help of Sam and the truth, things were going to be better for everyone. Everyone's lives were moving forward. There was hope for them all.

"Blaming ourselves and feeling guilt won't bring her back, Josh," Sam continued. "I know that now, but I didn't think that way that first day I saw you again at Mimi's house. I was in a bad place then too. I had lost her and you for the second time. I talk to myself every day and every night about you and her and the accident and what might have been, and I have to stop it and you do too."

His arms relaxed around Josh, but the boy continued to lean against him, absorbing his strength.

"I can't tell you how many times your mom and I biked together," Sam told him.

"And she was always way ahead of me. She had no fear. She never waited for anyone. You know that. I can see her turning around to wave to you, because she did the same thing with me at least once on every ride we took together, usually more, signaling me to hurry up. My God, she even walked faster than I did. And drove faster. She teased me for being so slow. On normal days, she had one speed, fast. On good days, faster. She had so much energy. She was a dare-devil, a hurling, free-for-all dare-devil. That's just one of the many things that I loved about her. She scared the crap out of me so many times, I can't begin to count them. And she was so strong in the face of everything. She had so much determination. She needed to be outside, Josh. You know that. She would have gone biking or jogging that beautiful day even if you hadn't wanted to. She needed to test her strength. She needed that sense of freedom. That's just the way she was."

Sam had described the essence of Josh's mother so vividly that Josh, in the shelter of his father's arms, could almost feel her there.

"She was so many things wrapped up all together, wasn't she?" He finally said. "Just when you thought you had her all figured out, she'd surprise you with something. Do...do you think she's in a good place now? Do you think that's possible? She has to be happy knowing we're together, don't you think?"

"Absolutely."

"So I'll be moving in with you as soon as Jess gets divorced," Josh thought out loud. "But it's going to be real hard to leave Jess and Ben and Katie. We're real close."

"I know that. But we're going to make things good for them too," Sam said. "I promise."

When Sam took him back to school, Josh didn't feel so alone as he had after the other visits, because he had answers he needed. He felt lighter. If Mr. Karnanski was any good at what he does, and if the judge would be fair, he'd soon be his father's real son again and Jess and Katie and Ben would be safe. Before they said good-bye, Sam handed him another note for Jess.

She read it in the privacy of her room before Steve came home.

Hi, Jess

Tomorrow is the big day, and I know that you're really nervous about it. That's understandable. But everything is going to be so good. You're going to enjoy Boake. He's a great guy, a no-nonsense guy, and I trust him 100% to do the job well for us.

I have another quote for you: "It is never too late to be what you might have been." It's so simple, isn't it? But it's a good reminder. George Eliot came up with that one. Someone gave it to me in the form of a bookmark. Just want you to know that I absolutely feel that you can be just about anything you want to be, and you're on your way. I'm looking forward to watching you become that "old" Jess I knew all of those years ago.

I'll see you tomorrow. Let's wear smiles.
Sam

Jess

Sleep was impossible for her the night before the meeting, and she fought to keep her body still. Slowly and painstakingly she crept out of bed. The living room glowed in the moonlight, and she walked herself into it and stood at the large bay window, hoping that this would be the last night that she would have to sneak to do what her body and mind intended for her. She felt Steve's presence before she saw him.

"So here you are," he said, moving closer.

Jess stepped away from him, certain what he was after, unable to hide the defiance and repugnance in her eyes. He pulled her back to him and studied her.

"You're different, Jess," he said. "What's going through that mind of yours? Tell me what you're up to." And even as he spoke, he stroked her breasts and reached between her legs. "Your little mystery makes you more exciting."

The thought of what he intended sickened her. I will not let him do it this time, she thought. I will have control over my own body and mind. She pushed him away, ready to take the blows that she had never been strong enough to fend off and fight the indignity of rape. Steve staggered backwards, a look of confusion on his face, and in that instant, Jess darted around him to run toward the stairs and find safety behind a locked door.

But there was movement there, another body moving hesitantly toward her in the shadows.

"No!" she yelled, and shook her head in warning to her son, even as Steve grabbed her from behind. She turned her body to her husband as her eyes watched Ben bring his hands to his head and rush away to the safety of his room.

PART SIX

Family

The next day, a very tall, totally bald man with an unlighted cigar tucked between his thumb and index finger walked confidently from his office to greet Jess and her family. Sam introduced them to his friend, Mr. Karnanski.

"Call me Boake," he said, and motioned them to the conference room.

The session began immediately.

"I want to make a couple of points very clear before we begin to discuss the procedures for getting Jess through the divorce," he told them when they were seated. "And that's what it is, by the way, right? It's a divorce. We're not taking the man to court to put him in jail. We're getting you, Jess, out of a bad situation with as little trouble as possible. Am I right on that?"

She nodded in agreement, feeling confident already by the lawyer's no-nonsense manner.

"Now, the reason why Sam asked me to help with your divorce is because, due to the nature of your marriage, things could get a little complicated. That's why I'm here and not a divorce attorney. I'm not going to whitewash the possible difficulties. Let's hope your husband is logical and wants to play nice once we confront him with our case against him. That way, the proceedings will go well with the judge, and we can all go home and get back to what we all like to do.

Several piles of material were stacked in front of him. He picked up the first of them and passed around lists of websites that explained abuse, as well as a list of ten specific and basic facts about the subject.

"I suggest that all of you do some research about the subject if you haven't already. The family's taking on a real responsibility for Jess and her children, and you'll want to know as much as you can so there aren't too many surprises."

He picked up another form from another stack in front of him.

"I wish we could have met sooner, Jess, so that we could have proceeded immediately, but I've been able to prepare a big chunk of our case based on our phone calls.

"Here are copies of the divorce papers, Jess. Read them very, very carefully before you sign them. Any questions, call me by Monday. I'm prepared to serve them to Steve at his office at four-thirty on Tuesday if you believe that everything is in order. I've called in some chits to a couple of friends of mine in order to facilitate things."

"Wait," Jess said. "It will begin as early as that?"

He looked at her unflinchingly and answered her question squarely. "It's already begun. Tuesday. Yes. You look over everything on the weekend, call me Monday, we make whatever changes need to be made, and serve him Tuesday. I'd do it sooner, but I need a little more time to do something else, which I'll explain in a minute."

"It's just happening so quickly," she exclaimed and looked to her family for confirmation. But their expressions showed something different. Realizing that something of the old Jess was lurking there, she made a determined decision to dispel her fears and simply said, "You're right. Please go on."

"Let's summarize," Boake said, wanting to make sure that Jess was ready to proceed.

He picked off his points with his fingers. "You feel that you and your children are in danger. In fact, your husband has hurt you and your son recently, and the severity of his attacks on you has increased as has the frequency. It's going to get worse. It always does. Sam called me, and you and I began conversations, let's see now, nearly two weeks ago. I've done some homework, and we're ready to get started. There's no reason to postpone it if you want the divorce. The sooner we get started, the better."

All eyes were on Jess. "I know," she said. "I'm sorry. It's just hard to realize…it's taken such a long time to get to this point. But I understand. I'm sorry."

"You never need to apologize for anything with me, Jess. That's one of my ground rules. You say whatever you want to say, and I'll do my best to respond intelligently and fairly. I will always respond honestly."

He leaned forward, laid his cigar on one of the piles of paper in front of him, and addressed the family like a fatherly professor might do.

"One of the things you'll find in your research from that list I gave you is that a huge percentage of women who begin the process of leaving their abusers return to them an average of four times. He threatens, plays on her insecurity, scares the hell out of her. That's one scenario. Another is that he makes nice for a while. Says how he loves her, he needs her, he'll be different, maybe even go in for more counseling. He'll revert back to the wonderful person she thought he was to begin with, turn on the charm, and make her feel that the relationship could and should be saved. Once he has her, it starts all over again."

Jess recognized the scenarios all too well. How many times had Steve played out all of them over the past thirteen years? She had never known what to expect from him after his assaults. That very morning she had expected him to be conciliatory after the previous night's attack. But he had left without even so much as a good-bye, adding to her confusion and fear of him.

"The wife hasn't made major decisions for a long time," he went on. "Or if she has, she's been punished for them. She's been isolated from friends and family, for the most part, for all of the years she's been living with him. He's told her, when it's convenient, that she'll lose the children if she goes forward, which, by the way, is boloney. So as your lawyer and advisor, I'm telling you that waiting will do you absolutely no good. If you want to give the marriage another try, do it. That's entirely up to you. There are good family counselors to whom I can refer you. And if you want to see another attorney to help, I'll certainly understand."

Jess wanted to tell him that she trusted him, but the words were stuck behind the thick lump in her throat and all she could do was nod. Luckily, the lawyer took her silence as assent to move forward.

Boake smiled at her. "Good. Now. In addition to filing the divorce papers, I want to suggest that I also file with the court for a Protection Order, because there's always the chance that once the divorce papers are presented to your husband, he'll threaten you and do everything he can possibly do to keep you from going through with this. That's what's causing us to take longer than I'd like.

That was exactly what Jess had feared all along. A Protection Order. The violence could get worse. The confidence she had felt just minutes ago began to fade.

"You and the children need to be protected against him," he continued. "He'll be ordered by the court not to contact you or come near you and your family. He cannot go to your children's schools and threaten them or leave with them, he can't go to your place of work, and he cannot possess a gun or other weapon. I can see that he moves out of your home if that's what you want, and I can see to it that he gives you use of an automobile, which I understand he has taken away from you. He will definitely have to pay child support and give you living expenses during the proceedings. In other words, we can make sure that, for at least two weeks – the duration of the P.O. - you and your children are safe from him and that you have some money and transportation. I'll explain other alternatives later."

He passed out copies of the rules governing a Protection Order, and Jess watched Sam study it carefully.

"The only thing that we need to prove to the court for the Protection Order to be awarded is that he continues to be a threat to you. If you think that there should be no contact between Steve and the children, then we will also get a Protection Order for them. The information that I'm giving you pertains strictly to the laws of Ohio. Other states have similar orders. How are we doing so far?"

Maddie asked how he would prove that Steve had abused Jess since she had never filed a complaint with the police. And she asked if Jess would have to appear in court with Steve and personally present her case.

Boake picked up his unlighted cigar and took a puff.

"Good questions," he said. "Within the next several days, Jess needs to document all of the information that she has.

Skipping STONES

We'll need to ask witnesses to document what they know. If there have been calls to 911, we need to know that. If there have been doctors involved, we need to know that too and ask if they'll support you. We'll get all of the information together and put our case together to present to the court. I've already started."

He turned to Jess and asked her, very seriously, if there had been any threats or any violence against the children.

"I'll need as much specific information about his interaction with them as I can get," he said. "You have to tell me if we should move to keep him away from them or if you want him to have the privilege to have supervised visits with them while we go through this initial two-week process. The judge on the case will arrange for another hearing to get Steve's side of it all as soon as he or she is able to schedule it. You'll have to be there. If the judge feels that a permanent order needs to go through, then it will be drawn up. If not, then Steve will have visitation rights. Do you feel that the children are in danger?"

Jess couldn't begin to imagine leaving the children with Steve.

"Usually, I've been able to turn his anger away from them. There have been times, though, when that wasn't possible."

She summarized what the children had gone through and how the years of emotional abuse had affected them.

"I can't stand the thought of their being alone with him," she concluded.

It was very quiet in the room as Boake made some notes on his legal pad.

"I'll file a separate request for a Protection Order for the children then," he said.

He sat back and took another thoughtful non-puff.

"Jess," he said. "You and I will need to get to know each other very well. I need to know everything about your marriage. Everything. You can't leave anything out. I don't want any surprises. You have to tell me if there's anything he might bring up that could form the basis of a case against you as an unfit mother. Anything at all. Don't hold back.

"And if you have anything to say, anything at all, after any of the times we'll talk, email me from someone else's computer. My email is secure."

He rubbed his bald head as if he were smoothing hair down and looked back to the others. "We've covered a lot. Give me your questions."

No one spoke.

"Okay, then. Know where you're going to stay while all of this is taking place?"

Jess told him that they would stay with her parents.

"Get there early Tuesday. The important thing right now is that Steve has no indication whatsoever what we're about to do. Nothing must get out to him before I get the divorce papers filed and we get the PO from the judge."

"He suspects something," Jess said. "I don't know how, but he's said that he knows that I'm up to something."

"Has he threatened you about that?"

"Yes."

"It's a good idea to have a plan in place in case you need to get in touch with any of your family immediately and get out of the house if you need to – a safety plan. Get together documents, photographs, papers, medical records, birth certificates, anything that you will need and want to keep. Get them together and get them to a safe place as soon as possible, probably in one of your family's homes or a safety deposit box.

If there are any special mementos or things you and your children want to make sure are saved, get those to a safe place too."

Papaw spoke up. "What if she were to move in with us now? How would that affect everything?"

"She can certainly do that. My only advice would be to make certain that she's absolutely safe there. I would say that the majority of women who decide to leave go to shelters where they can get counseling, legal advice, and absolute safety. They leave their homes when it's safe, often take only what they can carry, and find safe haven in the shelters. I understand that Jess doesn't want to do that. As long as you can protect her in case her husband decides to go after her and the children until we get the order, you could do it."

"Would it impact her case against him?" Maddie asked.

"He could always turn it into abandonment and go after her in court on those terms, depending on how long she's gone, but not in the timeframe we're talking about. I doubt that he'd do that. We're only talking a couple of days and hopefully we'll have enough proof of abuse that it would never hold up."

"What would you advise?"

"If he's suspicious and you're afraid, Jess, get the hell out of there."

꽃

The family had an early lunch together on the way home, and Mimi and Papaw decided that they would help Jess that very afternoon to find the papers and documents that Boake had referred to and would take them to their home for safekeeping. When they walked into her house, the beeping of the answering machine immediately drew them into the kitchen.

There were four messages: three from Steve and one from Ben's school principal, Mr. Lewis. Steve's first call was a demand for an explanation of where Jess had been all day.

"Things are bad enough around here without me not knowing where you are and what you've been doing," he'd said. "I want you to call the minute you get home. Do you understand me? Your attitude towards me is disruptive. I will not put up with your arrogance anymore."

He simply hung up the other times when the machine clicked on.

Instead of calling him back, Jess called the school and was immediately put through to Mr. Lewis. He got right to the point.

"Ben got into a fight with another boy during lunch period. He apparently initiated it. Both boys were roughed up before two of the teachers on duty were able to stop it. I've taken Ben out of class for the day. He's sitting in one of the nurse's stations with his cousin, Josh."

Blood pounded through her temples. She breathed deeply and fought to hold her tears back. Ben had never been in a fight. Never. She understood that what he had seen the previous night had finally set him on a very bad path.

"Is he all right? Is Josh hurt too?"

He's doing well. The nurse took a good look at him, and he'll be fine. Just a cut on his lip. His eye is going to be black and blue. Josh wasn't involved. He heard about the altercation and refuses to leave Ben. They're both pretty upset. I'd like you to come and pick them up. I'll be happy to answer any of your questions here at the office."

Only then did she call Steve's office to tell the receptionist to leave a message for Steve that she was still with her parents and that everything was fine. She also told her that the three of them were going to pick the kids up at school later and take them out for a snack as a special treat. Her parents stood beside her, their arms around each other for support. They were in the midst of her tumultuous life.

Mr. Lewis was waiting for them at the school and asked to speak with Jess alone before she went to see the two boys, and Jess remembered to ask how the teacher who broke up the fight was. He explained that one of them fell during the altercation when Ben shoved her away from him, but that nothing was hurt but her dignity.

"His teachers reported that he had been agitated all morning and had been aggressive," he explained. "He let loose in the cafeteria. I guess an older boy said something to him in line, and he exploded. We've reported to you several times in the past month, according to our records, about his teachers' concerns about him. He's always been somewhat of a loner, but lately he's become more withdrawn. He's been to the counselor several times on the advice of his teachers, and she's written you notes and has called you. I understand that you weren't able to come in. I'm sure that you were concerned. I think the time has come for us to sit down with you and your husband. We're concerned about Ben. He's a very bright boy and could be a fine student. But he's distracted. He deliberately pulls away. And his aggression is becoming a disruption."

"There are some things that I need to explain," Jess told him. "I'll do it soon. I know that I should have come sooner, but…I couldn't. I'm very sorry for all of the problems we've caused."

"No apologies necessary," he said more kindly. "The important thing is that we help Ben. We've seen this kind of behavior before. There are a lot of things that can bring it on."

He paused and looked at her, opening the opportunity for her to speak. She couldn't. Not then.

"The important thing," he continued, "is that we get Ben back on track. I'm sure that if we all work together, we can do it."

They stood to make their way to the nurse's station. "By the way," he said, "we wouldn't ordinarily permit someone to stay with a student in detention, but we made an exception here." He chuckled. "Actually, we really had no choice. Josh refused to leave Ben. Simple as that. And we thought, in this case, having his cousin with him might calm Ben down and be a positive thing."

They entered the small room and found the two boys sitting at a large metal desk. Josh was writing on a notepad and Ben was staring off in space. Neither of them spoke.

Ben's bottom lip was swollen and red, and there was a cut on the right side. His left eyelid was puffy and was turning an ugly blue over the red mark the other student's fist had made.

Jess remembered the boy Ben had attacked and asked the principal how he was.

"He's all right. His parents came earlier and took him home for the rest of the day. You might get a phone call from them."

Ben wouldn't look at his mother, and after it was apparent that he was not ready to talk about any of it, Mr. Lewis told Jess to take her son home and keep him there another day. He reminded her to set up an appointment for the following week.

The ride home was completed in absolute silence. Ben walked quickly inside and went straight to his room; Josh fixed himself a soda and looked disconsolately out the French doors at the barren garden. His silence worried Jess. She had never seen him so despondent. Her response to the incident at school would be incredibly important. She needed to give herself time to consider what it should be.

There were more messages from Steve on the answering machine. His final call had come just ten minutes earlier.

"What the hell's going on?" he said. "You'd better have a good explanation for ignoring me, Jess. A very good explanation, or there's going to be hell to pay."

Mimi and Papaw made Jess sit down at the table and asked Josh to go check on Ben, a ruse, he knew, to give the adults some time to talk.

Papaw took his daughter's hand into his and rubbed her shoulder for a moment, and she was reminded of those times in her youth when he had needed to reprimand her. She was a child again.

"Jess, things have come to a head here," he said calmly. "Your home has just become more dangerous for you and the children. You shouldn't be here. None of you."

Of course, he was right, and Jess knew it. And she knew that once she stepped out of the door, this place would never be home to her and the children again. Her father lifted her face and gently wiped away her tears.

"Honey, I know it's hard," he said quietly. "I know you're afraid. But you need to leave. Now."

He waited patiently, and she looked at him and nodded with as much resolve as she was capable of.

"You need to leave now," he continued. "I want you and the children to come home with your mother and me and stay until we get all of this worked out. And we need to call Boake and fill him in on everything to see if there's anything else we should be doing."

She told Boake everything then, including the incident with Ben the night of the Christmas concert and his attempt to protect her from Steve the previous evening. He instructed her to document everything, including the talk with Mr. Lewis, and to record the messages from him and Steve. He would do what he could to escalate things on his end.

∽

Papaw went to Ben's room and brought him and Josh to the kitchen table. Ben was a coiled spring, and Josh clearly misunderstood the reason for the conversation.

"He couldn't help it," Josh said. "He didn't mean to hurt anybody. He's just mixed up because of everything else that's happened. It was partly the other kid's fault. He said something to Ben he shouldn't have said, and Ben just couldn't help himself."

"I understand, Josh," Jess answered. "I'm not angry with Ben. And I'm not angry with you for sticking up for him."

She turned to her son. "I know why you lashed out today, Ben, and I know why you stood by him, Josh. But you boys can never be like Steve. It's never right to hurt someone. I know you both know that.

"Mimi and Papaw know everything now," she continued. "I've told them how we're living here. We can finally speak openly to one another. No more secrets. No more lies. No more pretending. It's over."

She took a deep breath as she finally broke through the barrier that years of pain and pretence and silence had put between her and her son.

"You've lived with the abuse from your father ever since you were born, Ben," she went on. "I won't offer excuses, but maybe someday you'll be able to understand and will forgive me for waiting so long to get to this point. Your father is an abusive man. He always has been, but I found excuses for him. I really thought that I could change him. We had counseling years ago, when we were first married, and we had it again after you were born, Ben. But, obviously, nothing changed. I don't understand what makes him the way he is; I probably never will. But I do know now that I was wrong to stay, to keep hoping things would change. You've wanted us to leave, and I knew you were right. But I had loved him. We had some wonderful times together. We had such exciting dreams. I couldn't let go of those memories."

She turned to Josh, her son's protector and staunchest ally.

"I should never have allowed you to come into this house, Josh. It was wrong of me. But you've been a blessing. You boys and Sam and Katie opened my eyes and made me see. You've been right all along."

It was impossible to know what they were feeling, but she could see that they were hanging on to every single word.

"Remember your New Year's resolution, Ben?" she asked. "You said you'll be strong and never let anyone hurt you. And you said that you'd help the rest of us. I wrote your resolution down, and Josh's too, and I look at them every single day to remind me what we're all capable of and to help me be strong. You children made a commitment to be the gull. I've made it too. Our strength will come from within, not through fists and hurtful words, but from love and confidence and empathy. You boys must grow to be gentle men and strong leaders."

She fought back tears, determined that they see her as the calm, confident person she had every intention of becoming. It was time to let them know about her plan and how quickly they would be impacted by it.

"Ben, we've talked to a man who knows all about homes like ours. We found out about him through Sam. If it weren't for Sam and Josh and Mr. Karnanski, we wouldn't be having this conversation. Maybe Josh has already told you about that."

"I didn't tell him everything because I figured it was up to you," Josh said. "But I wanted to."

She assured Josh that he had done the right thing, regardless of what he did or didn't tell, and then she turned to her son, to give him details of how their lives would further change within the hour.

"Ben, we're leaving your father. I'm in the process of filing for a divorce. Maybe he'll try to get help if we do that. He's very angry right now, and we have to get away so that he can't hurt us again. I'm not making any more excuses for him. We need to leave the house today. If your dad finds out about the fight at school, he'll have another reason to punish us. He's mad at me for being with Mimi and Papaw all day and is demanding answers about what we've done. I can't tell him. Things aren't going well for him at work. He's angry about so many things. For our own safety, we have to leave and go live for a while with Mimi and Papaw. Maybe we'll come back to this house sometime. Maybe not. But the important thing is that all of us are together and safe from your dad."

Ben's face showed no sign of what he was thinking. She reached out to him and hoped that he would let her into his heart again.

"Ben, honey," she said, "tell me what you're feeling. Please say something."

He gripped the counter's edge and tried to steady himself, his father's voice booming in his mind, saying that boys never cry. Jess stood up and walked to him, and the shield he had worn for years to hide most of his emotions slid off him. He cried uncontrollably for the first time since he was a toddler and had witnessed his father bring his mother to tears. At last, they were leaving the man.

Jess turned his face to her, and he walked into her arms and held on.

༄

They brought out suitcases and boxes and began packing what they thought they would need for the next two weeks, when Katie rushed through the door. They had lost track of time. She ran into her Papaw's outstretched arms and then asked what everyone was doing there. Then she took a good look at her brother.

"What's wrong, Ben?" she asked. "What's happened to your face?"

He allowed her to touch his bruises.

"See. It doesn't hurt," he said.

She looked slowly from him to the boxes and suitcases around her.

"Where's all this stuff going?"

Jess would have to tell Katie the truth, but not there. Not then. There wasn't time.

"We're going to have a sleep-over party at Mimi's and Papaw's," she told her. "We might even stay longer. Aunt Maddie and Uncle Bill might come for a while too."

"Why are we taking so much stuff?" She asked.

She took another long look at the anxious faces around her.

"Is Daddy going too?"

Papaw answered quickly. "Nope. Not this time. He can't come so I get more of you for myself. Can I spoil you rotten?"

The family hurried to finish the packing and were about to begin loading the car when the phone rang. It was Steve. He was curt. And he was on his way home.

"We can get it done," Papaw said. "Everyone grab as much as you can carry and throw it inside. We'll take ten minutes. We'll simply leave whatever we can't get in."

They were half-way down River Road when they saw Steve's car coming from the opposite direction. Jess and the children ducked down in their seats, and everyone but Katie prayed that Steve hadn't noticed them.

෴

The family felt as though they had been launched, and they held on tightly, dizzy from the momentum and afraid of falling off, as they settled into the temporary sanctuary of Mimi and Papaw's home.

Maddie and Bill joined them that night, and all of them threw themselves into showing strength for one another. The phone rang non-stop, and they knew whom the calls were from, but ignored them and focused on each other. As long as Steve's calls continued, they knew that he wasn't about to knock on the door.

The calls continued long after the children had gone to bed. It was nearly eleven when the phone rang for the last time. And against her parent's strong advice, Jess took the call. Steve was drunk.

"What are you doing to me, Jess?" he demanded, slurring his words.

"It was so late when we came back from having dinner out that we decided to spend the night here," she explained. "I'm tired, Steve. So are the children."

Skipping STONES

He spun the web.

"You've never gone off and left me before," he muttered in a maudlin tone. "I need you here, Jess. I need you, and you're not here. Why aren't you here?

"Everything's going wrong at work," he continued. "And then you leave, just like that, and you take the kids. What are you doing? Why have you done this to me at one of my worst times? You're my wife. Dammit. I'm hurting, Jess."

It was ironic, Jess thought. He was hurting, he said. He had no idea what hurt was.

"We'll talk tomorrow," she said firmly. "The children are sleeping. It's late. Go to bed now. Get a good night's sleep. It will be better tomorrow."

"Why are you doing this, Jess? What were you doing with your mom and dad? Are you lying to me? I can't believe you'd lie. If you're lying to me, you're a very bad girl. Tell me you're not a liar, Jess."

She couldn't answer. And still he pleaded with her, sounding so miserable that she handed the phone to her father, unsure whether, after all these years, she could keep herself from falling back into old patterns of behavior.

Papaw listened briefly, and, with a look of disgust, hung up. "He's done," he said, as he disconnected the phone. Jess prayed it was true.

֍

She and her parents were still in their robes, having their first cups of coffee at the kitchen table and worrying about their next step when the cheerful and insistent ding-dong of the front door bell made them freeze.

"It's him," Jess exclaimed. "He's come for me."

Papaw stood, and Jess thought how much older he looked in his thin leather slippers and faded robe.

"I'll talk to him. We'll take it one step at a time," he said, starting for the door. "Stay by the phone. Call 911 if there's any trouble."

"May I come in?" Jess heard Steve say in the pleasant and deceptive voice he always used for her parents. "I'd like to say hi to Jess and the kids before school starts."

"We're letting the kids sleep in this morning," her father replied. "I'm taking them to school later. They didn't get to bed 'til late. They're dead tired."

There was an uncomfortable lapse in the conversation.

"I see. Well, I'll just say hi to Jess then. I have a few minutes before I need to take off. I rushed to get here and haven't had my morning coffee yet. I could use a cup if you have some brewed."

"Look here, Steve..." Papaw began, but the younger man pushed past him, and before Jess could leave the kitchen, he was there, taking her in his arms.

"Nice that you can spend some time here," he said, releasing her and pouring himself a cup of coffee. "Glad you're getting out. I was thinking maybe I could take off work early. There's a meeting this morning, but after that, I could pick you and the kids up and we could have the rest of the day together. Maybe we'll have dinner at the club."

He turned to Papaw, oozing concern.

"Things have been hectic at work. The five of us haven't had a lot of time to relax together. I'll be real glad when I'm off the hook with this client."

The conversation was interrupted by the sound of small feet scooting across the floor.

"Daddy?" Katie asked, wiping sleep from her eyes.

Skipping STONES

The man held out his arms to her, and she looked at her mother before she approached him. Jess wondered how much Katie really understood about leaving her home and staying indefinitely with her grandparents. She would have to be honest with her daughter very soon in order to protect her.

"How are Ben and Josh?" Jess heard him ask the child.

She glanced at Jess again and answered carefully that they were all right and were fast asleep.

Steve hesitated, considering his options, and decided to accept her tight answer.

Papaw was turning the key in the door behind Steve when Ben and Josh came into the room from their hiding place in the hall.

"What are we going to do now?" Ben asked.

༄

They waited until eight-thirty to call the attorney.

"Boake here," he answered. "What's up?"

Jess explained what happened.

"Okay," he said. "We'll need to expedite things if we can. You have the divorce papers. Sign them now and courier them to me as soon as possible. We'll present them to him late this afternoon at his office. I'll see what I can do about the P.O."

He called back within twenty minutes.

"I put a call in to the judge and talked to her about the Protection Order. She's a friend of mine. Unfortunately, her docket's full and she can't meet with us until Tuesday. She's going to call to give me a specific time."

Jess was surprised at the depth of her disappointment. Once she had made up her mind that she would leave her husband, she had wanted all the pieces to be connected immediately.

"I'm going to declare that you have been abused emotionally, physically, and sexually," he continued. "Here's what you can be doing: make a detailed report of his attacks on you; list when the rapes began; give dates when he took away your money and your transportation; and think objectively about when he started to separate you from family and friends. Details matter, Jess. Be objective and thorough. Okay so far?"

She hadn't wanted to share the sordid details, had hoped that she could simply file for a divorce and it would be over. But she realized now that none of it would be simple. She would expose all of the ugliness to one more person to get herself and her children away from it forever.

"You have to give me details for the kids too. Getting the orders is a big thing. You have to satisfy the judge's objectives and prove that your husband is a danger to you and them. You'll have to appear before her, and you can't look vindictive or angry. I know you aren't that type, but judges don't just pass these orders out on a whim. I'll meet with you before we see her." And then, pausing, he added, "Did you record his messages from last night?"

"Not yet. But Dad will work on that while I work on the papers for you."

"All right," he said. "But in the meantime, until we get the orders, Steve has every right to see you and the kids. If I were you, I'd disappear this afternoon. Get out of there to some safe place and wait for me to get back to you. And, Jess, one more thing. I'll need to know if you've been involved in any extra-marital relationships. I also need to know your drinking and drug habits, if you have any. Over this weekend, prepare a report for me. Give me anything that he may be able to use against you when he gets his day in court. Remember that I told you the Protection Order lasts no more than two weeks. At that point, when the judge sets up the court date for both of you to argue your cases for and against the Permanent Protection Order, I need to know everything about you that he might bring up. We don't want any surprises."

Drinking and drugs. How much did Steve know about the pills and the flask? And what would he do with the information?

༄

When they called Maddie at work to fill her in on what had happened, she offered to have Jess and the kids stay at her home, but they decided against it, sure that Steve would look for them there.

"I know about a lodge at a state park nearby," she told Jess. "It's not the Ritz, but it's inexpensive, and Steve wouldn't have a clue about it. The kids would have something to do while you work on everything. I'll meet you there and stay over the weekend to keep you company."

Papaw booked two rooms for five days.

Jess signed the divorce papers, and Papaw recorded the messages Steve had left the night before and arranged for a courier to pick up the packet of materials to take to Boake.

It was time for another talk with the children.

"We're going on a little vacation," Jess told them. "Maddie told me about a park close by that we haven't been to before. There's an indoor pool there and a game room. There are lots of trails to hike. We can take our sleds. It'll be fun. We might even stay a couple of days next week. We'll see. Mimi's going to loan me her car so I can get you to school if we want to stay longer. Can you pack up again? Don't forget your bathing suits and boots. You can pack some of your games too and books if you'd like."

The boys understood far more than she was telling them in front of Katie. They looked frightened, but determined.

"By ourselves? We're going by ourselves?" Katie asked.

"Well, Maddie's going to meet us there and stay overnight with us tonight. Mimi and Papaw will be there part of the time too. They'll come later. Some of the time it will just be us."

"What about Daddy?"

Katie was trying very hard to figure it all out.

"Daddy won't be there, Katie," Jess said. "He'll stay at home this weekend and will work like he always does next week."

Everyone around the table waited for Katie's reaction.

She stunned them all. "Are we running away, Mama?" She asked, and Jess realized that all pretenses had to end now for this little girl.

"Yes, Katie," she said. "We're running away for a while."

"He's going to be really mad."

"Yes, he might be," she admitted.

"Do you think he'll be sad?"

Jess took some time to think about her daughter's question. Would he be sad? Relieved? Or simply enraged?

"He might be sad, but he'll be all right. Everyone will be a little sad, but we'll be okay.

Katie put her elbows on the table, cradling her face in her hands, deep in thought. No one spoke, giving the child the time she needed to process the information.

"We're getting divorced, aren't we?" Katie said finally. "You don't love each other anymore."

"Sometimes adults fall out of love, Katie," Jess told her. "It's a very sad thing, but it happens."

"Like Sam and Aunt Becky."

"Yes. Like them. It makes everyone sad for a while. I suppose in some ways, everyone is sad forever, but sometimes it's just the best thing to do when nothing you try really makes you happy. We'll be okay. When we get settled in at the park, you and I will sit down and I'll explain everything to you, Katie. But right now we need to leave as soon as possible. Is that all right with you?"

Katie threw her arms around her mother and hung on. "I don't care where we are, as long as I can be with you and Ben and Josh."

And with that simple statement, she sealed the commitment that they had all made.

An hour later, Jess and the children were headed for their safe place with Mimi and Papaw. To Jess, the flight away from her previous life felt like passing into another dimension through time and space. And it was. In two days, she had walked away from her past and her present and into a misty future. The children were fearful but relieved. Clearly they had no reference point on how to define their emotions. But she was sure that deep inside they, like her, were feeling a new sensation, light as a seed carried on a breeze and filled with life: *HOPE*.

୨୦

They got themselves moved into their new home away from home and were headed for the pool when Boake called. He had rushed the papers through, and his assistant was on his way to Steve's office, which wasn't more than fifteen minutes away in heavy traffic. At four-thirty, Boake called again to say that Steve had the papers, and an hour later, Maddie called from her car to say that Steve had been trying to get in touch with her and Bill.

They ordered pizza and found a movie the kids could watch on TV as soon as Maddie arrived. Bill called just as the children were going to bed. Steve had been to his home, looking for Jess. He had been belligerent, practically pushing his way into the house, but once he was satisfied that no one but Bill was there, he became almost supplicant. He admitted that Jess was divorcing him and actually seemed perplexed by it.

"He was incredulous," Bill said. "I couldn't figure him out. He's either totally unaware of what he's done to Jess or is very good at shamming. He almost had me believing that there was no reason for her to leave him."

Bill asked what Papaw and Mimi's plans were for the night, and, after a lengthy debate, everyone agreed that they should go back to their home. Part of the reason was unspoken: their place may need protection.

Maddie and Jess and the three children shared one of the rooms Papaw had reserved. No one, not even Jess and Maddie, wanted to be alone. At one-thirty, unable to sleep, Jess went to the other room and worked for several hours on her notes for the hearing for the Protection Order. She fell asleep in the chair sometime in the early morning in the middle of a prayer.

Waking dazedly before the sun came up, she took a shower and put her robe back on. The coffee she made tasted good, and she gave herself permission to sit and sip it in the luxurious quiet and solitude of the simple room. When she was ready, she picked up the notebook she had used just several hours before to complete her list of Steve's greatest assaults. There they were: incidents from most of a married lifetime, listed objectively and in chronological order. The list, however, was by no means complete. As she read, she wondered how anyone could possibly understand the deep emotions and the deeper scars that those attacks had left in her mind and the minds of her children. Would she be able to adequately explain the insults, the hurt, the degradation, loss of pride, and humiliation to a stranger? Be objective, Boake had said. But was explaining years of abuse objectively possible?

It was 7:30, and they had just finished breakfast when the phone rang.

"Our answering machine was filled with messages from Steve. He'd called here all afternoon yesterday and into the evening," Papaw said. "I'm glad we came back. We kept the drapes drawn and the lights on in the front of the house. A little past ten, he parked in the drive and rang the door bell. We thought he'd never stop. I was sure he was going to force his way inside. Finally, he gave up, but he came back at six-thirty this morning. I wouldn't open the door. I just yelled at him to leave or I'd call the police. He demanded to see you and the kids and absolutely refused to believe that you weren't here. I told him I had just dialed 911, and he backed off. But I went out to pick up the paper on the porch not more than fifteen minutes ago, and his car was parked down the street. He was watching the house. Thank God you aren't here, Jess. The kids wouldn't be able to handle it. Anyway, I went ahead and called the police and explained the situation. You may think I did the wrong thing, but Mimi and I were just about at our wits end. An officer came by and made him move on. I wouldn't have bothered you about all of this, but Mimi and I agree that we can't come back there until we're sure he's gone and isn't coming back. We don't want to take the chance that he'll follow us."

It was Saturday – four days before Boake and Jess could go after the Protection Order.

Sunday morning, Maddie and Jess did their best to entertain the children. For lunch, they headed in the opposite direction of their homes and found a small out-of-the-way restaurant that specialized in Italian food and fried chicken. It was a safe diversion, and they were able to relax for a while, but when they returned to the lodge, Bill called to say that he was on his way to Mimi and Papaw's home. Someone had tried to break in while they were at church, and the police were on their way. It had to have been Steve.

"What should we do, Jess?" Bill Asked. "Should we call the police or not?"

Maddie and Jess talked it over quickly and decided to try to get to Boake through Sam.

"I can't get him," Sam said when he called Jess back. "But I think we should let the police do their job. At least let them see the damage that was done. I mean, it's against the law to try to break down a door no matter who's doing it. At least everything will be documented. I can't get across town in time to help. You want me to come to the lodge later? Maybe I could do something with the kids while you and Maddie relax a little. I could be there in less than two hours with no traffic."

Jess called her parents and asked them to tell the police to document their report but not to encourage them to go after Steve even though the evidence from yesterday and this morning pointed to him. All she wanted was to get away from him, not to put him in jail or to damage his career; he was, after all, her children's father.

The children's spirits were raised significantly when they saw Sam walk in, and the pool and game room took on a different atmosphere that evening. There was no opportunity for the adults to have a meaningful discussion, but that was all right; everyone agreed that Katie and Ben and Josh needed attention and male security. At nine o'clock, Sam and the boys took over the extra bedroom, and Jess and Maddie comforted Katie in the other one.

Skipping STONES

"Will we go back to school tomorrow?" Katie wanted to know. "Are we going back to Mimi and Papaw's?"

"Two more days, honey," Jess answered. "Two more days and we'll be able to go back. Will you be okay for two more days?"

"I'll be all right," she answered in a sleepy voice. "Do you think Daddy's okay?

Katie's concern about her father surprised Jess and alarmed her. The child had suffered right along with her and Ben, and yet she still cared. What would his impact on her continue to be?

"He'll be just fine, honey," Jess assured the child. "Don't you worry. We're fine too, aren't we? Maybe Mimi and Papaw can come here for a visit tomorrow."

"That would be good," Katie yawned. "Maybe Sam will stay with us too."

༄

Finally, Tuesday came. Boake told the family that he was sure that they had enough information to present to the judge to get the Protection Order, especially with everything that had happened over the weekend. Jess wanted it to be over. Once more, she told herself, one more time to try to explain her sordid life. "Please, God," she prayed. "Please make this the last time."

Responsibilities had been defined. Mimi and Papaw would go with Jess to the Judge's offices, Maddie would get everything from the lodge moved into her parents' home for an easy transition, and Sam would take care of Ben and Katie and Josh until the hearing was over.

"I'll put them to work," he teased. "They can make milkshakes and flip burgers. Katie can learn how to wrap silverware. I'll teach them the restaurant business in under four hours. They could become my first franchisees."

※

When Jess and Mimi and Papaw pulled into city hall, they found Boake waiting for them just outside the judge's court room. He explained the procedures again to Jess.

"There are no jurors, no other lawyers," he reminded her. "It's just us and Judge Abrams and the stenographer. I'll present our request for a Protection Order for you first, and then the judge will ask you for facts relating to the abuse and the potential danger from Steve. She might ask you to elaborate on certain things. Remember to stay objective. After the order has been awarded, I'll ask for one for the children."

Jess felt like she had just jogged five miles at full speed. Could she present a convincing case, she wondered? What if she failed?

Judge Abrams entered the room after Jess and Boake had taken their seats at the desk. After a brief exchange of pleasantries, they got down to business.

"Mr. Karnanski has explained that you've asked for a divorce from your husband, who has been abusive," Judge Abrams said. "Will you explain the nature of the abuse?"

Jess told her that it started as emotional abuse and escalated, over a period of fourteen years, to sexual and physical abuse. And when the judge asked her to explain the nature of the emotional abuse, Jess told her how Steve had gradually taken control of every aspect of her life, beginning with keeping her from working and having no social interaction with others, including, finally, with her family members.

The judge wanted to know more about her claim that Steve had attempted to isolate her, and Jess explained as clearly and concisely as she could.

"I haven't had real friends for a very long time. He never wanted me to go out on my own socially. Even from the beginning. I've lost them all. These past several months, he's cut off my time with our children. I'm alone with them no more than two hours a day. I can't take them anywhere because I have no car. He wakes them up and makes sure they're in bed every night. I have no means to interact with the rest of the family unless they come to me, and if he doesn't like what I've done with them, he punishes me. Because he's taken away my check book and credit cards and the keys to the car, I'm really confined to the house. He monitors all calls."

"And the children?" Judge Abrams asked. "Are they socially active?"

Jess explained the trouble they were having at school academically and socially.

The judge quickly changed direction, asking about the precise nature of the sexual abuse, and Jess worked her way through her embarrassment to explain that she was not allowed to decline Steve's advances.

"So you felt that you were being raped by your husband," Judge Abrams said, looking at Jess over her glasses. "We must be very clear about this, Mrs. Selby."

The interrogation was precise, and Jess was careful to answer questions objectively, the way Boake had instructed her to do. The judge referred to the list of physical assaults Jess had provided. She then asked whether Jess had witnessed any physical abuse to the children, and Jess explained the gradual escalation from pushes and shoves to the final incident with Ben.

"You said that he frequently goes to the children's rooms after he sends them to bed," the judge said. "You said that he's done that for years. Do you know what was said or done at those times when they were alone?"

The question took Jess's breath away. She didn't know.

Judge Abrams simply looked at her and made notes.

The final question Jess was asked was why she had finally decided, after all these years, to leave her husband. Jess referenced again the final two acts of abuse to herself and Ben and Ben and Josh's reactions to them. She also explained her sudden awakening at the doctor's office.

"What was your husband's reaction to your filing for divorce?" The judge asked.

Jess explained the phone calls, the threatening messages, his drunkenness, his forced entry into her parents' and sister's homes.

Judge Abrams didn't hesitate.

"I'm issuing the Protection Order, Mr. Karnanski. I assume that you will also request a Protection Order for the children. The paperwork that will be presented to your husband, Mrs. Selby, will spell out exactly the conditions of the orders," she said crisply. "I'll have a copy for you also. Your husband will be required to stay away from your domicile – wherever you will be living temporarily - and the children's schools. He cannot come within fifty feet of you or the children regardless of where you are. He cannot threaten you or the children; he cannot possess a firearm or any weapon and cannot stalk any of you. Writing letters, sending emails, sending faxes and making calls to you or any member of your family constitutes stalking. For now, he will be required to move out of your home, if you ask for it, give you the keys back to your car, and pay you immediately for the expenses you've incurred this week and for what you may require over the next two weeks.

"Once in place," she said, "the orders cannot be changed until the formal and decisive hearing where both of you must be present to present your cases. In fact, if either of you disobeys the order, you will be breaking the law and will be subject to fines and or arrest. The police will be notified of the order.

"Perhaps Mr. Karnanski has told you this, Mrs. Selby," she said, "but I must also warn you that quite often, the issuance of a Protection Order, whether permanent or temporary, further upsets the defendant. This can be a very desperate time for all of you. You and your family have the responsibility to protect yourselves and act in a conscientious way regarding your husband and your personal safety. If you or your children are approached by your husband, you need to remove yourselves and call the police. Under no circumstances are you to interact with him without talking with your attorney or other authorities first. Do you understand?"

Boake said that he would deliver the orders to Steve immediately, and they agreed on a date for the review for a Permanent Order with Steve and his attorney. As they stood to leave, Judge Abrams had one more point to make.

"You and your children will need counseling, Mrs. Selby, she said. "Especially the children. Violence has a domino effect on children. The abused often become abusers and/or they are so troubled that they become non-functioning adults. Your children have been traumatized – possibly more than you understand - and are going to need professional help. I'm making that an order of my court. Mr. Karnanski will be able to suggest the best family counselors for you and them to see."

Jess realized then that the process would be even more harrowing than she had anticipated. She suddenly understood Boake's warning to her and her family that women often go back to their husbands as many as four times before the cut is finally made. She couldn't imagine doing that, but really leaving, getting away from Steve once and for all, would be an incredible challenge to her and the children in so many ways. She would need everyone who loved her to help her keep her resolve. Without love and understanding from family and friends, she understood how a woman could stumble.

◈

Jess called both schools from the car and told them that the children would be there the following morning and that she needed to meet with their principals as soon as possible.

Then she called Sam from the car to tell him that they were on their way to his restaurant.

He asked how things had gone, and she told him that she'd give him the details when they got to his place.

"They want to stay for a while," he said. "We've had a great time. Katie's become a master at milkshakes, Ben flips burgers with the best of 'em, and Josh is a whiz with the dishwasher. Why don't the three of you rest for a while and get yourselves settled. Meet me at my place for dinner at 5:00. I'll whip up something simple. I remember your dad likes scotch. Tell him I have a bottle of McCallan's Single Malt that's at its best age and needs to be enjoyed by someone who knows the difference."

Four hours later, Jess and Mimi and Papaw made their way through the historic section of Rocky River to the small street leading into the Yacht Club. The gate guard motioned them through, and they found themselves looking out over a narrow channel overlooking Lake Erie. Driving down the lane that ran along the harbor, they turned onto a steep driveway that led to a charming Victorian clapboard house that overlooked the marina and a view so beautiful that it took Jess's breath away.

They climbed the stone steps to a simple veranda that swept around three sides of the home. A single large Adirondack chair had been left outside there, and Jess imagined what it would be like to sit all bundled up against the early morning wind and cold, a cup of coffee in hand, watching the half-frozen waves make their cumbersome way to the shore.

The children ran to greet them and showed them through the home as proudly as if they lived there. Surprisingly, the interior was contemporary in style, one spacious room opening into another. Linen-white walls, decorated with colorful abstract art, would, on bright days, reflect the sun entering through the doors in the main space and skylights in the kitchen and bedrooms. Wide-planked wood floors grounded the structure throughout, and aqua and emerald green rugs provided paths to the various living spaces. Buttery leather chairs arranged in a circle surrounding a large sculpted burled-wood table ensured comfortable lounging. It suited Sam precisely, and she found herself yearning for the time when she could exercise her artistic skills as she had once planned to do.

But it was the kitchen that dominated the interior, with floor to ceiling white cabinets with a rub of pine taking up one entire wall, and an aqua glass backsplash behind the stove and sink repeating the colors of the rugs. It was an inviting room with its pine island and matching bar stools. Josh grinned proudly as his father pointed out the "Sam's Place" sign that he had made for him, now carefully mounted over the stove.

Jess thought about how far Sam had come over the years and what Becky had missed. And then it occurred to her that this had been the real Sam all along but the family had never looked closely enough at his dreams, let alone embrace them.

Sam was pouring himself and Papaw their second round of scotch when the cell phone rang. It was Boake, calling to tell them that Steve had been served the Protection Order and that he had reacted first with disbelief and then with outright rage.

"He didn't seem to see it coming," Boake said. "None of these guys can believe that their wives would actually be capable of leaving them, and when the courts get involved like this, it's a real blow, a real downer. They honest to God think they're invincible and justified in everything they do. It's never easy."

The family listened as Boake took a big drag on his cigar and blew it back out. The tinkle of ice in a glass followed, as he went on to explain that Steve knew now exactly what he can and cannot do. "He has to move out of the home within two days," he concluded.

Jess quickly thought about her old home and, surprisingly, told Boake that she wasn't ready to return to it yet. His response was that she could do whatever she thought was best, that the decisions were hers, and although he didn't use the word "freedom," Jess was suddenly aware that, for the first time in a very long time, that was precisely what she thought she had. Her happiness was premature.

৩৯

As soon as they were back at her parents' home, Jess put the children to bed and joined Mimi and Papaw in the kitchen. "Listen to this," Papaw told her, and they listened to the seven messages on the answering machine, the last one sounding like a receiver hitting a wall, the caller silent except for heavy breathing. When they checked the display that told where the calls came from, they found that the caller was listed as "unknown."

"It has to be Steve," Papaw said. "Where could he be placing the calls from?"

No one articulated their fear, but Jess and her parents made sure the doors were double-locked and the windows were secure. They kept the lights on dim. They were peering between the living room drapes one last time to make certain there was no one outside in the yard or down the street, when Ben walked up behind them, wanting to know if his father was out there.

Jess had just begun her assurances that everything was all right when Katie, carrying her piece of blanket and Ariel tucked under her arm, joined them.

"We're lonely," Katie said, and with a whisper, she added, "We're afraid."

Jess let all three children sleep in their sleeping bags on the floor at the foot of her bed as she lay awake throughout the night, worrying if she would really be able to keep them safe.

༄

The children lived with the fear that Steve would still be able to fulfill his threats to take them away from their mother, and Jess and her parents realized that it was important for them to experience some normalcy by interacting with other people. So when Sam asked that Jess provide permission for him to pick both boys up from school on Wednesday and take them out for a quick lunch, she eagerly accepted. Grandma Annie, Sam decided, could add a different kind of calm, and he asked her to go with him for the short outing.

"I know I'm going to embarrass you, Grandson," she said to Josh when he walked to her, "but I don't care. Get over here and give me a big hug." She focused then on Ben and complimented him on being such a strapping young man.

They headed for a small diner in an ethnic neighborhood the boys hadn't seen before, and Annie made the two of them sit across from her so that she could see them both straight on at the same time. Once the pizzas and salads were ordered, the talk never stopped, and none of it had anything to do with the divorce or the history of the marriage or what either boy did or didn't do, but simply good-natured bantering back and forth.

Sam teased his mother about her inability to make decisions about redecorating her living room, and she good-naturedly countered that she had lived with most of her furniture and those colors in that house for close to thirty-five years and that changing it wasn't something to take lightly.

Josh thought about his old home and the new one he just moved out of. "Where will we go next?" he wondered. And he wondered if anything about his life would ever be as permanent as Grandma Annie's.

"Some new ideas are beginning to rattle around in my head finally," Grandma Annie teased. "I'll let you know what they are as soon as I'm sure about them."

"Mom could help you," Ben muttered. "She's good at that stuff."

"Well, now, there's a great idea," Grandma replied. She looked to her son and smiled. "Why didn't you think of that?"

And then she remembered the book she had brought for Josh.

"It's all about rabbits. I think the rest of the family would enjoy it too."

She hugged her grandson again when they got back to school. "Everything is going to be really good really soon," she told him. "I feel it, and when I feel something this deeply, you can count on it."

Then she turned to Ben and gave him a long look.

"You're a fine, handsome young man. Tall and strong. Looks to me like you could be quite a basketball or football player. And I can tell you're real smart too," she assured him. "I've had strong feelings about you too, and they were all good." Then she pulled him aside and whispered, "You need to take a full inventory of yourself. And once you do, you'll see amazing goodness and strength there. Don't waste yourself, Ben."

That night, the family squeezed together in Papaw's den and escaped into the world of *Watership Down*.

༄

Just a week had gone by since the proceedings for the divorce had begun, but it seemed like forever. Jess talked by phone with Boake and discovered that, even though divorce in Ohio was "No Fault," she could still ask for particulars, including the house. If Steve agreed to the divorce and would settle with Jess outside of court, he told her, details could be kept out of court records and the media. That, he said, would certainly be best for Steve, an attorney himself. Boake would have to dig deep to find exactly what Steve's net worth was to come up with a settlement that would include, of course, child support. So far, he said, Steve and his attorney had been difficult to pin down. It appeared that, since Steve was apparently still in denial, negotiations could go on for a very long time.

Jess and the children had rushed away from their home with very little, and Boake assured them that there was no reason for their not going back to get the things they needed and clearly belonged to them.

"Just make sure Steve isn't there," he reminded Jess. "He isn't supposed to be, but we have to be careful. If you run into him, you could both be seen as violating the terms of the PO."

The next morning, after they took the children to school, Jess and her parents phoned the house to make sure Steve was gone and, for good measure, called his office to ask if he was there. When the receptionist told them that he had just walked in and suggested that she forward the call, they hung up.

They drove past the house to make doubly sure that no one was there and then pulled slowly into the drive. Cautiously, they stepped inside.

"I feel like an intruder," Jess whispered to her parents.

Carrying the cartons they had brought to pack, they crept to Ben's room first to gather the rest of his clothes and other personal items he said that he wanted. What they saw shocked each one of them. Everything – toys, games, books, clothes – was gone. The room was tidy and sterile.

With dread, they walked to Katie's room. The cheery pink and white little girl's room resembled a show place in a furniture store. It too was emptied of all personal belongings. Further down the hall, Josh's room had become an impersonal guest room once again. There was no indication of what had happened to any of the children's personal belongings.

Overcome with shock that Steve would have tried to eradicate any reminder of his own children, they made their way to the master bedroom. At first glance, everything appeared to be normal, but then Jess's eye went to the large antique beveled mirror on the wall behind her dressing table. It had been

Skipping **STONES**

shattered. Her perfumes and cosmetics lay in pieces in a garden bucket on the floor.

But what they found inside her closet was the most terrifying. Every single piece of her clothing had been slashed into shreds.

"I'll take pictures," Papaw managed to say. "Boake will want pictures."

༄

That night, Maddie and Bill joined their family for dinner, and the adults focused on the children.

"Let's tell them about the rabbits!" Katie exclaimed after the meal was over and the dishes were done."

Jess invited her to tell her aunt and uncle what she understood about the book. It took her several false starts, but eventually she found the words to begin.

"Well, see, there's this family of rabbits. Actually, there's a whole bunch of them. They're all family and friends. It's called a warren where they live. So anyway, one of the rabbits can see into the future. He's a… a… what is it Mama?"

"A seer?" Jess suggested.

"Yes. That's it. Good. So anyway… I forget his name."

"Fiver," Ben reminded her.

"Yes. That's right, Ben. Good work. So anyway, Fiver sees into the future and tells all of his family and friends that their home is going to be destroyed and that they should all leave their houses to escape the danger and to look for a new place to live. Most of the rabbits don't believe him. They have a big fight about it. Some are just afraid to leave because it's really scary for rabbits to go far from where they've always lived. But Fiver and his brother and a really big rabbit and a couple others who were really brave left anyway. Fiver's brother becomes the leader. He's real smart and very brave. He's really nice too. Everybody likes him because he's quiet and smart and wants everybody to be happy. So anyway, they leave their home and start out on an adventure. It's really dangerous. But they know it's the right thing to do. And. Let's see…"

Katie crossed her arms and put her finger up to her lips and thought hard.

"I'm a little mixed up about the rest, I think."

Josh spoke up. "Right. But, see, the whole warren was in trouble. Fiver could see that, but it took a long time for everyone to believe him. Most of the rabbits didn't. Only his brother really believed him. Moving away was really hard for them, but some of them could see that it was the best thing to do. The really big one, the one who likes to fight and argue, is Bigwig. He goes along. But only for the adventure. The others aren't so sure it's a good idea for Bigwig to go because he's a real tough guy and would rather fight than think things through and follow orders, but they need all the help they can get because of the danger."

"They don't really like him a lot," Ben added, "but they figure they need his strength. Bigwig is huge and would be good in case they all ran into trouble."

"It's a little hard to understand," Katie pointed out, "because it's about rabbits in England, and some of the words sound funny and I don't know what they all mean. The writer made up the story for his kids. Mama said it's a…what is it again?"

"A parable," Jess said.

"It isn't really about rabbits," Ben interjected. "Well, it is, but it shows how people act with each other too. It's about leaders and followers and smart people and tough guys and how they figure out what's right and what to do about it. They're

Skipping STONES

all scared, but they have the guys who know what to do, I think. That's as far as we got."

The adults looked at each other in veiled surprise. They had never seen Ben so involved in a conversation.

"We could read more now if you want to. Want to?" Katie asked.

And so, before the children went to bed, the family sat in the living room and listened to Papaw read several chapters from the book Grandma Annie had given them, and at some point into the reading, Josh realized that the story had been chosen with great care.

"Grandma Annie is a sort of seer too," he thought. "She makes us see things we couldn't see ourselves. She might even be able to see into the future."

༄

Jess made sure that the children were settled into their sleeping bags again in her room and had just made her way to the den to talk with her parents when the phone rang. Papaw insisted that she ignore the call, but she was adamant.

"Maybe he's calling to say he wants to end it all. Maybe he wants to tell me that we'll move forward with the divorce."

She pushed the "Talk" button.

"Don't hang up," Steve said quickly. "Don't tell your dad who this is. You're my wife. We have the right to talk."

She listened to his litany, his ranting about his concern about what people at work would think when they learned that she had left him and had taken the children. He accused her of being ungrateful for everything he had given her, of never having told him how she felt, and finally ended with an offer to see a counselor again.

She listened to it all, and when she hung up, she felt a touch of sadness that a man she had once respected so much had come to this.

༄

After she and Papaw delivered the children to school the next morning, Jess turned on her laptop and eagerly read the message from Sam.

"Hi. How's it going? Dumb question, right? I'm calling you because Mom's in the mood to make some of her candied apple dumplings. Of course, she'll add her baked chicken and au gratin potatoes and all of the trimmings. Problem is, she always makes enough for an entire army platoon. She needs guests to fuss over. Three kids and six adults, counting me, would be great to help her get rid of it all. It should be ready by Sunday afternoon. Can you think of any takers out there? Give me a call when you have a chance. Hang in there! Oh, by the way, there's still some of that Scotch left, and I have a couple of bottles of an unbelievable Puligny-Montrachet and a cache of Silver Oak, in case anyone is interested."

And then, as she started to respond, another message popped up.

"Don't turn your back on me. Our children looked sad this morning. They should be in their own home again with you. And with me. We need to talk. Where shall we meet?"

The message knocked the wind out of her. Steve had been there, watching. How many other times, she wondered, had he been close, spying on her and her family? Her fear was mixed with anger, and she and Papaw wasted no time and immediately called Boake. She asked again what could happen if Steve and she communicated to each other.

"Here's the deal," the attorney said after listening to their questions. "First, as I said before, he can't talk to you. Can't happen. Once the Order is made, neither party can break it. If he violates it, he can go to jail. Pure and simple. You can't go to him either. You must never even so much as respond to him if he calls or writes. Why are you asking? Is he stalking you?"

Boake wouldn't promise to keep what she said confidential because of the law behind the PO, but he did say that he would give her his best advice. She told him about the calls and emails from Steve.

"Not good, Jess. Not good at all. I'm surprised. I thought he was smarter than that. He's an attorney and knows the law. Even if he didn't, it's stated right on the Order. You didn't write back, did you?"

She said that she had not, but that she had listened to him once on the phone.

"You could get in serious trouble, my friend. And in more ways than one. Think about it, Jess. You've broken the law, and you've encouraged Steve just by listening to him. Promise it won't happen again. If he calls and leaves a message, record what he says. And promise you won't email anything to him. Don't even open his emails. I know guys who've recorded phone calls and changed email messages to make it appear that the spouse had put the call or message through and then used it against them in court. I know you think he wouldn't stoop that low, but, believe me, I've seen it happen a lot. His emailing you could be looked upon in some courts as a form of stalking. He's not helping himself here at all. Has he shown up anywhere except for that first time your dad saw him down the street?"

He was watching her, and she knew it, but she didn't tell Boake.

"I can take him to court right now if he's called, emailed, or stalked you in any other way.

"No. I want us all to agree to the divorce in a civilized way. I don't want my children's father to be thrown into jail. I can't do that. I just can't."

"We don't have to send him to jail, but we can use the information to get this all over a lot sooner."

The next day, Jess received a typewritten note through the mail: You're making a big mistake. Think about it. It was not signed.

⁂

Every night, the children and the adults read from the book Grandma Annie had given them, and the rabbits and their search for a good home gave Josh and Ben strength and inspiration to dream about their own futures. The adults knew the right questions to ask that would help lead the boys further into the various themes of the novel and help them begin to resolve some issues, large and small, that loomed in the backs of their young minds.

"I wonder why Fiver, who had the vision and the plan to search for a new home and save his warren, would let his brother lead their family and friends on the journey," Papaw said. "I think a lot of us would want to take the lead on an idea we developed. What does that say about him?"

Each of the boys tried to express their views, and Jess clung to their answers while formulating her own questions about Roundwort and Bigwig, both powerful and strong rabbits, who used their strength for different purposes. And she asked what made Hazel such a good leader.

Josh had his own questions. "They could have stayed at any of the warrens if they had wanted to, but they didn't. What were they really looking for?" Josh asked. "Why were they willing to keep moving? Why did they keep going on to Watership Down?"

Even after the family sessions about the book ended, the boys continued to think about the issues it raised.

"A leader doesn't have to be big and strong or even the smartest," Ben told Josh when they talked in their room at night. "It took Hazel a lot of time to make decisions, and he never asked the others to do something he wouldn't do. He wasn't the biggest or even the strongest.

"He even stood up for the smaller, weaker rabbits and did everything for the group," Ben went on. "He even tried to be friends with the other rabbits from the other warrens if they were nice. I think it shows that you can leave the bad guys alone or try to win them over unless they hurt you or your friends or family. But sometimes you don't have any choice but to fight them if you have to. I like Bigwig. He's smart and he's big. He's getting a lot better, you know?"

"Yeah," Josh agreed. "If you're going to do something like what they did, you have to be smart about it. You can't just take off and hope it all works out. You need to be able to think for yourself. You can fight for something in a lot of different ways. And you're a better fighter if you're fighting for something you believe in."

༄

All eight of them wanted to go to Grandma Annie's for dinner on Sunday, and each one was determined to make it a comfortable and important event. Papaw decided to take a special bottle of his own wine with him to share, and Jess and Mimi put together a small basket of before-dinner snacks for a hostess gift. Katie felt that she should wear a pretty party dress for the occasion, and she and Jess rushed to the mall to find something suitable. Ben checked his appearance in the mirror one more time and practiced standing tall and squaring his shoulders. Josh attempted to act nonchalant and failed.

Annie welcomed them all warmly, even though these same people had rebuffed her and her son years earlier, and dinner turned into a long and lovely event. When the dishes were finally cleared, Annie deftly asked Jess to go with her on a tour of the home and was quick to present the idea that she had gradually developed over the past months. Pointing out the new piece of furniture Sam had given her for Christmas, she told Jess that she knew that she needed to redecorate, but she didn't know where to begin. The new chair had made everything else look tired and worn, she said. Jess had already made an easy assessment of what she would do to the warm and simple home and the cared-for older pieces of furniture there to make the place even more beautiful. She shared her ideas and excitement with Annie, and the agreement was made right there and then. Jess would take over Annie's decorating project.

The family party broke up late, and Jess and Mimi were putting the three tired children to bed when the phone rang. Jess checked the number of the call on the answering machine's display and hurriedly answered. It was Sam. His voice was tight with tension.

"Make sure your doors are locked," he told her. "And close all the curtains. When I got home, I found that someone had thrown a rock through one of the doors off the deck and had tried to break the lock. It can't be a coincidence. Don't answer the door until you hear my voice. I'm coming over there now."

Skipping STONES

Warning calls went out to Maddie and Bill, and the family spent the night hours on high alert. Sam followed Jess and the children to school in the morning, making certain that Katie and Ben and Josh were safe inside and that Jess wasn't being followed, and the two of them stopped by a Starbucks to call Boake to get further advice on how they should live with the threat of Steve. Sam was advised to report the rock-throwing incident to the police even though there was no proof that Steve was the perpetrator.

༄

The following day, determined to "live without fear" and to hold onto her new-found strength, Jess insisted to her parents that she get out on her own for a few hours.

Since most of her clothes had been destroyed, she did a little shopping for herself and made her way to a fabric shop to see what might work for Grandma Annie. A quiet, leisurely lunch alone seemed a fine idea, and before she knew it, it was time to go after the children. Putting on her best cheerful voice, she phoned Mimi and Papaw and assured them that she was fine and that she was looking forward to stopping somewhere for a special treat with the children after school.

Picking Katie up first, and then the boys, Jess made several furtive passes through the parking lots, searching for Steve's car. Finally satisfied that he wasn't there, she concentrated on acting normal and told them her plan to go for hot chocolates before heading home. The children were excited.

They made their way to a Caribou Coffee house on Cedar Road, piled out of the car, and quickly sloshed their way through the dirty wet snow to get inside. The place was near-empty.

They dumped their coats on the chairs of the table closest to the big fireplace and walked to the counter to order their three hot chocolates and a skinny decaf cappuccino. Ben and Josh took inventory of the pastries. Chocolate chip cookies at least five inches in diameter looked too good to pass up. They bought six and settled in.

Katie lowered her head and took a big slurp from her cup and came up with a frothy white mustache. The boys copied her. "You too, Mommy," Katie urged, and Jess plowed through the foam of her cappuccino and brought some up, a part of her lip and tip of her nose. Josh showed them how to make their spoons stick to their noses, anxious to make their fun last.

Time passed quickly and it was suddenly growing dim outside. They all reluctantly agreed that they should get back before dark and began to gather up their belongings. And then, glancing out the large window to assess the weather conditions outside once more and to help remember where her car was parked, Jess saw a lone figure walking briskly between the few cars there, his coat collar turned up high against the cold, and heading their way. She recognized the figure and the walk.

There was little time to think through what her actions should be. The door of the café burst open, letting in a blast of icy air. And there was Steve. He smiled and walked with confidence toward her and the children.

"It's Daddy!" Katie cried out and then looked at her mother anxiously while the two boys jumped to their feet.

"Well, well. Look here," Steve said. "If it isn't my little family."

He walked first to Katie and picked her up and held her tightly in his arms, dampening her clothes. "How's my little princess? Miss me, girlie-girl?"

Skipping STONES

Jess reached for her daughter. "Steve," she said, "we're not supposed to…"

He cut her off.

"You don't have to remind me about the PO," he said. "I'm a lawyer too, remember?" He shifted Katie in his arms. "A man needs to see his family, Jess."

She fought for control. "We could both get into trouble if we talk like this."

He looked at Katie. "You're mother's causing the trouble, isn't she? If no one tells, no one will know."

He stepped over to Ben and reached out his free hand to him and gripped his shoulder.

"How are you doing, son? Is your mother taking good care of you? How's Mimi and Papaw?"

Ben turned to Jess, fear in his eyes.

"I'm talking to you, son. You don't need to get approval from her.

"And what's up with you, Josh? How's that dad of yours?"

The boy looked away, knowing the man didn't expect an answer.

Steve turned back to Ben. "You can tell me if Josh can't. How is he? How's Sam, your old buddy, Sam?"

Jess made an attempt to stand.

"We're leaving," she said, with more confidence than she felt.

He reached out and pushed her down.

"No. We are not leaving," he said. "We're going to talk."

He turned toward his daughter. "You want to talk, right little princess? You want to spend some time with your daddy."

Katie sat rigidly in her father's grip, her thumb finding her mouth.

Steve reached across to Jess and ran his fingertips down the inside of her arm and turned her palms up and stroked them. His monologue was the same as his email: he needed her; she was bringing him down, destroying his career. He would forgive her. The children watched it all, filled with dread and indecision.

"You're still wearing my ring," he said. "We're still man and wife, Jess." He folded her hand in his. "My beautiful wife," he fawned. "You're making me crazy. After all these years, even after these last two weeks, you're still beautiful to me. I still love you.

"Remember how it used to be with us? Remember when we couldn't get enough of each other?"

His touches repulsed her, and she pulled away again, searching for her and her children's surest way to escape. The change in him was instant. He grabbed her arm, but this time, it wasn't done lovingly.

"I know what you're thinking," he said between his clenched teeth. "You think you can have it all - Sam, the house, the kids, the car. Well, I have news for you. It won't work. You're mine, and so are these kids. That will never change. You took a vow seventeen years ago, and you'll stick with it. You can call off your little dog, Sam. None of this is any of his business. And you can hang it up with the rest of your family. You're acting crazy. There is no proof of your allegations. You're going to lose this battle, and you'll be very sorry. The game's over, Jess. I'll take you back, and we'll start all over."

The words sickened Jess and Josh and Katie. But they had a far different effect on Ben. His body finally did what his mind had for years told him to do. He took the three steps necessary to reach his father, quickly pulled Katie away from him, and

Skipping STONES

took position in front of her and Jess, shielding their bodies with his. And he found his voice.

"What is it that you don't understand?" He growled at his father. "We don't want you. All you do is hurt. You don't love Mom. You don't love anyone. You don't know how. And you know what? We don't love you either. We've been afraid of you. But we're not afraid anymore."

Steve's shock was written all over him, and, for a moment, he stood open-mouthed in front of his son. Then the rage took over.

"You puny little whiney brat of a child. It all changed when you were born," he hissed. "You should never have been born."

He grabbed his son around his neck.

"Say you're sorry. Say you're sorry, you little bastard."

Ben's first reaction was to pull away, but his father tightened his grip and sneered at him.

"You're way out of your league, boy."

And something happened inside Ben. He would not be held captive and he would not be silenced. The emotional and physical power that surged through his body and mind was thoughtless and instantaneous. Without thinking about the consequences, he kicked his father's shins and kneed him and pummeled his sides with his fists. And, feeling his father's hold on him loosening slightly, he stood his full height and battered his head into his neck, directly below his chin.

The fearlessness and the strength of the blows took Steve by complete surprise, and he staggered backwards against a chair and fell awkwardly on his back to the floor. Stunned, he made no attempt to get up.

Ben stood over him in a fighter's stance.

"Get up, you coward," he said. "I want to beat you like you've beat her. But I won't do it while you're down. I won't do it the way you do."

The man backed himself further away, crab-like on his elbows.

"I'm going to tell them all," Ben hissed. "I'm going to tell the lawyer and everybody else what you've done. Especially what you've done to Mom. They'll know what you are. They'll all know. And everyone will turn their backs on you. You'll be nothing. No one."

Steve looked up at his son in astonishment.

"You wouldn't do that," he choked. "You wouldn't do that."

"Oh yes I will. I'll do it, and I'll love every minute of it."

The family watched as Steve got to his knees and pulled himself up to stand, putting the chair between him and the boy. He dusted off his slacks and readjusted the sleeves of his shirt and ran his hand through his hair, giving himself time to consider his options.

Finally, he made his decision.

"You're not worth it," he hissed. "None of you. I've tried to help you, but I'm done."

He looked directly at Jess. "You'll want me back. But it's too late. It's too late."

Ben cut him off.

"You'd better get out of here fast before the police come."

Then, following his son's glance, Steve turned and saw Josh on his cell phone, giving the final details of their location. The last image he saw as he rushed out the door was his wife, his children, and his nephew standing together in a tight line of solidarity against him.

Skipping STONES

Katie was the first to go to Ben. She stood before him, tentatively and with respect, searching for his mood. Finally she reached out and placed her arms around the waist of her brother and held on. Nothing more. His posture was rigid, but he accepted her act of love. Then slowly and with great thought and dignity, for the first time ever, he bent his strong body down to her and embraced her.

The boys' roles had been determined.

Ben had finally found strength and courage and had used both for all of the right reasons. And he had known when to back off from inflicting pain when it was no longer needed. The love and gentleness in him that had been repressed most of his life were finally released and exhibited in a tender way toward his sister whom he had always loved unconditionally but to whom he couldn't show emotion for fear of his own stability. Jess knew absolutely that her son would be strong in positive ways. He would be their protector.

Josh had protected Katie and Jess emotionally and had been ready to back up Ben throughout the days and nights of their nightmare, and during his family's months of recovery, he would quietly and deliberately walk among them, solid and contemplative, ready to give reassuring words and acts of loyalty to everyone whenever and wherever needed. And he would continue to help them develop their imaginations and see possibilities that they couldn't. He would be their rock.

༄

Jess tucked Katie into her bed first. Katie had held up well throughout the evening, but when Jess put her down onto her bed and pulled the covers over her, she began to cry. Jess lay down with her and held her and waited for her to find her words.

"I don't know why Daddy doesn't love us; I don't know what we did that was so bad. I tried real hard not to be bad."

"We didn't do anything bad, Katie," Jess whispered. "You were always good to your father. You were never bad. If anyone could tell us why he hurt us, we'd find a way to help him get better. But I don't think anyone can tell us why.

"Is he sick?"

"Yes, honey, in a way he is sick," Jess told her. "But it isn't a sickness that just goes away. People with his kind of sickness need a lot of help to get better. It can take a very long time. But, honey, they have to want to get better and need to work hard at it. They have to ask for help. No one can do it for them."

"I hope he gets better," she whispered, nuzzling closer to her mother.

Would she, Jess wondered, ever heal?

"Katie," she said, "we're going to learn how to live in the sunshine. We're going to be happy and live like most other families do. You're going to have lots of girlfriends. You're going to dance and sing and laugh out loud and not be afraid to say what's on your mind. And I'm going to make sure that you are never afraid again and that you're surrounded by good boys and gentle men. We're going to be free to come and go whenever we want to. We're going to be happy, Katie. I promise you."

"Will we move back to our home again? Ever?"

"We're going to have a whole new beginning. We're going to start out fresh. We'll live here for just a little while longer, and then you and I and Ben and Josh will get ourselves a brand new house."

Skipping STONES

She had made a decision without even thinking about it. It seemed perfectly right to her that they would start all over again, completely fresh.

"But will I ever live with Daddy again?" Katie asked.

"I don't know, love. If he gets better and you want to see him that can probably happen. We'll just have to be patient and see."

The child nuzzled closer to her mother, and it took so long for her to speak again that Jess thought she had fallen asleep. And then she heard her whisper, "I was afraid of him today. Will he come after us and hurt Ben or you again?"

Jess pushed back her own tears.

"No," she said. None of us ever need to be afraid of him again. Our friend, Mr. Karnanski, will talk with the good lady judge, and she'll help us. The policemen we met will help us. Good people know that no one has to live in fear, Katie. Good people are going to make sure that no one hurts us. No one has the right to hurt us or make us feel bad."

"Where will our new house be?" The child's mind was everywhere.

"I don't know yet. But we'll start looking for one as soon as we can. We'll all do it together. Will you help me look?"

Katie sat up and smiled through the tears still covering her eyes and rolling down her lovely cheeks.

"Maybe we should get a place on the lake like Sam's," she said, eager to please. "Maybe we could have a boat and a huge porch and lots of windows that let the sunshine in, like his. Or maybe a small cozy house like Annie's. I like her house too. Would you like that?"

"I'd like anything and any place as long as you're there, Katie," Jess said.

"We'll be just like Josh and Aunt Becky, right?"

"Yes. Just like them. Josh will help us know what to do. It's been so long that I've kind of forgotten how to be that way, but I'll learn."

Katie lay her head on her mother's shoulder again and put her arms around her and held tight, trying to sort it all out.

"And our whole family can come see us and stay in our new house whenever they want to. Friends can come over too. Even Sam, right?" She asked. "He's family too. Everyone will come see us in our new house."

"Right. Our whole family can come whenever they want. Sam will be there absolutely and Grandma Annie too. And we can go to their houses whenever we want. It will be terrific."

Jess had thought that her love for Katie was as complete as it could possibly be, but the little girl's incredible effort to understand and to find some piece of happiness through the gloom of what had just happened caused more love to surge through her. She was amazed by her daughter's strength. And she would be strong, too, she told herself, stronger than she had ever been before. For Katie's sake. For Ben. For Josh. And for herself.

"I love you so much, Katie."

"I love you too, Mama. I love you happy."

༄

One full year had passed since Josh had left his mother's, then his grandparents', and, finally, Jess's homes. The new March winds had been mild, and the snow had melted early. The gentle rains of April had washed the earth clean, and the golden sun of May had prepared it for its bounty. Trees had gradually unfurled themselves, strong green grass had pushed its way up from rich brown soil, and colorful blossoms had finally popped over their strong stems. June ushered in summer at last, and the hearts and minds of the family grew fertile with the possibilities the season unleashed. Robins sang.

The family made their way to Sam and Josh's place for lunch and a long celebratory afternoon, carrying baskets of food from their own kitchens, games they wanted to play together, and walking shoes just in case they were needed, and each paused at the sign on the door that read, *Welcome to Ben and Josh's Place.*

Unloading their gifts, they followed Josh to his room where he proudly pointed out his very own new bed, chest of drawers, and shelves that held an untidy collection of books, family pictures, baseball gloves, a very special paperweight, address book, and yellow diary. NASCAR posters and prints of storms covered the walls.

Later, over lunch, the children announced the sports they had signed up for, the summer camps they had applied to, and the birthday parties they had been asked to attend. Katie proudly modeled her leotard for her new dance class, and Mimi and Papaw informed everyone that they were finally going to take the Baltic Cruise they had put off for years. Grandma Annie reminded them about her up-coming dinner in her beautifully refurbished home. They raised their glasses. Salud! They called out in unison.

Just before sunset, they headed down to the lake where the adults watched Josh and Ben teach Katie how to make small flat stones skip across the surface of the water.

"The key is finding the right stone," Josh told her while Sam watched, grinning proudly. "And then it's just about holding your hand and flicking your wrist in the right way.

Mimi and Grandma Annie walked slowly together along the narrow beach.

"I don't see how it can get any better than this," Mimi said.

"Oh, it's good all right," Grandma Annie answered. "But it's going to get better. You can count on it."

After everyone had gone, Josh and Sam made their way back down to the darkened beach and looked out onto the moon-sparkled water.

"Things are really good, aren't they?" Josh said.

"Things are better than good," Sam replied.

"I'm happy."

"I'm happier than I've ever been. And this is just the beginning."

They walked in silence for a while, simply enjoying the companionship and the warmth of the evening breeze. Then Josh turned directly to his father, ready, finally, to say some things that had been on his mind all day long.

"I haven't told you straight out before," he said, "but I want you to know that I'm real glad you're my own real dad."

"And I'm so glad that I'm a part of your life again," Sam answered. "You have no idea what it means to me."

The healing that Josh so desperately needed was taking place, but there were still profound questions remaining in his young mind.

"Do you think Mom knows?" He asked. "Do you think she sees us and knows we're all right?

Sam had always wrestled with his beliefs, in spite of his mother's strong faith. Lacking solid conviction about life after death, he would not answer his son's question directly.

"I think she's at peace," he said instead. "I think things have turned out the way they were meant to. I think we are the way we were meant to be. I believe that."

Skipping STONES

"Maybe it's wrong," Josh continued, "but I don't worry so much about her anymore. I think she's happy. I think her spirit's free."

"It isn't wrong. It's the way it should be. Hopefully you'll finally be able to concentrate on all of the wonderful memories you have of her. That's what she would have wanted."

The boy's thoughts were splintered.

"I wonder if...," he began but couldn't finish, afraid that what he was thinking was somehow a betrayal to her.

Sam understood. He had lost track of the nights when all of his what-if's filled his mind and pushed away the comfort of sleep. Of course his son would have the same demons.

"I think I know what you're feeling, Josh," he said. "You lost your mother, and I lost my best friend and the woman I had hoped I'd live with forever. Our lives would have been so different if that hadn't happened. And yet, here we are. Happy. And it's okay for us to be happy. We've lost a mother and a wife. But as a result of that, the rest of our family has joined together in ways we never thought they would. Would Jess and Katie and Ben have walked away from Steve if all of this hadn't happened? Who would have shown them the way if you hadn't been pushed into the middle of their awful lives? Would you and Grandma Annie and I have been as close to them as we are now? Would Mimi and Papaw?"

He stopped and watched the small waves slap onto shore.

"I don't know, Josh. It's a mystery how things turn out, isn't it? Your Grandma Annie says that things are the way they are meant to be. She said that God works in mysterious ways and that it doesn't do us any good to second-guess His plan. She said that we have to latch onto whatever happiness and gifts He gives us and simply be glad. And not be angry about our losses.

"Someone else once said to me that life is a journey, not a destination, and we have no way of knowing where that journey will lead us. We have to choose to be happy and try to be the best we can be no matter what's thrown at us. And we have to treasure every single day and hold onto every opportunity that we have for happiness."

"Kind'a like grabbing the tail of the wind and enjoying the ride," Josh murmured.

"That's right. We have to open ourselves up to everything life has to offer us – the good and the bad – and decide to live life to its fullest, no matter what."

The two walked on in silence, each vowing to stop questioning why the wife and mother had been taken away and why they had been thrown into the lives of Jess and her children. And they vowed to live, finally, with joy.

Josh had more to say – words that he had never spoken before, not even to his beloved mother because she hadn't dared to let her guard down and say them to him. He turned to his father again.

"Maybe men aren't supposed to say this to each other," he finally said, "but I just want you to know that I love you, Dad. I just think you should know that."

Sam's happiness got stuck in his throat, and for a moment, all he could do was put his arms around his son and hold onto him. "Dad," he had called him. "Dad." Finally, he answered.

"And I love you, my son. Always have. Always will. Now, let's grab hold of that wind and really get started on our exciting journey together."

Made in the USA
Lexington, KY
13 November 2012